# PRAISE FOR THE FIRST B[ ] [ ] TRILOGY

"*Three Fugitives* pulls readers into a fantasy realm with action, adventure, and characters that are easy to love. Even though Howler has created a world full of monsters, mayhem, heroes, and heroines, the novel is also a mirror of our own disturbing reality where the borders of good and evil are not clearly defined."

—Lee Gooden, ForeWord Clarion

The riveting story of Orren and his friends that began with
*Three Fugitives* continues in the second book of this trilogy:

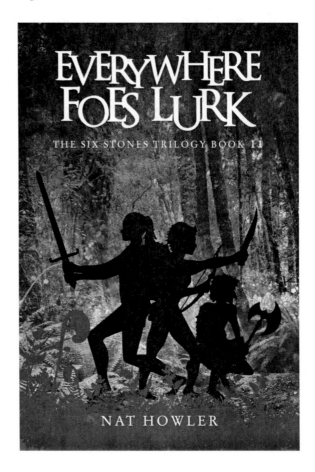

EVERYWHERE
FOES LURK

THE SIX STONES TRILOGY BOOK II

NAT HOWLER

# CURSED QUEST

# CURSED QUEST

## THE SIX STONES TRILOGY BOOK III

### NAT HOWLER

**TATE PUBLISHING**
AND ENTERPRISES, LLC

Published by Tate Publishing & Enterprises, LLC
127 E. Trade Center Terrace | Mustang, Oklahoma 73064 USA
1.888.361.9473 | www.tatepublishing.com

Tate Publishing is committed to excellence in the publishing industry. The company reflects the philosophy established by the founders, based on Psalm 68:11,
*"The Lord gave the word and great was the company of those who published it."*

Book design copyright © 2013 by Tate Publishing, LLC. All rights reserved.
*Cover design by Jan Sunday Quilaquil*
*Interior design by Honeylette Pino*

Published in the United States of America

ISBN: 978-1-62854-891-4
1. Fiction / Fantasy / General
2. Fiction / Action & Adventure
13.11.06

# TABLE OF CONTENTS

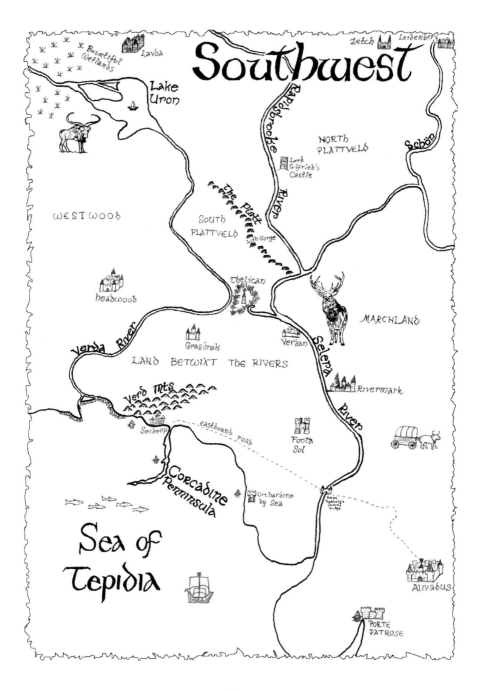

Southwest

Zetch
Leidenberg
Bountiful Wetlands
Lavda
Lake Uron
Rapidsgroshe River
NORTH PLATTVELD
Schön
Lord Gilfried's Castle
WEST WOOS
The Platz
SOUTH PLATTVELD
Sith Gorge
Thelican
Headwoos
Verda River
Grasbrak
Verdan
Selera River
MARCHLAND
LAND BETWIXT THE RIVERS
Verd Mts
Rivermark
Seidenp
eastbound road
Fonta Sol
Corcadine Peninsula
Orchardine by Sea
Baron Tapkerg's Sweret Hideo
Sea of Tepidia
Alivadus
PORTE PATROSE

10

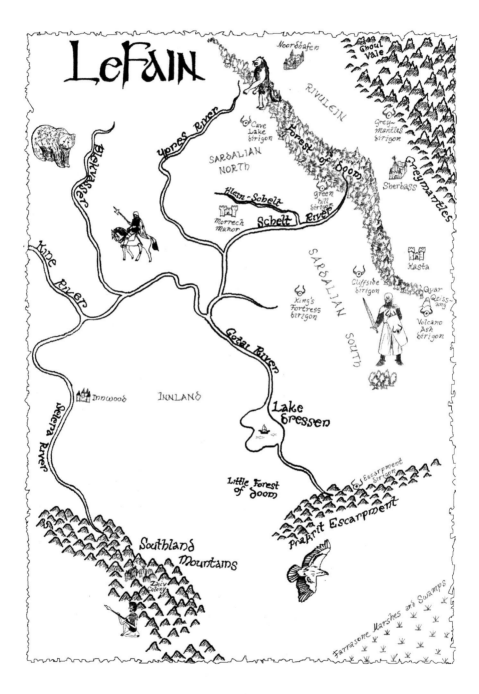

# LeFaIN

Noordhafen

Sea Ghoul Vale

RIVULEIN

Cave Lake birigon

Forest of Doom

Greymantles birigon

SARDALIAN NORTH

Sherbass

Hern-Schelt

green hill birigon

Morrech Manor

Schelt River

Kasta

SARDALIAN SOUTH

Cliffside birigon

Qyar Qeissang

King's Fortress birigon

Volcano Ash birigon

Vpres River

Blakwasser

Kine River

Gozar River

Innwood

INNLAND

Lake Gressen

Selorra River

Little Forest of Doom

Escarpment birigon

Prakrit Escarpment

Southland Mountains

Drov Colony

Farrasone Marshes and Swamps

# Western Greymantles

Ghoul Vale

Mount Solvard

Peat Bogs

hidden pass

Kegelmont

Gorge of the Leafy Curse

Lake Bolle

Granite Tors

Hargash River

Vulture Canyon

Lake Lovaggi

Schud Glacier

Kraan Glacier

Rivulein

Ring Valley

Fallagourn Falls

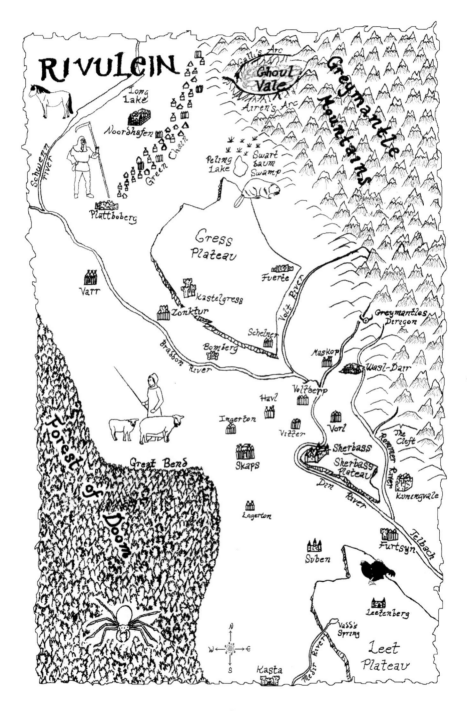

RIVULEIN

Long Lake

Noordhafen

Green Chain

Plattboberg

Schwenn River

Galli's Arc

Ghoul Vale

Airen's Arc

Greymantle Mountains

Peling Lake

Swart baum Swamp

Cress Plateau

Varr

Fverre

Kastelgress

Zonktur

Volt River

Schelner

Brabbon River

Bomberg

Maskop

Greymantles Diregon

Wasl-Darr

Volfserp

Havl

Ingerton

Vizter

Vorl

The Cleft

Forest of Doom

Great Bend

Skaps

Sherbass

Sherbass Plateau

Romner River

Kuningvale

Din River

Lagerton

Suben

Furtsyn

Telbach

Leetenberg

Vass's Spring

Kasta

Mesir River

Leet Plateau

N W E S

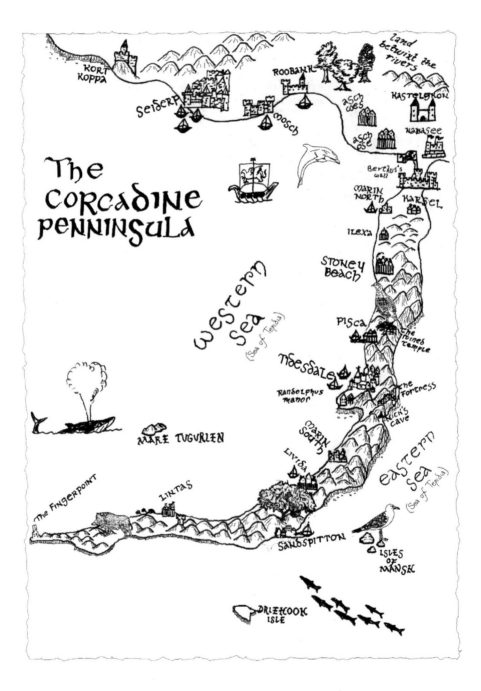

The Corcadine Penninsula

# A DREAMSCAPE BATTLE

Orren Randolphus woke up early one morning to discover that he was floating hundreds of feet above the earth. Above him was a clear, pre-dawn sky, filled with thousands of stars, and illuminated by a full moon. Below him was a bank of filthy clouds. Around him was a ring of mountains, with jagged, blue-white peaks cutting into the heavens.

Panic welled up inside him. What if he fell crashing to the earth? What if the wind carried him away, and dashed him to pieces on a mountainside?

He forced himself to snap out of it. If he was to find a way to escape this predicament, he had to keep his wits. Figuring out how to get out of sticky situations was his strength. Thus had he survived and overcome the adverse conditions that had always prevailed in his life.

There had to be a reason why he was up here. He decided that the only way to figure it out was to review the events leading up to this point.

It had all started with his father, Lorien Randolphus, lord of the Corcadine, a narrow peninsula hundreds of miles to the southwest. Lorien desired to protect the people of his peninsula from the rapacious Framguth lords of the mainland. The Framguth lords had magic at their disposal—magic derived from evil deities called the *odia*. Such deities included Adnari,

Globullum, and Mortistia, whose very names struck terror into the hearts of people throughout LeFain continent.

Long ago, the *astra*—benevolent star deities—sought to protect the *yelia*, or Sun Children, commonly referred to as 'elves,' from the very same odia the Framguth lords worshipped. These kind gods bequeathed upon that legendary race, seven stones called the *gwellen*, whose magic was unequalled. Each gwell had power over a particular element of nature. Sham, the Motherstone, whose power coordinated the magic of the other six gwellen, was later taken away by the astral gods for reasons unknown. The yelia, however, continued to flourish, with the six remaining gwellen as their power sources.

It was these six gwellen that Lorien desired, and he set out to find them. His task would not be easy; the yelia had hidden the stones before their doomed race disappeared entirely from the face of Urth. Moreover, the only non-yelia with the ability to handle the gwellen, were those favored by the yelia with chosen status, or selected descendants of such chosen individuals. No one else could even lift a gwell, much less use it.

Lorien, however, had a family tradition that he was one such descendant and, together with his companions, succeeded in finding three of the stones. After an ambush by unknown assailants, however, he was seriously wounded and lost one gwell over the Fallagourn Falls. His surviving companions brought him back to the Corcadine, but before reaching home, Lorien hid the other two gwellen.

In his absence, his despised older son, Berthus, took over Lorien's estate, and forced Orren, the much younger son, into the swinery to live among the manor hogs. Lorien was too weak to combat Berthus, who cruelly subjugated all of the Corcadine, with the aid of his toughs. Before dying, however, Lorien instructed Richard, the kindly steward of Randolphus Manor, to protect Orren from Berthus's wrath.

Richard became Orren's guardian and mentor, and taught the boy how to survive in the wild. He begged Orren to flee to the mainland, and there seek sanctuary in the city of Alivadus, under Baron Toynberg, a family friend. Orren, however, could not leave the beloved steward behind, and he stayed until Richard was on his own deathbed. It was then that Richard told Orren everything, and practically *commanded* him to flee.

While Orren was following his mentor's instruction, he discovered a beautiful, blue stone in Berthus's possession. He stole it, mainly as an act of revenge for all the abuse heaped upon him by his half-brother. What he did not realize was that the stone was Hesh, gwell of water, and that Berthus had discovered its hidden whereabouts, no doubt by some nefarious means.

Orren fled with the stone, the theft of which enraged Berthus, who mustered up an army of thugs to pursue the boy, kill him, and take back the gwell, before embarking on a quest of his own for the other five stones. Orren's situation was desperate, and in the course of his escape, he passed by the place where Lorien had hid another gwell, Kalsh of earth. The two gwellen were attracted to one another, and the attraction also created a telepathic connection between Orren and Berthus. That experience terrified the boy to his core, and he fled once more, not realizing that he had unwittingly led his half-brother to another gwell.

Orren made it to the mainland, with the assistance of Haxel, a young *zhiv*, or goblin, whose life he had saved. Berthus, however, had a great army of thugs and cutthroats, as well as the aid of *magic sniffers*, obscure persons whose specialty was tracking down magical objects. It was all Orren could do to keep ahead of his mortal enemy, but during the course of his escape, he discovered the true nature of the gwellen, and of Berthus's quest. He also discovered that both he and Berthus possessed the rare ability to handle the stones. He resolved to find the gwellen first, and to get them away from Berthus. Haxel, ever loyal, accompanied him. Their intended destination was Fallagourn Falls, where they intended to search for the gwell Lorien had lost there.

Together, Orren and Haxel rescued a sixteen-year-old girl named Marett. She was a *Duraline*, a member of a rare set of noble households, whose specialty was the knowledge contained within their family lores. Marett had lost her entire family in a Drammite raid, except for her estranged brother Perceval, who was absent at the time, but whom she refused to discuss at length, because he had joined the cult of Dramm years before. The tall, raven-haired beauty joined their quest, and her intelligence and skills helped them greatly, as together, they faced bandits, winter storms, peasant uprisings, beasts, and a sinister cult called the Order of Dramm, or *Drammites*. They narrowly escaped Berthus's army by entering the cursed Forest of Doom. There they fought off evil monsters from the distant past, while at the same time, discovering that a chosen individual could choose others to share the status, together with its accompanying abilities. They also found Orya, the gwell of fire, and rescued Quartz, a *sholl* or stone giant, from gradual death by erosion.

Their troubles did not end when they reached the other side of the accursed jungle. They endured a harrowing escape from a booby-trapped, Drammite-infested city, and were caught and nearly killed by Berthus; only Quartz's timely intervention saved them. They discovered, to their horror, that Berthus had made common cause with the Order of Dramm, and they also encountered a third gwell-bearer, a suspicious old man named Anselm.

Worn out, cold, and desperate, they wound up on Airen's Arc, overlooking the *Ghoul Vale*, a crater that was as cursed as the Forest of Doom. There, hideous birds called sordigryps attacked them. Quartz distracted the birds while Orren, Haxel, and Marett descended into the Ghoul Vale. In so doing, the rock giant violated the basic rule of his species, which was never to see the sun. As a result, he turned to stone, to face the same fate he had faced before Orren and his friends first rescued him.

Orren and Haxel were captured by shadow beings in the vale, and taken to the dark, walled city of Wardolam, situated in the crater's center. An assembly of shadow beings was about to condemn them to join the ghouls—the undead beings that guarded the city. Anselm, however, appeared, in company with Marett. It seemed that he was an errand runner for the shadow beings. It had been his job to find Ru'i, the stone of animal spirit, and to bring it to Wardolam. Berthus, however, had taken the gwell from Anselm, and had left the old man for dead, but Marett saved him.

The shadow beings were convinced that the loss of Ru'i was not Anselm's fault, but that of Orren, Haxel, and Marett. Anselm, however, defended the trio, with the result that he was thrown into prison together with them, while the shadow beings, who turned out to be the long-lost and supposedly extinct yelia, debated what to do with them. Orren, Haxel, and Marett thereupon accepted the old man into their fellowship. The four gwell bearers were now imprisoned together, in the dark yelian city.

Orren shook himself back to the present. None of his memories, he realized with disappointment, explained how he ended up in mid-air, several hundred feet above the Ghoul Vale. It was then that he felt a presence.

He spun around and saw, to his utter astonishment, Haxel, Marett, Quartz, and Anselm, floating in the sky together with him. Haxel was terrified; the little zhiv's eyes were wide with fear, and he flailed his long arms about in panic. He calmed down, however, when he saw Marett. The tall, raven-haired girl was calm and composed, with a serene look on her beautiful face. She placed a reassuring hand on Haxel's shoulder, a gesture that soothed Orren's nerves as well. Marett usually could make sense of anything that was going on.

Anselm seemed delighted to be floating in the air. He had a childish grin on his face and a twinkle in his eyes. Quartz, however, looked utterly bewildered. The sholl's presence was most astonishing to Orren, both because of his enormous, twenty-foot-tall bulk, and because his body had been petrified at the edge of Airen's Arc. Yet here he was in mid-air, floating as if weightless.

It was then that Orren recalled Marett describing a dream of her own, wherein she had flown out of her body, and was pulled into the clouds by an invisible force. Surely such a thing was happening now? If so, however, where was that force?

As if in answer, something began pulling all five of them away, in a southerly direction. Together, they floated over the Ghoul Vale's brown clouds, toward Airen's Arc—the natural ramp of earth and stone that formed the vale's southern boundary. Orren looked at Marett quizzically, but the girl only held out her right hand in a gesture that said, *just go with it.* They floated over the arc's edge. On the lip of the massive ramp was a black rock, partially covered in snow, which could only be Quartz's petrified body.

Suddenly, Quartz fell. His massive hulk grew smaller and smaller until it disappeared into his inert body. Orren looked at his friends in alarm, but there was no chance for them to discuss it, even using hand gestures, because at that moment, they were all pulled away to continue their southward flight. The invisible force carried them over Airen's Arc and the deep valley that lay between it and the mountains to the south. The whole landscape was covered in snow, and shone blue-white in the milky light of the moon.

Suddenly, Anselm hurtled downward. He disappeared faster than Quartz had, and in seconds, was swallowed up by the dim, pre-dawn landscape. Frantic, Orren searched for the old man, but he, Haxel, and Marett were whisked away.

The mountainous landscape that was below, rushed by, becoming a blur. After a few minutes, the force slowed down, and Orren realized that the pillar of dawn was visible in the west. In the increasing light, he saw brushy, wooded terrain, situated on mountain slopes.

Haxel fell. Orren caught a glimpse of the zhiv's terror as the vegetation below swallowed him up. The invisible force pulled Orren and Marett away. They soared over an open, snowy meadow that lay within a crater. In the middle of the crater was a strange, cone-shaped mountain. As soon as they passed over it, Marett plunged down toward it, and was seen no more.

Now Orren was alone.

He looked about, but all he saw in the purple sky were the waning moon and stars, and a single black cloud. There was something not right about that cloud. Orren stared at it and realized, to his horror that it was floating straight toward him, and he toward it.

The cloud drew closer and closer, and Orren's dread grew. He flapped his hands and kicked his legs in an effort to get away, but to no avail. Soon it engulfed him completely.

The black cloud was full of swirling wind and lightning bolts. Orren saw a human form appear in the gloom. It was a man, nearly six feet tall and quite broad in the shoulder. He came closer and closer, and Orren started to shake all over. His stomach clenched and he broke out in a sweat.

It was his half-brother, Berthus!

*I have you at last, swine boy!* Berthus's voice entered Orren's mind. *You won't survive this.*

Orren started to weep. During the course of his travels, he had overcome many dangers, and seemed brave enough to face anything. Berthus, however, was an entirely different matter. Orren's fear of his brother defied all rationality. In Berthus's presence, Orren lost all semblance of control, and what was worse, Berthus knew it. The tyrant fed upon his younger brother's terror, and derived power from it.

Waves of hatred assaulted the boy's mind, and with them came sad and terrible memories of being insulted, abused, beaten, and forced to wallow in the muck and filth of the swinery. What was worse, not all of the memories were Orren's own. Some of them came from Berthus. Berthus's memories of their father entered Orren's mind, and he experienced the abuse Berthus had suffered. He also saw Richard. He felt Richard's love for Berthus, and Berthus's love for the old man. Richard was the only good thing in Berthus's life, as he had been in Orren's.

Had Berthus suffered the same way Orren had? Was that somehow Orren's fault? Berthus certainly seemed to believe that it was, and his anger and pain assaulted Orren's mind. The boy clutched at his head, for it throbbed, and he felt himself drawn into his brother's power. Berthus would try killing him by attacking him telepathically, and there was nothing Orren could do about it.

*Nonsense, there is something you can do about it.* It was the mysterious voice that had been with Orren his entire life, and which gave him hope when hope was gone.

*I can't fight him!* Orren protested. *He's too strong for me.*

*Your friends will help you,* the voice said. *They can't defeat Berthus; only you can. But they'll be able to pull you away from mental attacks like this one.*

Berthus's assault felt like knives digging into Orren's psyche. Through the pain, however, Orren heard the voices of his friends, coming from far away. Haxel and Quartz cried out in anguish, while Marett and Anselm struggled to gain control. All four of them knew that Orren was in serious trouble.

*You're all too far away!* Orren cried out. *I'm done for!*

*Create the Bearers' Web!* The voice said in an emphatic tone. *Do it now!*

Marett had spoken of the Bearers' Web many times. It was a telepathic network by which the specially designated gwell-bearers supported one another, and buttressed each other's mental power. It was also the means by which all gwell-bearers knew when one of their number was using a stone. This was necessary because in the absence of Sham the Motherstone, no two or more gwellen could be used simultaneously, lest disaster result. Orren and his friends had considered the possibility of forming a Bearers' Web, once they acquired all six stones. Marett, however, cautioned that they should only do this as a last resort. The gwellen were extremely powerful, she said, and should be hidden in a sanctuary where no person, good or bad, could ever find them again. It was far preferable for the stones to be forever out of reach, than in the hands of a Bearers' Web, however benevolent and moral the bearers in that Web might be.

*I can't create a Web!* Orren protested, gritting his teeth from the mental attacks Berthus continued launching at him. *We haven't found all the gwellen, and besides, there are only five of us, not six! Anyway, we want to hide the stones, not take them for ourselves!*

*Your desire not to take the stones for yourselves makes you forces for good, which is all the more reason to create the Web,* the voice said. *Hiding them isn't feasible right now, since Berthus has two gwellen. You don't need all the stones to create the Web. Actually, you don't need any of them. And so what if there are only five of you? It will just be an incomplete Web—that's all—but you must create it now, or Berthus will overwhelm you! Proclaim the creation of the Web, and it will come into being.*

Orren was getting weaker by the second. Berthus was winning, and he knew it. The evil tyrant let out a whoop of joy, and Orren felt him rejoice. The mysterious voice, however, had never steered Orren in the wrong direction.

*I create the Bearers' Web!* he cried out through the darkness. *Haxel, Marett, Quartz, Anselm! Join my Web!*

He felt something grab him. It was a silvery-white cord of pure energy, and it pulled him away from Berthus. Berthus pulled back, but he was no match for the power of the Web. The mysterious voice cheered in triumph, as Berthus howled in rage. The black cloud disappeared, and Orren was once again floating above the Ghoul Vale, together with his four friends. Cords of silvery-white energy connected each bearer to the others.

Sobbing and shaking, he collapsed into his friends' mental grasp. They reached out to him and comforted him. Then Quartz disappeared back into his petrified body, and the rest of the group plunged downward into the cloudbank, which now was orange in the light of immanent sunrise. Orren, Haxel, Marett, and Anselm fell into the dark city, and back into their bodies.

Orren woke in a cold sweat. Haxel, Marett, and Anselm, now in physical form, ran over to him and embraced him while he bawled. The boy shook in fear even though he was safe with his friends once more, and despite the fact that they now had a Bearers' Web.

Orren, however, recalled the voice saying that the Web could only help him against telepathic assaults. It could not defeat Berthus entirely, particularly, Orren reckoned, if there were to be a physical encounter. One day, Orren would have to face his dreaded half-brother face to face. The question was, what possibility could even exist of his prevailing?

# Another Bearers' Web

"I had him!" Berthus hollered. He kicked over a chair and pounded his fists into the chest that sat behind his camping bed. "The swine boy was in my grip!"

"So why'd you let him go?" Iranda asked. The tall woman sat on another chair, her legs crossed and her eyes cast downward. Her hands rested in her lap, and in one of her palms, she held a small lantern. The soft yellow radiance it emitted, illuminated the interior of the tent, and added golden highlights to her long, brown curls.

"There was a silver-white light," Berthus hollered. "It grabbed the swine boy and took him away from me before I could kill him!"

A worried look appeared in Iranda's dark, mysterious eyes. Berthus's wrath drained away, only to be replaced by fear. If the woman was worried, then things were bad indeed.

Where Iranda came from, Berthus had no idea. She simply appeared one night, seemingly out of nowhere, at a time when Berthus's situation seemed hopeless. She had created the alliance with the Drammites, who had been intent on destroying Berthus's army. He was still very suspicious of the cult, but at least it was now working for him rather than against him. Iranda had assured him that the Drammites could be disposed of when they were no longer useful.

Ever since then, she had been with Berthus, encouraging him to persevere. Occasionally, she would disappear for a few days, but always for the purpose of strengthening Berthus's position.

She energized him and gave him hope, and she had the ability to soften his towering rages, which had been a liability in the past.

"Tell me everything," Iranda said with a sigh.

"I don't know how it happened," Berthus said. "I found myself floating above the earth. The mountains and valleys were below me, and I could flap my hands about and make myself move. Then I saw something in the distance. It was the swine boy, and he was coming toward me. I was afraid, so I chose to make a black cloud in which to hide, but he floated right into it.

"It was then that I remembered that the swine boy's afraid of me, so I decided that this was my chance to take him on, and maybe even kill him with my mental power. He panicked—I mean, he lost it completely. I knew that this was the best time to strike, so I recalled every bad memory of mine that he had caused, and I let the hatred and anger wash through me. I sent it at him like arrows, and he became weak.

"Just then he shouted something. I didn't hear what it was, but the next thing I knew, four strands of silver-white light entered my cloud. They were like ropes or cords, but made of pure energy. They grabbed the swine boy. I tried to pull him back, but the ropes were too strong, and soon he was gone. For a split second I saw exactly where the cords were coming from. One was from the goblin, and another was from the Duraline girl. The third one came from the old dodder, the one from whom I took Ru'i. I should have killed that old dodder, Iranda, but I didn't, because I wanted him to be eaten alive by the sordigryps. It was a stupid move, because now he's on the swine boy's side. Probably was all along."

Hot tears streamed down Berthus's face, but instead of allowing himself to break down and thus show weakness, he kicked the chest hard. This enraged him, for it hurt his foot, and he proceded to throw things about, in the tent. Vases, swords, furs, and even his own boots, flew around the small space until Iranda grabbed his hands. Berthus's rage dissipated, for as always, the beautiful woman had the instant and seemingly magical ability to calm him down.

"You need to think," she said. "You've accounted for three of the cords of light. What about the fourth?"

Berthus shuddered. "That was the worst thing of all. The swine boy's fourth friend was that huge shadow! The one that grabbed him, the goblin, and the girl, and deprived me of my just revenge. The thing was huge, Iranda! Couldn't have been less than twenty feet tall, and it was very wide. I didn't get a good look at it, but some of my men were able to describe its basic shape. They said it was wearing a long coat of some kind, and the top of its head was flat. Maybe…maybe it's not real, but something the swine boy created to frighten me."

"No, it's real alright," Iranda shook her head. "I know exactly what it is, now that you've described it to me. I'm afraid, Berthus, that your brother has a sholl on his side."

"A what?"

"A night guardian," Iranda said. "Sholls were the protectors of the yelia, but they were supposed to have died out even before the yelia did. They're the largest of all sabe races found anywhere on Urth, and they're stronger than you can possibly imagine. Somehow, some way, your brother's found one."

Berthus's heart sank. He collapsed on the chair. "Then all is lost," he said.

"Not necessarily," Iranda answered. "Sholls may be big and strong, but they're not invincible. Their inner ears are vulnerable, and they're also liable to develop cracks in their hide, particularly if they're old. Those cracks *can* be penetrated, either by sharpened sticks or by boiling pitch. Underneath their rocky hide, they have hearts just like ours, which are mortal.

"Another thing. Sholls are purely nocturnal. They cannot bear the sight of the sun, for if they see it, they turn to stone. Perhaps even more important, they're helpless before a gwell or a gwell-bearer. A sholl could kill all your men with just a few swipes of his hands, but he can do nothing to you, Berthus, *because* you're a gwell-bearer. Why do you suppose he grabbed the swine boy and his friends, and then disappeared without harming you?"

"When this 'sholl,' as you call it, did that, I only saw it out of the corner of my eye," Berthus said. "It moved so quickly, all I saw was a black blur, and I had no time to do anything."

"That's because if you *had* used the gwell, the sholl would have been finished," Iranda said. "It needed to grab the swine boy, the goblin, and the girl while you were preoccupied, and run for all it was worth. But Berthus, there's something worse than the fact that your brother has a sholl. The swine boy has created a Bearers' Web."

"A Bearers' what?"

"Let me explain," Iranda said. "Long ago, when the yelia were alive, each gwell had its own designated bearer, who was solely responsible for the stone and for all magic that emanated from it. There was only one bearer per gwell, because while bearing more than one gwell is possible, it's extremely difficult."

"I can do it," Berthus blurted out without thinking. "I'm gonna bear all six."

"Berthus, don't you find the gwellen to be a burden?"

"Yes," Berthus had to concede with an exasperated sigh. "I'll never forget the day I found Hesh. It was like I fell in love with the stone. From then on, Hesh was on my mind all the time. I kept it by my side when I slept, and when I was awake I took it out of my pouch again and again to gaze at it. There was only one thing I loved more than Hesh, and that was Richard. I put Hesh under Richard's bed in the hopes that it would heal him, which it did not.

"When the swine boy stole Hesh, it was the worst thing anyone has ever done to me. It felt like he had stabbed me through the heart, but that I didn't die and was forced to suffer. Never before or since have I felt so much pain and anguish. That's why I want Hesh back, Iranda. I must have it back! And I want Orya too!"

"And you will get them," Iranda said, "but at least the swine boy's theft of Hesh enabled you to find Kalsh, and now you've got Ru'i too."

"My connection to Kalsh is deeper than my connection to Hesh was," Berthus said. "You see, I never used Hesh's magic, not even once. I didn't think to. I was so happy when I found it that I skipped like a mountain goat back up to the manor house, and showed it to Richard, Shelton, and Lumus. I even showed it to Staffords, the fat lout whom I left in charge of the Corcadine while I'm gone. Richard convinced me to wait for the right moment to use Hesh, when everyone would be watching. They would see that I, Lord Berthus Randolphus, am the true master of the Corcadine, and all of LeFain! That's what Richard said, so that's what I did.

"But I *have* used Kalsh's magic, as you know, and because of that, my bond to it is special. Kalsh is like a heavy weight that I bear, Iranda. It's a huge burden, but I can't imagine not bearing it. I feel like Kalsh is part of me and I'm part of it.

"I don't yet have the same connection to Ru'i, because I haven't had that gwell for as long. When I first used Ru'i's magic to send the sordigryps after the swine boy, it made me ill. I vomited and fell to the ground shaking all over. Took a long time to regain my balance. I'm just not used to Ru'i's magic, that's all, but I'm sure I *can* get used to it if I use it enough. Yes, bearing Ru'i in addition to Kalsh is very, very difficult, but I must get used to it. The gwellen are mine, Iranda, all six of them, including Hesh and Orya, which I will take from the swine boy's corpse."

"You'll find the burden of all these stones too much," Iranda said. "The swine boy understood this, and that's another reason why he was informed, probably by the Duraline girl, of the Bearers' Web. A Bearers' Web is a mental network by which the bearers of the stones have a bond with one another. They can communicate telepathically and detect strong emotions in each other, and they can also support each other through their mental power. The Bearers' Web is essential, so that each bearer knows when another bearer is using his gwell's magic. That way, they can prevent two gwellen from being used simultaneously. As we both know, only one gwell may be used at any given time.

"When the swine boy called out, he created a Web. There was no way you could fight it, because it's way too strong, even though his Web has only five members, and needs a sixth in order to be complete. If you have any hope of overcoming him now, you'll have to do it physically, Berthus, because his friends have gained the ability to protect his mind from your assaults. The Web is what enables them to do that."

"So now what?" Berthus wailed. "Am I to get a Bearers' Web of my own?"

"Just what I was about to suggest," Iranda said, "and here's something I know that the swine boy surely doesn't. He bears Hesh, and I'm also sure that he's given Orya to one of his friends, probably the goblin. However, there's another way for you to have a Web of bearers and nonetheless be in charge of all the stones. If you designate a person as bearer for a gwell, and that person agrees to it, then as bearer, he becomes attached to his designated stone. You've already chosen Dargun Rodrick to possess the gwell-using ability. If you designate him as Ru'i's bearer, and he accepts, then he's tied to the stone *even if Ru'i remains on your person!* In essence, by physically keeping Ru'i, you bind Dargun Rodrick to you, and then *he'll* be responsible for Ru'i's magic, and he'll also get the burden that goes with it. He'll feel compelled to serve you, because he'll be dependent on the gwell, but whenever you desire to use Ru'i's magic, all you have to do is call upon the dargun, and he'll come running."

"So I get all the benefits, and Eric gets the burden?" Berthus said. "I keep Ru'i, and Eric serves me?"

"Yes," Iranda said with a smile. "The only burden you'll bear is that of Kalsh, for that is your stone. Best of all, Berthus, you can create a Bearers' Web without even having a gwell, so you need not worry that you currently possess only two. Also, you can designate particular bearers for particular gwellen even before you possess the stones in question. For instance, you can bind someone to Magna before you've even found it. All that's required is the consent of that person whom you want to bear Magna."

"What if Eric doesn't agree to it?" Berthus asked. "His family lore might warn him of what will happen if he joins my Web."

"I've already spoken to him about the general subject of gwell bearing," Iranda said. "He has no clue. This dependency secret I've revealed to you is hidden from even Duraline family lores. Bring the dargun in now, Berthus, and I promise you, he'll join your Web, and agree to be Ru'i's bearer."

"But where am I to find four other bearers?" Berthus asked. "After Eric told me his story, especially after he tied it to the swine boy, I couldn't help but choose him as a brother to me. I felt a bond to him because of it, Iranda, even though I knew he was using my weakness. And now I feel that he has a hold on me, and through him, the cursed Order of Dramm has a hold on me too. I can't imagine anyone else having such a story, one that could create a feeling of kinship in me, unless…Iranda, what about *you*?"

"No!" Iranda shouted. For the first time, Berthus saw real fear in the woman's eyes. She went pale and started to tremble. "I can't be a gwell-bearer, Berthus! I can't touch any of the stones! Don't ask this of me!"

"Why not? Iranda, what's wrong?"

"Just don't ask it of me," the woman said in a voice that resembled a menacing growl. "I can't be a gwell bearer, and that's that."

"Then who will be?"

"You just leave that to me," Iranda said. "I'll sound the candidates out. You will soon have your very own Bearers' Web, with six members, as opposed to the swine boy's five. With the dependency factor I told you about, you can even have five bearers who are mortal enemies of one another, for once you have each one's individual consent to bear a particular gwell, you will become the glue that binds them together, whether they like it or not."

"No more Drammites," Berthus said. "Dargun Rodrick may be tied to me. He may become dependent upon me, but I don't like the idea of being beholden to his cult any more than I already am. I've got other groups in my army, Iranda, and mostly, they distrust the Drammites, as quite honestly, do I. One Drammite in my Bearers' Web is enough."

"Absolutely understood," Iranda said. She stood up, flashed Berthus a beautiful smile, and left the tent.

# THE COUNCIL'S DECISION

Orren woke up inside the dark prison cell he shared with his friends. He stood up, walked over to the tiny, barred window, and looked out, but all he could see were the vague outlines of neighboring buildings. The sky above was black, an indication that dawn was still hours away.

In truth, there never was much to see. During the day, the sky was light brown, thanks to the roiling cloudbank that perpetually covered the Ghoul Vale. The part of the city visible from the prison cell was always deserted. The buildings outside, while beautifully carved into organic tree-like shapes, seemed to be slowly crumbling away.

The only activity in the vicinity took place inside the vast prison complex. The yelia used the wide passageway outside the cell as a thoroughfare of sorts. They silently and solemnly went about their business, going back and forth from one place to another. Orren and his friends rarely saw any of the yelia conversing with one another, and none of them ever laughed or even cracked a smile. They were a morose race, and though polite, were standoffish.

As far as Orren could tell, the only inmates in the prison were Haxel, Marett, Anselm, and himself. The Wardolam prison was, however, as benign as a prison could be. The cell that Orren and his friends inhabited was huge, with soft piles of straw to lie upon, and illumination from lit torches in the passageway. The yelia had also provided blankets, though these proved unnecessary, given the mild temperature of the Ghoul Vale.

On the right side of the cell was a little door, behind which was a small room containing a privy. There was also a spigot from which clear water ran, with a basin. Nearby was a large bathing chamber, in which the prisoners were allowed to bathe privately, one by one.

The three humans had been given several changes of new clothes. These included soft, knee-length undergarments, as well as comfortable leggings, and long shirts. The yelia furnished Haxel with raw flax, from which he made new clothes for himself. Every day, the Sun-Children took the prisoners' used clothes to be laundered, and brought the clean ones back.

Twice a day food was brought to the prison cell, together with dishes and spoons. The meals consisted of spongy pot bread, groats, various stews, fresh fruits and vegetables, nuts, and a spicy butter-cheese. Clay vessels containing goat's milk, flavored water, and fruit juice accompanied every meal. Every day, the prisoners ate and drank to their satisfaction. They also were allowed out of their cell twice a day, to exercise in the dark thoroughfare.

All in all, the treatment Orren and his friends received at the hands of the yelia, was exemplary. It was a source of pride for Anselm, who continuously boasted of the kindness and fair ways of the Sun-Children. Their internment also served to heal wounds. Still, Orren was discontent, for he and his friends had spent three weeks inside the Wardolam prison, and there was no telling how much progress Berthus might have made during that time.

A week had passed since the night Orren experienced the terrible dream. He had, however, recovered from the trauma thanks to the ministrations of his friends, who used the mental power the newly created Bearers' Web gave them.

The most peculiar and even disturbing aspect of their sojourn was the yelian community itself. Orren had always been taught that 'elves' were beautiful beings, and when he first laid eyes upon them, he was indeed dazzled by their appearance. Over the past few weeks, however, he had seen enough of the Sun-Children to be able look past the bejeweled eyes with their elliptical pupils, and the glossy, lustrous hair. What he slowly came to realize was that in actuality, many 'Sun-Children' were quite ugly.

There were yelia who were magnificent and exceptionally tall, but almost all of these were white-haired elders. The younger Sun-Children were shorter and less attractive, and there were also fewer of them. It seemed that the younger a yelius was, the uglier he or she appeared. What was even more bizarre was that there were no yelian children. A handful of yelia had childlike appearances, but Anselm insisted that these individuals were actually between twenty-five and forty years old.

Shann-Rell, the yelian lady who had defended Orren's group during their trial, was a case in point. She was the same height as Anselm, which was somewhat short for a yelius. Her pointed ears poked up out of her shimmering black hair, but one of them was floppy and down-turned. She also had many wrinkles, even though she was clearly quite young.

Other younger yelia had similar defects, or else different ones. A yelius might have one arm shorter than the other. Another would be squint eyed, and a third would have a chin that curled upward.

One time, Orren made the mistake of asking Anselm to explain this phenomenon. The old man lost his temper, and let loose with a tirade of insults, calling Orren a 'stupid, narrow-minded boy with typical human blindness.' Marett, however, smoothed things over, explaining that Orren meant no disrespect. Mollified, the old man gave Orren the answer.

Basically, Anselm said, the yelia were in hiding, for they didn't want humans to discover their existence. The clouds above the Ghoul Vale admitted enough sunlight to enable crop growth, but the yelia themselves were forbidden to leave. Thus it was that generations of yelia had come and gone without ever laying eyes upon the Sun Father they loved so much.

Deprived of direct contact with their deity, the yelia became a sullen, glum race. Most of them refused to have children, and the handful who did had few partners to choose from. This trend worsened with each passing generation. The result was a serious limitation in bloodlines, and birth defects among those babies who *were* born.

Anselm then launched into an anti-human tirade, blaming humans for the plight of the yelia, and for the deterioration in the health of their population. Orren, however, ignored the old man. The boy could not help feeling that the yelia were doing this to themselves. What could be the purpose of having an entire race stay in the shadows, never to bask in the Sun Father's light? Surely the yelia, reputed to be extinct, would *truly* make themselves so by obeying this stupid decree? He dared not voice his opinions, however, lest he anger Anselm once again.

The sound of a key turning in a lock brought Orren out of his reverie. He looked up to see Shann-Rell and four shadow-clad yelian guards, enter the cell. Haxel and Marett stirred and opened their eyes, and Anselm leapt to his feet, ever ready to obey the yelia like the 'Slave' he was.

"Greetings, prisoners," Shann-Rell said in her fluty, lilting voice. "The Wardolam city council awaits, for we have made our final decision regarding your fate."

Orren and his friends filed out of the cell and walked alongside Shann-Rell and the guards, down the wide, torch lit passageway. The walls were lined with columns, which had been stylized to resemble tree trunks. Between the columns were numerous arches, and the ceiling contained multiple vaults. The vaulting had been carved in the likenesses of spreading branches, complete with leaves of stone. Between the pillars were colorful reliefs depicting forest birds, animals, and flowers. It seemed to Orren as though the complex had been carved in this manner so as to make it into some kind of artificial forest.

After twenty minutes of twists and turns, they entered the enormous council chamber, with its ninety-foot high, domed ceiling. Tree-shaped pillars ringed the space, and the mosaics and frescoes here were particularly beautiful, depicting all manner of animals, including some Orren could not identify. Fires blazed out of four cone-shaped, golden structures that resembled piles of fallen branches. The flames illuminated a grand, sky blue dome with a shimmering golden sun at its apex.

On the side of the chamber farthest from the entrance, sat an elevated dais, upon which was an elaborately carved, high-backed chair, with ivy-like patterns in the woodwork. A live peregrine falcon perched upon the chair's back, preening its feathers. A huge red mastiff with slavering jaws, lay on the dais, and sitting on the chair itself was Narx, the city council head.

Narx was effectively the ruler of the yelia. He was a severe man, who, besides for Berthus, probably inspired more fear than anyone Orren had ever encountered. He was nearly six-and-a-half feet tall, with a very broad forehead, which tapered downward into a long, thin face that ended in a sharp-pointed chin. His nose was unnaturally long, so much so that it drooped down over his lips, though it bent to the right, probably the result of a birth defect. His hands were gnarled and perpetually curled almost into a fist. Most disconcerting of all were his eyes. They were pure gold, and shimmered in the firelight, but they were cold and harsh, displaying hostility.

An enormous frame of silver-white hair framed the council head's face. Orren figured that the hair, the falcon, and the hound were symbols of authority. Narx wore a floor length gown of brilliant yellow, with golden sparkles that shimmered in the firelight, and a golden, sun-shaped pendant around his neck.

The other council members stood in a circle around the gwell-bearers. There were sixty of them in total, and whereas during the trial, they had worn elaborately embroidered robes, this time they all wore floor length gowns. The majority of the council members,

Shann-Rell included, wore yellow gowns similar to Narx's, but a few wore green, brown, or purple ones. One man wore a blue gown and one woman, a red one.

A gong sounded, momentarily startling the red mastiff.

"The Wardolam city council has come to order!" Narx's voice boomed through the chamber. "Stand to attention, prisoners, for the council has decided your fate. It will not, however, be proclaimed here in the council chamber, but in the city forum, before the entire community of the Sun-Children. Every last member of our blessed race that still inhabits Urth, shall be witness to your sentencing, as will the sacred Staff of Diktat, upon which you, the accused, must swear."

A doorway opened behind Narx's throne. Nine shadow-robed guards entered the chamber. Four of them took up positions behind Orren and his friends, and the other five grabbed hold of handles that were attached to Narx's throne. They swiveled the entire dais around and, to Orren's surprise, wheeled it, together with Narx, the falcon, and the mastiff, out the door. The council members followed their leader, and then the shadow guards instructed the prisoners to do the same.

When Orren and his friends emerged from the council chamber, they found themselves on a wide platform some two-hundred feet wide, and extending from the council building to another structure of similar size and design. A wide staircase led down to a massive city square, which was ringed by large, decrepit buildings shaped like tree trunks.

The vast space was illuminated by hundreds of torches, resulting in a blaze that enabled Orren to see everything and everybody who was gathered there. Above the city, the ubiquitous cloudbank roiled. The sky was as dark as ever, indicating that this was still the middle of the night.

Hundreds of yelia were gathered in the forum. Despite the size of the crowd, however, the city square appeared empty. It had clearly been designed to accommodate much larger crowds than the one present on this night. Haxel, however, was impressed.

"There must be 2,000 yelia here!" he exclaimed.

"2,348 to be exact," Anselm corrected him. "Before you, my zhiv friend, are gathered all of the Sun Children. 860 of the Magg tribe, 550 Kell and the same number of Rau. The Nebb number 180; the Haas 155, and the smallest tribe—the Orr, 60."

"Each tribe, I presume, corresponds to a gwell," Marett said.

"Right," Anselm nodded. "Each tribe specializes in the element that governs its gwell."

The tribes were easily identifiable, because members wore robes the color of their tribes' respective gwellen. The Magg were clearly in a position of dominance, for they were situated closest to the steps, and the others stood behind them, with the small Orr tribe all the way in the back.

The council members stood on the steps facing the platform. Alongside the walls were twenty shadow guards in their dark raiment, surrounded by shimmering yellow nimbuses. Narx's throne was situated against the back wall, facing the yelian assembly. The council head looked as though he might explode in rage at any second. At his feet, the red mastiff still lay, and the falcon was still perched on top of the throne.

To the right of Narx's throne was a wooden post about nine feet tall. Its base had been sunk into the stone of the platform, and it was unadorned, save for the likeness of a golden sun at its apex.

"The Staff of Diktat," Anselm whispered in Orren's ear.

"Prisoners," Narx's voice barked out. "You are to hear and obey the sentence passed by the Wardolam city council. The council's decrees apply to all members of your party. It is only fitting therefore, that your entire party be present. Guards, bring forth the Moon Child."

Orren's heart leapt at those words. Haxel and Marett let out cries of joy. The gaze of the entire assembly was upon the door.

An awed hush fell over the yelia as the gigantic shape of Quartz materialized in the doorway. The sholl crouched down onto his hands and knees, and crawled out. He then straightened himself to his full, twenty-foot height. A collective gasp of astonishment passed through the yelian assembly.

Quartz looked much the same as he had when Orren, Haxel, and Marett last saw him, though the cracks in his hide appeared to have deepened somewhat, and there were bits of debris caught up in his skooch. A warm feeling of pure love emanated from him, and washed over Orren and his friends. Unable to control their emotions, Orren, Haxel, and Marett ran over to the sholl. Each one grabbed a giant finger and caressed it.

"What happened, Quartz?" Marett asked. "How did you get here?"

"The Great Master Narx and his shadow men ascended the arc during the night, Madam Marett," Quartz explained. "Great Narx pressed two Sun-Stones onto me and spoke, thus reviving me. When I returned to my proper sholl-form, the yelia instructed me to follow them into the vale, and I did, for it is a sholl's duty to serve. They gave me fruit wine to drink and fruits to eat. I am overjoyed and humbled by the presence of my masters and the Sun Father's progeny."

"We missed you, Big Friend," Haxel said with tears in his eyes.

"Quartz, I think it's time you met Anselm," Orren said, waving toward the old man. "Anselm's gonna be our guide, and I promise you, we can trust him."

"I am aware of this, Master Orren," Quartz said. "Master Anselm, it is a rare privilege to make your acquaintance. We may never have met in person, but I saw you in the dream we all shared. I cannot thank you enough for the kindnesses you have shown to my masters. You too, are now my master."

"I was only acting in obedience to the Guiding Light of my people," Anselm said. "I too, saw you in the shared dream, Quartz, and I felt your love. These youngsters have told me all about you, and I can see that you deserve all the praises they heap upon you and more. I was always taught that the sholls went extinct. Never did I imagine I would meet one, and I must say, you are magnificent, regal, and awe-inspiring."

The emotions that emanated from Quartz in response to Anselm's words basically amounted to a sholl's version of blushing. "I do not deserve your kind words, Master Anselm," he said.

"If you please!" Narx's voice boomed. "You prisoners are wasting the council's time. Stand at attention—humans, zhiv, and sholl. Turn to face the council head and the Staff of Diktat."

Orren and his friends did as they were told.

"You must each approach the Staff," Narx said. "Place your hands upon it and solemnly swear to abide by its authority, for through it, the council head's words will become binding upon you. When all of you have so sworn, the decree will take effect. Now approach!"

Anselm did as he was told. "I solemnly swear to abide by the council's decree and the authority of the Staff of Diktat," he said.

Quartz did exactly as Anselm had done. Marett went next. Haxel looked at his master with uncertainty in his eyes.

"Just a minute," Orren said. "You said that the decree takes effect only if all of us swear to it, right?"

"Correct," Narx said, "but do you dare challenge the council head's authority, young human male?"

"I want to know what happens if one of us refuses to swear."

"You young fool!" Anselm shouted, his face purple with rage. "What do you *think* will happen?"

"You will all be handed over to the ghouls," Narx said. "The undead ones will devour your souls, and you prisoners will join their number. The sholl's size will be no protection for him or for you, and neither will the Slave's preferred status."

"Does that answer your question?" Anselm asked in a sardonic manner.

Orren tried to think of a way out of this predicament, but he could come up with nothing.

"Master, I don't think we have a choice," Haxel implored.

"I don't want to be tricked," Orren said.

"Orren!" Marett yelled. "Stop being stubborn!"

"These are Sun-Children, you stupid young fool!" Anselm said. "They're far superior to anything you could ever hope to be. Now get yourself over to the Staff, and take the oath!"

"Pay heed to the Slave's words, young human male," Narx said in a dangerous-sounding voice.

"Master, what have we got to lose?" Haxel asked. "If we don't do it, we'll die. If we do it, we might have a chance at life."

"OK," Orren said. He strode over to the Staff, took it in his hands and said, "I swear on this staff and on whatever the council says." Then turning to Narx, he disdainfully asked, "Is that good enough for you?"

"It will suffice," Narx said. "Now zhiv, it's your turn."

Haxel grasped the Staff of Diktat. "I swear that this Staff and the council have authority over me."

"Very well," Narx said. "You have all accepted the binding nature of the council's decision, which consists of three decrees. The first decree is as follows. Orren Randolphus, Marett Reina Baines, Druba Haxel Kokolaminkokla, Quartz Moonchild, and Anselm the Slave, you have all been designated temporary gwell-bearers. Therefore, you will be allowed to continue with your quest for the Sacred Stones. In fact, not only will you be allowed to continue; you are *commanded* to continue. You will bring back Magna, Nebi, Kalsh, and Ru'i to Wardolam, even if it means confronting this Berthus usurper to do so."

Orren and his friends all let out a cheer. Orren felt a surge of triumph and excitement, though it was tinged with dread at the prospect of confronting his brother.

"Clothes, food, and other necessities, along with the Slave's donkey, have been provided for you in the foyer chamber inside the city's main gate," Narx continued. "All of you will have what you need, save for the sholl. The resources of Wardolam are not sufficient to sustain so large a being."

Quartz bowed his head in acquiescence. "I will provide for my own sustenance, Great Master Narx," he said.

"The second decree is as follows," Narx continued. "You gwell-bearers will not be allowed to take Orya or Hesh with you. The two stones hitherto found, belong to the Sun-Children, and with the Sun-Children they will remain."

"What?" Orren was outraged. "How do you expect us to find the other four? Don't you know the stones are attracted to one another?"

"That's not the council head's problem," Narx said. "That is your own. You have only yourselves to blame. What naugus is so presumptuous as to think he has the right to bear a gwell?"

"Would you prefer Berthus had them all?" Orren shouted.

"Orren, please don't argue," Marett begged.

"Yes, shut your mouth," Anselm snapped.

Orren grit his teeth and clenched his fists, but said nothing.

"The third decree is as follows," Narx said. "You gwell-bearers have sworn on the Staff of Diktat. It therefore has power over you. The Staff of Diktat is the object whose magic binds the ghouls to their state and to this vale. You five are now similarly bound. You have three months in which to obtain the other four stones and bring them back to Wardolam. That's ninety days from now, and midnight of that day is the Moment of Reckoning. Your task is to find all six gwellen and place them in the hands of the council head by then. If you fail to do so, the Ghoul's Curse will take effect.

"The Ghoul's Curse binds you to the Vale, and transforms you into undead beings in bondage to this place. No matter how far you may flee, you can't escape the Ghoul's Curse, so don't try, for you will of necessity, be drawn back into this vale. Therefore, gwell-bearers, your quest is under a curse."

"I knew it!" Orren hollered. "We were tricked by these lying, sneaky—"

"Remove the ungrateful human male and his friends from my sight," Narx said. "Take them to the foyer chamber to get their supplies and their donkey, and then throw them out of the city."

"*I'm* ungrateful!" Orren yelled. "Without us you'd never have gotten Orya and Hesh! You're the one who—"

The shadow guards grabbed the boy and muffled him. He kicked and scratched in an attempt to hurt them, but to no avail. Orren was quickly immobilized. The darkness of the shadow guards' raiment swallowed him up.

# GIFTS FROM THE TRIBES

Orren could not contain his rage. He kicked the city gate repeatedly.

"Curses on that Narx!" he said through gritted teeth. "He threw us out of the city like pieces of rubbish! How are we gonna find the other four gwellen without Hesh and Orya?"

"Oh, quit your melodrama," Anselm said with a derisive snort. "You're fourteen years old, but you're acting like you're four."

"Don't you get it?" Orren yelled. "The gwellen are attracted to one another! That's why we need Hesh and Orya, so we can find a third and—"

"You think I don't know all that?" Anselm said. "What do you take me for, an idiot? I tracked *you* down using that same mutual attraction you're talking about. I probably know more about it than you do. By the Guiding Light, young Ornery, for such an intelligent boy you can be a colossal idiot!"

Orren was about to retort with an insult of his own, but Marett shot him a warning look. He remembered what the Duraline girl had told him about respecting one's elders no matter how irritating they could be. He stayed silent, not wholly out of respect for Anselm, but in honor of the memory of another elderly person—dear, departed Richard.

"None of this is helping us," Marett said. "My friends, we have to look on the bright side. The yelia have allowed us to complete our quest. Not only that, but they've given us food and provisions, and fine clothes, and they've given Jasper back to us."

"Can't argue with that, can we?" Anselm said. He lovingly patted the head of the beloved little donkey that had traveled far and wide with him.

Orren also had to concede that Marett was right, for the yelia had fitted him out with fine new clothes to replace the lost ones. He wore a short tunic and comfortable hose that fit perfectly, as well as a pair of boots that were almost knee-high. A cloak of fine sheepskin, with large pockets, served as an excellent replacement for the vouzan garment he had lost in Sherbass. A pair of long gloves warmed his hands, while allowing his fingers to move freely.

The yelia had given Orren a water skin and a hunting bow, as well as a short sword similar to the one he had stolen from the Lith Gorge bandits. However, Grnoud, the council translator, who oversaw the gwell-bearers' expulsion from Wardolam, would not release the gwell-sacks that Haxel had fashioned out of Forest of Doom plants. Orren protested. He tried to explain that the sacks could conceal the gwellen from detection. Grnoud would not relent, explaining that the omission was Narx's decision. Apparently, the yelian ruler feared that Orren and his friends would use the sacks to run away with the stones. That, of course, made no sense, because all the gwell-bearers had the Ghoul's Curse hanging over their heads anyway. The whole episode convinced Orren that Narx was basically insane.

Marett was dressed in similar attire, though her tunic was longer than Orren's, extending to three inches above her knees. She had been equipped with a triple-looped belt exactly like the one she had stolen from Jurgan, and she had been given a sword and a dagger. The water skin she had found in a Rivulene village, with which she had saved Anselm's life, had been given back to her.

During their internment, the yelia had provided Haxel with raw flax. The zhiv had used his prison time well, deftly creating new garments for himself. He was now wrapped warmly in a thick shaspa, and he also wore plant fiber leggings and long gloves. He had even been given fresh new grasses for the short skirt he wore. Haxel now had a water skin of his own, as well as a new double-bladed ax, which he attached to his skirt belt. The yelia had returned to him his precious shlenki sack, with all the shiny objects he had obtained during the course of his adventures.

Anselm wore a traveling tunic made of goat hide, as well as matching leggings, and a pair of boots much like the ones Orren and Marett wore. The yelia had also given him a hooded cloak made of pigskin, as well as a water skin of his own, and a lantern that was now dispelling the pitch darkness of the Ghoul Vale. His only weapon was a slingshot, which he assured the others, he could use to great effect.

Quartz was the only member of the group wearing the exact same clothes that he had worn upon first entering Wardolam. The pensive rock giant did not seem to mind, however; being reunited with his friends was satisfaction enough for him.

The yelia had laden Jasper with sacks of food and medicines, quivers of arrows, coils of rope, and two extra lanterns. The little donkey seemed eager to act as a beast of burden. She balked when Quartz tried to take some of these things off her back, and thereby lighten her load. Anselm explained to the sholl that Jasper derived a certain sense of pride from her work.

"You know, we really ought to get going," Marett said.

"Yes," Anselm agreed. "It won't do us any good to stand around while Ornery throws a temper tantrum."

Orren seethed, but Haxel calmed him down with a hand on his shoulder.

"OK, Anselm," Marett said. "You know the way. Lead us."

"We'll walk in single file," Anselm instructed. He lit one of the lanterns Jasper carried, and handed it to Marett. "That's the best way to avoid getting lost in this impenetrable darkness. I'll go first, of course. Jasper will follow right behind me, and Marett comes next. Ornery and Haxel, you two keep your eyes glued to

Marett's lantern. Quartz will take up the rear. You don't mind that, do you, Quartz?"

"Not at all, Master Anselm," Quartz said. "It is an honor to follow your advice."

"Let's go then."

They walked through dense, foggy blackness. Despite his anger at Anselm, Orren understood that the old man had the best technique for traveling through the Ghoul Vale. The roiling clouds were so thick that the lantern lights were the only things visible, and even they appeared blurry.

There was a light shuffling sound. Several things were moving in the darkness.

"Good Sir Anselm!" Haxel yelled in a panic-stricken voice. "The ghouls are trying to get us!"

"No they're not!" Anselm shouted back. "We're under the council head's protection. The ghouls are forbidden to lay hands upon us."

Suddenly, six lights appeared in the gloom. They were lamps, similar to the ones Anselm and Marett carried, and each one was borne by a shadow guard.

"Wh-What's going on?" Haxel asked.

"Esteemed Sun Guardians," Anselm said. "To what do we owe the honor of your presence?"

"Gentle Anselm, it is I," a familiar, female voice spoke. "Shann-Rell, representing the Magg tribe." At that point, she removed her dark, shadow robe to reveal the customary golden-yellow one of her tribe.

With me are my fellow chiefs," Shann-Rell continued. "I introduce Ordam of the Kell, Diduann of the Rau, Thraix of the Nebb, Warah-Hoolah of the Haas, and Sha-Rax of the Orr. We come bearing gifts." All the other tribal chiefs removed their shadow robes. They stood in the swirling mist, illuminated by the torches, and resplendent in their tribal garb.

"What gifts could you offer us?" Orren asked with a derisive snort.

"To answer that, Orren Randolphus, I must provide you with an explanation," the yelian woman said. "I'm sure you noticed that we Sun Children are divided into six tribes. Each one derives its origins from a sacred gwell. My tribe, the Magg, is the largest, and we dominate the city council. Narx is our chief, and I rank second. We are the tribe of Magna, the yellow gwell of air."

"OK," Orren said. "What does that have to do with us?"

"Oh, show some respect, will you?" Anselm huffed.

"Honored Shann-Rell, I apologize for Orren's brashness," Marett said. "Orren, remember what I told you."

The boy did not respond, but Shann-Rell spoke in a soothing voice that caused his cynicism to dissipate.

"Narx is our leader," she explained, "but that does not mean we agree with everything he says. He and a small number of advisors despise you gwell-bearers, and want you to join the ranks of the undead ghouls. You should know, however, that among the yelian populace, you are hailed as heroes. You did, of course, restore two of our sacred Sun-Stones to us, after all these centuries. I promise you, noble gwell-bearers, you're very beloved in Wardolam."

"Funny way to show it," Orren muttered under his breath.

"My fellow tribal chiefs and I share your outrage over Narx's second decree," Shann-Rell continued. "We understood that it is very difficult, if not impossible, to find a gwell without having another gwell at hand. We could not, however, violate Narx's word, so we've done the next best thing.

"The gwellen are not the only magical objects possessed by our people, though they are by far the most powerful. There are other objects of lesser power, which in the human tongue, are called talismans. They are quite ordinary objects, but they became magical long ago, when their creators infused them with power from the gwellen. They've been with us ever since, awaiting the day when they would be of use.

"Each yelian tribe has a particular talisman that is that tribe's treasure. We offer these tribal talismans to you, noble gwell-bearers. Use them judiciously, for each talisman can only be used once, after which it crumbles to dust. Each one of you must choose a talisman. As we present the objects to you, look into your heart to decide which one to take. If you have borne a gwell, try to select a talisman that corresponds to a different gwell, lest the magic of a particular element overwhelm your senses.

"Only the bearer of a particular talisman can use it. However, a bearer can 'carry' other individuals. What that means is that a bearer can choose other persons to be beneficiaries of his object's magic. The more beneficiaries carried, however, the greater the mental effort necessary to keep the magic running, so be selective in who you choose to carry, at the time when you activate your talisman."

She reached into a pocket of her yellow robe and drew forth a small fan, of the variety that noble women use on hot days. "On behalf of the Magg tribe, I present the Fan of Invisibility. It weaves a whirlwind around its user, hiding him and anyone he carries, from his enemies' perception, and shielding its beneficiaries from injury. Who among you will claim it?"

Orren felt drawn to the flimsy-looking fan. He stepped forward and held his hands out. "I will," he stammered. "I'm the leader, and I drew all my friends into this quest and the curse. I've got to do what I can to protect these folks."

Shann-Rell smiled and placed the Fan of Invisibility in Orren's hands. The boy thanked her, and placed the talisman in one of his cloak pockets before stepping back.

Diduann, the purple-robed chief of the Rau was a very tall yelian male with sapphire eyes and bone-white hair. He drew a small object out of his pocket and revealed it to be a flute-shaped instrument on a chain.

"On behalf of the Rau I present the Whistle of Merging," he said. "Whoever chooses it must blow upon it while bearing a particular animal in mind. The mind of the user and the minds of any beneficiaries carried by the user will merge with the mind of the selected animal. The user can then direct that animal to do his bidding. Who will claim it?"

Marett strode forward. "Connecting mentally to certain creatures is an art that my ancestors practiced, but which was lost. Perhaps this whistle will give me some insight into how it was done."

Diduann smiled down at the girl and gently placed the chain around her neck. Marett fingered the whistle with pride, and stepped back.

Warah-Hoolah, a six-foot female with silver-white hair, brown eyes, and a wrinkled but beautiful face, spoke next. She reached into the dark robes that lay on the ground at her feet, and revealed a staff some five feet tall and carved with the likeness of flowing water. Because the blue-robed Haas chief could not speak any human tongue, Shann-Rell translated for her.

"Warah-Hoolah offers the Staff of Transport," Shann-Rell said. "It has the power to travel through water, and transports any user who grasps onto it, as well as any beneficiaries who grasp it together with him. This staff is stronger than the wildest river or the roughest tide. It can even climb waterfalls. Who will claim this talisman?"

"I fear water," Haxel said, as he stepped forward. "But the Master and the Miss have taught me to face my fears. Maybe this staff will help me."

When Shann-Rell translated his words, Warah-Hoolah nodded and looked at Haxel with warmth in her eyes. She handed the staff to the zhiv, who took it and caressed it before stepping back. He did not seem to mind the fact that the talisman was substantially taller than he was.

Thraix, the green-clad Nebb chief was tiny; he was almost a head shorter than Orren. His ginger hair was turning white, and he had a crooked nose, a curled chin, and blue eyes. Like Warah-

Hoolah, he could not speak a human tongue. He reached into the dark robes at his feet and drew forth a flask of thick glass, with a green liquid inside.

"Thraix offers the Salve of Recovery," Shann-Rell said. "It will heal all wounds and illnesses sustained by its user or by any beneficiary he carries, so long as that individual has not crossed over into death. Who will claim it?"

Suddenly, the great dark shape of Quartz blotted out the little yelian chief and his lantern from view. "I am most unworthy," the sholl said. "A yelian colony was destroyed under my watch and thus, I have inflicted hurt upon the world, but perhaps in some small way, I can heal it." He stepped back, with the flask in his huge left hand, and Thraix became visible again.

Sha-Rax, the chief of the Orr, was skinny and bald, except for a shock of black hair. He had golden eyes with narrow, elliptical pupils that made him appear reptilian. Only one of his ears was pointed; the other was round like a human ear. He wore robes of such bright red that in the torchlight, they were jarring to the senses. He held a small, silver tinderbox in his hand.

"Sha-Rax offers the Tinderbox of Warming," Shann-Rell translated for him. "It will bring warmth to anything, be it earth, water, or air, and whatever you warm will remain so for two days. You need not even designate beneficiaries to be carried, unless of course, it is people you're warming. After all, anyone can benefit from a warm object. Who will claim this talisman?"

"I will!" Anselm cried out. He ran up to the yelian chief with great enthusiasm, and then suddenly remembering his place, prostrated himself on the ground. Sha-Rax tapped the old man's shoulder, and Anselm rose to his feet.

"I've had many adventures," Anselm said, "and thank the Guiding Light, I'm still fit, strong, and healthy. However, I'm not the young man I once was, and every winter, I feel the cold a little bit more in my bones. I like the idea of lessening it."

Sha-Rax placed the box in Anselm's hands, and Anselm thanked him in the yelian tongue. He then put the talisman into one of his pockets.

Ordam, chief of the Kell, was tall, with golden hair and equally golden eyes. Her chin was unnaturally long, and her brown robes appeared drab next to the bright ones Sha-Rax wore. Her voice had a soothing quality, and she was able to speak the classic human tongue. In her hand, she held a small copper shovel.

"On behalf of the Kell, I offer you the Shovel of Tunnels," she said. "In the blink of an eye it will dig as long a tunnel as its user desires. I perceive, however, a problem, for there are only five gwell-bearers. Mayhap one of you will consent to bear a second talisman?"

Before anyone had a chance to respond, Jasper trotted forward. To everyone's astonishment, the donkey took the little shovel in her mouth.

"Well why not?" Ordam said with a broad smile. "Why indeed not?"

"Truly a remarkable beast," Marett said.

"Jasper's more than just a beast," Haxel chimed in.

"She traversed great distances with me," Anselm said with great pride. "She's probably familiar with every kind of terrain you get on this continent, so why shouldn't she bear the earth talisman?" He took the shovel from her mouth and placed it inside one of the sacks the donkey carried.

"How are these things supposed to help us find the gwellen?" Orren asked. "They're not attracted to the stones, are they?"

"No," Shann-Rell said, "but when you use them, your minds will become more attuned to the magic, and thus to the gwellen. We realize it's not much, but we feel it was important to let you have these talismans. After all, you're the ones doing this kindness for us."

"Richard would call it doing their dirty work," Orren whispered to Haxel. The zhiv nodded.

"And now farewell, gwell-bearers," Shann-Rell said. "May the Sun Father and the Moon Mother guide you along your way."

The chieftains all put their shadow cloaks on and disappeared into the darkness.

# FOUR STORIES

The Ghoul Vale was not the only location where important selections were taking place. At the base of Airen's Arc, in the early hours of the morning, Berthus sat in his tent, unable to sleep.

A week had passed since the dream that had alerted him to the need for his own Bearers' Web. During that time, his main camp had caught up with him, and thousands of tents were pitched on the mountain slopes and on the arc itself. Berthus's army now numbered over 10,000, and it consisted of an odd assortment of Drammites, Framguth knights, Gothma peasants, brigands, and other assorted hangers-on. There were also slaves, horses, dogs, and various beasts of burden, as well as four wolfards—huge, bipedal, slavering beasts with wolf heads, which Berthus had enslaved and kept as status symbols. Day and night, sordigryps soared over the campsite, completely in thrall to the Lord of the Corcadine and the purple gwell he bore.

Berthus was not intent on going anywhere right now. He was waiting for the swine boy and his friends to emerge from the dreaded vale. He also was busy searching the arc and its environs for a legendary hidden pass that was supposed to lead through the Greymantles, and directly to the banks of the Hargash, the river upon which the Fallagourn Falls were situated. Meanwhile, Iranda was searching for four more potential Web members.

The young tyrant did not really want to give anyone else the power to use the stones. It seemed, however, that he had no choice. Using Ru'i's magic made him violently ill, but that changed when Dargun Rodrick was there to help him. Iranda had succeeded in convincing the Drammite leader to become Ru'i's designated bearer, thus ensuring that he was in thrall to the stone. Berthus savored the fact that he could keep the gwell, yet place its burden on someone else's shoulders, and at the same time, make that person dependent on him.

"Berthus, are you awake?" Iranda's voice called out in the darkness.

"Of course," Berthus lit his lantern. "I can't sleep."

"Good," Iranda said. "I think I've found the third person for your Web." Then, addressing the individual she was with, she said, "Go on in."

The tent flap opened and a small figure entered.

Berthus immediately recognized Shelton Kassi, his right-hand man. Shelton was in his early fifties. He was an ugly little man who resembled a rat, but he, together with his hulking nephew Lumus, were among Berthus's earliest followers. Shelton was utterly ruthless, but as an administrator he was superb, and Berthus's men feared him.

It came as no surprise to Berthus that Shelton had been selected. Berthus had considered him many times, but he wanted Iranda to make that judgment.

"Greetings, m'lord," Shelton said.

"Greetings, Shelton," Berthus replied. "Please sit down."

Shelton sat on a chair facing his lord. The lantern light flickered in his little eyes, and made his bald forehead shine.

"You and Lumus have always served me well, Shelton," the young lord said, "but Iranda says I must feel a familial bond to you, which currently I don't. So tell me why I should. Why do you deserve to be a chosen one, a Web member, and responsible for a gwell, specifically Orya, gwell of fire?"

"M'lord, Iranda told me you'd ask this question," the little man said, "so I'll get right down to it. You see, m'lord, the Kassi family is one of the oldest in the Corcadine. During the early years of the Regnum—that ancient empire everyone talks about—we actually ruled the peninsula. Our fortunes, however, declined even before the Regnum fell apart, but we still kept our titles. We maintained great influence in the Corcadinian Council until your father came to our land, and built his wealth and power.

"The stupid folk of the Corcadine, despite being Gothma, fell for this Framguth usurper because he brought employment, and unlike most Framguth lords, worshipped the astra. His place was established right in the heart of House Kassi's former domain, and most of our family went along with it. The only ones who didn't were my cousin Klido, and myself. We kicked up a fuss, but the council overruled us and declared us subversives. Klido fled to the north and became an outlaw, but I wasn't so fortunate. I was flung into prison and languished there for eight years. Then you rescued me, and you gave my brother's son, Lumus, a purpose to his drunken, brawling life."

"So why do you serve *me*?" Berthus asked. "I'm pure-blooded Framguth."

"That's an accident of your birth," Shelton said, "however, unlike your father, you grew up in a Gothma land, speak with a Gothma accent, and were raised by Richard, who was a Gothma. Appearances mean nothing, m'lord. There are light-haired Gothma folk, , though not on the Corcadine, for our isolation has kept our blood pure. You also get dark-haired Framguth. Unlike Klido, who's a hothead with a backward mindset, I know that being Framguth or Gothma is not a matter of color or even blood. It's a matter of how you behave and how you lead, and you, my lord, lead like a Gothma. That's why you have such a large Gothma following. My people can recognize one of their own."

"Your brother, however, carries your father's spirit," Shelton continued. "The swine boy's a real Framguth pig. No wonder he makes common cause with Duraline upstarts, goblins, and Drammites. No Gothma would accept such dregs into his company."

"I've accepted the Drammites into mine," Berthus said in a warning voice.

"You're using them m'lord," Shelton said, "just as you used the Framguth pigs. I know you intend to discard them all when you're done with them—all except the Gothma folk."

Berthus nodded with satisfaction. Not everything the little man said made sense, but the mere fact that Shelton identified Berthus's father and brother as his own personal enemies, was enough to create feelings of kinship.

"What would you gain from following me, Shelton?" Berthus asked.

"When you become emperor of LeFain, m'lord," the little man said, "I would like the Corcadine as my own—my family inheritance, to rule as your vassal."

Morning turned to afternoon, and Berthus awakened. He did not normally sleep so late, but the night had passed in insomnia. The tent flap opened. "I see we've woken up at last," Iranda said. "And not a moment too soon. Berthus, the fourth member-to-be of your Bearers' Web wishes to address you."

"Send him in."

To Berthus's surprise, Lord Bertrand Hemric entered. He prostrated himself on the floor in front of his liege, his head so low it looked like he was kissing the earth.

Lord Hemric was a minor Framguth noble from the northeastern corner of the Land Betwixt the Rivers. His demesne was only fit for growing beans and flax, so House Hemric was not wealthy or powerful. They were, however, excellent fighters, and most of their income came from being hired as mercenaries by more powerful lords.

Lord Hemric was an unremarkable-looking man. He was of medium height, neither handsome nor ugly. His eyes were dull gray and rather lifeless. His hair was umber brown, as was his scraggly beard. He was missing his right ear and two fingers from his left hand. He wore a faded blue tunic and hose, with a similarly faded red eagle emblazoned on his chest.

Hemric had joined Berthus together with the other Framguth lords, and immediately impressed his new liege with his fighting prowess. He was effective at raiding villages for slaves, though his cruelty and ruthlessness shocked even Berthus. When the Framguth lords, upon learning of the alliance with the Drammites, rebelled against Berthus, Hemric was with them, but at some stage he switched sides. He later claimed that the rebel lords forced him to revolt with them, and that they had been the ones who had inflicted his injuries. Berthus was never sure what to make of that, but he allowed Hemric to rejoin his forces—one of only two Framguth lords to do so.

"This should be interesting," Berthus said. "Bertrand, rise. Sit in that chair and say your piece. I'm eager to see how Iranda thinks you could possibly become a Web member."

Hemric did as he was told, and began his story.

"M'lord," he said. "As you know, I'm a Framguth noble from a family that relies on our boys becoming mercenaries, but it wasn't always so.

"When the Regnum came into existence, we Framguth were primitive, tribal folk, who valued courage and honor. The Gothma legions invaded our lands repeatedly, and we suffered in many ways. They were our foes, but we were impressed by them and copied their farming. That's why our numbers exploded. We needed more room, so we expanded in the only direction we could—into the Regnum.

"The Gothma attempted to drive us back, so we organized under the leadership of our chiefs. The greatest chief of all was Hemric, my ancestor. Under him and his heirs, we drove back the Regnum, even raiding Metrus, the Gothma capital.

"What House Hemric and other great houses didn't realize was that while we were bravely fighting on the front, lesser chiefs stayed behind and seized all the land. They adopted the ways of the Gothma governors, living decadently in their castles. Great houses, like that of Hemric, were left with only peripheral lands. We've eked out a bare living ever since, and have suffered degradation at the hands of Framguth lords who live like Gothma apes, and aren't even worthy to lick the horse dung off my boots."

Lord Hemric spat on the ground in a display of disgust.

"What does all that have to do with me?" Berthus asked.

"You, m'lord were raised in a Gothma cesspool," Hemric said, "but you came out a pure Framguth, unlike so many of the old families. Framguth are clever folks. We had to be, in order to survive. The stupid lesser lords who followed you, however, couldn't even see that your alliance with the Drammites was merely for survival. I tried to tell them that you'd get rid of the Drammites when they were no longer useful, but the idiots wouldn't listen. That's why they cut me up."

"And the swine boy?" Berthus asked. "What do you see in him?"

"He serves the astra," Hemric said, "while we Framguth houses serve the odia. He's allied to the meddlesome baron of Alivadus, who wants to put a stop to our ways. He brought a goblin into our lands, bringing us misfortune. He threw the Drammites at us; were it not for him, they could have been destroyed easily. The Framguth lords rebelled against you because of him.

"The foolishness of the other Framguth lords was actually good for me, because it may mean that House Hemric will be restored to its rightful position in the world."

"It certainly will," Berthus said. "I'll give you all the Land Betwixt the Rivers for your own."

A rare expression of gratitude appeared on Hemric's face. "Iranda said you'd be gracious, m'lord. The hope of my family will come at last…" the Framguth lord's face then darkened. "Unless the meddlesome baron steps in, and if the swine boy brings him the gwellen…"

Berthus noted with pleasure that the Framguth lord's body tensed as he spoke these words. It warmed his heart.

"Hemric," he said, "I have a proposal for you, specifically having to do with Hesh, the gwell of water…"

Berthus remembered the very first time he saw Jurgan. The bandit chief had been caught up in the flows of a swollen river and, holding onto a log, struggled to stay afloat. Berthus rescued him by lassoing him and pulling him to shore, because he wanted to know whether the flash flood had something to do with the swine boy.

As it turned out, Jurgan had been the leader of a notorious group of bandits, who terrorized the Plattveld region. They proved, however, to be no match for the young thief, who used Hesh's magic to drown them all. Jurgan was the sole survivor.

Jurgan stood almost a head taller than Berthus, and was broader as well. His ugly face was scarred, and he had long black hair, bushy dark eyebrows, and a beard to match. He did not scare Berthus, however; in fact, when the Lord of the Corcadine first learned that the swine boy's escape was due to Jurgan's negligence, he flew into a rage and beat the bandit savagely.

Once Berthus's anger was assuaged, he allowed the bruised and bloodied giant to join his army, figuring that a man his size would make a good status symbol. Jurgan never showed any resentment for the beating he had sustained; quite the contrary, he showed deep respect for Berthus's dominance. Ever since then, he had served his new master loyally, and had been instrumental in bringing all of Berthus's pirates, bandits, and assorted criminal types, into line. So obedient did they become, that few of them deserted Berthus even when the Drammites were coming at him from all directions.

"M'lord," Jurgan prostrated himself on the ground at Berthus's feet.

"I'd ask you to sit on that chair," Berthus said, "but you're so big, I fear you might break it, so sit where you are and look up at me. I want to know why Iranda thinks I could have a familial bond toward you."

"Great Lord of the Corcadine," Jurgan said. "It may surprise you to discover that I was once a devout Astralite."

"Are you joking?"

"No, m'lord," Jurgan said. "I was born and raised in Salin, the land that lies in LeFain's western extremity, where my family, House de Burnoisse, a family of mixed Framguth and Gothma descent, produced fine wines and cheese, and gave abundantly to the Church. Not being the eldest son, I did not stand in line to inherit their domain, and neither did I desire to be a knight, so I took up religious vows. That's how I ended up in the Abbey of Sanct Ju'ann the Fisherman beside the Great Western Ocean, among the peaceful monks. Our lives were devoted to prayer, meditation, and copying manuscripts. We also preached in the villages, and the abbot especially favored me for this, because my size gets folks' attention, and I have a loud, booming voice. It was a pleasant, satisfying life, but it came to an end when the Vaaks invaded."

"Who?" Berthus asked.

"The Vaaks," Jurgan said. "Kinsfolk of the Framguth who live in the Isles of the White Bear, in the shadow of the Great Northern Ice. Their lands are practically useless, so they live by raiding, destroying, and loading up their dragon-prowed ships with slaves. The Vaaks cannot get to LeFain's southern coasts, because the mountainous Carrina Isthmus cuts off the Sea of Tepidia from the Great Western Ocean.

"The Vaaks are particularly attracted to churches and monasteries, because of the precious, sacred items they contain. The raiders came to our abbey and destroyed it, killing the monks. They burned the nearby villages, taking slaves by the hundreds. I was the only surviving monk, and that's because I crushed the life out of three Vaaks with my bare hands. The others left me alone, thinking I was a demon or something. Even so, my entire world was reduced to a smoking ruin. The astra did nothing to assist their faithful monks, so I stopped worshipping them.

"I returned home, but when my father discovered my loss of faith, he cut me off. I entered the service of a powerful Framguth lord named Claude LeSaxonne, who served the odia as faithfully as my family served the astra. In fact he was one of the biggest supporters of odia-worship in Salin. However, he lost his life in a battle with a rival lord. With LeSaxonne out of the way, the Church was able to suppress odia-worship in that area. The odia did nothing, for they too, are impotent.

"Being associated with an odia-worshipper left me without the means to support myself, and I couldn't go home, so I learned to live by brigandage. Others flocked to me, and we established our hideout in the Lith Gorge, and acquired swift horses, including several equatrii. Thus we became the most feared bandits from eastern Salin to the Sardalian. Our downfall came about thanks to the filthy girl we made our slave, and of course, your brother."

Berthus was not sure where this was all going.

"M'lord, the astra are worthless, as are the odia," Jurgan said. "Not by devotion or by worship does one survive, but by one's sheer might alone. I became mighty, but two children and a goblin destroyed my might. I pursue them, not out of a need for revenge, but to prove to myself that the power which I, through my own carelessness, lost, can be mine again.

"And yet, my lord, there is one mightier than me, and that is you. Despite my size and strength, you beat me. It was then that I knew that if I were to regain my might, then I must attach myself to the only person superior to me."

It was not the most emotionally moving story, but Berthus could appreciate the part about might and power. The swine boy had leeched away Berthus's own might, and only the lad's death could make things whole. Jurgan had a similar goal, albeit a much less sentimental one. However, the fact that they both desired the removal of the same obstacle to power was good enough for a familial connection to be established and for the selection of a bearer for Magna, stone of air.

There was no doubt in Berthus's mind that Felix Ramburgus was the most intelligent man in his entire army. Dargun Rodrick may have been a Duraline with a rich family lore, but he did not have the depth of practical knowledge or the experience that Ramburgus had, and he certainly was not as widely traveled.

Ramburgus was the same age as Shelton, but unlike Shelton, he was tall, handsome, and well built. He had short white hair, a youthful face, and startling blue eyes. He wore black boots and the fashionable doublet, loose breeches, and wide-brimmed hat of the urban bourgeoisie. Over all of this, he donned the purple cloak of the magic sniffer brotherhood.

Berthus first found out about the magic sniffers from Shelton, whose family had employed them in the past. He hired the obscure brotherhood to procure certain charms, with which he impressed pirates into his service. Ever since then, the magic sniffers had been very useful, for they were able to track down a magical object by detecting the psychic trail surrounding that object's bearer. The brotherhood had thus been Berthus's most powerful weapon against the swine boy.

Magic sniffers were intensely loyal to anyone who paid for their services, which explained how they were willing to follow Berthus into the wilderness. Originally there had been eight in his employ, but one was killed attempting to capture the swine boy. Four others found Berthus's alliance with the Drammites too much to bear, and in violation of Ramburgus's commands, joined the Framguth lords' rebellion. As a result, Berthus killed them with Kalsh's magic. Now only three were left—Ramburgus and two fresh-faced youngsters.

"So what do you have to tell me, Felix?" Berthus asked.

"My lord, it came as no surprise when Iranda explained to me how you wanted to create a Bearers' Web," the magic sniffer said, "I've been expecting this for some time."

"How's that possible?"

"The magic sniffers are a very ancient brotherhood," Ramburgus said. "We know the ways of the earth. In fact, prior to the time of the Regnum, we were the priests of the land, known to the people as *dru*. We knew the lore of the ground and the stars, and we worshiped astra and odia alike, as well as nature spirits, ancestral beings, and heroes. Whatever rituals and sacrifices were needed, we performed, including human sacrifices on rare occasions. We did not distinguish between good and evil, but merely sought harmony with the spirit world.

"When the Gothma came north from Metrus, they hunted down the dru, for we represented a competing religious authority, first to the Metran state priests, and later, to the Astralite fraters. Those of us who survived became petty magicians and rural witches. The fall of the Regnum was no relief for us, for the odia-priests of the Framguth persecuted us too. We were reduced to the status of mere treasure hunters, seeking out trinkets and baubles for whoever would pay for our services.

"The common folk of LeFain have forgotten about the dru of old, and view us, their descendants, as unholy profiteers. Magic sniffer families live apart from others, in a state of semi-secrecy. Our arts have been degraded, for we've been forced to ally ourselves with whoever may protect us. Some of us have become Astralites, some odia-worshippers, and a few even have turned Drammite. Thus we've become divided amongst ourselves as well.

"I, however, am the heir to the true ways of the dru. We dru are like the water, my lord. We flow wherever it's necessary for us to flow in order to survive. Under your rule, however, we may flourish once more, for you have shown yourself to be one who will flow as we do. You use the Framguth lords here, the Gothma warriors there, the Drammites over there—but you aren't loyal to any one of them. You control them; they don't control you, and thus you are exactly the kind of master that the dru need. When you establish your power, my lord, I will teach you our ways."

Berthus was happy to hear that, but he had one more question.

"What about the swine boy? What prevents you from offering your services to him?"

"Originally nothing, my lord," the magic sniffer said, "until he made common cause with a Duraline. The Duralines are foes of the magic sniffers, for they promote an absolute morality, and sole worship of the astra. If it's true that he's also made an alliance with the meddlesome baron, then that shows he's an even greater threat to us than we thought. If the swine boy rises to power, my lord, he's likely to become similar to the rulers of the Regnum, and that could be terrible for the remaining dru, particularly since he'll have the gwellen at his disposal. I cannot allow such a thing to happen."

Berthus nodded and smiled. He had already chosen the other four Web members. Each one represented a different faction of his army. Dargun Rodrick represented the Drammites; Shelton, the Gothma horde; Hemric, the Framguth knights; Jurgan, the bandits and pirates, and Ramburgus, the magic sniffer brotherhood wherever they could be found across LeFain. All of these factions could be used, and even if they fought amongst themselves, it would work to Berthus's advantage. He, being the glue that could bind them all together, would be supreme master.

Only one thing remained to be done to make the Web complete.

"Felix Ramburgus," Berthus looked right into the magic sniffer's blue eyes. "I accept you as my brother and fellow Web member. Swear absolute fealty to me, consent to become the bearer of the plant spirit stone, Nebi, when we obtain it, and I swear to you that the dru will rise again."

"I do so swear," Ramburgus had tears in his eyes. "I'll gladly accept upon myself the burden of Nebi. And now that I've heard these gracious words of yours, I have another gift to give you, one that I withheld from you until now."

"What's that?"

"My lord," Ramburgus said. "I know the exact location of the secret pass through the Greymantles."

# Mount Solvard

Orren woke up, pulled aside a fold of Quartz's skooch, and looked out. The Ghoul Vale's cloudbank was now sepia in color, which meant that the sun was setting. He saw the grotesque, skeletal shapes of ghouls milling about in the brown mist. None of them, however, dared come close to anyone on a council-entrusted mission.

The previous, eventful night had been long and exhausting. Once Orren and his friends received the six talismans, sunrise was at hand. Although the sun was not visible in the Ghoul Vale, enough of its rays penetrated the cloudbank to necessitate Quartz bedding down for the day. The sholl sat on the ground, wrapped his skooch around his body, and pulled the hood low over his face. In the middle of the dreary, featureless landscape, he slept much as he would have anywhere else.

Though it was not necessary for them to do so, Orren, Haxel, and Marett crawled under the giant's garment, for they found his steady heartbeat soothing. Jasper apparently felt the same way. She lay under the edge of the skooch, near Quartz's massive feet. Only Anselm remained in the open, though he lay in a crook formed by one of the sholl's folded arms.

At the back of Orren's mind was a tiny pinprick of consciousness that could only be described as gray and dreary. It was almost as if a miniscule poppy seed of gloominess had been planted inside his brain. He shook his head, but to no avail. Perhaps the best way to deal with it, he figured, was to focus on the positive energy generated by him and his friends being together.

"Awake already?" Anselm opened his eyes.

"Yes," Orren said. "As soon as it's dark, Quartz will also wake up. Then we can be on our way. I suppose, Anselm, that you know where the hidden pass is."

"Of course I do," the old man said. "And I know where it forks, dividing into two passes. However, my young friend, we're not going to use the hidden pass."

"Why not?" Orren was shocked. "Isn't it the fastest way to the Hargash River?"

"Yes," Anselm said, "but by now the whole of Airen's Arc is probably swarming with your brother's men, and there's no way to reach the pass without crossing the arc."

"Berthus might have moved on," Orren said. "He wants the stones more than anything else, and might have continued searching."

"Wrong," Anselm said. "He wants you dead more than anything else. Don't argue with me, Ornery. I know exactly what I'm doing. You don't."

Marett and Haxel poked their heads out.

"What are you two arguing about?" Marett asked.

"Ornery thinks he knows my job better than I do," Anselm said.

"Orren, Anselm's our guide. Remember?"

Orren seethed at the girl's patronizing tone, but said nothing.

"What's *your* solution, Anselm?" Marett asked.

"We're going to climb Mount Solvard," Anselm said. "It's at the eastern edge of the Ghoul Vale."

"But...but, isn't that the highest mountain in the western Greymantles?"

"So you know your geography," Anselm smiled. "I'm impressed."

"How are we supposed to climb it?"

"Quartz will climb for us," Anselm explained. "You three won't have to do anything, which sounds perfect for a princess like you. His skooch has three pockets, each of which can hold a person snugly and securely inside."

Haxel let out a gasp. "What about Jasper?" he asked in a jittery voice.

"Look at all the ropes she's carrying," Anselm pointed at the donkey, who at the sound of her name, emerged from beneath the skooch. "I'm going to make them into a strong, secure harness, which Quartz will wear under his armpits and over his shoulders. My Jasper will be affixed to our huge friend's chest. Believe me, she'll be perfectly safe."

With that, he took the rope coils off the donkey. He tied them around her middle and between her legs. When the harness was finished, long lengths of rope still remained.

"And you?" Haxel asked. "Will you also be in a pocket? One pocket can hold two people."

"No way!" Anselm smiled. "This is the opportunity of a lifetime. I'm going to ride on Quartz's shoulders, enjoying every second of the journey."

"You will, I hope, make a harness for yourself," Marett said.

"I will not," Anselm said with a childish grin. "Where's the fun without the danger?"

Haxel approached Orren. "Master, this Good Sir Anselm might be a bit crazy," he said softly enough so only the boy could hear.

Orren silently nodded.

The Ghoul Vale became dark. Quartz stirred and removed his hood. Anselm lit his lantern and explained his plan to the sholl. Quartz put Anselm on his shoulder, and then picked Jasper up. The old man tied the donkey's harness ropes securely to the giant's shoulders. She looked tiny against his enormous body.

"How do you know this plan will work?" Haxel whined. "What I mean, Good Sir, is how do we know the big friend can climb mountainsides?"

"He's a sholl, isn't he?" Anselm asked. "The Moon Mother made them out of the earth. Their hands and feet can actually adhere to bare rock, almost becoming one with it. You tell him, Quartz."

"Master Anselm is correct," Quartz said, "and as you know, my masters, my skooch alters the air quality so breathing will not be difficult for you. But Master Anselm, there is one problem."

"What's that?"

"My hands and feet cannot adhere to ice. There is bound to be snow and ice on Mount Solvard's slopes."

"That's the beauty of Mount Solvard," Anselm explained. "It has no slopes. It's just a sheer wall. Ice does indeed form on it, but you can break it with those strong hands of yours. Snow can't gather, because it just slips off. My big rocky companion, we're going to ascend straight upward for nearly eleven thousand feet."

Haxel let out an anguished wail. "There must be another way," he started to blabber. "We must try for the hidden pass. Maybe Berthus is no longer there."

"You want to take that risk?" Anselm asked in an aggressive tone.

"No," Orren was emphatic. Ascending a giant mountain sounded far better than the possibility of running into Berthus. The mere thought of Berthus caused the gray pinprick in Orren's head to flare slightly.

"But Master, we could—"

"I said no!" Orren yelled. He instantly felt sorry for his outburst, and promised himself that he would apologize to Haxel later on.

"Anselm, can you see Airen's Arc from Mount Solvard?" Marett asked.

"You bet."

"Then I suggest a compromise," the girl said. "How about if Quartz ascends just high enough for Haxel to take a look at the arc with his sharp eyes. If there isn't any army camp there, we'll go to the pass. If there is, then we carry on climbing Mount Solvard."

"You mean I'll have to look—"

"Haxel, don't whine!" Marett yelled. "If you're insistent that we not do as Anselm suggests, then you must be prepared to do your part. No one has better vision than you do, so you'll have to take a look."

Haxel said nothing. Orren was relieved.

"All right," Anselm said. "Enough jabbering. Quartz, I think you ought to put us in your pockets now. You can walk faster than we can, and the sooner we get to the base of Mount Solvard, the better."

The rock giant put Marett into his right pocket, Orren into his left, and Haxel into the inside pocket. Anselm rode on his shoulder while Jasper was strapped to his chest.

"OK, Quartz," the old man said. "Go this way."

The sholl walked through the Ghoul Vale with his passengers, following Anselm's instructions. After half an hour, he reached what appeared to be a sheer wall of rock, which disappeared into the roiling clouds.

"Here we are," Anselm said. "You can start climbing."

Orren watched as Quartz placed his hands on the rock. As Anselm said would happen, the giant's palms adhered to it as if sholl and mountain had become one substance. Quartz pulled himself up and placed his feet on the cliff face. His soles functioned as his hands did. He did not have to grasp onto anything or look for footholds. It was sufficient for his palms and soles to simply make contact. He made no sound as he ascended, and he dislodged nothing. Orren marveled. It was like watching a fly climb up a wall. Quartz made it look ridiculously easy.

Enraptured, the boy looked around. The sholl ascended into the cloudbank, and all visibility was cut off. Anselm's lantern light became a yellow blur in the roiling darkness. The only way Orren could tell that they were still ascending was by Quartz's movements.

Orren and Marett both let out a gasp of wonder as the sholl emerged into a glorious, starry night. Above them the heavens glittered like so many gems, and their light reflected on the Ghoul Vale's cloudbank, making it almost look beautiful. The lip of Airen's Arc loomed dark and ominous to the south, but above and around it, blue-white mountain peaks jutted sharply into the sky. The air was cold and crisp, and it smelled and even tasted of ice.

"No need for this anymore," Anselm put out his lantern light, clambered over Quartz's arm toward Jasper, opened one of the donkey's bags, and placed the lantern inside. He then fastened the sack shut. It unnerved Orren that Anselm was not firmly affixed to anything.

The mountain wall was dark, though here and there, frozen rivulets shimmered in the starlight. Quartz did not seem perturbed by these, but as he ascended, they became more and more prevalent. Orren knew it was only a matter of time before the sholl would have to start smashing ice.

They ascended past Airen's Arc, and kept going. The top of the arc was blue-white, but Orren fancied he could make out small, black dots. His stomach lurched at the idea that Berthus might be looking directly at him from there. There was no way that his brother would be able to see him or even Quartz, but the mere thought of being in the tyrant's line of vision was perturbing enough.

As if reading his mind, Anselm said, "OK, my fine zhiv friend. Time to take a good look and tell me what you see."

Quartz turned his body halfway around, and held the inside of his skooch outward so Haxel could take a look. The zhiv whimpered, but said, "You were right, Good Sir. The Wicked One has men all over the arc like ants on rotting fruit."

The little gray spot in Orren's head flared again.

"*Now*, my zhiv friend, maybe you'll learn not to argue with me," Anselm said with a huff. "Let's carry on, Quartz."

Silently the rock giant continued. The higher he climbed, the more excited Anselm became. He started to clap and sing.

"Um, Anselm," Orren asked. "Is it safe to do that?"

"Of course," the old man said. "No avalanches here, because there's no snow."

The wind began to howl. Anselm whooped with glee. As Quartz ascended, the wind became stronger, and in some places the gusts were so intense that the sholl had to pause until they calmed down. Thus, the climb took many hours.

"Um, Good Sir," Haxel said in a meek voice. "What if the sun rises while we're still climbing? Quartz will have to wrap himself up."

"Well then we'll just have to spend the day hanging from the mountain face. Sounds fun, no?"

"I really think he's crazy," Orren heard the zhiv say.

They reached an elevation where much ice had formed. Quartz smashed through it. This jarred Orren's nerves, and judging from the gasps and whimpers, it perturbed Haxel, Marett, Jasper and even Quartz himself, though not Anselm. The ice that the sholl broke, plunged into the Ghoul Vale thousands of feet below.

At one point, the rock face extended forward, and Quartz found it necessary to climb upside down in a horizontal manner. His skooch hung off of him, with the terrified passengers in its pockets. Anselm found the whole thing hilarious. "I'm the old man here," he said. "You're the young 'uns. You should be enjoying this adventure, and yet you're squealing like a bunch of hogs about to be slaughtered. Say, young 'uns, look at this."

Orren, Haxel, Marett, and Quartz all gasped as the old man slipped off the giant's shoulders. Holding onto the edge of the skooch with his hands, Anselm allowed his body and legs to dangle in thin air.

"Anselm, get back on top of Quartz's shoulders at once!" Marett shouted.

"He's crazy!" Haxel was almost hyperventilating. "He's just plain crazy!"

"Weee!" The old man swung back and forth.

Jasper let out an anguished, moaning neigh, as if begging her master to stop these dangerous antics.

"Master Anselm," Quartz said in a nervous voice. "I must respectfully request that you not do that."

"You're as bad as the young 'uns, Stone Head," Anselm said as he clambered back onto the giant's shoulders. "No wonder you're always so serious. I mean, have some fun for a change."

At the edge of the overhang, giant icicles dripped down. Quartz smashed through these. The sholl then pulled himself over the lip of the overhang, and grasped the rock above. For a minute, his tree-trunk-like legs dangled in the air.

"There, see how enjoyable it is?" Anselm asked.

Quartz said nothing, but Orren felt a strong sense of annoyance coming from him. The boy sighed. If Anselm tested even the *sholl's* patience, then they were all in for a trying time.

Above the overhang, the climb was no longer vertical. There was a slope, though very steep. Quartz, however, made short work of it. Orren admired the way he deftly avoided little patches and depressions where snow had accumulated. The going went quick, which was fortunate, because the stars were starting to fade. It did not take long for them to reach the top.

The summit of Mount Solvard was wide enough for the sholl to sit on, but not much wider than that. Orren looked out and saw a wonderland of jagged peaks, underneath a purple sky. Anselm climbed down toward Jasper's sacks, opened them, and started handing food out to everyone. The donkey ate a carrot and a turnip. At Anselm's insistence, Quartz accepted three apples and a barley cake. Everyone else dined on cheese, bread, and dried fruits.

"Dawn approaches," the giant said. "My masters, it is time for me to sleep. Might I humbly suggest that you do too? If you stay beneath my skooch, you will be able to slumber for the duration of daylight."

"I just want you to know that you exceeded my expectations," Anselm said to Quartz. "That was a very difficult climb even for a sholl, and yet you did it. You didn't quail in fear or question my judgment. The Moon Mother must be looking down on you, marveling at her child's skill."

The pride that emanated from Quartz at Anselm's praise, washed over everyone. Orren smiled. It was worth bearing the old adventurer's insults, badgering, and general annoyance, if only to hear him praise the sholl in this manner.

Quartz arranged the folds of his skooch tightly around his body and pulled the hood over his face. Jasper and Haxel were snug and cozy inside, while Orren was content with the outer pocket.

The sun rose. The sky went blue. The white cap of Mount Solvard, and those of its neighbors, sparkled gloriously, but none of the people camped upon it, witnessed the beautiful sight. They were all asleep.

"Good evening, everyone!"

That voice could really grate in one's ear!

Orren opened his eyes, yawned, and stretched. "Is it nighttime already?"

"You bet," Anselm said. "Time to go down the other side of this mountain."

"How?" Haxel asked.

"Take a good look, my deft-fingered companion," Anselm said.

"I'd rather not."

"It won't kill you just to look," Anselm said in his nagging tone. "There, what do you see?"

"Uh…it's a slope!" Haxel cried out. "Master! The other side of the mountain …it's a long slope! And it's covered with snow!"

"So what's your plan?" Marett asked.

"We slide down," the old man said with a mischievous giggle.

"We what?" Haxel screamed.

"Well, to be perfectly honest with you, *we* don't slide," the old man said. "Quartz will slide for us. His garment looks like it's got good friction. It should make a nice natural sled. Quartz, are you awake?"

"Yes, Master Anselm."

"Before you start sliding, hitch up the front of your skooch," Anselm instructed. "Arrange it so the pockets are lying on top of your stomach. That way, you'll slide on your back, while Orren, Haxel, Marett, and Jasper are safe on top."

"And yourself, Master Anselm?"

"I'll be on top too," the old man said. "Just not in a pocket or strapped to a harness."

"You can't do that!" Haxel gibbered.

"Anselm," Marett said. "If Quartz slides down, he'll pick up velocity and won't be able to control himself. Besides, take a look." She pointed at the base of the mountain. "Doesn't that look like a canyon to you?"

"Of course it is!" Anselm said. "Galli's Gorge. About three hundred feet wide. Friends, this will be an experience you won't soon forget. As far as speed goes, Quartz can control it by shifting his body from side to side, which will make him zigzag down the slope."

"Couldn't that cause an avalanche?" Orren asked.

"I'll say it might," Marett said, "It would be far bigger than the one you saved us from, Anselm, particularly with an object as large as Quartz, disturbing the snow."

"It's a risk we'll have to take," Anselm said. "Would you rather climb back down the way we came, head for the hidden pass, and face Lord Doofus?"

"No!" Orren snapped. The little gray spot in his brain was really starting to irritate him now. "We slide!"

"If we slide, we'll all be trapped under ice and snow!" Haxel flapped his arms about.

Orren took a deep breath. "Let's put it to a vote," he said. "Who says we slide? I do."

"Me too," Anselm said.

"Who says we look for the hidden pass?"

"I do," Haxel and Marett both said at once.

"What do you say, Quartz?" Orren asked.

"Please forgive me, my masters," Quartz said. He stood up, hitched the front of his skooch over his stomach, and eased himself off the summit of Mount Solvard.

Anselm whooped with delight as the sholl slid down the slope. Haxel screamed. Marett gasped. Jasper whinnied. Orren was terrified, but was relieved not to have to face Berthus.

The sholl picked up speed. He moved to the left and then to the right, in exactly the manner Anselm had advised. His body created snow sprays some twenty feet high, as he undulated down the eastern side of Mount Solvard. Orren saw moonlit mountaintops zooming by.

After some time, Quartz reached a part of the mountain where the snow was thicker. It was then that Orren heard an enormous rumbling sound. He knew then that all their worst fears had been realized. An avalanche was coming, a gigantic one.

The roar of sliding, falling snow soon drowned out all other sounds. An impenetrable sheet of blue-whiteness blotted out the starry sky and the mountains. Suddenly, however, these became visible again. Orren looked downward and saw to his horror that Quartz was flying through thin air. Below them was Galli's Gorge. In front of them, the canyon wall loomed, and it was getting closer and closer with every passing second.

At the last moment, Quartz flailed out. He grabbed hold of the canyon's rocky walls, and his huge hands and feet seemed to sink into them. His gigantic body absorbed all of the impact, and thus, his much smaller, frailer passengers did not have to.

The sound of the avalanche was deafening. Behind Quartz, an unfathomably huge quantity of snow plunged off the opposite canyon wall, and into Galli's Gorge. The air filled with blue-whiteness once again, and for several minutes, nothing else could be seen.

It took some time for Quartz to catch his breath. The experience had unnerved even the mighty rock giant, who remained clinging to the canyon wall. After everything settled down, the night went still and silent once again.

"By the Guiding Light, that was fun!" Anselm said. "Wasn't it, my friends?"

"Good Sir?" Haxel said in a weak voice.

"What?"

"You're definitely crazy."

# GRAY KERNELS OF DESPAIR

Haxel peeked timidly out of the inner pocket of Quartz's skooch. He watched in silence as the sholl made his way hand over hand, down the canyon wall. When Quartz reached the bottom of Galli's Gorge, his huge feet sank into the deep snow, followed by his legs and torso. Haxel watched in fear as the snow level, which had been greatly increased by the avalanche, passed the sholl's inner pocket, and eventually reached his neck. Were they all being buried alive? The mere thought exacerbated the pinprick of gray despair that had been in Haxel's mind since he and his friends left the Ghoul Vale.

The little zhiv was not sure how much more his nerves could take. He placed his hands on the Staff of Transport. During the course of the harrowing climb and the even worse slide down Mount Solvard, Haxel had been touching the talisman constantly. Its presence comforted him, possibly because it reminded him of a similar staff that Tchafla, the zhiv deity, wielded.

Quartz started shoveling snow with his huge hands to clear a pathway. Haxel closed his eyes and relaxed in the knowledge that this quest was in the hands of people stronger and wiser than he.

For a long time, the only sound to be heard was that of Quartz trudging through and clearing away snow. The only person who spoke was Anselm, and that was to give Quartz instructions. After that, the old man started snoring. There was silence, which told the zhiv that all his companions, except for Quartz, were completely worn out and had fallen asleep, so Haxel did the same.

Hours later, he woke up to find that Quartz was sitting down. The sky was beginning to lighten. Sounds of movement indicated that the sholl's other passengers were awake. Anselm and Jasper stood on the snow, where the old man was removing the donkey's harness. Jasper immediately started pawing the frozen ground. With her hoofs, she uncovered grass stubble, which she ate.

Galli's Gorge had widened into a broad valley, situated between lines of enormous peaks. A thick forest of larch, silver fir, and several varieties of pine grew within. The snow beneath the trees was covered in fallen needles and cones.

"Big Friend," Haxel said. "There's a feast for you here with all these cones."

"I have eaten, Master Haxel," Quartz said, "and I assure you that when I awaken, I will dine even more heartily, but now I must prepare myself to sleep for the day. You, my masters, have slept already, and are no longer tired. Might I humbly suggest that you carry on without me?"

"What do you mean?" Anselm barked. "You're not quitting, are you?"

Haxel and the others could feel Quartz's hurt at the old man's accusation.

"Not at all, Master Anselm," he said, "but we surely must spend all our time searching for the gwellen. I am sure you will agree that every moment counts, and you, my masters, may waste time if you wait for me. I will catch up to you, for I am bonded to all of you, and will easily find you. My passage through the woods will be slow, however, for I have to find a way through that will minimize damage to the trees."

"Damage to the trees?" Anselm said with a snort. "What kind of foolish notion is that?"

"The sholl way is to tread lightly upon the earth," Quartz said.

"That's ridiculous!" Anselm snapped. "I understand your need to sleep for the day. I understand and sympathize with your desire not to harm nature, but these are extenuating circumstances,

Quartz. We need to get those stones, and if it means you must knock down a few trees in order to do it, then that's what must be done."

"Please, Master Anselm," Quartz pleaded. "Trust me. I will not be separated from you and my other masters for very long, but I *must* do this the sholl way."

"Well then the sholl way's a stupid way!" Anselm said. "I know this land, and these forests go on for miles. You have to get through them if you want to reach the Hargash River. Unless you knock down a few trees, someone your size will take years to do that."

"OK," Marett held up her hands in a conciliatory gesture. "Let's try not to argue."

"Stone-Brain here's the one who's arguing!" Anselm shouted her down. "I'm the guide. I know the lay of the land!"

"Anselm," Marett said, "If you'd been with us in the Forest of Doom, you'd have seen—"

"This isn't the Forest of Doom, Miss Carrot!" the old man yelled in the girl's face. "Who do you think you are, imagining that you know better than me? And as for you, Stone Brain," he turned back to Quartz. "We can carry on without you, so just go ahead and sleep—for eternity if you so desire."

Quartz's emotions washed over Haxel. The sholl was so hurt from the old man's insults that he could not speak. Instead, he pulled his skooch around his body and lowered the hood over his face.

Haxel was outraged. How dare Anselm talk to Quartz in that manner, especially after everything the rock giant had done!

Painful memories came back to the zhiv, reminding him of all the times he had been misjudged in his life. He remembered his childhood peers calling him a "plopflutsk," the glunk elders expelling him from the colony, and even the humans, thinking that he, as a 'goblin', would bring them bad luck. Now Anselm was misjudging Quartz and insulting him, and it hurt Haxel almost as much as it did the sholl.

He turned away, so disgusted with the nutty old adventurer that he could not bear to look at him. He glanced at his master. Orren's face was red, and he was clenching and unclenching his fists.

"Let's go," Anselm commanded.

Haxel and Orren both looked at Marett. The girl shrugged and followed the old man into the forest. Orren and Haxel walked after her, taking care to remain some distance behind Anselm. Meanwhile, Jasper trotted along, seemingly oblivious to the tensions that were forming in the group.

The sun rose. The sky went orange and then blue. Fat, puffy clouds moved at a rapid pace over the mountains, pushed by a wind that rustled the trees. The air was still cold, but less so than it had been before, and it smelled of fresh pine. Red squirrels chattered in the branches. Haxel knew that the end of winter was nigh. The weather was glorious, but the zhiv's mood was not, and the gray seed in his mind throbbed.

"Just who does he think he is?" Orren whispered in a soft, growling voice. "I know Marett says we must respect him because he's older than we are. Well Quartz is older than *him*—a lot older! Haxel, why do we let Anselm walk all over us? One of us needs to stand up to him. Marett won't do it, so I'll have to."

Haxel had no answer.

They walked for some hours before stopping to eat. Marett passed out bread, cheese, dried fruits, and bacon. Jasper pawed about in the snow, and found more stubble. She seemed capable of digging up food wherever she went.

"Let's carry on," Anselm said when they were finished. "We've still got many miles ahead of us. If Stone Brain were here, he could carry us over certain cliffs, but we haven't got that luxury anymore."

"He'll catch up to us," Orren said. Haxel could see that his master was trying not to get angry. "You'll see."

"Yeah," the old man said. "When we're dead."

"He's not like that!" Orren protested.

"No, he cares more about trees."

"You know something?" Orren stood up and punched a tree trunk. "I'm sick of this! You're always saying bad things about us and calling us names!"

"Orren, please," Marett said.

"No, Marett!" Orren shouted. "I've had enough! Didn't you hear how he spoke to Quartz? If it weren't for Quartz, we'd be nowhere. *Quartz* climbed the mountain, not you, Anselm! He slid down the other side. He caught hold of the cliff. And while we were all sleeping, he kept going, shoveling the snow away! You act like he's your slave. Well he's not. He has his own feelings and you ought to treat him better. You treat all of us badly, because you think you're better than us!"

"I'm the servant of the Sun-Children!" Anselm pursed his lips. "That makes me better."

"You're just a bitter old man," Orren shouted. Haxel was alarmed. Anselm had pushed Orren too far, and now the boy's temper was getting the better of him. "You bow and lick Narx's feet, even though he doesn't respect you. You've got no respect for yourself, and that's why you don't respect us. Actually, Anselm, you're pathetic, so why *should* anyone respect you?"

The old man jumped to his feet. "How dare you!" His face was purple with rage. "You impudent, young human!"

"You're human too!" Orren shouted. "You always were human and you'll always be human. In fact you're the most human of anyone here!"

Before Marett could get between them, Anselm lunged forward and slapped Orren across the face. The boy was so startled he lost his balance and fell in the snow.

"Little ingrate," the old man snarled. "You won't lose your temper at me!"

Orren leapt to his feet, turned around and hit a tree.

"And you call *me* pathetic!" Anselm said.

"That's enough!" Marett shouted. "Stop fighting, you two."

"I will not speak to this nasty-tempered little boy anymore," Anselm said.

"And I won't speak to you!" Orren hollered.

"I won't speak to you either, Anselm," Haxel said. "Insulting Quartz! Hitting the Master!"

"No loss for me," the old man said. "I don't need conversation with anyone who has a chicken heart and freaks about everything."

Haxel seethed, but said nothing. He refused to make Master Orren's mistake, allowing the old man to goad him into anger.

Marett was at a loss.

She was a Duraline. Her family had a long history of settling disputes between rival noble families, and yet, she could not even keep her little group together. She felt like a failure, and this caused the seed of despair in her mind to throb.

She did not know what the little gray thing in her brain was. All she knew was that it had been irritating her ever since the group had left the Ghoul Vale. Whenever she had thoughts about her own inadequacy as a Duraline or about errors within her family lore, it became worse. Meditation and prayer eased it, but did not dispel it completely, and memories of her slain parents and her turncoat brother Perceval, worsened it.

Marett was angry at her fellow gwell-bearers. She was wroth with Anselm for his verbal abuse. She was upset with Orren for losing his temper, and at Haxel for adding to the flames. She was deeply disappointed in Quartz for having so low a self-image that Anselm's words could cut him deeply.

Right now, no one seemed to be listening to her. As they progressed through the woodlands, she spoke with Anselm, because someone had to keep communications open within the group. This, however, evoked nasty looks from Orren and Haxel. After a few hours, they stopped talking to her altogether.

When night fell, Anselm led the group to a small cave in the side of a cliff. Before entering, they allowed Jasper to graze, while they ate supper. Marett handed out food to her companions, but Orren and Haxel did not even thank her. When they were finished, they all entered the cave and fell asleep.

The next day was spent traveling through alpine forests. Orren and Haxel conversed with one another, but neither one would say a word to Anselm or to Marett. The boy and the zhiv walked a good distance behind, so as to minimize contact, which for Marett was very hurtful. Jasper was the only one who took no sides. The little donkey would travel with one group for a while, and then switch to the other. All the while, the gray seed in Marett's mind grew, until it seemed to occupy the entire back of her head.

Night fell and the group found another cave. They ate their meals and then bedded down. Once again, neither faction talked to the other, though Marett attempted to make conversation. She soon gave up and, turning onto her side to face the cave wall, went to sleep.

The third day passed in silence as well, though the terrain was much rougher than it had been before. Thus, it tired them out quicker. Anselm found a copse of firs and lay down in it, with Jasper by his side. Evening came. Owls hooted, and in the distance, a lone wolf howled.

Suddenly there was a rustling sound. The trees started to move. Marett leapt to her feet and drew her sword and her dagger.

"Get ready to fight!" she called out to her friends.

Haxel pulled his ax off his skirt belt. Orren drew his short sword. Anselm fitted a stone into his slingshot.

A giant hand pushed the trees aside, and Quartz peered into the copse.

"I am so sorry, my masters," he said. "I did not mean to frighten you."

Everyone heaved a sigh of relief.

"It's good to see you, Big Friend," Haxel said.

"Indeed it is," Anselm said with a warm smile. "You caught up with us quicker than I'd expected."

"Master Anselm," Quartz said. "I hope I have demonstrated my ability to track my masters' footsteps. I can and will follow you to the ends of the earth. Though my movement through thick woods may be slow, remember that I take enormous strides."

"He thought you'd given up on us," Orren said in a sarcastic tone.

"I did not," Anselm said. "I just didn't understand the necessity for not damaging trees when our quest is of utmost importance."

"Don't lie!" Orren yelled. "When we told you Quartz would catch up, you said, 'Yeah, when we're dead'!"

"He did say that, Big Friend," Haxel said. "I heard it with my own ears."

"I was in a bad mood," Anselm said. "Sometimes I say things I don't mean when I'm in a bad mood. Heck, we all do! Don't listen to them, Quartz. They're trying to turn you against me."

"Please, my friends, there's no need to fight," Marett said.

"We didn't start it," Orren said. "Anselm did. He always does."

"Watch your mouth, boy," Anselm snarled. "I'll slap that pretty face of yours again, and harder this time."

"You'll do nothing of the sort," Haxel jumped in front of his master.

"Folks, please!" The grayness grew until it filled up half Marett's mind. "Stop this!"

"No gratitude," Anselm said. "After all I did for them. Typically human."

A painful, searing sensation emanated from Quartz and washed over Marett and the others. The sholl fell to his knees. He clutched at his head. "I-I-I-can not!" he said in a pained voice.

"Quartz, what's wrong?" Marett cried out.

"Look what I have done!" the sholl said. "I have caused discord and division among my masters. I, who am not even worthy to be noticed, am the reason for a terrible fight that is ripping our fellowship apart. Oh, the Moon Mother must be so ashamed of me. That must be why she afflicted me with the gray seed of despair!"

"What?" Orren, Haxel, Marett, and Anselm all blurted out at once.

"My masters, I am at a loss," Quartz pleaded. "Ever since we left the Ghoul Vale, there has been a small, gray thing that has sat in my mind. I have tried to shake it off, but to no avail. It keeps getting worse, and now, it is taking over."

"You have it too?" Anselm asked in an incredulous tone. "I thought it was just me!"

"Anselm, what do you mean?" Marett asked. "What have you experienced?"

"Everything that Quartz described, has happened to me as well," the old man said. "There's this gray thing in my head. It was no bigger than a speck of dirt when it started, but now it takes up half my brain. If it gets any larger, I'll no longer be able to see in color."

"I have it too," Orren said, "and every time I think of Berthus, it gets worse."

"I have one of my own," Haxel wailed. "Mine gets worse whenever I think of my plopflutsk ways."

Suddenly, Marett remembered some of the ancient legends her grandfather told her. A long forgotten part of her family lore popped into her mind, and she knew what these 'gray seeds' were.

"My friends," she said. "I've been suffering from the same thing, and now that you've all described yours, I know what they are. The family lore refers to them as hex-seeds."

"Come again?" Anselm said.

"There's a certain type of curse that exists within particular magical objects or persons," Marett explained. "When a person makes physical contact with that object or person, it causes the germination, in one's mind, of a kernel of despair. It's like a seed, but it's actually a parasite in one's mind."

"But...but how could such a thing happen?" Anselm asked. "We haven't touched anything cursed."

"Haven't we?" Marett asked. "What about the Staff of Diktat? Narx wanted us to make contact with it, because by doing so, we placed ourselves under its power, and the Ghoul's Curse became a reality in our lives.

"The hex-seed is the manifestation of the Ghoul's Curse. As time goes on, and as we get closer to the three-month deadline, it's going to get stronger and stronger. When the gray despair takes over our minds, as it will at the end of the three months, we will become ghouls."

Haxel wailed.

"Is there no hope?" Anselm asked.

"We can't drive it out of our minds," Marett explained. "The only way *that* can happen is for us to succeed in our quest. However, we can minimize the growth of our hex-seeds.

"Hex-seeds are nourished by fears and personal weaknesses. Anselm, every time you insult your fellow gwell-bearers, you feed your hex-seed. Orren, your hex-seed loves it when you lose your temper or when you focus on Berthus. Haxel, you've already admitted that your fears are feeding yours. Quartz, you need to stop telling yourself that you're unworthy. Then there's me. I've been constantly obsessing about the errors within my family lore. I've been worrying about whether I'm living up to my expectations as a Duraline. I can no longer afford to do that, because now I have this thing in my mind.

"Above all, we need to put an end to the fighting and bitterness that's tearing us apart as a group. The gray kernels of despair *are* going to get stronger, and we're going to need one another for mutual support if we're to cope with them while we continue our quest. Anselm and Orren, you two need to make peace and apologize to each other."

"I warned you folks what I was like," Anselm said. "I told you that I'm intolerant of humans, because of my background. Of course, I realize that's no defense. There's no excuse for how I yelled in your face, Marett, or how I mocked your fears, Haxel. There's certainly no excuse for all the hurtful things I said to Quartz. As for slapping Orren, I'm simply disgusted with myself for doing it. I've been insulting, abusive, and downright nasty. If you can't find it in yourselves to forgive me, I'll understand, especially you, Orren."

"I could have ignored you," Orren said, "but I let myself lose my temper, and in my anger, I said shameful things to you. For that, I really am sorry."

"Miss Marett," Haxel said. "You were only trying to keep the peace when you kept talking to Anselm. I should have recognized this. Instead, I shot you nasty looks. I stopped talking to you. I'm sorry, Miss."

"It's OK, Haxel." Overwhelmed by emotions, she grabbed the little zhiv and embraced him. Orren then embraced her, and Anselm embraced Orren, while Jasper nudged each person. They all then turned to face Quartz.

"I will try my best, my masters," the sholl said. "I now see that I have to help you by giving you emotional support. I cannot do that if I am constantly putting myself down. Hey, Madam Marett, the gray seed in my mind just became much smaller!"

"Mine did too!" Haxel cried out.

"And mine!" Orren said.

"Mine has gone back to the size it was when we first left the Ghoul Vale," Anselm said. "Amazing and scary. These hex-seeds bring out the worst in us."

"I respectfully disagree, Anselm," Marett said. "It is us who give the hex-seeds strength, but now that we've promised to support each other, we can mitigate the worst effects."

Light seemed to flood Marett's head. The gray kernel of despair was driven to the back of her mind, where it sat, brooding. Marett thanked the astra for enabling her to recall a long-forgotten detail from her childhood stories. She also prayed to the gods for strength to continue being a sure vessel for her family lore, as she had been on this night.

# THE WALKING
# BUSHES

After two weeks of traveling, Orren and his friends reached a cliff overlooking the Hargash River. The sun was setting over the Greymantles, and it bathed everything in a red light. The river appeared crimson, but it was actually white and brown, due to rapids and eddies, which carried vast amounts of mud and ice down from the mountains. This created a strong, earthy smell, which filled the cold air.

It was not a wide river, but it was strong and vigorous, as evidenced by the roaring sound it made. Over the eons, it had cut a deep canyon through the mountains. The Hargash undulated like a snake, appearing and then disappearing behind steep cliffs. Thick alpine forests grew on its banks, but the rocky cliffs that overlooked the river were covered in vegetation of a very different kind. These consisted of bushes and thickets, dominated by winter-bare green alders and buckthorns, evergreen hollies, and smaller shrubs such as heaths and brooms. Due to the snow and river spray, these plants were tall enough to conceal a sholl.

Everyone except Quartz, who was asleep, stood in awe at the sight of river, mountains, and sunset. A few miles to the south, a column of clouds rose from what appeared to be a gorge, and this captured Orren's attention.

"That's the Gorge of the Leafy Curse," Anselm said.

"Why's it called that?" Orren asked.

"Remember me saying that the hidden pass divides into two?"

"Yes."

"The Gorge of the Leafy Curse is the northern branch," Anselm said. "The southern branch is called Vulture Canyon. If we had been able to take the hidden pass, we would have gone through Vulture Canyon, which, incidentally, ends maybe five miles south of the Fallagourn Falls. No one in his right mind would *dare*, however, to venture into the Gorge of the Leafy Curse."

"Why not?"

"The vegetation is particularly thick there," Anselm said, "and some of the bushes are said to be able to uproot themselves and attack. I've even heard that they shoot arrows at people."

"Richard told me that walking bushes attacked my father and his men," Orren said. "Most of them were killed, and Father later died from his wounds."

"Didn't you tell me that your father was ambushed near the Fallagourn Falls?" Anselm asked.

"Yes."

"The bushes must have followed him all the way down there," Anselm said, "the question is why?"

Orren shrugged, and Anselm did the same. Since the discovery of the hex-seeds, their friendship had improved drastically. They hunted together, resulting in stews of partridge, hare, marmot, and squirrel for the humans in the group.

The non-humans also ate well. Jasper found grass stubble and tubers everywhere. Haxel used his sharp claws to dig into tree bark for mushrooms, dormant termites, and beetles. Quartz subsisted mainly on cones, except for one evening when the group stumbled across a large peat bog, situated in a bowl-shaped depression. So excited was Quartz at the prospect of a change in his diet, that, forgetting to put his passengers down, he charged into the bog. With his huge hands, he scooped up great quantities of peat, which apparently is a delicacy among sholls, and ate more of it than anyone could have thought possible. In the process, he carelessly dumped cold bog water all over his friends. He could not stop apologizing as they dried themselves out beside a blazing fire.

The weather continuously improved. The air seemed slightly warmer each day, and the snow on the ground less thick. Little rivulets of freezing water ran off the cliffs. Wildlife was increasingly active, with squirrels running about gathering nuts, and hares and partridges everywhere.

Hex-seeds continued to grow in the gwell bearers' minds, but Orren and his friends found that talking about them was helpful. Marett said that the hex-seeds were actually a blessing in disguise, because they forced everyone to bond, thus strengthening the Web.

There was a loud thunderclap, followed by another, and then a third.

Orren looked over his shoulder and saw ominous gray clouds amassing to the southwest. A storm was coming, and it was moving quickly, rapidly blotting out the glorious sunset. The clouds seemed to swallow up the mountain peaks.

"Oh no!" Anselm cried out. "Not here! Not now!"

"What's wrong?" Orren asked.

"I feared this might happen," the old man wailed. "My friends, the Brakenstürm is here."

"The Vomit Storm?" Marett asked. What's that?"

"It's the reason no one in their right mind travels through the Greymantles at this time of the year," Anselm said, "though due to the Ghouls' Curse, we had no choice. The Brakenstürm marks the end of winter in these parts. Caused by warm winds that blow over LeFain from the Great Western Ocean, the huge clouds get bigger and bigger as they move east. When they reach the Greymantles, they pick up great quantities of snow from the peaks. The bloated clouds literally vomit out their contents—rain, snow, and ice, all over the mountains. I know a refuge some miles south of here, but we need Quartz to take us there, and he won't wake up in time."

"So what do you propose?" Marett asked.

"We have to wait for him," the old man said. "There's no other way. I can direct him toward certain sheltered niches, which might be just large enough for him to fit inside."

The next five minutes were agonizing, for the group had to wait for darkness to come. When night fell, the clouds became closer and the thunder louder. Finally, Quartz woke up. Anselm quickly explained the situation to the rock giant. Without any delay, Quartz put his friends into his pockets, with the sole exception of Jasper, who he carried in the palm of his left hand. He moved rapidly over the scrub-covered hills. He climbed cliffs and descended into ravines. All the while, the storm came on quickly.

Rain and ice started pouring out of the skies. The winds mercilessly battered the sholl, and caused his skooch to billow about. Freezing rain entered the garment's pockets, chilling the occupants within.

"Master Anselm," Quartz said after a few minutes. "Here is shelter."

"What is it?"

"A canopy," the sholl said. "Tangled moss and creepers thick enough to keep out rain and snow. I can crawl underneath."

"Then by all means, do so," Anselm said.

Whatever Quartz had found, provided shelter. Underneath the canopy, it was warm and smelled of plant growth. The sholl's passengers climbed out of their respective pockets.

Orren strolled through the space that the canopy covered, and noticed that it was full of unidentifiable objects, many of which had been crushed by the giant's feet. In his desperation to find cover, Quartz had been unable to follow his rule about not destroying things.

"We'll be here awhile," Anselm said. "The Brakenstürm usually lasts an entire night plus some." He took food from the sacks the donkey carried, and distributed it. The gwell bearers ate, talked, and joked.

After many hours, Quartz pulled his skooch around himself, explaining that another day had come. Even though it was storming outside, he needed to sleep, for the sun's rays still percolated through the clouds. Orren, Haxel, Marett, Anselm, and Jasper followed his example.

Orren woke up to discover that he was outside, in broad daylight, unable to move. He was in a standing position, propped up against something. His hands and feet had been bound. Though he still had his short sword, he could not reach it.

He looked to his right and saw Haxel and Anselm, similarly bound, to wooden posts. The zhiv and the old man looked back at him helplessly. Special precautions had been taken to ensure that Haxel's fingers and toes were completely immobile.

Orren looked to his right and saw Marett trussed up in the same manner. A few paces away, Jasper stood with a miserable look in her eyes. There was a rope around her neck, which was suspended from the branch of a turpentine tree. More ropes bound her legs to stakes, and the poor animal could not move.

There was no sign of Quartz.

Tall bushes and leafless green alders grew in profusion upon the snow and ice. Sheer cliffs soared on all sides, and the sky above was blue, with a few puffy clouds. Clearly, their captors had brought them into a narrow canyon.

"Wh-Where are we?" Orren asked.

"Never been here," Anselm said. "I just woke up and here I am."

"M-Master," Haxel cried out. "G-Good Sir Anselm! Look!"

The bushes rustled, and to Orren's shock, began moving. Shrubbery uprooted itself and closed in on the hapless prisoners. Everyone was dumbfounded, shocked into horrified silence.

Suddenly a tendril reached out and grabbed Haxel, who screamed. The zhiv was pulled into the growth, and he disappeared from view.

Haxel could see nothing but tangled branches and briars. The plants engulfed him, and passed him to one another. For what seemed like miles, he was conveyed in this manner, until he reached a round clearing, surrounded by bushes. He was placed, still trussed up, on the snow-covered ground, where he trembled, wept, and prayed to Tchafla.

The bushes stopped moving. Small, lithe figures stepped out of them. It only took a few seconds for Haxel to recognize the vulturine noses, tapering chins, clawed fingers, and plant-fiber clothes. His heart leapt. *Zhivi!*

The zhivi numbered many hundreds, and included heavily armed warriors and gray-haired elders. There were beautiful, hulking females clad in long reed shirts. Some of them had babies in plant fiber slings. With them were smaller males, many of them muscular and wiry.

The mass of zhiv heads created an ocean of unkempt dark hair, though Haxel noticed to his surprise, that there were a few individuals whose hair was red like what some northern humans had! *That* trait did not exist in Haxel's Southland Mountain colony.

There was a hubbub of noise, as the zhivi conversed in a language that, while somewhat different from the one used by Haxel's folk, was understandable.

Two zhivi made their way through the crowd toward Haxel, who meekly stared up at them. One was a wizened male with long white hair and a similarly white beard. He wore a robe that appeared to be more shells and feathers than plant fiber. The other was a big, plump female with iron-gray hair, whose clothes were dyed blue and red in the style of her glunk. Both zhiv elders wore wooden *tchefei*, the four-oval symbols of Tchafla.

"Prisoner!" The big female poked Haxel roughly in the ribs. "Why did you lead the humans and their giant thing to our temple to destroy it?"

Haxel's mouth dropped open. He should have known that the strange canopy was the ceiling of a zhiv temple! The objects that Quartz's feet had crushed were probably altars, votaries, and sacred vessels. What a foolish, hapless plopflusk he was!

"I-I had no idea," he blubbered. "The storm came and we needed shelter. It was dark. I couldn't see. Oh Tchafla, please forgive me!"

The zhiv mob murmured in anger. Haxel was sure he was about to be killed.

"You haven't truthfully answered the question Mother Tiblitz asked you," the male elder said. "Are you a traitor to your kind like the spider-zhivi of old?"

Tears streamed down Haxel's cheeks and his body trembled at so horrible a suggestion. His hands shook and his heart pounded. There was a buzzing sound in his head, an indication that his life was in danger.

"His silence is an admission of guilt," Tiblitz said. "Father Veshkel, let's execute him now."

"No, you've got it wrong!" Haxel cried out, struggling to express himself in the unfamiliar tongue. "I'm not from here. Listen to my speech. I had no idea a zhiv colony existed in these parts!"

"Then what are you doing with the human enemy?" Veshkel asked. "And the giant who trampled our sacred items—what is that thing? It lies prostrate in the ruins of our temple, and we've placed sharpened stakes, coated with pitch, into the cracks of its hide. The smallest flamed arrow will set it alight."

"No please!" Haxel begged. "He's my friend, and he loves zhivi. Don't hurt him. And these humans—they're not like most humans. We're on an important quest. We're searching for the ancient Sun-Stones of the yelia!"

The crowd gasped.

"The gwellen?" Veshkel asked. "Why do you want such powerful objects?"

"*We* don't want them," Haxel said. "Another human wants them—the chief of a human army. We must make sure he doesn't get them."

"Wise elders," a black-haired, male warrior, barged into the clearing. "I have news to bear."

"Speak, Tubuz."

"A human army marches through the Southern Gorge—many humans on their riding beasts. We saw four bipedal wolves with them. Clawed birds fly above. The leader of this army bears a close resemblance to the one who swept through this area ten season cycles ago."

"The Southern Gorge?" Haxel gasped. "The leader you speak of is Wicked Lord Berthus. He's found the hidden pass! This is terrible!"

"There's something else, wise elders," Tubuz said. "Two humans separated from the main army and came here, into the Northern Gorge. Normally we'd kill any human passing through our lands, but we were sure that you Honored Ones would want to question them."

"Bring them in," Tiblitz commanded.

Two humans were brought, trussed up, into the clearing. The zhiv warriors roughly threw the captives to the ground. One was a youngster, not much older than Miss Marett. He was handsome, with white-blond hair, and terrified blue eyes—he actually bore a chilling resemblance to the man Haxel and his friends knew as Darga Eric, but who was now refered to as Dargun Rodrick. The other, Haxel noted with shock, was the 'man in black,' Miss

Marett's longtime nemesis! He was bigger than the young man, and he wore a black cassock with a veil that covered his face.

"You recognize these humans," Tiblitz said. "I see it in your eyes."

"I only recognize the big one," Haxel said, "though I've never seen his face. He's the enemy of the young human female who travels with me. He's followed her across the wilderness, and now he's tracked her here, into the mountains. The other human, I've never seen before. They're not our friends, Honored Ones. They're our enemies."

"So you say," Veshkel said, "but what assurance have we that anything you say is true?"

"I will submit to a teita-tara," Haxel said in a resolute voice.

"A what?"

"A teita-tara," Haxel said. "Don't you have it? It's that berry that you ferment—"

"Oh, a tutta-tu'a," the elder said, using his own language's term. "We had considered forcing a tutta-tu'a upon you, but now you say you'd submit to one of your own volition?"

"Yes, if it will prove my innocence and that of my friends." Haxel's stomach sank as he spoke these words. No zhiv ever wanted to undergo a teita-tara, for the fermented berry drink was a truth potion. A zhiv under its influence could spill out his most closely guarded personal secrets. Haxel had suffered once from such an ordeal, when the Drammites compelled him to undergo a modified version of the teita-tara.

A hubbub rose from the zhiv masses. Veshkel raised his clawed hand for silence. "Fetch the tutta juice," he commanded. A young zhiv female left the clearing. After twenty minutes, she returned with a gourd.

"Rudub," Tiblitz called out. "Please administer the tutta juice to the prisoner."

A big, red-haired female zhiv stepped forward. The younger female gave her the gourd. Rudub picked Haxel up and held him with one muscular arm, while with the other hand she forced the gourd into his mouth, and made him drink its contents. She then put him back on the ground.

Haxel's head swam. The ground seemed to fall away. A kaleidoscope of colors and shapes filled his vision. The faces of the assembled zhivi looked green, blue, and red. Veshkel's voice entered his mind.

"What is your name and where do you come from?"

"Druba Haxel Kokolaminkokla," Haxel said. "I'm from the Southland Mountains."

"I've been to the Southland colony in my travels," a squeaky voice spoke up from among the crowd. "I know the language, and 'kokolaminkokla' means 'he whose limbs do not coordinate.'"

The zhiv crowd burst into laughter. Haxel was very embarrassed.

"How did you get such a title, Druba Haxel Kokolaminkokla?" Veshkel asked in what seemed like a mocking tone.

Against Haxel's will, the entire story of his childhood came out, along with detailed descriptions of the many foolish things he had done. The words spilled uncontrollably from his mouth, causing him intense humiliation. The squeaky-voiced zhiv translated from Haxel's language to the closely-related but somewhat different local tongue so everyone could understand. The zhiv crowd laughed, jeered, and taunted him, enjoying themselves at his expense.

"OK," Tiblitz's voice spoke in his head. "We now know about you. That doesn't explain what you're doing with humans."

Haxel told the assembled zhivi about his expulsion from his colony, followed by how he came across Orren and Marett. He explained what his master was trying to do, and the danger that Berthus posed. At first, the zhivi made fun of him, but as his story progressed, they became quieter and more serious. By the time he had reached the part where he, his master, and the Miss entered the Forest of Doom, the crowd was listening to him with respectful silence. Then when he talked about the giant spiders that Miss Marett called arachodi, their mouths dropped open in awe.

He finished by telling them about Wardolam and the roles that Quartz and Anselm played in their fellowship. The zhivi were astonished to discover that the yelia still existed, and they were fascinated by Haxel's descriptions of the gwellen. When he finished telling his tale, the teita juice was beginning to wear off, and he was able to see hundreds of awestruck faces.

"Rudub," Veshkel said when Haxel was finished. "Take his sack and open it."

The big, redheaded female did as the elder told her. She emptied the sack's contents, much to the amazement of the assembled zhivi. Haxel explained what each shiny object was. He quickly learned to use the term *shlant,* which was *shlenk* in the local tongue. The golden pelt of the Spider Queen astonished the crowd more than anything else.

"Rudub, cut his bonds at once," Veshkel commanded.

The red-haired female pulled out a brush-knife and sliced off Haxel's ropes. Soon he was free, and he stood up straight. Father Veshkel, Mother Tiblitz, and an assortment of other elders talked silently for a few minutes. When they were finished, Veshkel spoke.

"Druba Haxel Kokolaminkokla," he said. "You are a true son of Tchafla. You're brave, loyal, and noble, and we offer our sincerest apologies for the way we've treated you. The title 'kokolaminkokla,' however, is a demeaning one, which no longer fits you. We've decided that you need a new title. Your new name is Druba Haxel Spakiwakwak, which means, 'he who slays the spiders.'"

Tears streamed down Haxel's cheeks as he received more accolades. His shlenki were placed back inside his sack, which was returned to him. Never would he have imagined being honored among his own people.

"And now, Druba Haxel Spakiwakwak," Tiblitz said, "We will question these two humans, and you can help verify or disprove what they say." Turning to the two human captives, she spoke in the human tongue, not the Allamene spoken in Rivulein, but the one Master Orren spoke, which was known as Vulgalquor. "You, prisoners, who are you, and what human army marches through the pass? Why did you separate from them?"

The man in black did not respond, for perhaps, Haxel reckoned, he did not speak Vulgalquor. The blond one, however, did. "The army is that of Lord Berthus Randolphus," the young man said, "who is an oppressor in the lowlands. We joined it in an effort to find out where they're going, so we can relay that information back to those in the lowlands who resist tyranny. As to why we separated, it was because my companion detected the presence of friends. These friends also fight Lord Berthus, and we knew that they would need our help. We had no idea a goblin colony existed in these parts."

At Father Veshkel's command, Tubuz hit the young man on the side of his head with a spear butt. The young, blond human cried out in pain.

"*Zhiv* colony!" Veshkel corrected the young human. "Use the proper term for Tchafla's children. 'Goblin' is something you filthy humans call us, but we are *zhivi*! Remember that or Tubuz will run you through with his spear."

"I mean no disrespect," the blond captive said. "I never learned the proper term for your people. I honor and respect zhivi, and in fact, one of our friends is a zhiv named Haxel."

Haxel leapt forward with indignation. "I'm Haxel!" he shouted, "and these 'friends' as you call them, are nearby. But you're no friends of ours." He pointed at the man in black. "I've already told my fellow zhivi about *your* friend here. He has chased Miss Marett across the country. He wants to kill her."

"No, I don't!" the man in black said through his veil. His words were spoken in Vulgalquor!

The blond man looked at Haxel. "Haxel, if that's truly you, your friends would have told you about me. I'm Iskander from Sherbass!"

"Liar!" Haxel shouted. "Iskander's a hero. He snuck my Master and Miss Marett out of the city. Iskander would never be friends with a Dramm human!"

"Marett misunderstood this man here," the blond man said. "I love him very much, for he's part of the resistance. Tell your zhivi friends to take us to Marett and Orren. I promise you they'll recognize me, and I'll vouch for my friend here."

Veshkel and Tiblitz conferred with their fellow elders. After a few minutes, they spoke to Haxel in the zhiv tongue. "Druba Haxel Spakiwakwak, do you advise we do as this human suggests?"

"I don't see why not," Haxel said, "and I really want to see my friends again."

"Come with us."

Haxel was ushered out of the clearing and back through the tangled mass of bushes, until he reached the spot where Orren, Marett, Anselm, and Jasper were still bound.

"Haxel!" Orren cried out. You're alive!"

"Thank the astra!" Marett heaved a sigh of intense relief.

"We thought you were a goner," Anselm said.

Haxel noted that all three of his human friends had red faces, indicating that they had been weeping for him. Jasper whimpered and stared at Haxel with doe eyes.

"My friends," Haxel said. "These walking bushes. They're zhivi!" He suddenly felt a cold sensation in his heart, for at that moment, he realized that *his people* had been responsible for the death of Orren's father, and for the awful childhood that the Master had to endure.

As if on cue, masses of zhivi emerged from the bushes. Tiblitz, Veshkel, Tubuz, Rudub, and many warrior zhivi flooded the space around the wooden posts. The zhivi cut his friends' bonds.

"Whatever you did, Haxel, you saved us," Marett said.

"Yes," Anselm nodded. "We're in your debt."

"Master, Miss, Good Sir," Haxel talked quickly. "The Wicked One has found the hidden pass, and he's heading down the Vulture Gorge."

"What?" Orren cried out.

"Human friends of Druba Haxel Spakiwakwak," Mother Tiblitz said. "Haxel informed us of the nature of your quest. He also said that you might recognize these two human captives, who split off the main body of the big human army, and ventured up the Northern Gorge."

The zhivi brought out the blond captive.

"Iskander!" Orren and Marett both cried out at once.

The zhivi then pulled the man in black into the clearing. Orren and Marett both gasped. "That's my pursuer!" Marett yelled. "He's tracked me all the way here to kill me. Haxel, tell the zhivi to execute him at once."

"Marett, he's not what you think he is!" Iskander protested.

Before the girl could respond, however, Tiblitz spoke up. "It appears that you have reason to trust the blond human, and he, in turn, trusts the black-clad one. However, we zhivi don't trust any of you, so you must earn our trust. Humans, you—all five of you, and your giant, and even this beast here," she pointed at Jasper, "will now do something for us."

"What's that?" Orren asked.

"You will cleanse the Mount of the Cone."

"What?" Anselm screamed. "That's outrageous!"

"Honored one!" Haxel was shocked. "I thought I'd proven to you—"

"You've proven that *you* are noble and true, Haxel," Veshkel said, still speaking in the human tongue, "but we have no such assurance about the humans and their giant. For all we know, they may have tricked you, in order to gain your trust. If they wish to complete their quest, they will do as Mother Tiblitz asks. Otherwise we'll kill them all."

Haxel was flabbergasted. His mouth dropped open. All he could think of was to say, "We'll do whatever you ask, Honored Ones."

"No, Haxel," Father Veshkel said, "*They'll* do it. You will remain safely with your people, while these 'friends' of yours show us their worth."

One look at the zhiv elders told Haxel that nothing he could say would change their minds.

# THE MAN IN BLACK UNVEILED

A very confused Orren was forced, together with the other captives, to hike for three miles through dense, bushy terrain. Whenever they slowed down, the zhivi jabbed them with sticks and spear butts, despite Haxel's constant and tearful pleas that his friends be treated with kindness. Eventually they reached the wrecked temple, where Quartz sat on the ground beneath the canopy, asleep in his skooch. He had no idea that fierce zhiv warriors had crawled under his garment and had thrust pitch-coated stakes into the cracks in his hide. Neither was he aware that zhiv sentries stood nearby with blazing torches, in case their giant captive woke up and posed a threat.

"Wake the giant," a large female zhiv with red hair, commanded. She poked Orren obnoxiously in the ribs.

"Sholls can't wake up during the day," Orren said.

The zhiv female became angry, but Haxel explained to her that his master was telling the truth. With a sigh, she made a hand motion, and the other zhiv warriors withdrew. Haxel begged to be allowed to stay, but the redheaded female said something in the zhiv language that Orren understood as a 'no'. Haxel then sat down and stubbornly refused to leave, but he was no match for the female's superior size and strength. She picked him up and dragged him out.

Orren, Marett, Anselm, and Jasper sat outside the canopy, waiting for sunset. Iskander and the man in black sat some twenty feet away. Neither group conversed with the other. When Anselm took food out of one of Jasper's sacks, he distributed it to his friends, and fed the donkey several carrots and a turnip, but offered nothing to Iskander or to the man in black.

As the sun started to sink, Orren broke the silence by asking Anselm, "Just what is the Mount of the Cone?"

The old man let out a sigh, clenched his fists and said, "The Kegelmont. It used to be a fortress, but now it's home to the largest sordigryp colony in the Greymantles, and most likely, in all of LeFain. No one in his right mind would dare approach it, especially because, according to legend, a gigantic and terrible sordigryp queen lives on top, though no one has ever seen her.

"The Kegelmont sordigryps are the main reason so few humans live in these mountains nowadays. Over the ages, one prince or another has attempted to dislodge the birds, but something—usually freak winds—always prevents their reaching the top."

Quartz awoke as soon as the sun disappeared. At that moment, swarms of zhiv warriors reentered the temple. Haxel was with them, and he explained the situation to the giant. The warriors removed the stakes from Quartz's hide, whereupon he crawled out of the temple and stood up. The zhivi gasped, for they'd had no idea how large he was. They disappeared, together with an unwilling Haxel, into the shrubbery.

Silently and obediently, Quartz placed Orren, Marett, and Anselm into his skooch pockets. He grasped Jasper in his left hand; his huge fingers wrapped around her in a protective embrace. He glowered at Iskander and the man in black, in a manner that Orren had never seen before. Iskander went pale and broke out in a cold sweat, while the man in black's reactions could not be determined, for his Drammite garb concealed him completely.

"Both of you will hand your weapons to me," Quartz said to the two men. It did not matter that he spoke in his typical rumbling manner. Merely by directing his speech toward someone, a sholl could make himself understood. Iskander and the man in black quickly gave Quartz two swords, a dagger, a small bow, and a quiver of arrows.

Quartz picked up Iskander and, glaring at him, said, "You shall ride on my shoulders, only because you saved my masters in the city. I will hold your black-clad friend between my thumb and index finger. Any untoward moves against my masters or Jasper, and I will squash you both to death. Understand me?"

"Yes," was all Iskander could utter.

Orren was taken aback. He never would have imagined the gentle, polite sholl uttering threats. It didn't seem part of his character, but it *did* illustrate the extent of his devotion to those he called his 'masters.'

"OK, Quartz," Anselm said. "The Kegelmont is in a U-shaped valley. It won't take you long to get there. I'll show you the way."

Directed by Anselm, Quartz made his way through the scrub and brush, climbing up cliffs, and descending into ravines. After three hours, he reached a particular hilltop that overlooked the valley.

"There it is," Anselm said, "The Valley of the Cone, and in its center, the Kegelmont."

The Valley of the Cone was situated some twelve miles, as the crow flies, east of the Gorge of the Leafy Curse. The Hargash River was no more than two miles east of it, also as the crow flies, but the raging torrent was cut off from view by a line of jagged mountains. Mountains and cliffs surrounded the valley. It appeared flat at the bottom, and was filled with dark forests, interspersed with snow-covered meadows that shone blue-white under the moon.

The Kegelmont, a lone mountain shaped like a cone with its head lopped off, was in the middle of the valley. The remains of a formidable fortress stood on top. Orren estimated the Kegelmont to be five hundred feet tall, puny in comparison with the towering peaks surrounding its valley. Still, it had a sinister appearance, which was accentuated by a thin, eerie, blue-gray mist that lingered beneath the summit. Scores of small black shapes, which had to be sordigryps, flew to and from the mountain.

Quartz descended into the valley. When he reached the bottom, he put his passengers down on the ground.

"Nasty-looking place," Orren said.

"And what makes it nastier is the fact that the zhivi have forced us to accept enemies into our midst," Marett said in a hostile tone.

"Marett, it's not what you think," Iskander protested. "We're here to help you. That's why we came into these mountains."

"And yet your silent companion has tracked me all the way from the Plattveld," Marett said. "He wants to kill me. Don't deny it, Iskander. By taking up with him, you've proven that you too, are our enemy."

"Marett, I've been thinking," Orren said, "I'm not so sure that—"

"No, Orren!" the girl yelled. "Don't be fooled just because he saved us in Sherbass. Anyway Iskander, why doesn't your friend talk? Why does he keep that veil on him? What's he trying to hide?"

Without warning, the girl lunged forward and ripped the hood off the large man's head. She let out a gasp and said, "I knew it! I just knew it, though I didn't want to admit that it could be true! My friends, we've been betrayed!"

She punched the big man in the stomach before Orren could get a look at him. The man in black fell to the snow-covered ground with a groan of pain. Iskander tried to come to his friend's aid, but Quartz seized the young man, lifted him into the air, and held him tight.

Marett pulled out her dagger, but Orren grabbed her arm. "Didn't you hear what the zhivi said?" he hissed at her. "These men *have* to help cleanse the Kegelmont, or we can't continue our quest."

"Let me go, Orren!"

"No," Orren said, though he did not know how much longer he could control her. Anselm rushed to his aid, and Jasper grabbed the girl's cloak in her mouth.

Orren took a good look at the man in black, who was on the ground, clutching at his stomach. The boy let out a gasp as he stared transfixed at the man's features, which were clearly revealed in the bright moonlight.

The man in black was in his mid-twenties. He was very handsome, with olive skin, dark eyes, and long black hair tied behind his head in a ponytail. Except for his darker complexion and masculine appearance, he looked almost exactly like Marett.

Orren suddenly realized who he was.

"That's some wallop you've got there, sis," Perceval said, still holding his stomach.

"I'm no longer your sis!" Marett hollered. Orren had never seen her like this before. She had lost all sense of rationality, and would surely murder her brother if Orren, Anselm, and Jasper released their grip.

Marett struggled, but to no avail. Anselm was much more powerful than he looked; Jasper's jaws were clenched tight on her cloak; and Orren's muscles had been greatly strengthened due to his many physical ordeals. They would not permit the girl to do what needed to be done, so she had to content herself with verbally abusing her former brother.

"It *had* to be you!" she snarled at him. "Came back to finish what your fellow Drammites started, didn't you? It wasn't enough that you betrayed your family and besmirched an unsullied bloodline! You had to make sure you completed your work, which is why you followed me across the country! Well, Orren and Anselm can't hold onto me forever, and when they release their grip, I shall kill you."

"Before you do that, sis, at least let me speak in my own defense," Perceval said.

"Why should I?" Marett yelled. "Your actions say everything! You can't be trusted! You can't—"

"Marett, be quiet!" Orren yelled in her face.

Marett went silent and stared at the boy.

"Marett," Orren said in a calmer voice. "You need to listen. If you kill him and he didn't do anything wrong, what will that make you? Come on, Marett. Be the smart, strong person we all love so much. You always listen to us no matter what we say. Why can't you do the same for your own brother?"

Tears streamed down Orren's face. "For all you know, he could still be your brother, who loves you," he said. "I wish I had that. Instead I have Berthus. Please, Marett, you may have something I don't, but you won't know unless you listen."

"The young man's right," Anselm added. "You should be aware by now, my warrior princess, that everyone has a story to tell."

"But I can't know whether or not he's lying," Marett protested. "Neither will you."

"No we won't," Orren agreed, "but Quartz will."

"Master Orren speaks correctly," Quartz said. "Madam Marett, as you well know, a sholl cannot do this 'lying' thing you humans do, but we *can* listen to someone's speech, and determine whether words and thoughts are one and the same."

Marett looked up at her enormous friend's stony face. "Listen to your brother," Quartz's voice was gentle and coaxing. "If his words and thoughts do not match, I will inform you."

"OK," the girl said. She sat down in the snow. Orren sat to her right, with his hand on top of hers, while Anselm was on her left, with a hand on her shoulder. Jasper lay down by her feet, and Quartz, still holding Iskander immobile in his hand, positioned himself protectively in the back.

"Marrike, you were too young to remember this," Perceval began, "but one night, when I was thirteen, Ma and Pa received Drammite visitors. Their leader was a woman who, at the time, was about twenty-eight, by the name of Cinda Lowny. You know her all too well."

Marett nodded, wondering where all this was going.

"Darga Lowny was a dark Duraline. Her mother was from House Federi. Lowny was a bit of a renegade among the dark Duralines, because she wanted to spread the Drammite movement into the western Duraline families, probably for her own self-aggrandizement."

"Anyway, Ma and Pa chased her off, and I'll never forget Lowny's last parting words. 'One day, you'll regret your decision,' she said. Her words haunted me ever since. They gave me nightmares about human sacrifices and things of that nature."

"When I turned eighteen, I went out into the world, which, as you know, is the tradition among Duralines when they reach that age. You were forced to do it at sixteen, Marrike, but that's another story. I visited nobles, peasants, and clergymen, and what I found, to my horror, was that Drammite infiltrators were everywhere. Wherever I went, I found them.

"When I reached Sherbass, I was fortunate enough to make the acquaintance of Biskop Weilar there. Weilar was well aware of the fact that Drammites were infiltrating the Church, and he wanted to do something about it. The tragedy, of course, was that the biggest infiltrator of all was Weilar's own assistant and successor, Yorell, and Weilar had no idea of it until he was on his deathbed.

"Anyway, I took a vow before the biskop—and fortunately, Yorell was not present—to do to the Drammites what they were doing to others. I infiltrated the infiltrators—the very first person to ever do so. I gained their trust and became a darga."

Marett felt sick to her stomach. She could not see how Perceval's actions were justifiable. She knew she would need to ask him the toughest, harshest question she could think of. "Did you perform human sacrifices?" she blurted out.

"Yes," Perceval said in a solemn voice. "You can't be a darga if you don't."

"Is that how you alleviate your guilty conscience?" she asked.

"Marrike, you must believe me when I tell you the following, even though it may sound like a bunch of platitudes," Perceval said. "First, I made sure I sacrificed only wicked people—bandits, slave traders, and the like. Secondly, I did not torture them. I used to whisper in their ears, telling them to scream as if I *was* torturing them, and in return, I would make sure they died quickly and painlessly. Also, I trained others whom Biskop Weilar picked, to infiltrate the Drammites as I did. Through Weilar also, I helped Iskander create the anti-Drammite resistance movement, which he has done admirably."

Marett shrugged, not sure what to make of that.

"The cost of what I was doing nearly broke me," Perceval continued. "I came home and informed Ma and Pa. They went ballistic, and told me to go away, for I was no longer their son. As far as they were concerned, I had brought dishonor to House Baines, contaminated our pure bloodline, and compromised our family lore. There are instances of our ancestors infiltrating evil societies, but Ma and Pa refused to entertain such a justification, telling me that I wasn't one of my ancestors. Therein, sis, lies one of the problems we Duralines have."

Marett was outraged that Perceval would insult their parents' memories. She was about to tell him what for, when he held up a hand for patience.

"Before you rush to their defense, sis, heaven forefend that I would ever blame Ma and Pa. We were both very lucky to have them in our lives. They were themselves victims of a mentality that has been ingrained into us Duralines for generations, and that is the notion that somehow we're the elite of mankind. The original Houses of the Oath saw themselves as servants of mankind, not the elite. Once we started seeing ourselves as elite, we lost our relevance."

"We're *still* relevant!" Marett yelled at him. "No one's more relevant than us!"

"Are we so?" Perceval raised an eyebrow. "Look at us. We go to great lengths to ensure that our bloodlines are 'pure,' and that we marry only into 'good' families. How many rewarding, fulfilling relationships have Duralines been prevented from having, due to such stupid rules? And there were instances where Duralines have entered into abusive marriages, because the prospective spouses had good bloodlines. That's exactly what happened to Cinda Lowny's mother, sis, which may explain how Cinda ended up the way she did."

Marett felt a pain in her stomach when she remembered how Orren, who had fallen in love with her, was shattered when he learned of the pedigree rules. Of course, she would not consider marrying him now, because he had become like a brother to her. Still, he had been hurt, and so had she.

"This attitude has had other side effects as well," Perceval continued. "The dark Duralines use it to justify alliances with evil powers, saying that it will result in absolute Duraline dominance. That, of course, was never the goal of the original Pact of the High Meadow. Western Duralines, on the other hand, have a different problem. We see ourselves as pure-blooded, and we put our family lores on pedestals. We don't consider the possibility that errors may have crept in. We tend to think that if something is not contained within the family lore, it's not worthy of consideration."

"Duraline family lores have always been enriched by the experiences of our ancestors. That's what makes them so potent, but when we calcify them, we compromise their effectiveness. Errors might creep in to a family lore, but so what? As we learn more, we correct those errors, and thus the family lore grows and becomes greater. What's important, Marrike, is the Wisdom Core that guides us all. That's what sits at the heart of every Duraline family lore, even the dark ones, though they try to suppress it."

Marett suddenly felt as if an enormous burden had been removed from her shoulders. She hated admitting it, but Perceval had found the answer to the dilemma that had afflicted her for the past few months. Moreover, Marett herself had lived up to what Perceval claimed was the family lore's original function, for it was she who had figured out, purely through her own inference, that a chosen person could designate others as chosen by accepting them as family. That discovery had been *hers*, not her ancestors', and it had resulted in the creation of the Bearers' Web, that had saved Orren from Berthus's telepathic assault. However, there was more that needed to be clarified.

"Perceval, why did you do nothing when Ma, Pa, and everyone else was killed?" Marett asked. "Why didn't you use your influence in the cult to stop it?"

"As a darga, I studied under Cinda Lowny," Perceval said. "She was destined for greatness within the order, but she discovered who I was. She planned out the attack on our family, and I only found out about it when she was already on her way to the Plattveld to carry it out. I would never have discovered it were it not for two idiots with flapping lips—Dargas Henry Voss and Guida Fellini. Iskander tells me you've encountered them too."

Marett nodded, remembering well the two foolish and violent dargas in Sherbass.

"I rushed home to warn Ma and Pa," Tears streamed down Perceval's cheeks as he spoke. "But I was too late. The deed was done. Hysterical, I searched through our home, and found the bodies, which I buried as best I could. I could not find you, though, Marrike, and when I went to the stables, I found out that Rima, your steed, was gone. I knew then that you were away from home during the attack. The fact that you were alive was the only thing that kept me going. Protecting you became my life's goal."

"I waited for you to come home, but I dared not remove my veil, for I would be recognized by enemies. Sadly, you mistook me for a foe, and you even took refuge from me among those nasty bandits. Still, I remained in the vicinity, hoping for an opportunity to come into the Lith to save you.

"My months of waiting, however, were not entirely wasted. I made my way to the nearest town, and found the local Drammite infiltrators. By that time, I had a high status in the order, so I dispatched these individuals to dirigons throughout the country, carrying the 'urgent' message that Cinda Lowny was teaching heresies about the Blood Master, and that she was trying to orchestrate a Duraline takeover of the order. My ploy worked. Lowny became dishonored, her dreams and aspirations destroyed. That was the beginning of my revenge upon her, which has not yet reached its full fruition."

"I was jubilant when I discovered that you'd escaped, thanks to this brilliant boy here. As soon as I saw the swollen river drag the bandits to their deaths, I knew that a gwell had to be involved. It was Iskander who later filled me in on *those* details."

At the mention of Iskander's name, Quartz put the young man down. Iskander sat in the snow, by Perceval's side.

Marett could not help feeling a surge of pride. She smiled at Orren. His resultant blushing was evident even in the moonlight.

"I followed you through the wilderness, but you always stayed ahead of me," Perceval said. "And if I may say so myself, I saved your lives twice. The first time was when you attempted an ill-thought-out escape from Skaps during a time of high alert. You would have run right into the village patrol, who, not recognizing you, would have shot you with their arrows. I was stomped on the foot, elbowed in the stomach, and bitten on the hand for my trouble."

"We're really sorry about that," Orren said.

"The second time was in Sherbass, when Lowny cornered you. Iskander and I rescued you together. I must say, I derived great satisfaction from breaking the jaw of that wicked witch, and would have killed her then, except that I had to fight off the warriors that were with her. One day, however, I'll catch up with her and she'll pay for what she did.

"When young Orren started that melee, the resulting chaos spread. Sherbass exploded into riots between Drammite factions, and the resistance took advantage of it. The movement spread to the smaller towns, and because its leadership was most capable, Iskander and I left them so we could follow Lord Berthus's army up to Airen's Arc. We were sure we could find you and help you with your quest."

"It was around the time you climbed Mount Solvard that Berthus found the hidden pass. Iskander and I joined his army incognito. We slipped away at the place where the pass divides into two. We came up the northern branch, intending to meet up with you on the riverbanks, but things turned out slightly differently, as we've seen."

Marett was speechless. She had no idea how to react, so she turned to Quartz.

"Your brother's words and thoughts match," the sholl said. "He truly loves you, Madam Marett, and everything he has done, he did for you."

"Thank you…Quartz, isn't it?" Perceval said. "You see, Marrike, the sholl understands."

"Perc, did you ever think that your decisions were the wrong ones?" Marett asked. "I mean, once Ma and Pa expressed their disapproval, didn't it make you stop and think twice?"

"I've been haunted by doubts for years," Perceval said, "but one night, not long, in fact, after you fled into the Forest of Doom, I had a dream. Some invisible force pulled me out of my body and transported me through the clouds. A golden cloud appeared, on top of which was an opal palace. Ma and Pa were waiting for me there, and they were pleased to see me."

"I started explaining myself to them, but they stopped me, for they now understood why I did what I did. They said it was the right decision—someone *had* to infiltrate the Drammites. They told me to act as a sure vessel for the family lore, and after that, they said, 'Always know that we love you children.'"

Perceval's voice broke and he wept. Marett stood up, stepped forward, and sat down right in front of her brother. She took his head in her arms and embraced him. He embraced her back, and together they wept tears of grief for their lost loved ones, followed by tears of joy at their reunion. Then Marett told Perceval about her own, similar dream.

"And now I understand the 'children' reference," she said. "They loved both of us. Ma and Pa are even wiser now than they were while alive, because they're so much closer to the Wisdom Core."

Iskander placed a hand on Perceval's shoulder, and Marett put her hand on top of his. Their eyes met. Marett had to resist the urge to reach up and stroke the young man's pale blond hair, which appeared blue in the moonlight. She tore her gaze away from him, unable to say another word.

"Perceval," Orren cut in, "I've got questions."

"Yes?"

"How did you track Marett across the country? How did you keep finding us even after we went into the Forest of Doom and the Ghoul Vale? And how did you know we climbed that mountain?"

Marett's brother put two fingers in his mouth and let out a shrill whistle. There was the sound of beating wings, and seven ravens landed in the snow at Perceval's feet. Marett's and Orren's mouths both dropped open.

"You probably saw them as you traveled," Perceval explained, "I learned the art of avian communication from a certain Darga Dahry, whose acquaintance I made. Dahry was from a Framguth noble family that worshipped the odia Mortistia and Adnari. He became a Drammite, and rose to prominence in the order, before being murdered by Astuval Telleri."

"You raise birds of a particular species—each person must choose one species—from the time they hatch, so they imprint upon you. Then, using certain meditative techniques, you learn their nature and attune your mind to theirs. Eventually, you're able to communicate with them telepathically, by passing onto them, images and sensory data. The birds communicate in the same way back to you. Because their intelligence is different from yours, it takes a while to learn what they're telling you."

"I chose the raven as my species because it's an intelligent, inquisitive bird. Also, they can travel very far, very quickly. And then there are the loud caws they make, which, as it turns out, communicate thoughts over long distances in a very effective way.

"These ravens first saw you, Marrike, when you fled from our destroyed home. I gave the birds your image, and they were able to pinpoint your location in the Lith Gorge, though with bandits everywhere, there was no opening for me to come rescue you."

"The ravens followed you, Orren, and Haxel through the Sardalian. At first they lost you when you entered the Forest of Doom, but I had them fly over it. They sighted you and then lost you a few times, but that was sufficient for me to predict the rough whereabouts of where you would emerge. Of course, being a Drammite, I had access to fast horses too, for the cult's messenger and spy network have much use for them."

"We never noticed the ravens until we came out of the forest," Marett said.

"My birds take full advantage of tree cover to conceal themselves," Perceval said. "The only reason you noticed them in Rivulein is because I sent them into the meadow, so they could be close to you. I needed them to hear your speech because it was the best way I could determine what your subsequent plans were."

"They lost you when you entered the Ghoul Vale, but that's a relatively small area, and there's high visibility around it. They saw Quartz climb Mount Solvard. As you can imagine, this avian communication skill is extremely rare and potentially dangerous. I believe that Telleri murdered Dahry, because Dahry refused to teach it to him."

"Perceval, can your birds scout the Kegelmont?" Orren asked.

120

"I love my birds, and would not send them into the colony itself, but they could certainly gather information from outside."

"Good," Orren said. "Have them fly over and around it. Find out everything you can from them, about this nasty mountain."

"What have you got in mind?" Perceval asked.

"The beginnings of a plan," Orren said. "I'll figure out the rest once your ravens tell us more."

# SORDIGRYPS OF THE KEGELMONT

Orren anxiously waited and watched. It had been three hours since Perceval's ravens had flown off toward the Kegelmont. Orren's plan, or what there was of it, was purely dependent upon the information the birds brought back.

He was relieved to hear a loud cawing sound, as the seven ravens finally flew into his vision. They landed on Perceval's shoulders, atop his head, and upon his outstretched hands. Orren watched, transfixed, as Marett's brother went into a sort of trance. He spoke to the birds in an odd series of clicks and clucks, and now and then cocked his head to one side. The birds made similar noises and movements, which were accentuated by spreading of the wings and ruffling of feathers.

When this whole procedure was finished, sunrise was near. Perceval collapsed, exhausted on the ground. The effort from having to glean information from the birds, apparently took a physical toll. With great care, Quartz pulled the large man into his skooch and then wrapped the garment around his own body.

"Let's also go under the skooch," Orren said to the others. "We must sleep, because we'll need all our energy for tomorrow night."

When the sun set that evening, Orren was ready, for he had been awake for several hours, mulling over ideas in his head. Quartz stirred. Jasper emerged from beneath the sholl's skooch, and Marett, Anselm, Perceval, and Iskander also crawled out.

Everyone gathered on the snow-covered ground in front of Quartz, who pulled the hood off his giant head. The cawing of Perceval's ravens could be heard, coming from nearby trees.

"I think I have as much information as we're likely to get," Perceval said. "Firstly, my birds could not fly over that mountain. The winds prevented them from doing so. The way they saw it, the mountaintop is impervious to approach by any creature, due to these winds, which are strongest on the south side. That's where we are."

"Perc," Marett said. "Do you remember the legends Grandpa used to tell us about force fields? He used to say that maintaining one requires the continuous presence of a wizard. There could be a wizard living in the Kegelmont, who's making these winds."

"Then we're in trouble," Perceval said, "because we have no magic of our own."

"Yes we do," Orren said. He told Perceval and Iskander about the talismans.

"Those talismans should only be used as a last resort," Iskander said in a cautionary tone, "especially if they can only be used once."

"Well, we'll see about that," Orren said. "What else did the birds tell you, Perceval?"

"They were able to find out more by flying around the sides of the mountain," Perceval said. "They even went into the tunnels, though I did not tell them to do so. Apparently, the sordigryps carry their prey into the Kegelmont, and eat it there. The smell of carrion attracted my birds, and they gorged themselves."

"The Kegelmont has three entrances, one on the north, one on the west, and then there's the main one, which is on the south side, facing us. The tunnels lead into chambers, and it's there that the sordigryps congregate. Every square inch of the tunnel and chamber floors is covered in a carpet of feathers, dried dung, and other assorted debris. One of my birds found the tunnel that leads to the top, but she had no desire to go up there."

"That's OK," Orren said, "in fact, it's great. My plan is in place."

He turned to Quartz. "You must carry us up there, Quartz," Orren said. "Make your skooch take on the color and look of the mountainside. We want to remain unnoticed by the sordigryps for as long as we can. Once reach the south entrance, I'll tell you what to do."

"I hear and obey, Master Orren," Quartz said.

"Also, you need to give Perceval and Iskander their weapons back," Orren said. "They'll need them." Quartz did as he was told.

"Anselm, please take everything off of Jasper and leave it in Quartz's pockets, except for a coil of rope—just in case we need it—and a lantern. Tie the lantern to her neck. She'll light the way through those dark tunnels."

Anselm did exactly as Orren instructed.

"You've got some good pieces of flint, don't you?" Orren asked.

"I never go anywhere without them," the old man said.

"Good," Orren said, "Sometime, you'll need to make a fire, which *you* do faster than anyone else I know. You could, of course, use the fire from the lantern, but I'd rather you didn't. We don't want to risk losing our light."

"You're very thorough, my cunning friend," Anselm said with an admiring smile. "No wonder your plans succeed."

Orren smiled at him and then turned to the others. "Iskander, are you good with a sword?"

"Yes," the young man said, "all Duralines are."

"Then you'll go first," Orren said, "Perceval will come next. I'm sure you're more agile than he is, because you're smaller, while he's probably stronger. You two are gonna cut down any sordigryps that get in our way. Marett, you'll be behind me. I have a feeling I'll need your support. Perceval, tell your ravens to stay in the trees. There's no need to put your birds in danger."

"I appreciate your concern for my birds," Perceval said.

"That's it," Orren said. "Let's go."

Quartz placed Jasper and Anselm inside his inner pocket. He put Marett and Perceval into the one on his right. The left pocket was full with the cargo Jasper usually carried. Orren and Iskander rode on Quartz's shoulder, but remained concealed beneath his hood. Quartz then strode forward. When he reached the Kegelmont, he transformed his skooch so that it took on the look of the mountainside.

He climbed the mountain face slowly and methodically. As usual, his huge hands and feet adhered to the rock. It took half an hour or so for Quartz to reach the main entrance, which was a black hole slightly more than the height of a man. It was only wide enough for one person at a time to enter.

"OK, Quartz, a few things," Orren whispered. "First, you must duck your head down and place your shoulders at the same level as the tunnel, so we can walk in. Second, as soon as we're inside, I need you to go to the bottom of the mountain. I saw big boulders down there. Get some, find the other two entrances, and plug them shut so the sordigryps can't get out. Kill any sordigryp that comes out of the tunnels or gets close to you. When you've finished, come back here and wait for us. If we succeed in removing whatever's making those winds, you'll have to climb up to the top to get us."

"Yes, Master Orren," Quartz whispered back, as he placed Perceval, Marett, Anselm, and Jasper on his shoulders. "Please be careful, you and the rest."

Orren pulled the Fan of Invisibility out of his pouch. Iskander looked at him doubtfully, but Orren nodded, indicating that the time had come to use his talisman. Iskander drew his sword and stepped out in front of the boy, and Perceval took up his position behind his friend. Orren motioned for Anselm and Jasper to go next, followed by himself and then Marett.

"Anselm," Orren whispered. "As soon as I've waved the fan, light the lantern on Jasper's neck. We have to get to the top of this mountain. I need *all* my energy to keep the fan's magic going, and to 'carry' all of you, so *you're* gonna be our leader."

"Right," the old man said.

Orren waved the Fan of Invisibility. Whirling air emanated from it and formed a protective cocoon around the boy. Orren directed it to expand forward so that it covered Anselm and Jasper. Then he extended it more, to embrace Perceval and Iskander. Finally, he stretched it backward to encompass Marett.

Anselm lit the lantern. "Go," the old man commanded the others.

One by one, the group stepped off Quartz's shoulders and into the dark tunnel of the Kegelmont.

Were it not for the lantern, they would have been unable to see a thing. The tunnel sloped upward, so that the group had to go down on hands and knees. Orren placed the Fan of Invisibility in his mouth and held it between his teeth so he could crawl.

The tunnel floor was soft and spongy, but it was not pleasant to the touch. The masses of feathers, dried manure, dust, and other debris made one filthy, and it stank. The air in the tunnel was musty and thick. As the group went farther into the mountain, the stench worsened.

A sordigryp hobbled its way through the tunnel. Orren saw the bird by the lantern light, and he nearly gagged. This bird had a body as large as that of a man, with immense wings. Where its wing joints were situated, it had wicked-looking claws, with which it moved itself along. Its head was bare, with gray, wrinkled skin, and its feathers were matted and greasy. Its beak was as long as Orren's forearm. It opened its mouth slightly, and Orren saw filthy, yellow fangs. It gave off a rank odor akin to that of rotting beets mixed with mildew and manure.

Orren turned away. He needed all his concentration to keep the magic going. He heard a thump and a screech, which told him that Iskander had dispatched the nasty bird.

As they continued going through the tunnels, now walking, now crawling, more sordigryps appeared. Some had feathers like the first one, and others were bare, with mottled, leathery skin and bat-like wings. None of them made it past Iskander, who killed them quickly, with little resultant noise.

After some time, the group entered a chamber. The space was two hundred feet wide on all sides, with a ceiling some forty feet high. There were hundreds of sordigryps, including numerous chicks. The chicks were perhaps the vilest of all. They were bare of feathers, and their beaks had not been formed yet. Instead, long fangs jutted at diagonal angles out of their heads. The chicks fed by grasping onto adults and sucking their blood, or by killing and cannibalizing one another. Once again, Orren had to tear his gaze away from these terrible sights, so he could focus on maintaining the talisman's magic.

The problem here was that the stench was almost overpowering, and there was a cacophony of awful noises—shrieks, grunts, snarls, and hisses. Hardly an empty space existed inside the chamber, and the group members found themselves stepping on sordigryps. The birds lashed out with their claws and beaks, but could not penetrate the shield of wind.

"Iskander, Perceval, clear us a path to the nearest tunnel," Anselm said. The two young men hacked with their swords, severing heads and cleaving through bodies. The evil birds panicked, for they had no idea where their doom was coming from. The result was general pandemonium. Sordigryps fluttered about and killed one another in an effort to get away from…they knew not what.

The old man took the lantern off Jasper's neck and held it up until he located another tunnel. "That way," he told Iskander. As soon as the young man saw where Anselm was pointing, he began hacking another pathway through the mass of wicked birds. He became soaked with blood and covered with feathers, and Perceval was not much better off.

As the group entered the tunnel, a dozen or so sordigryps came down into the chamber. They fell to the swords of Iskander and Perceval, and one was killed when Anselm downed it with his slingshot, using a sordigryp bone as ammunition.

The effort from so much crawling began to take its toll on Orren. He was not sure how much longer he could continue, while at the same time, 'carrying' all his friends. Marett seemed to detect his distress, because she placed a hand on his shoulder, which calmed him, and enabled him to concentrate better.

Anselm seemed quite capable of directing, because they continually ascended. They entered a second chamber, which was half the size of the first one. Again, Iskander and Perceval chopped a pathway through the sordigryps. The group reached another tunnel, and made their way up into a third and then a fourth chamber. The effort to maintain the magic was almost more than Orren could bear.

They walked upright down a twisting, winding tunnel, until they reached an intersection. Three tunnels met in one place, which was some twenty feet wide on all sides. Above them was a hole, and through it, stars could be seen.

"What do we do now?" Iskander asked.

"We go up," Anselm said. "Marett and Orren first." Perceval lifted the girl and thrust her through the hole. Orren felt the big man lift him next. He rolled onto the top of the mountain, but kept his mind firmly focused on the Fan of Invisibility.

A loud, shrill squawk seared into his mind, breaking his concentration. The talisman's magic failed, and the Fan of Invisibility disintegrated into fine dust. A terrible voice yelled in Orren's mind, in a foul, unknown language, which the boy could somehow understand.

*Intruders! Attack them! Kill them!*

Orren heard a multitude of shrieks and snarls, and he knew that hundreds of sodigryps were rushing down the tunnels toward his friends. "Stand and fight!" Anselm commanded. Orren heard Iskander and Perceval slashing with their swords,

Anselm barking out commands, and Jasper whinnying in terror. He picked himself up.

"We've got to help them, Marett!" he yelled, but the girl was transfixed on a swirling fog that was rapidly blotting out the stars.

A shape appeared in the fog. Orren saw a sordigryp, but this one was far bigger than any of the others. Its head was larger than his torso, with a beak nearly six feet long. Its sinuous neck was longer than Marett was tall, and the size of its body could not be guessed.

*Intruders!* The monster screamed in his mind. *You die now!*

Marett stood in shock as the sordigryp queen lunged at her. Its beak opened, revealing fangs at least six inches long. Orren grabbed the girl and threw her to the ground. The sordigryp queen's jaws snapped thin air.

At that moment, he heard Anselm scream, "No Jasper! Stay with us! Jasper, come back! Jaspeerr!!!"

The sordigryp queen lunged again. Marett drew her sword. She parried the huge beak, but lost her grip on her weapon. It flew through the air and landed twelve feet away. There was no way to get it now. Orren drew his short sword and Marett her dagger, but these were insufficient against the monster.

"They've killed her!" Orren heard Anselm wail in extreme anguish. "They've killed my Jasper! Perceval! Iskander! Protect me while I light a fire. I'm going to burn these nasty birds to ashes."

The sordigryp queen prepared for a third strike.

"Marett!" Orren yelled. "The whistle! Use the whistle!"

Many thoughts raced through Marett's mind as she locked gazes with the horrifying sordigryp queen. She held the Whistle of Merging to her lips. Her brain displayed a series of images in rapid succession—images of Perceval, Orren, Haxel, Anselm,

Quartz, and finally Iskander, who caused her heart to flutter. Through the images, she saw the sordigryp queen lunge.

Marett blew the whistle.

Suddenly she was looking down upon herself and Orren. She saw Perceval and Iskander scramble out of the hole, and then bend down to lift Anselm through it and onto the mountaintop. She smelled burning flesh and feathers. The carpet of debris that covered the floor of the tunnels and chambers within the mountain was very flammable, and Anselm had set it alight. She heard the panicked screams of sordigryps. Dozens of the winged fiends burst through the hole. The impact of so many birds flying out at once knocked Perceval and Iskander to the ground.

The sordigryps surrounded her friends and her own unconscious form, on all sides. She heard the twangs of Anselm's slingshot, and saw Iskander and Perceval swing their swords, cutting down birds left, right, and center. However, more sordigryps were emerging every second. She had to plug the hole, but with what?

She tried to move and discovered that her body was huge and heavy, and that it was covered with—feathers!

Of course! She had blown the Whistle of Merging, and now controlled the sordigryp queen's mind. With every effort she could muster, she moved the enormous body toward the hole. As she went, she snapped about in the air with her beak, killing the attacking sordigryps. She repeatedly swept through the mass of birds, destroying several each time.

She moved her body over the hole and placed herself on top. She grit her fangs and ignored the sharp pecks of trapped sordigryps on her abdomen. She felt flames licking at her feathers, burning them, and she screamed in pain, for she was being roasted alive.

She had to get out of this body, but how?

She saw Iskander slice through the neck of a sordigryp. She made a lunging motion toward the young man.

"Iskander, look out!" Orren yelled.

Iskander swiveled around. Marett looked into his eyes for a split second before he drove his sword deep into her neck. She then blacked out.

Marett woke up in her own body. She felt the Whistle of Merging disappear, chain and all, in a puff of fine, powdery dust.

Only a handful of sordigryps were left, and Anselm, consumed by rage and grief at the loss of Jasper, was shooting them down with his slingshot.

"Marett!" Iskander shouted. "Thank the astra, you're OK."

She picked herself up and stared at the immense body of the sordigryp queen. The huge corpse plugged up the hole, and the ugly head lay on the ground, surrounded by the broken bodies of smaller birds.

The smell of burning feathers intensified. There was smoke coming out from underneath the sordigryp queen. Marett realized to her horror, that the roof of the Kegelmont was covered in a compacted-down version of the debris carpet. It would only be a matter of minutes before it caught alight, and she, Orren, Perceval, Iskander, and Anselm would be caught in the blazing inferno.

Quartz seemed to realize it as well, for she heard his voice cry out, "Madam Marett! Master Orren! Master Anselm!" He was close to the top of the Kegelmont—that much was certain, but he could not get to his friends, because of the barrier formed by the strange winds, which even now whistled above them.

What did her family lore say? Wherever there is magic, there's a source for that magic. It was up to Marett to find that source, and it wasn't a wizard.

"After me!" she commanded the others. She ran to the spot where the sordigryp queen had nested. Orren followed her, and so did Iskander and Perceval, both of whom supported the weeping Anselm.

The nest was composed of the same material as the debris carpet, except that it was thicker. It was full of eggs, each one the size of Marett's head. All of them were an ugly, blue-brown color.

Marett heard an explosion. The sordigryp queen's carcass went up in flames. By the firelight, she saw that one of the eggs was much smaller than the others, and that it was a different color. It appeared to be a golden yellow, the size of Marett's fist, and smooth. She reached for the strange object, which popped into her hand. Marett's jubilation could not be contained. At the top of her lungs, she screamed, "Magna!"

The flames roared across the top of the Kegelmont, but Marett took the gwell—the magnificent golden gwell of air that had been hidden in the sordigryp queen's nest for astra-knew-how-long—and concentrated on it. A surge of wind emanated from the stone, and drove the fire back.

She then realized what the invisible barrier was. The Kegelmont was repeatedly hit by winds, most of which came from the north. These reached the mountaintop and activated Magna, resulting in a barrier of air on the fortress's southern side. However, a lesser amount of wind bounced off the mountaintop and fanned out in all directions, which is why the air shield was on *all* sides of the cursed mountain. That was *one* way around the gwell's directional limitation!

Marett concentrated again and pulled the air barrier away. Within seconds, Quartz pulled himself over the mountaintop and, with a swoop of his giant right hand, grabbed all five humans. He placed them on his shoulder, and then shimmied down the mountainside as fast as he could go.

As soon as Quartz reached the base of the Kegelmont, he put the humans down on the snow-covered ground. Anselm collapsed, weeping and screaming, "They killed my Jasper! My Jasper distracted those evil birds, and caused many of them to go for her and not us. She sacrificed her life so we could live!"

"Master Anselm," Quartz said. "I have Jasper right here."

He took the donkey out of his inner skooch pocket, and put her in the snow. Everybody gasped.

Jasper was unconscious. Her breathing was shallow, her heartbeat weak. She had sustained terrible injuries. A sordigryp beak had gouged out her right eye. Her left ear and her tail had been ripped off, and she had deep wounds all over her body, including a leg injury that exposed the bone.

"She raced through the tunnels until she reached me," Quartz explained. "She lost a lot of blood, my masters. By placing her inside my skooch pocket, I have been able to keep her alive, but she will not live for long. I greatly desire to do something for her, but I need my masters' permission."

"For what?" Anselm asked.

"For using the Salve of Healing—the talisman that I carry."

# THE OLD
# ADVENTURER'S
# STORY

A soon as they saw flames atop the Kegelmont, great masses of zhivi poured out of the woodlands and bushes. Haxel was among them. He ran as fast as he could toward the mountain, uttering tearful prayers to Tchafla as he went, for he was anxious about his friends.

He spotted the immense form of Quartz kneeling in the snow. His three human friends and the two additional humans who had been forced to join their group, were gathered in a circle in front of the sholl. Their expressions, illuminated by a lantern that Anselm carried, were grave, and their discussion seemed heated.

"I'm aware that you loved her," the one named Iskander said. "I don't blame you, because she was special, but please be rational. The success of this quest is vital to the future of all LeFain continent, and right now the odds are against us. These six talismans are among the only things working in our favor, and they're rare. Already, two of them have been used up."

"She was a most excellent animal," the man in black, who no longer wore his veil, added, "and we'll all remember her with great fondness, but she was exactly that—an animal. Should we use a talisman on a mere animal?"

Haxel joined the circle. He let out a horrified gasp when he saw Jasper's gaping wounds and the missing eye, ear, and tail. He shook all over and began to bawl, and the hex-seed in his mind grew to the size of a walnut.

"She isn't just an animal," Anselm snarled. "She's my friend, and she's Quartz's friend, which is why we both want to save her."

"I'll do everything in my power to save her," the man in black said. "I have experience working with animals. Just don't use the Salve of Healing."

"I say we *should* use the Salve," Marett said with a defiant glare at her pursuer.

"But sis—"

*Sis?* Haxel took a good look at the man in black's face and gasped. Miss Marett's pursuer was a larger, darker, male version of her! It could only be one person.

"Don't 'sis' me!" Marett yelled. "You have no idea what this 'animal' as you call her is capable of. Anyway, the vote's not up to you, but is limited to Web members alone. Quartz asked for permission from his 'masters,' and that excludes you two. Orren, what do *you* say?"

"Use the Salve," the boy said in an emphatic tone.

"And, ah, I see Haxel's back with us," Marett said.

"Use the Salve of Healing," Haxel said before the girl could ask him the question.

"You're making a big mistake," Perceval said.

"Surely you'd reconsider—" Iskander began.

"Who do you two think you are?" Anselm hollered. "You!" He turned to face Perceval. "By your own admission you performed human sacrifices. Your brain has been so warped by the Drammites that you now think like them."

"And you!" He addressed Iskander. "You were assistant to a traitor, a turncoat! His influence has rubbed off on you! Get out of my sight! Both of you!"

Anselm picked up clumps of snow and threw them at Perceval and Iskander. Anything he could find, he flung at the two young men—sticks, pinecones, and pieces of bark. "Go away! Get out of here!" he hollered.

The two men walked away quickly, into the zhiv crowds. Had it not been for the fact that they both towered over the zhivi, Haxel would have lost sight of them.

Quartz took the Salve of Healing out of a skooch pocket. He uncorked the flask, and gently poured the thick liquid onto the donkey's body.

"Quartz, pick her up," Orren said. "Hold her so we can rub that stuff on both sides of her."

The sholl held Jasper upright, while the others frantically rubbed the salve into her wounds. Anselm took the right side, and Orren the left. Haxel slid under the donkey and rubbed salve onto her belly, while Marett carefully rubbed her back, neck, and head, including the empty, bloody eye socket. Within seconds, the thick, green liquid disappeared into the donkey's skin. The flask that had contained the salve disappeared in a puff of smoke and dust.

The talisman's effect was instantaneous. Jasper's wounds closed up, and new skin grew over the protruding bone. However, she still lacked her right eye, left ear, and tail. "Will she grow those back?" Haxel asked.

"The yelia created this talisman using the power of Nebi, gwell of plant spirit," Marett explained. "That's the element of growth and development. I think Jasper *will* grow her eye, ear, and tail back, because such is the power of a gwell, but it will take time. Meanwhile, I think she needs rest. Quartz, why don't you put her back in your inner pocket?"

Before the sholl could do as Marett asked, however, a multitude of zhivi swarmed into the space where Haxel and his friends stood. Thousands of zhiv men, women, and children covered the snow and uttered praises to Tchafla. They formed a tight circle around Jasper and looked at her with awe and wonder.

"Gwell bearers," Veshkel, who was at the front of the group, said, "You have cleansed the Dreaded Cone. No more will we zhivi spend our lives cowering beneath our covered walkways and in our moss-domed city, fearful of going outside. Many times, zhivi have attempted to drive the clawed birds from the Cone, but for every clawed bird we killed, more would take its place. The Greymantle zhivi are grateful to you. You can now pass through our lands to resume your quest."

Tiblitz made her way through the crowd and bent down to whisper something in Jasper's ear. The donkey stirred, opened her one eye, and licked the zhiv elder's clawed fingers. Haxel stared, dumbfounded, as Tiblitz spoke to Jasper, and he was sure that Jasper understood. He thought he overheard the elder telling the donkey to "keep us informed," or something to that effect.

Mother Tiblitz gave Jasper a final, affectionate pat, and then withdrew, returning to the woods. The rest of the zhivi followed. Within minutes, the throng disappeared into the brush and forest. Only the churned snow bore evidence that so large a crowd had been present.

Iskander and Perceval sat forlornly at the forest's edge, some two hundred feet away from the gwell bearers.

"Are they coming with us?" Haxel asked.

"Hopefully not," Anselm said.

"Master Anselm, I implore you not to blame them," Quartz said. "They are ignorant and have no idea who or what Jasper is. I forgive them for their short-sightedness."

"So do I," Orren said. "It wasn't their choice to make anyway."

"The man in black—he's your brother, Miss, isn't he?" Haxel asked.

"He is indeed," Marett said with a smile. She looked as though she had found some sort of inner peace. Haxel had never seen the girl like this before. It warmed his heart and caused the hex-seed in his mind to shrink once again. There was something special about being reunited with one's family, and it gave Haxel hope that one day, the same thing would happen for him.

There was also something else about Marett. She had a dreamy look in her eyes, and she periodically glanced at Iskander. There was something going on between her and the blond, young man. It reminded Haxel of the way Grispel used to glance at him, but would Grispel be proud of the fact that the Kegelmont had been cleansed without his help?

"I wish the zhivi had let me join you," Haxel sighed and stared at the ground. "I'm ashamed that I was safe while you all risked your lives."

"Um, Marett," Orren said. "I think you ought to show Haxel what you found."

Marett took something out of her pouch. In her hand, she held a fist-sized, ovular-shaped stone that Anselm's lantern revealed to be bright golden-yellow. Haxel's heart wanted to sing for joy. "Is that—"

Marett picked Haxel up, embraced him with enthusiasm, and planted a kiss on his cheek. "It's Magna!" she cried out. "Gwell of air, weaver of shields, the warriors' boon!" She proceeded to tell him the entire story of what had transpired.

"And you know what?" she said when she was finished. "None of this would have been possible without you."

"What do you mean?" Haxel was confused.

"You agreed to do that berry juice thing," Orren said. "You told me that going through something like that is very scary, but you did it, Haxel. Because of that, the zhivi spared us and made us cleanse the mountain, and we got Magna."

"That's right," Anselm said. "You told your whole life story to perfect strangers. You even told them the most embarrassing parts, and in doing that, you've inspired me. My friends, sit down. Make yourselves comfortable. There's something I want to tell you."

Quartz sat back on his haunches. Orren, Haxel, and Marett propped themselves against the sholl, while Anselm stood up and started speaking in a highly animated way, holding the lantern in front of him so they could clearly see his face in the darkness.

"I know the life stories of each one of you," the old man said in a tender voice. For the first time, Haxel saw tears in Anselm's eyes. "But you don't know anything about me. I know it hasn't been easy traveling with me. You've had to put up with my insults and abuse, my general crankiness, and my hatred for humanity. My life story is tragic, and it's not something I generally like talking about. However, after the united front you all showed, standing solidly by me while I defended the need to save my Jasper, I think I owe you an explanation.

"You folks may think, by looking at me, with my dark complexion and aristocratic nose, that I'm of Gothma heritage, but I'm not. I'm Jangurth. My birth name is Ansai Arra. 'Anselm' is a Gothmization that I've simply gotten used to.

"The origins of us Jangurth are shrouded in mystery. We don't originally come from LeFain. We're a wandering folk, never staying in one place for long, and we've made our livelihoods through horse and dog breeding, small scale trading, craftsmanship, and magical charms.

"Naturally, our occupations and differentness made us feared and despised, and the subject of many foolish stories. We've been attacked by mobs, chased out of demesnes by armored knights, and condemned by clergy of all persuasions. Jangurth life is always on the road, our caravans rumbling from one end of LeFain to another. Our living conditions are often terrible.

"As if all that wasn't bad enough, we fight among each other, particularly when resources are scarce. Blood feuds are common, as are disputes over where members of a particular clan can travel so they don't run into the turf of another, rival clan.

"My clan was known as the Arra. Ragged, destitute Arra groups still eke out a meager existence far east of here. When I was a mere lad of five, a famine forced my clan to wander into the territory of an enemy clan, the Tura. To say the least, they didn't want us there."

Haxel could identify with everything Anselm was saying. His *glunk*, or clan, the Druba, had its enemies in the colony, particularly the Fraka glunk. Among zhivi too, clan rivalries could turn nasty and violent.

"The Tura attacked us one night," Anselm said, though with great effort, for he kept choking up. "We were unable to mount an adequate defense. Our adults were killed, and the children forced into slavery. The Tura chained us to their caravans at night, gave us worn rags to wear, and fed us scraps. We had to take care of the latrines, clean the pens where livestock were kept, and do other filthy, unwanted jobs.

My elder brother Rigedd, however, made an escape plan, and one misty night, we all fled into the forests. The children went their separate ways, but Rigedd, myself, and my sister Klida—the last surviving members of a once large family—stayed together. Rigedd was convinced that the Guiding Light would bring us better lives.

"We lived off nuts and berries and whatever we could steal, until we came to a Gothma town. The townsfolk, however, drove us off. The Gothma, you see, have an irrational and venomous hatred for our kind, so we kept moving.

Rigedd decided that we should try our luck farther north, in Framguth lands. We avoided the Framguth peasantry, who shot us dirty looks and threw things at us. Instead, we headed for the largest castle we could find. The lord, Berrendonn Kleiter, took us in, fed us, clothed us, and had his frater teach us to read and write. Lord Kleiter's kindness, however, had a sinister motive, for we were groomed to become his tax collectors and record keepers.

"Lord Kleiter had acquired new lands, and he wanted to squeeze every ounce of blood and sweat out of his new peasants. He figured that with us as tax collectors, *we* would be the ones with whom the peasants associated their suffering. Their hatred would be directed not against Lord Kleiter, but against us. He didn't even provide us a detail of knights for protection, but instead hired men who were basically common criminals.

"One day we were out collecting, when the Drammites came. They whipped the peasants into a frenzied state. We were attacked. The men who were supposed to guard us, deserted us. Rigedd's genius saved us that day, for he had us jump into the nearby river, which was swollen with springtime runoff."

"The water was cold and icy, and I became ill, but Rigedd and Klida would not let me rest. We had to keep going, they said, until we found a place to settle. I walked until I could walk no more, and then I collapsed. Fortunately, Sereida found us."

"Who was she?" Orren asked.

"She was a forest witch who lived by herself," Anselm said. "Sereida was feared by the local folk, though they came to her for charms and incantations. She nursed me back to health, but then she put us to work, slaving for her. At the same time, she taught us magical arts. With all the chores, however, I couldn't concentrate on what she was trying to teach, and all I wanted to do was wander wherever the Guiding Light might take me."

"Sereida was vexed with me. This made Rigedd and Klida very uncomfortable, for they feared I was endangering our relationship with her. They bullied me, called me names, slapped me, and rubbed my face in manure. They wanted me to do Sereida's bidding, but I just couldn't. Eventually I ran away, never to see Rigedd or Klida again."

Anselm paused. His eyes misted over. After a few minutes, he continued.

"I returned to Gothma lands. I had a strong command of the language, because Gothma was what Lord Kleiter's frater had taught us, and it was the language in which we kept records. Also, members of my clan are relatively tall and light-skinned as

Jangurth folk go, so I was able to disguise myself as a Gothma. I took the name Anselm and have stuck with it."

"I started out as a small scale peddler, then apprenticed myself to a leather-maker. I became particularly adept at tanning, but I also wanted to learn other skills. I bribed journeymen from different guilds to teach me their trades even though it was in violation of their guild rules. Thus it was that I learned metalworking and medicine. Ever restless, I moved from town to town, but was unable to make friends or to build any lasting relationships."

"I was very unhappy, for I had no one in the world. That was when I decided I hated humanity, and that I didn't want to live in a human world. I climbed a tall cliff, prepared to throw myself off, but there was someone waiting for me at the top."

"He was my height, with a grotesquely wrinkled face, club feet, sharp, pointed ears and chin, a miniscule nose, and weird orange eyes with elliptical pupils. He had a mane of white hair, but was bald on top. He was positively the ugliest person I'd ever seen, and he introduced himself as Varshing."

"Varshing?" Marett asked. "Why does that name sound familiar?"

"I've heard it too," Orren said, "but I can't think where."

"As it turned out, Varshing was a yelius," Anselm said. "In fact, *he* was the Wardolam council head before Narx. In those days, the council head used to wander the countryside collecting information—the only yelius allowed to do so. It was the knowledge and experience acquired during wandering that originally gave the council heads their authority. Varshing, however, was getting too old for this, and the world outside the Ghoul Vale was deteriorating. It was necessary for the yelia to have a *naugus*—a non-yelius—do it for them. That way the Sun Children could remain pure in their city."

"Varshing brought me back to Wardolam, where he promised me that if I faithfully served the yelia, performing errands and gathering information, I would transcend my lowly human origins and become a yelius."

"*You'd* become a yelius?" Marett was incredulous.

"Yes," Anselm said. "Just think of it! Me, a Sun-Child."

"Anselm," Marett said. "I'm not sure that's possible."

"Of course it's possible, you stupid girl," Anselm said. "If it weren't, Varshing never would have said it. And so ever since then, I've served the Sun Children. They call me their Slave, but I don't care. I'd rather be a slave to the yelia than a prince among humans."

"On my first errand, it was necessary for me to take more things than I could possibly carry, so Narx, who was Varshing's second, provided me with a beast of burden, one of a number of animals they keep. That's how I acquired my Jasper, and somehow, we connected from the moment we became acquainted."

Tears streamed down Anselm's face. "I nearly lost my beloved Jasper on this night, but now she's with me, hopefully for years to come."

"And finding Ru'i was one of your errands?" Orren asked.

"Yes," Anselm said. "Orren, my boy, you should know that Varshing, in the course of his travels, found out about your father. I don't know how, but he did. It disturbed him greatly that a human leader could find not one but *three* sacred Sun-Stones. Varshing made it his mission to pinpoint the locations of the gwellen, and thus prevent anyone like Lorien Randolphus from doing this again. However, he was too old to get the gwellen himself, so he made me a chosen one, and instructed me to do it."

"Varshing died and Narx took over, and I'm under Narx's orders now. It was Narx who figured out that Ru'i was in the Valley of the Beasts. No one, however, knew where the valley was, so I had to find it. It took me a full ten years to do so, but when I did, I obtained Ru'i, and made my way back to Wardolam with it. Running into you folks was a completely unexpected stroke of luck; it was pure coincidence."

"It was no coincidence," Marett said. "It was the will of the astra."

Orren groaned.

"Orren, don't you see?" Marett cajoled. "The astra put all of this together. You, Orren, set out to find the gwellen, equipped with nothing but your desire to stop Berthus. Then you and Haxel 'happened' to find me. I just 'happen' to have vast knowledge contained within my family lore, with which to assist you. Then we 'happen' to come across Anselm, who just 'happens' to serve the lost yelia, and who 'happens' to have acquired another gwell. The astra planned all of this out, because they don't want Berthus getting the stones. Honestly, where's your faith?"

Orren didn't want to argue with her, so he stayed silent. He figured, however, that if the astra really needed to save the gwellen from Berthus, then they ought to have come down to Urth to do it themselves.

"I am honored, Master Anselm, that you would tell me your story," Quartz said.

"I agree," Marett said, "and clearly it wasn't an easy thing to do."

"You've had such pain," Haxel added.

"But now the sun is about to rise," Quartz said. "I must sleep, and I recommend that you, my masters, do the same."

"Perceval, Iskander," Marett called out. "Come under the skooch. We must bed down for the day."

"Why would you invite *them* to join us?" Anselm shrieked. "They didn't want my Jasper to live."

"Anselm," Orren said. "They were stupid about that. They saw Jasper the wrong way, just as folks saw *your* people in the wrong way. Don't make the same mistake they did. Teach them better."

"Please forgive them, Master Anselm," Quartz pleaded.

"If they apologize for their foolishness and admit they were wrong, I'll forgive them," Anselm said, "but not before."

Haxel recalled Ferthan, the poor human miller whom he had befriended in the Sardalian, and who had been misunderstood his whole life. Ferthan ended up being betrayed by a cause he believed in, and Haxel had been unable to save him. Somehow, however, by listening to Anselm tell his story, Haxel felt that he and his friends were giving the old man something that Ferthan did not get—a chance to heal.

# GOING FOR HELP

Orren marveled at how well Jasper looked the next evening. All traces of the donkey's gaping wounds had been erased. A stump of a tail was growing, and a small ear was poking up out of her head. There was even a white substance developing in her empty eye socket. The Salve of Healing had surely done its work.

The little donkey seemed to have a voracious appetite. Not only was she eating her usual stubble, but also, for the first time, she had adopted Quartz's habit of devouring pine, fir, and larch cones. These lay about in abundance.

"Are we ready to go?" Marett asked.

"Before we do," Perceval said. "You should know that Iskander and I were talking to Tubuz, the zhiv general, while you all were having your discussions. He informed us that there's heavy snow in Vulture Canyon, particularly after the Brakenstürm."

"That shouldn't be an issue for Berthus," Marett said in a gloomy voice. "He could use Kalsh to clear it all away."

"Not really," Anselm cut in. "Avalanches and rock falls are a big problem there, and anything, including a blast of magic, might cause one. Lord Doofus has brilliant advisors—including that Duraline Drammite—who would not let him make such a mistake."

"So he's delayed," Marett said. "That's one factor's in our favor."

"No it isn't," Anselm growled.

"Why?"

"My original plan was to follow the Hargash River down to the Granite Tors," Anselm said. "Quartz would take us over the Tors until we reached the southern stretches of Vulture Canyon. I had intended to travel through Vulture Canyon until we reached the river below the Fallgourn Falls."

"Now Doofus has spoiled my plans, which means we're going to have to travel down the banks of the Hargash itself. For most of its length, the river is bordered by steep cliffs, upon which thick forests grow. Traveling through such terrain is not a problem for humans, zhivi, or donkeys, but it will be a nightmare for a sholl. I shudder to think how long it will take Quartz to get through the forest, especially if he doesn't want to destroy trees."

"And now we have Magna," Marett said. "And because Narx wouldn't let us take our gwell-sacks, which were so effective at concealing the stones, Berthus will be able to detect Magna with the two gwellen he already has."

"Don't blame the great Narx," Anselm snarled. "Who do you think you are, daring to criticize the leader of the Sun-Children? Don't you know that Narx has reasons for everything he does? Honestly, the presumptuousness of these humans!"

Orren was about to retort, but Iskander held up a hand for silence. "Even if we find Nebi and escape with it," he said, "there are more problems. Back in Rivulein, everything has gone insane. The resistance is brave and well organized, but the Drammites are much stronger. Yorell has disappeared, so he's an unknown factor, and if Berthus returns to Rivulein…" He shook his head.

"The Drammites are drafting peasants into their fighting force," Perceval added. "The peasant folk fear what will happen to their families if they refuse, and they're too terrified to support the resistance. Certain villages that *have* rebelled, have been made examples of by the cult, and…Orren and Marett, there's no easy way to tell you this. One of the destroyed villages is Skaps."

"What?" Orren and Marett both cried out at once.

"I'm afraid it's true," Iskander said with a sad shake of his head. "Darga Stefan Drugger came to Skaps and established the town as a Drammite stronghold. It didn't take long for the village folk to realize their error. First, Darga Drugger sacrificed some villagers, in order to consecrate the new dirigon. Then the Drammites seized all property and livestock. Most of it they sent to their own warriors, and the remainder they rationed out to the village folk. The people of Skaps soon discovered that their poverty had worsened, and now their freedom was gone too."

"So they rebelled. They destroyed the new dirigon, and Darga Drugger was driven out, but he came back, this time with a battalion of warriors. The village was burned to the ground. Chief Marvin and his whole family, as well as many others, were killed."

"Poor, poor Kenner and Fama!" Marett cried out. Tears streamed down Orren's cheeks and a lump developed in his throat as he and Marett remembered the kind peasant couple in Skaps who had adopted them. He and Marett embraced each other and cried.

"Refugees are streaming from the villages, into Sherbass," Iskander said. "They know the fighting's bad in the city, but they figure it's the only chance they have. They're getting into the city any way they can, even through the sewers. The influx of peasants is exacerbating the already dire food, housing, and sanitation problems. For now, the Drammites have their hands full with all the fighting, but that will end if Lord Berthus returns to Rivulein with the gwell Nebi. If that happens, then all hope is lost, and Rivulein will plunge into dark tyranny, followed by the rest of LeFain."

"But isn't Nebi a healing stone?" Haxel asked. "Frater Gissel's poem says it cures all kinds of wounds. How can it be dangerous?"

"Sis," Perceval said, "I think you'd better tell your friends what our family lore says about Nebi's powers."

Marett dried her eyes and let out a deep sigh. "Nebi is the gwell of plant spirit," she said. "That's the element of growth and development, and it's something inherent even in animals. Nebi can heal wounds, but it's also capable of creating tumors, cancers, lesions, and rashes."

Orren, Haxel, and Anselm all let out cries of dismay.

"As with all the other gwellen, the way to activate Nebi's power is by making contact between the stone and its element,"

Marett continued. "Plant life is found not only in trees, shrubs, and grasses, but in the dust of the earth. My family lore states that in every handful of soil, there are thousands of plants so small that they cannot be seen with the eye. All Berthus has to do is throw dust into the air, use Nebi on it, and the tiny plants in the dust will do the rest."

Haxel sat down, dejected, on the snow-covered ground. "So there's no hope, is there?"

"And what is worse, my masters, I have become part of the problem," Quartz added. "I will hinder your progress through the forest and toward the falls. It makes me feel ashamed, for I am now a liability on this quest."

"There's one source of potential hope," Iskander said, "the Baron Alfred Toynberg of Alivadus."

"His name keeps popping up over and over again," Orren said. "Richard used to tell me to escape from Berthus and go to Alivadus. He told me that the baron would take me into his service. Berthus also knew about him. He told the Framguth lords that I was doing Toynberg's work, even though I've never met him. Marett wanted Yorell to send a message to Baron Toynberg, so that his knights would help us. Just who is this Baron Toynberg anyway, and what can he do for us?"

Perceval smiled and put a hand on Orren's shoulder. "The Baron Toynberg," the big man said, "is the hope of all us faithful Astralites."

"He's the descendant of a Framguth chieftain who swept into Gutimia during the declining years of the Regnum. The chieftain was driven back from that land, but he and his tribal warriors settled in the region around Alivadus. At that time, there was a Gothma regional governor in the ancient city itself. Chieftain Toynberg married the man's daughter, and their families became one. House Toynberg is thus of both Framguth and Gothma heritage."

"The Toynbergs were originally odia worshippers, but Marquel Toynberg, the father of the present baron, received communion into the Astralite Church. He drove the odia priests out of the city, and established Astralism as the official religion. He also founded an order of knights to protect the Church from its enemies."

"The present baron has expanded the size of his father's state. The Barony of Alivadus now stretches from the Orchardine Coves in the west, to the Southland Mountains in the east, and from Kastelberg in the north to the Moreido Escarpment in the south. That makes Alivadus the largest state in all of LeFain, with the sole exception of the Kingdom of Salin. Unlike Salin, however, Alivadus is ruled by a man of virtue. Baron Toynberg is brave and humble. Even his title—that of a baron—is a holdover from the time of the Regnum, when the rulers of the city, vassals of the Regis, were called barons. Toynberg's loyal subjects have begged him to name himself king, for his state is completely independent, but the baron won't do it. He does not see himself as better than Alivadus's previous rulers. Thus it is that Alivadus is *still* called a barony."

"Protected by the baron's brave knights, Alivadus is an island of peace and tranquility, justice and righteousness, in our otherwise unhappy, chaotic world. The baron marches forth every now and then from his state, to suppress forces inimical to the holy astra. That's why the odia-worshipping Framguth lords hate and fear him."

"The baron has been aware of the Drammite threat for some time. When I learned this, I made contact with him, and he supported my efforts to infiltrate the cult. He's also been the sponsor of the resistance movement, as Iskander here will confirm."

"So why doesn't he send his knights into Rivulein?" Orren asked. "They can surely help the resistance movement defeat the Drammites."

"Rivulein is far from Alivadus," Iskander said. "The baron can't be everywhere at once. Otherwise his forces will be spread thin, leaving his own nation open to attack. He has to choose his battles wisely, or Alivadus could suffer, and then the last powerful bastion of Astralite faithfulness will be lost. However, if the baron learned that the gwellen are involved, it would change everything. I'm sure he'd march up into Rivulein with at least a portion of his knights, in order to combat such a threat."

"Baron Toynberg has no idea that even one of the gwellen has been found, let alone five. Moreover, he's not given to believing reports that are unsubstantiated. Somehow, we need to convince him that Berthus is a threat to all of LeFain. He also needs to know that the gwellen are now involved, with five of them having been obtained by one side or the other. The trouble is, how are we going to cross the vast stretches of wilderness to get to the baron and let him know what's going on?"

Orren's head spun. It was all so much to take in. Berthus marching down Vulture Canyon, the Drammite repression in Rivulein, Skaps destroyed, Quartz being unsuited for the next leg of the journey, and Berthus being able to detect Magna. The boy felt dizzy and sat down in the snow, clutching at his head.

Suddenly, something clicked. Orren jumped to his feet.

"You'll go!" he said to Perceval and Iskander. "You two will go to Alivadus and tell the baron everything. You told me you met him, didn't you, Perceval? He'll know who you are. Then Iskander can tell him whatever he needs to know about the resistance movement."

"But how are we supposed to get there?" Iskander asked.

"Quartz will take you," Orren said. "The baron will be impressed when he sees a sholl, even though everyone thinks that they died out with the yelia."

"You want to separate Quartz from us?" Anselm cried out.

"How can you send him away?" Marett asked.

"Master, would sending Quartz with these men help?" Haxel asked.

"I'll tell you what *won't* help," Orren said. "It won't help if Quartz has to travel with us through lands he's not good at traveling through. He'll help us much more by going to Alivadus with Perceval and Iskander. They'll ride on his shoulders. He can go faster than any horse, and he can climb up and down mountains."

"And pray tell, young man," Anselm asked. "What if they run into trouble? In case you haven't noticed, Quartz is not invulnerable. He's got deep cracks all over his body, from his face to his shoulders, to the backs of his hands. Didn't you see how the zhivi were able to immobilize him with pitch-covered stakes? If Quartz and these two clowns run into an army, a battle, or even well equipped bandits, and they shoot just one flame-coated arrow…I don't even want to think about what might happen to our giant friend here. The point I'm trying to make is that he needs some means of self-protection."

"Marett," Orren said. "I think you should give Magna to Quartz."

The girl raised her eyebrows.

"Think about it, Marett," Orren said. "Quartz needs the protection. The stone will only give us trouble anyway, because Berthus can detect it with Kalsh and Ru'i. This way, we take care of *both* problems."

Marett smiled. "Brilliant!" she exclaimed. She handed the yellow stone to Quartz. "Quartz, you're now the bearer of Magna. I relinquish it to you. It really isn't hard to use. Just remember, this is the gwell of air. All you have to do is concentrate on the stone and its element, and think about what you want to achieve."

"Madam Marett, Master Orren," the sholl said, "Am I worthy of—"

"Oh stop that!" Orren shouted. "You're a member of our Web! Of course you're worthy!"

"Remember what I said about believing in yourself, Big Friend?" Haxel asked. "This is your chance. Take the stone. Then take these nice humans to see the baron."

Quartz took Magna and held it in the palm of his gigantic hand. By the light of Anselm's lantern, it appeared to have a golden sheen. It looked as small as a mustard seed when held by the sholl, but Orren knew there was no danger of him carelessly losing it. Quartz silently placed the gwell in the pocket of his inner skooch.

"Are you sure Perc and I can—" Iskander looked up at the huge sholl doubtfully.

"Of course," Marett said. "Quartz now knows you're both friends. He'll do whatever he can for you. Just promise me you'll look after him."

"Looks to me like he's more than capable of looking after himself, sis," Perceval said, "but we'll do our best."

"Oh Perc!" Marett fell into her brother's arms. They embraced warmly. Then, looking up at Quartz, she tearfully said, "Take care of my brother, will you? And Iskander too." Orren saw her smile sweetly at the young, blond man, and he could not help feeling jealous. Iskander looked at the ground, blushing.

"I promise you, I will, Madam Marett," the sholl said.

"Go north," Anselm advised. "That way you'll avoid Doofus detecting Magna. You'll have to take the long way around, Quartz, but it's worth it, and *you* can do it with speed."

Perceval hugged Orren and Haxel. He wanted to embrace Anselm as well, but the old man shot a warning look, so he kept his distance. Then Quartz picked up Marett's brother and put him on his shoulders. Though Perceval was a big man, he looked tiny in comparison to the rock giant.

Iskander embraced Orren and Haxel, while Anselm turned away in disgust. The young man then approached Marett and planted a tender kiss on her cheek. Marett embraced him and kissed him back. This brought back to Orren, unpleasant memories of the time in Sardalian, when he learned that the black-haired beauty would never be his, because he possessed the wrong blood.

"Take care of yourself," she said to Iskander. Orren grit his teeth, but forced himself to remember that Iskander was a loyal friend, who was deserving of the love of a girl like Marett.

Quartz then placed Iskander on his shoulder, right next to Perceval. He took the cargo that Jasper normally carried, out of his right pocket, and placed it on the ground.

"Goodbye, my masters," the sholl said, "and goodbye, dear Jasper. May the Moon Mother's spirit guide your steps."

"And yours," Orren said, admittedly relieved to see Iskander gone.

Without another word, Quartz strode northward. Orren watched the sholl until he disappeared around the opposite side of the moonlit Kegelmont.

"Well, there he goes with those two unworthies," Anselm said. "And now, my friends, I think it's time we also got going. Come Jasper."

The old man started walking southward, out of the Valley of the Cone, with Jasper trotting alongside him. Orren, Marett, and Haxel followed Anselm into the bushes. Together, they ascended the steep hills, leaving the cleansed Kegelmont far behind.

# THE POOL BENEATH
# THE FALLS

The next nine days were spent traveling through the forests along the Hargash River's banks. Orren found the going less difficult than he had expected, but the terrain would have been completely unsuited to Quartz. Still, he missed the rock giant, and wondered how he was faring. The gwell-bearers traveled by day, and made camp at night, sleeping in lean-tos of fallen logs and branches. To keep warm, they wrapped themselves in thick blankets that the yelia had provided, and huddled together.

As they traveled south, the weather became warmer. Nights were still bitterly cold, but in the day, temperatures were high enough to affect snowmelt. The icicles that hung from the trees dripped with water, and there was less snow on the ground. Cheery white pasqueflowers, with yellow centers, poked their way through the snow, as did purple snowbells, with their down-turned heads.

During the day, the forests resounded with the chorus of renewed life. The drumming of woodpeckers could be heard everywhere. Redstarts, song thrushes, crossbills, blackbirds, and warblers were common in the mountain forests, as were little tit birds, of both the great and blue varieties. Alongside the riverbanks, gray wagtails could be seen hunting for the insects of early spring. Herds of elk browsed in the alpine forests. In rockier, more open areas, there were chamois, as well as marmots and golden eagles.

Despite the abundance of wildlife, however, hunting was difficult because of the dense tree cover. The alpine forests of the Greymantles did not have a canopy like the Forest of Doom or even the mixed woods of the lowlands did. Needle-laden boughs jutted out at every level, so it was very difficult to aim for anything. Anselm, however, proved adept at bagging snow voles. These, together with river trout and char that he caught in riparian pools, constituted most of what the three humans ate. Haxel fed on mushrooms, tubers, and the grubs of bark beetles. He shared the grubs with his human friends.

Everyone continued to be troubled by his or her respective hex-seed, which now perpetually occupied the back of one's mind. It was a relief to speak about them, but everyone felt sorry for Quartz, who for sure, had to suffer alone. Every now and then they used the Web to connect with him and send him comforting thoughts, but he was so far away that such contact was ephemeral. Had the sholl chosen to concentrate on Magna, it would have been different, but he clearly never did.

Jasper continued healing. It only took two days for her ear to regenerate fully. Her tail was also growing out, and her eye, while slower to develop, showed steady progress. Her appetite did not let up, and she continued to devour copious amounts of pine, fir, and larch cones, as well as grass, lichens, tubers, mosses, and even tree sap. Her stomach sagged from all the food she was eating, but it did not appear to slow her down.

She developed another, much stranger behavior, however, which was of great concern to Anselm. Whenever night fell, she disappeared into the woods. The little donkey could be gone for two or three hours before she returned to her master's side. The group conversed about it a great deal, but nobody could come up with any reason as to why Jasper was acting this way. In any case, it did not matter, because she always rejoined the group.

One day, when the sun was in the middle of the bright blue sky and the snow-covered mountain peaks shone gloriously, Orren heard a loud, steady roar. He asked Anselm about it, but the old man smiled and told him to keep going. As Orren walked, he noticed that the forest was becoming moister, and that there appeared to be a white spray in the air and the smell of fresh water and pine. Anselm led him, Haxel, Marett, and Jasper through a break in the dripping trees, and out onto a rocky ledge. What Orren saw took his breath away.

There, before him, was the largest waterfall he had ever seen in his life. It was a full 150 feet tall, and some 30 feet wide. The entire Hargash River, ice flows and all, plunged over this single cataract. It produced a roar, which, combined with the loud cracking of falling ice flows, drowned out all other sound. The water was brown and white in color, and its spray lessened the blue of the sky above. The falls carried the rich smell of earth and ice, and when seen from certain angles, produced rainbows.

Anselm motioned for the others to return to the forest, so they could hear him speak. When they were once again beneath the pines-scented boughs, the old man put one hand on Orren's shoulder and said, "Behold the Fallagourn Falls. We have arrived."

"You did it!" Orren cried out. "Anselm, you're the best!" He gave the old man a warm hug. Marett and Haxel copied his example.

"Somewhere down there, lies Nebi," Marett said, "the green gwell of plant spirit."

"I think it most likely that Nebi fell into the Orientation Pool," Anselm said. "That's the body of water that lies at the base of these falls. It's a long pool, and quite wide. Its waters are calm, except where the falls feed into it, of course."

"Why the funny name?" Haxel asked.

"The Orientation Pool lies on a perfect north-south axis," Anselm said. "In days of yore, travelers used it to gage direction. The Hargash empties out of the pool at its southern end, but then curves sharply to the east, almost at a right angle. Come, I'll lead you down to the water."

The gwell-bearers descended steep slopes, using trees to prevent themselves from slipping and falling. The snow was very thin here, and ferns and rhododendrons grew in profusion. When they reached the edge of the pool, Anselm took off one boot and put his foot into the azure-blue water.

"Yikes!" He quickly pulled his foot out and clutched at it in an effort to warm it up. "By the Guiding Light, that water's cold enough to freeze your limbs off."

"Then how will we search the water?" Marett asked.

"The Tinderbox!" Orren said. "Anselm, use the Tinderbox of Warming. It will make the entire river warm for two whole days!"

"You brilliant young man," Anselm said. "Of course!"

The old man reached into one of his pockets and pulled out the small, silver tinderbox. He opened it and took out a single piece of flint. Then he lay down on his stomach with his hands over the water. He struck the flint against the box and into the pool.

An enormous quantity of steam rose from the water. The Tinderbox of Warming, including the flint, turned to a powdery dust, which floated on the water's surface. Anselm took off his other boot, and then removed his traveling clothes until all he had on were his long undergarments. He put his weapons into one of the sacks Jasper carried, and then waded into the water. He let out a sigh of intense pleasure.

"Come in," he told the others. "It's not only warm, but it's also healing me. My bones feel stronger than they have in years."

Orren and Marett placed their weapons in Jasper's sacks. Orren then took off his clothes except for his knee-length underpants. Marett removed her outer garments. Her underclothes left her calves and shoulders exposed. Both Orren and Marett waded into the water.

The Orientation Pool was now in essence, a warm bath, and as Anselm had said, it had a healing effect. Orren felt certain aches dissipate—old aches from beatings administered to him by Staffords and the swinery workers, which he nowadays barely even noticed. Welts on his skin from those blows, and old bite marks from the mice and insects of the swinery, disappeared. All over his body, his skin turned flawless, and it even glowed.

He ducked his head underwater and luxuriated in the warmth. When he resurfaced, he saw Marett staring at him.

"Wow, Orren!" she exclaimed. "You look most handsome, and your hair is shining like red gold!"

Orren blushed and felt giddy at her praise.

Marett and Anselm promptly ducked their heads under the water. When Marett came up, her hair was a rich, glossy black, and her fair skin was flawless. The water had a similar effect on Anselm. The old man was not handsome, but the wrinkles on his face lessened, and his bald pate shone in the sunlight that refracted through the mist and steam. He now looked distinguished and regal.

"Haxel! Come on in!" Orren cried out.

The zhiv was scared of water, but Orren saw him steel his nerves and remove his shaspa, stockings, and gloves. He placed his ax into one of Jasper's sacks, and tied the Staff of Transport to another. Then, wearing only his grass skirt, Haxel waded into the pool. He too, exclaimed in pleasure, and wet his head. His leathery, brown skin was rendered clean of scratches, and his umber hair became rich and fine. Even the black claws on his hands shone.

"You too, Jasper!" Anselm called out. "Join us in the water!" The donkey, however, lay down on the banks. Orren could tell she did not want to soak the cargo she carried.

"The warmth in this water is from the talisman," Marett explained, "but the healing power has an entirely different source. My friends, Nebi is present, and it's the cause of the wholesome goodness contained within this pool. Even if the water were cold, we'd heal in it. Now all we have to do is find the gwell."

Orren felt about with his feet. The bottom of the Orientation Pool was completely covered in small, rounded pebbles, the largest of which was the size of a walnut.

"Feel these stones," Orren said, "They're all small. It shouldn't be hard to find one the size of a fist. I say we should each choose a part of the pool, and feel about in it with our feet, pushing the pebbles around until we find Nebi."

"I'm the tallest person here," Marett said, "so I'll search the area by the falls, where the water is probably deepest. Haxel, because you're the shortest, I suggest you take the shallow end. Anselm and Orren, you two search the middle."

"Sounds like a plan," Anselm said.

Each gwell-bearer subsequently waded toward his or her section of the pool. At its deepest, the water took Orren up to his chin, so he found it easy to keep his feet on the bottom. He swept through the pebbles, searching every square inch for a large, smooth stone. He walked back and forth, from one side of the pool to the other. He then shifted one pace to his right, and searched there. This went on for a long time, but Orren was unable to find anything. He looked toward Marett on his right hand side, but the girl shrugged. He looked to his left, but the creased looks on Anselm and Haxel's faces told him that they too, had no luck. They waded over to him with looks of defeat. In anger, Orren slapped the water with his hands, creating a loud splash. "Drat on Narx!" he yelled. "If he'd let us take Hesh, we'd have been able to part the water and find Nebi that way."

"Don't be a stupid fool!" Anselm retorted. "The Great Narx knows what he's doing. If he'd let us take Hesh, Doofus would have found us. When are you going to learn not to question the council head?"

"We're gonna come across Berthus anyway," Orren cried out, with a cold shudder at the impact of his own words. "We have to if we want to get Kalsh and Ru'i away from him. A month has gone by since we were cursed; we now have sixty days left."

"Oh, so you can do simple math, but you can't recognize a superior being?" Anselm said.

"Calm down, everyone," Marett said. "This isn't helping. We need to put our heads together and figure this out."

"The healing magic comes from somewhere," Haxel said, "and because it's from a gwell, it can only move one way."

"That's it!" Marett said. "Haxel's got it!"

"I do?" the zhiv asked.

"Yes, you do," Marett said. "My friends, the magic of the gwellen has to be acted on by an outside agent. That agent can only push the power in one direction at any given moment. In Nebi's case, the water is that agent, and the magic moves directly southward, along the axis upon which the Orientation Pool is situated."

"Then if the magic is moving south, the stone must be to the *north*," Anselm said. "The falls are directly north."

"Maybe Nebi's under the falls?" Orren asked. "If so, how can we get it? There's so much water coming down that we'd be crushed to death if we tried."

"Nebi can't be directly under the falls," Marett said. "The impact of the water would have dislodged it from there long ago."

"I thought only a chosen person could move a gwell," Orren said. "Or a yelius."

"Those are the only *individuals* who can move a gwell," Marett said, "but a natural force is not an individual. It's inanimate. We've already seen that the magic can be activated by nature. Winds blowing through the Forest of Doom entered the gregarious fig chamber where Orya was, producing the Hot Spot. The invisible barrier around the Kegelmont was created by wind hitting Magna."

"It's true what she's saying," Anselm said, "and that, my friends, is how I found Ru'i. I figured that the gwell's presence had to be the reason so many animals and birds were attracted to that otherwise unremarkable valley. Jasper and I observed the animals' movements, and by doing so, pinpointed the location of Ru'i, which was right inside the hollow of a dead chestnut tree. Wind blowing through the tree would have produced the attraction."

"So taking all these factors into account," Marett said, "The only logical conclusion is that Nebi is *behind* the falls. As to how we can get to it, remember that waterfalls are not uniform. Most of them have sections where less water is coming down. Usually these sections are on the sides, but sometimes, they're under a rock overhang."

"Then let's go," Anselm said. "We don't have much time. We're lucky to have gotten here before Doofus, but he's on his way."

That thought propelled Orren toward the waterfall. Marett followed him, and then Anselm. The old man let Haxel climb onto his shoulders. They waded toward the falls.

"There," Marett pointed to the left side. "That's our entry point." She led her friends toward the spot, and then disappeared under the curtain of warm water.

Orren, Haxel, and Anselm stared at one another. Marett reappeared and, unable to speak over the roar of the falls, motioned to her friends to follow.

Orren closed his eyes and swam under the falling water. A moment later, he felt air above his head. He brushed his soaked hair away from his face, and opened his eyes.

He was standing in neck-deep water, behind the great curtain that was the Fallagourn Falls. Marett stood next to him, and Anselm and Haxel also appeared. On their left was a cavern wall seemingly composed of various kinds of moss. The light coming through the falls gave the place a cheery, green glow. No sound could be heard save that of the great waterfall, and the moist air smelled and even tasted of loam. Since hearing one another's voices was impossible here, they used hand gestures to communicate.

Haxel spotted something and gestured toward it. Marett sloshed through the water toward where the zhiv was pointing. Orren followed, and then came Anselm, still carrying Haxel on his shoulders.

They found a staircase. It appeared to have been deliberately carved into the rock, and was completely covered in a thick layer of moss. Marett began ascending, followed by Orren. Anselm took Haxel off of his shoulders, put the zhiv on the staircase, and they both ascended. The moss cushioned their feet as they climbed.

When they were twenty feet above the water, they found themselves inside a large chamber. The ceiling was at least eighty feet high, and the chamber's width was some thirty feet. It was impossible to determine how far back the cave went, because its depths were lost in the darkness. Moss grew in profusion all over the floor, walls, and ceilings. Amid the moss bed, were large numbers of ferns and epiphytes. There were even a few small trees. Water poured off the ceilings and into the cave, and the rich flora was perpetually soaked.

Using hand signals, Marett indicated that everyone should begin searching. Orren, Marett, Haxel, and Anselm got down on their hands and knees in the soft, springy moss, and searched through the plants. Orren was closest to the falls, but the thickness of the moss seemed overwhelming. In frustration, he kicked at it, and his foot hit something hard. He did not have time to focus on the pain; however, for he instantly recalled the time, underneath Richard's bed, when he had hit his foot against Hesh.

Excited, he tore at the moss, ripping bits of it away and throwing it over his shoulder. He saw something smooth and green underneath, which reflected the light from the waterfall. He reached for the object, and it popped into his hand.

He ran over to Anselm and showed Nebi to him. They both alerted Marett and Haxel. The four gwell-bearers marveled at the stone. Then Marett motioned for everyone to descend the stairs. This they did, and then they ducked under the waterfall and made their way to the shore, where Jasper lay on the ground, waiting.

"Well done, you young geniuses," Anselm said as he sloshed through the warm water. "And now we can get out of here and make plans for the remaining two stones that Doofus has."

They emerged from the water and dried themselves with the blankets. They put their clothes back on, and walked into the bushes. Orren took one last admiring look at Nebi, and put it into his pouch. Then he and his friends entered the thick part of the woods.

Something jumped out from behind a tree and knocked him down. Orren struggled, but whatever had grabbed him was large and powerful. It pinned him to the ground so he could not move. To his horror, he felt his captor reach into his pouch and remove Nebi. Orren was then jerked to his feet and spun around, only to look into the bearded face of the bandit Jurgan!

Jasper bolted into the forest, which came alive with armed men. One of them, a bearded Framguth lord of medium height, had Haxel in a headlock so tight it looked as though the zhiv's neck would snap if he moved. There was a flash of red. Dargun Rodrick emerged from the woods, holding a sharp knife to Marett's jugular, and sporting a triumphant grin. Anselm then came into view, his right shoulder gripped by Shelton, and his left, by a distinguished-looking magic sniffer.

To Orren's abject horror, Berthus stepped out of the bushes. His red-gold hair was pinned behind his head. He wore a deep purple cape, a rich, maroon doublet, and dark blue hose. His boots were knee-high and shiny. He carried a jeweled sword with a golden double-headed griffon emblazoned on its sheath. A pendant with a similar design hung from his neck.

Orren froze. He could not bear to look at his half brother's face, so he stared down at the shiny boots. He tasted bile in his throat and vomited on those boots. Berthus backhanded him across the face. Orren saw stars, especially because Jurgan's iron grip prevented him from falling. Thus he absorbed the full impact of the blow. He wet himself from fear, and the hex-seed grew until it encompassed half his head.

"You're disgusting, swine boy," Berthus spat. "This world will be better off without you, and don't think you'll get away this time. Your rock giant is nowhere near us, and I know that, because Ramburgus here," he pointed at the magic sniffer, "says that they can't easily make it through thick forests like these. That donkey of yours ran off into the forest when it saw us, so now your beast of burden's gone too, and with it, all your supplies and tools, including your weapons.

"You may wonder how I snuck up on you when you were carrying Nebi. Why didn't it detect my Kalsh and Ru'i, you ask? It's very simple. The stones aren't here. They're back in Vulture Canyon, in my main camp, and Iranda, whom you've met, is guarding them. I couldn't risk you detecting the presence of the two gwellen, and I had no idea how to find Nebi, so I had *you* do it for me. That reminds me," he turned to Jurgan. "Hand it over, Jurg."

Jurgan gave Berthus the green gwell.

"He does exactly what I tell him," Berthus said with a grin, "for he knows who has the power, and you will too."

Orren's head spun. He could barely breathe.

"And now, men, take the other prisoners to the banks above the falls on this side," Berthus commanded. "Jurgan, Eric, Bertrand, Shelton, and Felix will come with me. My puppies are going to carry us and the swine boy across this pool, and we'll climb up the opposite bank until we reach the ledge on that side, which hangs over the falls. Then I'm going to do something I should have done long ago."

"What's that, m'lord?" Jurgan asked.

"I'm gonna throw the swine boy off."

# BROTHERLY HATE

Orren's stomach churned. His throat was dry. His heart pounded so furiously, that it caused his head to throb, worsening his hexseed. His legs were unable to hold his body up, and he collapsed on the rocky ledge that hung over the Fallagourn Falls.

His reduced state contrasted sharply with the beauty of his surroundings. On both sides of the river, white, snowcapped peaks cut into the blue sky. Below the ledge, the falls roared, resulting in a white spray that hovered over the conifer forests and the blue Orientation Pool, and created a brilliant rainbow. For Orren, however, the falls were no longer magnificent, but held the promise of death.

The ascent had been quick, achieved by dozens of wolfards at the gwell-induced command of Berthus and Dargun Rodrick. The tyrant and the Drammite had commanded the huge beasts to transport themselves, as well as Orren, Shelton, Ramburgus, Jurgan, and the savage Framguth lord named Hemric, up the slopes on the river's eastern bank. The wolfards climbed to the top, and then deposited them all on the ledge.

From this vantage point, Orren could see the opposite bank clearly. There, Haxel, Marett, and Anselm were each tied to a stake. Drammite warriors and various assorted thugs were there too. Orren winced when he saw a darga slap Anselm across the face twice. There was no sign of Jasper.

He looked away, unable to bear the sight. Berthus, however, grabbed him by the back of his neck and forced him to look. Dargun Rodrick, Jurgan, Shelton, Ramburgus, and Hemric, all stood grinning behind their lord.

"These gentlemen are my Bearers' Web," Berthus said with pride, "and unlike you, I have six in mine. You only have five, but not for long. First, we're gonna dispatch that disgusting old dodder. He'll be sacrificed to Blood Master Dramm."

Orren started to weep.

"Next, we'll skin the goblin while you watch. Then you'll be cast over the falls to your long overdue death. We'll use the girl as bait to lure the sholl, who we'll be waiting for in a narrow cleft. When he comes, we'll pour boiling oil into the cracks of his hide, frying him from the inside out. Then I'll keep the girl for myself; it would be a pity to let something so beautiful go to waste."

Orren wept so hysterically that he was practically choking. Berthus's companions mocked him.

"Upset, swine boy?" Berthus asked. "There's only one way to save your friends. Tell us where you've hidden Hesh and Orya."

Orren could barely speak. He could not even think straight. He had fallen into his brother's hands, and was now about to suffer the doom that had always been in store for him. However, the slightest chance of saving Haxel, Marett, Quartz, and Anselm, gave him some hope.

Orren's friends were aware of what Berthus was saying, for their voices entered the boy's mind by means of the Web.

*Don't betray the yelia!* Anselm said.

*I'd willingly die with the secret!* Haxel chimed in.

*Orren, be strong!* Marett said. *Don't accept the offer.*

From somewhere far, far away, he felt a pinprick of consciousness from Quartz, begging him not to give in.

*I can't help it,* Orren spoke through the Web, *you all must carry on without me, my friends.* Then turning to Berthus, he said, "Hesh and Orya…are with the yelia."

Berthus hit him on the back of his head, and he saw stars. "Don't play games with me!"

"I-I'm not," Orren stammered, struggling to speak clearly. "Th-The yelia never died out. They're in the…the Ghoul Vale. There's a c-city there called Wardolam. The g-ghouls guard the city and the yelia live in it. The city c-council head has Hesh and Orya. Y-You've got to b-believe me." Orren felt sick as he betrayed the wherabouts of the yelia to Berthus, but he reminded himself that Berthus's army would never be able to take the dark city. The ghouls would make sure of that! The boy knew he was about to die, but he took comfort in the possibility that before his death, he would lure Berthus to his own doom.

"I think he's telling the truth, m'lord," Ramburgus said.

"I don't," Dargun Rodrick said with a defiant glare at the magic sniffer. "Everyone knows the yelia are extinct."

"Well there's one way to find out for sure," Ramburgus said. "There's an old art form, unique to us magic sniffers, by which we can enter someone's mind to determine if he's telling the truth. The art form requires a very powerful magical object as a focal point—an anchor of sorts—so we'll use Nebi. Let's activate our Web, and I'll guide all of you."

Orren squirmed, but Berthus's grip held him immobile. The boy tried to steal his thoughts against the mental onslaught, but as soon as he felt Berthus's presence, his resistance dissipated. Berthus entered his mind, and the hatred and anger he brought, seared into Orren's brain and swelled his hex-seed. The hex-seed, in turn, gave Berthus strength, transforming him into an overwhelming presence. As if that was not bad enough, Orren felt his head also being invaded by the probing, searching presence of Ramburgus; the sharp, analytical consciousness of Dargun Rodrick; the cruel keenness of Shelton; the dull brutality of Hemric; and the unpleasantly surprising intelligence of Jurgan.

Then suddenly, Haxel, Marett, and Anselm were also in his head, along with a weak pinpoint consciousness from Quartz. Orren's Web pushed back against Berthus's. Though outnumbered, his friends proved too strong for the enemy.

Suddenly, Orren felt his arms twisted violently behind his back, and realized that it was not his own pain he felt, but Anselm's. He felt something burn Haxel's flesh, and heard the zhiv scream. Whips cracked against Marett's back. The Web faltered.

Berthus's men were torturing Orren's friends, thus compromising their ability to focus on the Web and support him. Quartz's consciousness disappeared entirely; as far away as he was, he could not assist without the presence of the others. Berthus and his companions took over, and Orren felt all his resolve crumble. His enemies pulled mental images out of his mind—images of the Ghoul Vale, Wardolam, and the yelia. They laughed and rejoiced as they plundered Orren's inner self.

Orren's head swam and his body went limp, as he felt Berthus drag him over to the precipice, ready to throw him into the Fallagourn Falls' deathly embrace. He heard and felt his friends' distress, but there was nothing they could do. Neither could *he* do anything. All was lost.

*All is not lost!* The mysterious voice suddenly spoke. *You must fight.*

*I can't!* Orren cried out in his mind. *Berthus defeated my Web.*

*But he hasn't defeated me,* the voice said. *Concentrate on me, Orren. With my help, you'll drive your enemies out.*

The voice started to hum. It was the same humming that Orren remembered from his childhood, which had sustained him through all the misery of those nights in the swinery. He focused on the humming. His hex-seed shrank, and he fought the six individuals who were invading his mind. One by one, he drove them out.

He opened his eyes to see Dargun Rodrick doubled over and coughing blood. Ramburgus's hands clutched at his face, and he screamed that he'd been blinded. Jurgan was on the ground, gasping for breath. Shelton looked as though some invisible force was pinning him down. Only Hemric remained relatively intact, though he appeared somewhat dizzy. Orren knew from the mental onslaught, that the Framguth lord was the least intelligent and most brutish member of Berthus's Web, so it was no wonder he was less affected than the others.

Berthus trembled all over. He could barely keep his hold on Orren.

"Finish him off, m'lord!" Hemric growled as he stood up.

"I'm trying to!" Berthus snarled.

"You're not trying hard enough!" Hemric shouted. "If you don't do it, I will!"

Hemric lunged for Orren. Orren yanked himself out of Berthus's tenuous grip, and kicked Hemric in the right knee. The Framguth lord let out a bestial yell. He knocked the still-shaking Berthus aside, and attempted to grab Orren once again. The boy ducked, and as he did, he stuck out his left leg and tripped Hemric, who lost his balance and fell screaming off the ledge, into the falls.

That action brought Berthus back to his former self! "You killed my Web member!" he hollered. With his right hand, he grabbed Orren's throat, and clamped his left hand over the boy's nose, preventing him from breathing. At that very moment, however, Orren saw, out of the corner of his eye, masses of zhiv warriors rushing out of the shrubbery on the opposite bank, in time to save his friends. Berthus's men on that side were about to be overwhelmed and slaughtered. Screams of terror and rage came from the other side of the river, and Orren saw, in his mind's eye, masses of zhivi cutting down his friends' captors.

*You see?* the voice said, *there's always hope.,*

The voice was right. There *was* always hope…and rage!

Orren bit Berthus on the hand as hard as he could. Berthus howled in pain and let go. Orren stumbled backward and fell off the ledge, but at the last moment, grabbed the rock and launched his body upward, so that he landed on top once more. Berthus lunged. Orren sidestepped him and punched him in the stomach, his anger giving him extra power. Berthus fell back and rolled over. He pulled out a knife and attacked once again. Orren dropped to the ground and landed a kick to his brother's groin. Berthus doubled over in pain, dropping the knife.

Consumed by rage, Orren began kicking his half brother in the ribs repeatedly.

*Snap out of this!* The voice said. *Berthus's friends will recover in a few minutes, and they'll finish you off! Remember what's most important!*

Orren grabbed Berthus's knife and cut the pouch containing Nebi, from his brother's belt. Taking the small sack and the green gwell within, he then ran for his life, while Berthus, still writhing in pain, shrieked curses. The boy raced down the hill toward the river, leaving Berthus and the four remaining members of his Web, who were also still immobilized, far behind.

His friends' cheers resounded in his mind.

*Head upstream!* Anselm commanded. *And don't worry about those of Doofus's men who had captured us. The zhiv army killed them all.*

*You'll find a shallow spot,* Marett said. *The zhivi will be waiting on the other side.*

*Tubuz will shoot an arrow over the river,* Haxel said. *Grab it and let them pull you across.*

He ran until he reached the spot where the zhivi were gathered, and when the arrow with the rope was shot, he grabbed it. He let the zhiv throng pull him across the river, which was still warm from the talisman. He emerged, dripping and exhausted, on the other side. Haxel, Marett, and Anselm were nowhere to be seen.

"No time to rest!" Tubuz's voice rang out. "Rest when we reach safety." The zhiv warriors hustled Orren into the bushes. They tore through bracken and thickets, until they reached the side of a cliff. The zhivi indicated a small cave, hidden by a large holly bush. Orren crawled inside, and the zhivi followed him.

There was a light in the tunnel, and it revealed that the space within was large enough for Orren to stand up in, so he did. He and the zhivi followed the light into a wide cavern, illuminated by two lanterns. At least two hundred zhiv warriors were there, as were Haxel, Marett, Anselm...and Jasper!

Orren collapsed at the feet of his friends, all of whom glowed with pride.

"You conquered him," Marett said.

"You fought your greatest fear," Haxel said.

"And you won," Anselm added.

"I did," Orren suddenly realized the impact of what he had done.

His friends embraced him, tears in their eyes.

"How did Jasper get here?" Orren asked.

"This creature of yours," the zhiv general Tubuz said, "what Mister Anselm called a 'donkey'—is very brave. She's the reason we were able to come to your aid."

Orren looked at Tubuz in confusion.

"The elders were very impressed with how she sacrificed herself at the Mount of the Cone," Tubuz said. "So Mother Tiblitz spoke to her."

"I thought I heard Mother Tiblitz say something to Jasper," Haxel said, "It sounded like 'keep us informed,' or something like that."

"That's exactly what happened," Tubuz said. "You see, my human friends, we zhivi are lousy trackers. We can't follow a trail. We don't need that skill, for we don't hunt large animals."

"But if you can't track, how did Haxel follow me through the woods of the Corcadine?" Orren asked.

"I used my eyes, Master," Haxel said. "I didn't track. But if you'd traveled through forest like this, I'd have lost you."

"That's where Jasper helped," Tubuz said. "We followed your footsteps, but every night, Jasper came to us and guided us to where you camped. That's how we kept up with you."

"So *that's* why she kept disappearing!" Anselm said. Then turning to the donkey, he said, "You, my dear, are a genius." He leaned over and kissed Jasper on the nose. Then Orren and the others embraced the donkey as well.

"When she ran away from your captors," Tubuz said, "she came and found us. She led us back to you, and that's why we were able to save you."

"But if you zhivi can't track, what happened to my father?" Orren asked. "The 'walking bushes' attacked him by the falls, which are far from the Gorge of the Leafy Curse."

"I remember your father," Tubuz said. "He came into the northern branch of the pass, some ten season cycles ago. We showed his party aggression, so they wouldn't enter our gorge, but he used the brown gwell on us. He killed several zhivi by burying them in dust. He and his men then retreated, and went through what you humans call Vulture Canyon. We followed him, intent on revenge. We didn't attack his group *in* the gorge, because we'd be vulnerable in that enclosed space. We waited until he ascended the slopes that straddle the falls. We climbed higher than he and his men were, and we shot our arrows at them. Your father jumped into the river, and we always thought he'd drowned."

Orren cast his eyes downward, not sure what to make of this information. On the one hand, the zhivi had inflicted the wounds that eventually killed his father. On the other hand, his father seemed to have killed some of *them* first.

"I think we all need to rest," Anselm cut in.

"Agreed," Tubuz said. The zhiv warriors settled down. Orren lay on the cave floor and fell asleep.

He awoke hours later, and the first thing he heard was Anselm asking Tubuz, "How long do these tunnels extend?"

"We don't know, Good Sir Anselm," the zhiv general said. "The khain built them. Unlike them, we zhivi are not subterranean creatures. However, we do know of one tunnel that goes on for some distance, before reaching an exit that faces the river."

"Then we'll take it," Anselm said. "And we should do it now. That magic sniffer can still detect Nebi's psychic trail. We don't want Doofus upon us again."

Anselm took one lantern, and Marett, the other. Then the gwell bearers and the zhivi walked through the tunnels, until they reached the exit. For the entire way, Orren could not stop thinking about the implications of the fact that zhivi had mortally wounded his father.

It took less time to reach the entrance than everyone had thought. Before they left the tunnel, the gwell bearers bid the zhivi goodbye, and expressed their gratitude. Then they traipsed through the forest until they reached the riverbank.

"What do we do now?" Haxel asked.

"We need to get to the Gorge of the Leafy Curse," Anselm said. "Then we'll go up the hidden pass, back to Wardolam."

"But we don't have Kalsh or Ru'i," Orren said, "or Magna."

Anselm put a hand on Orren's shoulder. "My boy," he said in a paternal voice that reminded him of Richard. "I know you didn't have a choice in the matter, and I don't blame you for one minute, but when Doofus found out from you about Wardolam, that put the Sun-Children in danger. Doofus and his cronies will go there. It will only take them a week to traverse the pass, until they once again reach Airen's Arc. We must warn Narx and the council of the threat they face. Ghouls or no ghouls, they need to know."

"But the Gorge of the Leafy Curse is far away," Haxel said. "Vulture Canyon's the short cut. Remember?"

Anselm detached the Staff of Transport from Jasper's packs, and placed it in

Haxel's hands. "It's time, my nimble friend," he said. "All of us will grasp onto this talisman. You make it travel upstream. I'll tell you where to stop, by tapping your shoulder twice."

Haxel grasped the front part of the staff. Anselm walked behind him, and then came Orren, Marett, and finally Jasper, grasping the end of the stick in her mouth. Together they waded into the river. The warm water was wild.

"Grab the staff, everyone," Haxel said, "and hold on tight."

Orren and the others did as Haxel instructed. The zhiv closed his eyes and focused on the talisman.

The mountains, cliffs, and forests raced by, as the staff transported its passengers upstream. Haxel, Anselm, Orren, Marett, and Jasper practically flew, their bodies hovering slightly above staff and the water. The roughest rapids and wildest eddies were no match for the talisman, which traveled so quickly that everything became a blur.

After about half an hour, Anselm tapped Haxel on the shoulder. The zhiv directed the talisman toward the shore. As soon as the gwell bearers emerged onto the pebble-covered banks, the Staff of Transport disintegrated into powdery dust that the river carried downstream.

"The Gorge of the Leafy Curse is one mile to the west," Anselm said. "Come, everybody. Narx will be enraged at this news, but that doesn't matter. It's time to do what's right, and to face the consequences of whatever mistakes we've made."

# THE COUNCIL HEAD'S WRATH

It took two days for the gwell-bearers to travel through the Gorge of the Leafy Curse. They encountered no zhivi there, but the normally thick bushes had been moved to the sides, leaving a clear path. Orren and his friends reached the Hidden Pass without incident, and they traveled northward through it for four days.

The events of the past month had worn everyone out to such an extent that no one was willing to take on the burden of becoming Nebi's bearer. The green gwell was left inside the pouch that Orren had cut from Berthus's belt. The pouch itself had been placed inside one of the sacks Jasper carried.

North of the fork where the Gorge of the Leafy Curse and Vulture Canyon came together, the Hidden Pass was very narrow, and ascended continuously. In some places, the gray canyon walls rose more than one hundred feet above the travelers' heads.

It was bitterly cold in the pass, but mercifully, the snow cover was thin. Anselm explained that this was due to there being little precipitation at the higher elevations. Flora and fauna alike was scarce, and the travelers were forced to ration their food supplies. They obtained water by loading water skins with snow, and melting it with their body heat. Jasper fared better than the others, because she had fattened up in the forests, and she obtained all the water she needed by eating the snow as it was.

When they once again gazed out over Airen's Arc, it became immediately clear why the pass was so difficult to find. First, the entrance was more than one thousand feet above the valley that lay between the arc and the mountains. Second, it was concealed by a veritable maze of boulders. Third, there was a monotone of color among the rocks, which gave the impression of a continuous wall.

Mercifully, Airen's Arc was deserted. Thus, the gwell-bearers were able, free of hindrance, to walk directly into the valley, before ascending the arc, and then descending into the Ghoul Vale.

When they reached the city, Anselm spoke a few words in the yelian tongue, and the gates opened. The gwell-bearers entered the foyer chamber, where three shadow guards greeted them and told them to wait for the city council to convene. Two hours later, they were summoned by a single guard who, carrying a torch, led Orren, Anselm, Marett, Haxel, and Jasper through the long, dark tunnels into the great hall.

The familiar pillars, dome, and mosaics came into view, as well as the strange woodpile-shaped sculptures out of which flames lit up the chamber. Narx sat on his throne with a cold look in his golden eyes, and a stern expression on his face. The peregrine falcon preened itself atop the back of the throne, and the red mastiff snoozed at the council head's feet. However, most of the council members were missing. Out of the original sixty, there appeared to be a mere twenty present. They wore the colorful embroidered robes that Orren had first seen them in, rather than the monotone gowns that signified their tribal affiliation, but even so, Orren could tell that everyone present was a member of the Magg tribe. Shann-Rell, however, was nowhere to be seen even though she too, was a Magg.

Narx's glare sent shivers down the boy's spine. It was immediately apparent that the council head had no concern for the lives of the gwell-bearers, including the one he referred to as the "Slave." Narx's mind was on one thing only—he wanted the gwellen.

"So where are they?" he asked.

"He doesn't even ask where Quartz is," Haxel said quietly so that only his master could hear. Orren nodded.

"O Great Narx," Anselm said, "We have obtained Nebi, the gwell of plant spirit."

The council head descended from his throne, walked over to Anselm and held out his hand. Anselm removed the green gwell from Jasper's packs, and placed it in Narx's hand.

"And where are Ru'i, Magna, and Kalsh?" Narx demanded.

Anselm's body trembled as he prostrated himself on the ground. "O Great Narx," he said. "There is much that the council needs to know." The old man proceeded to tell the council head, who stood over him the entire time, the story of their foray to the Fallagourn Falls.

"...so there you have it, Great Narx," Anselm looked up, pale-faced, at the yelian ruler, as he finished his tale. "Lord Doofus now knows of Wardolam's existence, and he's heading this way. The Sun-Children must prepare themselves."

Narx backhanded Anselm across the face so hard that the old man fell backward onto the floor. He then seized Anselm by the collar and lifted him to his feet. Orren, Marett, Haxel, and Jasper all rushed to their friend's defense, but the shadow guards quickly seized them and removed their weapons.

A trickle of blood ran down Anselm's chin. Narx started shaking him by the collar and yelling in his face. "You were sent to obtain all four remaining Sun-Stones, and you came back with just one? Do you think that by bringing Nebi to me, you somehow atone for your negligence in losing Ru'i to this Berthus?"

"No, Great Narx, I—"

Narx backhanded him again.

"My predecessor, Varshing, took pity on you!" The council head growled. "He elevated you far above your lowly human origins, making you a Slave to the yelia. You were fed, healed, and honored, and all we ever asked from you in return was that you carry out our errands. Yet, you couldn't even do that! You lost Ru'i, and then you brought your lousy human friends here. You also brought us a zhiv, despite the long-standing enmity that exists between the zhivi and us Sun-Children. Worst of all, you bring the most foul humans in the world, to our hallowed doorstep!"

"I'm sorry!" Anselm wept. "I'll make it up to you!"

Narx flung him aside. Anselm fell hard to chamber's stone floor, where he lay in a pathetic heap, crying.

"What apologies can be accepted, coming from a lousy human?" Narx growled. "What promises can be relied upon? Our forebears trusted certain humans, bestowing chosen status upon them, and look what happened!"

The other council members murmured angrily in their flute-like language. Whatever they said seemed to encourage Narx further, for he lunged at Anselm once again, and jerked him to his feet.

"Leave him alone!" Orren shouted.

"How dare you speak so brazenly toward the council head," Grnoud, the council translator said. "We ought to execute you where you stand!"

"No," Narx said. "If they couldn't serve us as living beings, then they will serve us as ghouls. Hand them over to the undead ones. They will spend eternity protecting the city of Wardolam."

"You can't do that," Marett said in her first show of defiance toward the yelia. "We swore on the Staff of Diktat to carry out this mission within ninety days. Fifty-three days remain for us to complete this quest and hand the stones to you. You have to allow us another chance."

"The council head doesn't *have* to do anything," Grnoud said. "At least not with regard to naugai. Besides, Narx has the support of every member of this body."

"Not everyone," Orren blurted out. "Most council members aren't here. Where *are* they, Narx? Where's Shann-Rell? Where are the folks from the other tribes?"

"Get them out of my sight!" Narx's already ugly face was contorted with rage. "Throw them to the ghouls—the Slave, the two young humans, and the zhiv. Throw the donkey out too. Her long association with the Slave contaminates her, and I can't bear her sight or smell any longer."

The shadow guards pulled the gwell-bearers toward the door. At the last moment, Orren saw a wicked grin on Narx's face. "One more thing, Slave. All promises that a council head makes are for the good of the Sun-Children, including false ones. You were our chattel, to do with as we liked, so there was no need to ever be honest with you."

"What?" Anselm went deathly pale. "You mean you never intended to turn me into a yelius?"

"It's not possible to do that," Narx said. "You're a human and a human you'll always be, at least until you become a ghoul."

"You deceptive, hypocritical, betraying, thieving scum!" Anselm struggled against his captors as he screamed.

"Goodbye, Slave," Narx said in a mocking voice. "Enjoy your undead state."

Anselm continued to swear at and insult the yelia. A shadow guard, however, clamped a darkened hand over the old man's mouth. Orren also lost his temper, but he could not vent his outrage, for he was gagged, and his arms and legs were rendered immobile.

The shadow guard unceremoniously dumped Orren and his friends on the black earth outside Wardolam's gates. In front of them, the Ghoul Vale's brown mists swirled.

Orren jumped to his feet and started punching and kicking the walls in anger. Meanwhile, Anselm buried his face in his hands and wept hysterically. Marett and Haxel put their hands on his shoulder, but he would not be consoled.

"So this is how it ends," the old man said through his sobs. "Why did the Guiding Light lead me to Varshing in the first place?"

"Just a minute," Marett said. "Varshing…Varshing…that's it!"

"What's it, Miss?" Haxel asked.

"Orren, do you remember Iskander telling us how the dark Duralines came to be?" Marett asked. "He said that his great-grandfather met a very deformed old man named Varshing."

Orren turned around and looked at her. "Do you think it's the same person?"

"I'm sure of it," Marett said. "Varshing was the last council head to wander about in the outside world. He must have wanted something from humans. The question is what?"

"Why does it matter?" Anselm asked. "We're going to suffer a fate worse than death anyway."

Marett went silent.

"Master?" Haxel asked.

"Yes?"

"I'm sorry it was zhivi who gave your father the wounds that killed him."

"I'm sorry he killed some of your kind," Orren said. He held out a hand toward the zhiv, and Haxel took it. "If we're gonna be ghouls, at least we'll all be ghouls together."

As if on cue, a mass of skeletal shapes appeared in the fog. The ghouls walked toward their victims slowly and solemnly. Their empty eye sockets stared at Orren and his friends, who could feel their hunger and longing. Orren kept a firm grip on Haxel's trembling right hand. Haxel reached for Marett, who took his left hand in her right. With her own left hand, she made contact with Anselm. Jasper lay down by Anselm's side, and he put his hand on her mane.

Suddenly six black shapes darted out of the city gates and drove the ghouls away. The fiends disappeared into the fog.

The black figures removed their hoods. It was Shann-Rell and the chiefs of the other yelian tribes. "Gwell-bearers," Shann-Rell said, "return with us into the city."

Orren, Marett, and Haxel stood up to follow her, but Anselm remained seated.

"Anselm?" Shann-Rell said. "Won't you come inside?"

"To keep company with you lying, manipulating yelia again? No thanks. I'd rather be a ghoul."

Marett and Haxel looked to Orren in desperation.

"Anselm, come inside the city," Orren said. "Not for the yelia, but for *us*."

Without another word, the old man stood up. He took Marett's hand and Orren's, and walked with them into Wardolam. Jasper trotted by his side. When they were all once again in the foyer chamber, Sha-Rax, the emaciated-looking chief of the Orr, shut the gate behind them.

Shann-Rell opened a door, which was not the same as the one that led to the council chamber. She motioned for everyone to follow her. Marett went first, followed by Orren, Haxel, Anselm, Jasper, and finally the six tribal chiefs. Sha-Rax shut the door behind them and locked it.

They followed Shann-Rell down a narrow, twisting passage that had no ceiling, and was therefore open to the brown sky. In some places there was only enough room for them to walk in single file. The walls around them were constructed of packed earth and stones, and the corridor seemed to go on forever.

Eventually, the narrow passageway ended, and they emerged onto a road that, while wide, was deserted. The familiar buildings, which resembled tree copses, came into view. Everything was derelict. The structures were falling apart, and the cobblestones that covered the streets were loose.

At one point, they turned a corner, and Orren knew exactly where they were. It was the empty part of the city that he and his friends had seen from their cell. He located their cell window, which was now blocked with stones.

They walked a few hundred feet down the road, which ended at an arched doorway. Shann-Rell opened the door and ushered the gwell-bearers into an open space several hundred feet wide. Over one thousand yelia were present, wearing the gowns that bore the colors of their respective tribes. When they saw Orren and his friends, they let out a cheer.

The yelian crowd included tall, beautiful elders and shorter, less attractive younger ones. There were a few who resembled children, though Orren knew that they were old enough to be his father or mother. Every tribe, including the Magg, was well-represented. All of the yelia had the same empty look in their eyes. This time, however, there was a glimmer of hope.

"See?" Shann-Rell said. "I told you that you're heroes to most of the Sun-Children."

"Who cares?" Anselm grunted. He turned away and folded his arms across his chest.

"Shann-Rell, what's going on?" Marett asked. "The council condemned us, but you saved us."

"Narx and his followers have gone way too far," Ordam, the Kell chief said, anger flashing in her golden eyes. "Shann, I think you'd better explain everything."

"Wardolam is a very ancient city," Shann-Rell said. "At one time it was one of the homes of the *shamari*."

"The who?" Orren asked.

"The shamari were the priests of the yelia," Diduann, the chief of the Rau tribe, said. "And just as each of the six subordinate gwellen has its own tribe, so the shamari were in essence, the tribe of Sham, the Mother Stone, though they weren't really a tribe as such."

"A dispute arose between two candidates for the office of *shamar'nark*," Shann-Rell said. "That's the high priest. The loser in the argument was a man named Ortrax, a powerful and skilled magician from a respected lineage. Embittered by his defeat, Ortrax took his followers to Thelta, the evil god known for his foul, distorted creations."

"How can that be?" Marett said. "The Sun-Children don't act in such a manner."

"You humans have such an idealized view of us," Diduann said with a sad smile. "The reality is that our history is besmirched with warfare and violence."

"A pact was created between Thelta and Ortrax," Shann-Rell said. "Ortrax would benefit from Thelta's legions of foul creatures, and his own followers would be transformed into more such monsters. Ortrax, in turn, would utilize the powers of the Sun-Stones for Thelta's benefit, since no odius can bear a gwell."

"In yelian law, a pact is sealed by creating a talisman," Diduann said. "The talisman that sealed the pact between Thelta and Ortrax, was the Staff of Diktat."

"You mean we're now servants of *Thelta*?" Marett shrieked.

"No," Shann-Rell said. "Thelta's no more, and Ortrax is one of the ghouls—no one knows which one he is, and it doesn't matter anyway, since the ghoul state basically erases individuality. The Staff of Diktat, which was created using the magic of Ru'i, makes the ghouls possible, for anyone who swears by it and violates his oath, becomes a ghoul."

"After Wardolam was destroyed, the divine astra cursed Ortrax and his followers, turning them into ghouls fated to guard the ruined city. No one lived here then, so the ghouls were essentially doing nothing. That's part of the punishment, for it's a terrible thing when one's entire existence is futile. We yelia live in Wardolam now, but for the ghouls, existence is still futile; after all, no one feeds them, pays them, or honors them for what they do, and they remain bound forever to the Staff of Diktat."

"During the latter years of the Regnum, decadence and inso-lence were everywhere, and it even afflicted even the Sun-Child-ren. Only the Magg tribe resisted the corruption and adhered to traditional ways."

"When the decay started even seeping into Magg society, our chief, Prarx, decided to isolate us from the humans and the corrupted yelian tribes. He led us into the vale, where we rebuilt Wardolam."

"The corrupted yelia were unprepared for the upheavals that came when the Regnum collapsed. Many died in the resulting chaos and wars. Most of the remnants fled to the Ghoul Vale, and begged us Magg, who were already here, to let them in."

"At the time, Prarx the Second was council head. He felt compassion for the refugees, but didn't want them corrupting the Magg, so he worked out a compromise. All Kell, Orr, Rau, Haas, and Nebb then alive, and all future generations of those tribes, had to swear on the Staff of Diktat, to be subordinate and obedient to the Magg. Disobedience meant being handed over to the ghouls, to be devoured by them, and to join their number."

"That's awful," Marett said.

"Actually it didn't affect us so much at first," Ordam said. "Relative harmony existed between the tribes, with each tribe carrying out its specialty. For instance, the Nebb grow and harvest crops. The Rau raise livestock. We Kell plough the soil and build. If more than one element was required, tribes collaborated."

"The problem, however, was that we yelia don't thrive when we're cut off from the Sun Father. Many of us didn't want to bear children because of it. That's why our numbers plummeted. When Prarx the Second admitted us to Wardolam, the population here rose to 75,000. By the time Shibbia became council head, we were down to 10,000."

"Shibbia was a tyrant," Diduann said. "He reduced all who weren't Magg, to servitude and poverty, and removed our representation on the city council, except for a few who acted as advisors."

"And life among the Magg became increasingly regimented and restricted," Shann-Rell added. "The elderly died out, and fewer children replaced them. By the end of Shibbia's rule, the population of all our tribes together, was reduced to 4,000."

"Varshing was Shibbia's successor," Ordam said. "He continued Shibbia's policies, and forced even the Magg to swear on the Staff of Diktat. All yelia alive today live under the Staff of Diktat save for two, both of whom were born before Varshing's rulership. One is Narx, and the other is Grnoud, the council translator. Grnoud is the only one who can stand up to Narx, but instead, he merely does Narx's bidding as though he too, were under the Staff."

"Shann-Rell seems able to stand up to him," Marett said.

"Only because I know him so well," Shann-Rell said. "He's actually my uncle, and I know just how far to push him and how to placate him when he's angry. Every year, however, he gets less and less patient and tolerant, and harder and harder to deal with."

"And just who are these shadow guards anyway?" Marett asked.

"They're actually drawn from all the tribes," Shann-Rell said. "They're individuals who are eager to gain favor with Narx, so they seek to impress him by enforcing his decrees. The more ruthless they are, the more Narx is impressed. Grnoud coordinates and plans their actions."

"We yelia of all tribes were on the verge of losing hope," Ordam said. "Our situation worsened constantly, birth defects increased, and then we stopped breeding altogether. No child has been born in Wardolam for 25 years. We were ready to face true extinction, but then, unexpectedly, hope returned. You gwell-bearers brought it."

"How did we do *that*?" Haxel asked.

"For centuries, the most powerful object in the life of every yelius has been the Staff of Diktat," Ordam replied. "The staff cannot be damaged, for it was made with powerful magic. Now, however, it's no longer the most powerful object, for you have brought back three of our sacred gwellen. That's why you're heroes to us, and that's why we will hide you from Narx, and help you as best we can, to complete your mission."

"Varshing knew about your father, Orren," Shann-Rell said. "He made it his business to know everything he could about Lorien Randolphus. It was the last thing he did before he became too old to leave the Ghoul Vale on errands. On his deathbed, Varshing begged Narx to find the gwellen, and to bring them back here. Narx, however, refused to leave the vale, so Anselm did his work."

"His dirty work, you mean," the old man spat. "*Your* dirty work."

"Anselm was the one who searched for clues to the stones' whereabouts," Shann-Rell said. "When Narx was satisfied that Anselm had enough information with which to locate Ru'i, he made Anselm a chosen one, and sent him to fetch the stone."

"I was their dog," the old man said. "They said 'fetch' and I'd fetch."

"Narx never had to bring Anselm under the Staff of Diktat," Ordam said. "The promise of becoming a yelius was a better motivator. We weren't supposed to know about any of this, but Narx made the mistake of not swearing Anselm to silence. Anselm is a very friendly person, who loves to converse, and that's how we found out what Narx was up to."

"Truth to tell, we didn't take Anselm seriously," Shann-Rell said. "The gwellen have been gone for so long, we believed they could never be found. We thought that Narx had fed Anselm a pack of lies about finding Ru'i, just as he did about Anselm becoming a yelius. Imagine our surprise, therefore, when you three arrived in Wardolam bearing Hesh and Orya."

"Narx became paranoid after you left," Diduann said. "He threw out all the council members—Magg tribesmen included—who weren't slavish supporters of his."

"And now you know our full story, Anselm," Shann-Rell said, "I understand that you're angry and disappointed, and you have every right to be, but if we'd revealed the truth to you about Narx's lie, your anger at him would have been revealed, and then you *and* us would have become ghouls. So knowing what you know now, can you find it in yourself to forgive us?"

The old man looked at her, cracked a smile and said, "I suppose I can."

# THE GHOULS TURN

Lord Berthus Randolphus sat at the entrance to his tent, overlooking the Ghoul Vale. The brown clouds that concealed the valley stood in sharp contrast to the gray, early spring rain clouds that covered the sky above. The air was cold, but less so than it had been when Berthus's army had last camped upon Airen's Arc.

Warmer conditions had caused most of the snow in Vulture Canyon and the Hidden Pass, to melt. Thus, the return journey only took eight days. Hundreds of tents were now pitched upon the arc.

The three magic sniffers had insisted that the gwell-bearers came through the pass and into the vale, carrying Nebi. The psychic trail they left was apparently still fresh. Berthus therefore sent the magic sniffers into the Ghoul Vale, so they could find more clues. Five-dozen Framguth knights went with, to protect them. Berthus eagerly awaited their return.

Three figures suddenly appeared on the edge of the arc. They were pale, bedraggled, and exhausted. Their clothes were ripped, torn, and covered in black soot. Berthus immediately recognized one of them as Felix Ramburgus, the magic sniffer leader. The other two were Framguth knights, whose names were of no consequence.

"Where are the others?" Berthus demanded.

"The ghouls took them," Ramburgus said, his eyes wide with fear, "and that includes Torgen and Brenco, my disciples." Then the head magic sniffer's face contorted with rage. He pointed an accusing finger at Berthus. "*You* killed my men, Berthus Randolphus!" he shouted. "Nine magic sniffers set out from the Corcadine with you—nine! Now I'm the only one left."

"Calm down, Ramburgus," Iranda said. "We've all had to make sacrifices."

"What do *you* know of sacrifices, woman?" Ramburgus shouted at her. "You weren't there to see those skeletal beings coming out of the fog. They fell upon us, and literally sucked the lives out of Torgen and Brenco. Torgen and Brenco stood up; their eyes empty, their souls vacant, and they attacked us. We escaped by running as fast as we could, up the slope. I've never seen anything so ghastly and horrible!

"You, Berthus Randolphus, promised to bring the *dru* back to glory. Instead, what have you done? You've sacrificed my men as though they were cattle—as if we were victims of the Drammites. Is this what it means to serve you?"

Berthus had heard enough. He leapt to his feet and lunged at the magic sniffer. He grabbed Ramburgus by the collar, flung him to the ground, and kicked him in the ribs. Ramburgus doubled over.

"How dare you point fingers at me, Felix!" Berthus growled. "Your men died because of your own negligence. You know more about things like ghouls than anyone else. I *rely* on you for information. You should have taken into account what might happen, but you didn't. And you're not the only one who's lost men. I lost fifty-eight of them to those ghouls. How do you think I feel?"

Actually, Berthus felt nothing. The 700 or so remaining Framguth knights had become a source of constant worry. Lord Hemric had been appointed their leader, but now, thanks to the swine boy, Hemric was dead. Only one Framguth lord, Martin Kannover, remained, but Berthus did not trust him, and certainly would never admit him to his Web. Berthus was happy to send some knights into the vale, to face the ghouls. Leaderless and volatile, they were now expendable. Even so, they were useful as a defense against Ramburgus's wild accusations.

"The deaths of my men are on your head, Felix," Berthus said. "You deserve execution!"

The magic sniffer looked up at Berthus with pleading eyes. Ramburgus was pale and trembling once again, but now it was because he feared his lord. That was exactly as Berthus wanted it to be. The Lord of the Corcadine had faced down yet another challenge to his authority.

"You've lost all my respect, Felix," Berthus said, "but you're part of my Web, for I still feel connected to you. I'm gonna give you one chance to regain your standing in my eyes. You complain that the goblin killed your best man back in the Corcadine? That goblin's been a constant source of bad luck, so find it, Felix, and kill it. Now!"

Ramburgus picked himself up and, clutching at his side, disappeared into the camp.

"Iranda?" Berthus said.

"Yes?"

"Bring Eric here."

Iranda walked into the mass of tents. After a few minutes, she reappeared, together with the young, blond dargun. "How can I be of service?" he asked.

"Eric, I presume Iranda told you what happened to the men I sent into the Ghoul Vale?"

"Yes, my Lord," the dargun said, "and I assure you, it's no loss. It was just a pair of magic sniffers, selling their services to the highest bidder, and a bunch of odia-worshipping Framguth knights. You still have the favor of Blood Master Dramm, and that's what matters."

"Eric, what do you know about the ghouls?"

"My family lore says they were created long ago by elvish magicians. Basically a ghoul is a being whose soul is trapped inside his body so that it can't leave, even after the body dies. Ghouls are not alive or dead, but something in between. They have no free will but follow their instinct, which is to be bound to the place they're charged to protect, and to devour anyone who falls into their hands, turning them into fellow ghouls."

"What was that word you just used?" Berthus asked. "*Instinct?* Explain it to me."

"Instinct is the natural compulsion of an animal to behave in a certain manner," the dargun said.

"Instinct...animal," Berthus said. "Eric! Iranda! I have our solution!"

"Yes?" the dargun and the woman both said at once.

"Animals have instincts," Berthus said, "and these ghouls do too. I have Ru'i, the gwell of animal spirit. Surely it will command the ghouls, the way it does animals, forcing them, by their own instinct, to obey my every word?"

"That, my lord, makes perfect sense," Dargun Rodrick said.

"It does indeed," Iranda smiled.

"There's no need for us to attack the elvish city," Berthus said with a cruel grin. "The ghouls will do it for us."

Orren was awakened by the sounds of high-pitched fluty voices and running feet. He fumbled about in the darkness for Anselm's lantern. A blazing torch, however, came into view. It was carried by a black-haired female yelius from the Nebb tribe, and it illuminated the interior of the dark tunnel in which Orren and his friends hid. Fourteen other yelia accompanied the torchbearer. One of them was Ordam, the Kell chief.

The yelian faces were stricken with fear and confusion. Ordam's golden hair was a mess, and she was out of breath. Clearly, she had been in a hurry, and was desperate to speak to the gwell bearers.

"What's going on?" Anselm asked, as he threw off his blanket and groggily struggled to his feet.

"O gwell bearers, the ghouls are acting strangely!"

"What do you mean?" Haxel shrieked. Marett, however, put a hand on the zhiv's shoulder, and calmed him down.

"The undead ones are amassed against the city walls," Ordam said. "Some of them are climbing upon the backs and shoulders of others. They've never acted in this manner before. The Sun-Children are confused and frightened, and are all gathered in the city forum. They're demanding answers from the council, which has convened to discuss the problem."

"And you've come to us *naugai* for answers," Anselm said in a mocking tone.

"So much for the yelia knowing everything."

"I want to see what's going on," Marett demanded. "Ordam, is there a vantage point from where we can see outside the city?"

"There are towers built along Wardolam's walls," Ordam said. "I'll take you into one, so you can have a look out the window."

"Then let's go," Marett said.

Orren, Haxel, Marett, Anselm, and Jasper followed Ordam and the other yelia through a maze of tunnels. The dark passages had been the gwell bearers' home for the past two days, where they hid from Narx and the shadow guards. Their yelian rescuers brought them food and water, and gave them blankets and cushions to lie upon. Even so, it was a terrible thing to be forced to remain in the darkness like this, doing nothing, while the date of the Ghouls' Curse came ever closer. Everybody was on edge, and half of each gwell bearer's mind was occupied by his or her hex-seed. The usual means of reducing the gray nodules of despair were of no effect now.

Orren lost his temper more times than he could count over the past two days. Anselm was constantly irritable, and shot insults at everybody and everything. Marett remained silent the whole time, and spoke to nobody, while Haxel had fits of weeping. Jasper patiently stayed by the gwell-bearers' sides, and resisted any attempts by them or by the yelia, to remove the sacks and ropes she carried. She also ate an untold fortune, obliging the yelia to bring her large amounts of hay and vegetables. Her body seemed to be broadening, and her coat was shaggier. Orren even thought her hoofs were larger.

Lanterns were the only sources of light in this darkened world. The gwell-bearers had to rely on the yelia to guide them through the underground tunnel network, for if they tried to find their own way, they were sure to get lost. They were thus stuck in the darkness, which was maddening.

For what seemed like an eternity, Ordam led the gwell-bearers through tunnel after tunnel, until they reached a staircase of solid stone. They ascended, half blind, with only the torchbearer to guide them. When they reached the top of the stairs, however, there was light, albeit the gloomy brown light of the Ghoul Vale.

"Oh, to see blue skies again," Haxel moaned.

"Get used to this," Anselm snapped. "In fifty-one days, this will be all any of us Web members will ever see for the rest of our miserable existences."

They ascended another stone staircase, this one spiraling upward. After climbing for at least one hundred feet, they reached a room that was illuminated by the ubiquitous brown light. There was a large window, which Orren and his friends approached and peered through.

The window was only a few feet below the filthy, swirling cloud cover. It afforded a view of the walls below, where there was a scene that made Orren want to vomit. Hundreds upon hundreds of ghouls had accumulated against the wall. The fiends were climbing on top of one another. Slowly but surely, they were creating what resembled scaffolding, composed of masses of boney limbs. Though the piles collapsed now and then, there was steady progress upward.

"No doubt about it," Anselm said. "The ghouls are trying to scale the city walls."

"But how can that be?" Ordam asked. "The Staff of Diktat binds them to the vale and the city. They *have* to protect us. It's all they know how to do—all they ever knew how to do. They're like animals; unable to conceive of doing things differently from the way their instinct teaches them."

"You see?" Anselm snapped. "Right there is the problem with you yelia. You see the whole world as there to serve you, until one day, the truth comes out. I was fooled for many years, but now the ghouls have finally seen the truth, and want to get rid of the source of their suffering."

The yelia went silent.

"I don't think that's it," Marett said. "I have another theory. Ordam, did you say that ghouls are like animals?"

"Only in the sense that they don't have free will," the Kell chief said.

"They're completely subservient to the Staff of Diktat?"

"Yes."

"But the Staff of Diktat is merely a talisman," Marett said. "It's inferior to the gwellen."

"Then Berthus is here," Orren said, "and he's got Ru'i. The ghouls aren't obeying the Staff anymore; they're obeying Ru'i, which is much stronger. At the same time, the ghouls *exist* because of the Staff…Ordam, take us to the council chamber now!"

"We came from another part of the city," Ordam said, "and you won't survive an encounter with Narx's Shadow Guards if you go through the main passage, but I believe there's a passageway that leads directly into the council chamber from here. Zarell!" She addressed a small, young-looking yelian male in brown Kell robes. Ordam gave him instructions.

Zarell nodded and then motioned for everyone to follow him. The Nebb female with the torch followed immediately behind. Ordam came next, with her entourage, the gwell-bearers, and Jasper.

Zarell led them all down the spiral staircase and back into the dark passageways.

"The network of tunnels is so vast, no one knows all of them," Ordam said, "but to the extent that *anyone* knows them, Zarell does."

Everyone followed the little yelius through a mind-boggling series of twists and turns, gates and doors. They climbed another staircase, which led into a wide passageway, decorated with the familiar tree-shaped pillars, vaulted ceiling, and colorful mosaics. Zarell turned a corner, and everyone burst into the council chamber.

The twenty council members, in their resplendent, embroidered robes, stared with shock and horror at Ordam and the gwell-bearers. Outraged, Narx sprung from his throne. His mastiff growled and the falcon shrieked.

"What are the humans and the zhiv doing here, Ordam?" Narx screamed. "I threw them to the ghouls!"

"We saved them," Ordam said in a defiant tone, "and they're here to help us solve this problem. Narx, we're in great danger. The ghouls have turned on us."

"Guards!" Narx said. "Grab the humans, the zhiv, and the donkey. Grab Ordam and these other upstarts! They're going to discover what comes of disobeying the council head."

Twenty shadow guards moved toward Ordam and the gwell-bearers, who stepped backward until they were up against the chamber's rear wall. The closest one was about to make a lunge at Marett, when suddenly there was an ominous sound in the passageway. It was the shuffling sound of thousands of running feet, combined with the clicks of bones.

"The ghouls are upon us, Narx!" Ordam shouted.

Suddenly, the foul, empty eyed fiends burst into the council chamber. There were hundreds upon hundreds of them, and more entered with every passing second. The shadow guards charged them, but the ghouls were no longer obedient, for they now answered to a gwell.

The shadow guards disappeared under the ghoul mass. Bone chilling shrieks resounded through the council chamber. Most of the council members were frozen stiff in terror, but Narx bounded toward the door that led out onto the city forum. His mastiff and falcon followed him, and Ordam, the gwell-bearers, and the other fourteen yelia, followed close on their heels. One of Ordam's companions, a golden haired female in blue Haas robes, was not fast enough. Orren looked over his shoulder in time to see the ghouls grab her and literally suck the life out of her face. Before she was transformed into a ghoul, she let out an ear-piercing scream. The same fate befell the council members and the remaining shadow guards.

Narx threw the council building's door open and, together with his big red dog, fled outside. Ordam, the thirteen remaining members of her escort, and the gwell-bearers, followed, bursting out onto the wide platform. There, Grnoud was trying to placate the restive citizens of Wardolam. Behind the council translator, stood the Staff of Diktat, nine feet tall and foreboding, even with the golden sun on top. Narx's peregrine falcon flew onto the sun symbol.

Ordam slammed the door shut, and stood against it. Orren and his friends, and many yelia, ran to her assistance. It soon became apparent, however, that their efforts would be in vain. The ghouls pressed against the door on the other side. Their combined weight was proving too much. Skeletal hands reached through the opening, evoking terrified screams from the yelian crowd in the forum.

"Narx!" Orren screamed.

The tall council head swiveled around and glared dangerously at Orren.

"Destroy the Staff of Diktat!" the boy said.

"I don't listen to naugai!" Narx yelled. "You naugai brought the ghouls upon us. Besides, the staff can't be destroyed."

"Yes it can!" Orren shouted, "with a gwell!"

Grnoud, Narx's lackey, turned to his leader and said, "I think we must do as Orren suggests."

"I will not listen to a filthy human!" Narx said.

Grnoud then tackled Narx. The Wardolam council head fell to the ground. Though Grnoud was a head shorter, he was much more well-built than Narx was, and the military training that had been a necessary aspect of his shadow guard background, ensured that he was physically stronger. While Narx yelled threats and obscenities, Grnoud searched through his friend's clothes until he found Orya, the gwell of fire. He drew out the red stone and, leaving Narx lying in the dust, darted over to the Staff of Diktat.

At that exact moment, the ghouls forced the door open. The yelian crowd screamed and scattered in all directions, while the undead beings, whose number now included the council members and shadow guards, poured out onto the forum. Grnoud, however, shooed Narx's falcon away from the Staff of Diktat, and touched the red gwell to it.

The Staff of Diktat burst into flames. Within seconds, it was reduced to ashes, which crumbled to the earth. The ghouls also fell to the ground. Their corrupt and mottled flesh disintegrated. Within a matter of a few minutes, all that was left of the dreaded ghouls of the vale was a mass of bleached and truly lifeless skulls and bones.

Grnoud vomited. He then fell on the floor and coughed up blood. Several yelia ran over to him and helped him to his feet. The council translator was pale and trembling, but insisted that he would recover.

"What's happening to him?" Haxel shrieked.

"Grnoud is a Magg," Shann-Rell said, "Magna is the stone of his tribe. Anyone who uses the gwell of another tribe becomes ill."

"That's what happens to us gwell-bearers," Orren said.

"Yes," Shann-Rell agreed. "Grnoud, of course, has no Web. He braved illness for the sake of his people, which is much more than I can say for Narx."

# INSURMOUNTABLE ODDS

Orren's hex-seed occupied half of his mind, and it throbbed in response to the wide range of emotions he experienced around him. On the one hand, the yelia were relieved that the ghoul threat had been removed, but on the other, there was fear and apprehension about what future Wardolam might have, now that it was deprived of its spectral guardians. There were also intense outpourings of grief when it was revealed that eighty-four yelia had been killed in the ghoul invasion. Though the council members and shadow guards were widely disliked, their losses were keenly felt, due to the fact that the Sun-Children were so few in numbers.

The council chamber was full of whitened skulls and bones, which spilled out into the forum. Dust from the decayed ghouls' flesh had settled in the open space. Narx lay on the dusty floor, his mane of white hair soiled, his embroidered robes filthy. Orren and his friends stood in shock. Meanwhile, Shann-Rell and the tribal chiefs conferred among themselves. Above the city, the brown cloudbank roiled, oblivious to the upheavals that had taken place beneath it.

"Is that the end of the Ghouls' Curse?" Haxel asked.

"Maybe," Anselm said, "but the hex-seed in my mind is as strong as ever."

"So is mine," Marett added.

Narx let out a high-pitched, somewhat demented laugh. He stood up and brushed the dust off of his clothes. "You're still under the Ghouls' Curse, humans and zhiv, and so is the sholl."

"How can that be?" Marett asked. "The Staff of Diktat is destroyed, and with it, the ghouls. The Thelta-Ortrax Pact has been annulled, because the talisman that seals it is no more."

A malicious grin appeared on Narx's face. "You five naugai were given ninety days in which to obtain the gwellen, of which fifty-one are left. Though you were originally bound to the Ghouls' Curse through the Staff of Diktat, it was not the *only* talisman that sealed your fate."

"Your time runs out at midnight on the Fifteenth of the Month of the Skylark," Narx continued. "If you don't place the Sun-Stones in the council head's hands by that time, you will be transformed into ghouls. That moment—the Moment of Reckoning—takes the place of the Staff of Diktat, and *it* is the talisman that now seals you to the curse. The Moment of Reckoning is not the kind of talisman that you can destroy the way you destroyed the Staff of Diktat, because it exists within time, rather than within space. The five of you will form a nucleus for the rebuilding of the ghoul hordes. You will subsequently add more ghouls to your number, by sucking the lives out of others who venture into the vale."

Orren and his friends looked at Shann-Rell and the tribal chiefs, but could see only sadness on their faces. Murmurs of outrage went through the yelian crowd. "I'm afraid Narx is correct," Shann-Rell said. "I'm sorry, gwell-bearers. I wish it were different."

"It's a bit late for wishing," Anselm glared at her.

"We aren't defeated yet," Marett said. "We have fifty-one days within which to obtain the three remaining gwellen. Berthus will be here long before then, and Quartz will return to Wardolam with Magna."

"However, when the Moment of Reckoning arrives, the council head need not *accept* the gwellen from your hands," Narx said. "I may just allow the five of you to wither. Once you become ghouls, you will no longer be chosen. You'll be unable to handle the Sun-Stones, which I'll get back anyway."

"That assumes that you're still the council head by that time," Grnoud cut in.

"What?" Narx's face went red.

"I was a fool," Grnoud said in a contrite tone. "I simply allowed Varshing, and then you, Narx, to control this city. I've been complacent. I bear part of the responsibility for the fact that our numbers continue to dwindle, and I'm partially to blame for the deaths of eighty-four yelia on this day. However, the fact remains that you, Narx, are the primary perpetrator, which was particularly apparent when you refused to destroy the Staff of Diktat. I knew that I had to take matters into my own hands. Had I allowed you to have your way, as I have done for far too long, the Sun-Children would be extinct at this very moment. It is therefore my opinion that you should be removed from office."

"Don't be absurd," Narx said. "No council head has ever been removed from office."

"That may be true," Grnoud said, "but there is a legal means by which this can be achieved. If the entire body of the Sun-Children votes to remove the council head, and that vote is ninety-nine out of one hundred of us, or its numerical equivalent, then the council head loses his office."

"You wouldn't dare!" Narx went pale.

"Sun-Children!" Grnoud addressed the crowd, first in the human tongue and then in the fluty yelian speech. "Approach me one by one, and be counted. If you favor the removal of Narx from office, raise your left hand, and extend your thumb and index finger outward. If you oppose the motion, raise your right hand, and maintain a closed fist."

Narx was the first yelius to approach Grnoud, and his vote, unsurprisingly, was no. Shann-Rell and the tribal chiefs came next, and all of them voted for Narx's removal. The Magg tribe then approached Grnoud one by one, and their final tally was

817 in favor of Narx's removal, and three opposed. The other tribes came next, and among them the vote against Narx was unanimous. Finally, Grnoud raised his own left hand, with his thumb and index finger extended.

"The final tally is 2,260 in favor of Narx's removal from office, and only four opposed," Grnoud said. "That's well in excess of the numerical equivalent of ninety-nine out of one hundred. Narx, you are no longer council head."

Narx hollered curses. He spat at Grnoud, and then fled the forum by entering the building opposite the council chamber, whereupon he disappeared. The mastiff and falcon did not go with him, but stayed in the forum.

"And now, Sun Children," Grnound announced, "the time has come for us to choose a new council head. Let anyone from any tribe, who wishes to be a candidate, ascend the steps and stand here. I myself will *not* be a candidate, because my longtime support for Varshing and Narx renders me unworthy. Whoever gets the highest acclaim from among the candidates who *are* standing, however, will be the new council head."

All of the tribal chiefs except for Warah-Hoolah, chief of the Haas, stood as candidates, and a total of thirty yelia from different tribes, joined them. At the last moment, Shann-Rell added herself to their number.

Grnoud first approached Sha-Rax, the emaciated-looking Orr chief, and made a pronouncement in the yelian tongue. Sha-Rax's tiny tribe shouted their acclaim, but hardly anyone else joined them. The next candidate was the Kell chief Ordam, who received almost unanimous acclaim from his large tribe, but no one else. The other candidates had less impressive results, until only Shann-Rell remained.

Enthusiastic cheers arose from yelia of all tribes. Grnoud added his own voice to theirs, as did the other candidates. When the cheering died down, Grnoud spoke in both the human and yelian tongues. "It has been decided," he said, "Shann-Rell is the new council head for the Sun-Children of Wardolam. Gwell bearers, your task is to place all six Sun-Stones, not into Narx's hands, but into Shann-Rell's, by the time the Moment of Rekoning arrives."

The yelia cheered, and Orren and his friends joined them.

"My beloved Sun-Children," Shann-Rell said, "It's a rare privilege and honor to serve you. I promise you that under my headship, this office will once again act as servant to the people, rather than master. My first act as council head will be to confer with the gwell-bearers, as well as my fellow tribal chiefs and brave Grnoud here, who was able to admit the error of his ways."

The aforementioned individuals gathered in a circle, in front of where the Staff of Diktat once stood. Shann-Rell addressed the others. "I'm under no illusion that we're safe," she said. "The ghouls may be no more, but I fear that Berthus Randolphus has more plans."

"You bet he does," Orren said. "His army is huge. He's got all kinds of bandits and pirates following him. He's got Framguth knights and Gothma fighters, and the Order of Dramm. Plus, there are wolfards, sordigryps, and who knows what else. Worst of all, he's got two gwellen—Ru'i and Kalsh—and a Bearers' Web to support him when he uses their magic. I killed one of the Web members at the Fallagourn Falls, but Berthus still has four others."

"What do you think Berthus's next step will be?" Shann-Rell asked.

"You can never tell for sure what Berthus will do next," Orren said, "but I think it likely that he'll use Kalsh to knock down this city's walls. If that happens, we'd all better get into the tunnels, because that will be the only way to escape him. Even then, he'll come after us, hunting us through the tunnels until he kills us all. He'll do that no matter how many of his own men get killed."

"The odds against us are insurmountable," Diduann cried out in despair. "If Quartz can't get Baron Toynberg to come to our assistance, we're finished."

"We need to get word to him," Anselm said. "Quartz needs to know how dire things are. Come, Web members, and let's put our heads together."

Orren, Anselm, Haxel, and Marett all closed their eyes. They felt the silvery light of the Web encompass them, and sent it forward. They found Quartz, but the cloudbank of the Ghoul Vale made the connection very weak, and it also fed the hex-seeds, which expanded to cut contact off entirely.

"It's no use," Marett said. "If it were only the cloudbank and only the hex-seeds, then we could probably do it, but both of them together is too much. If we could leave the Ghoul Vale entirely—"

"I promise you that Berthus has the vale surrounded by now," Orren said. "After all this time, I know how he thinks. It's impossible to slip by him unnoticed, unless… Haxel! You could do it!"

"Me?" the zhiv said.

"Yes," Orren said. "No one sneaks around in the dark better than you do. No one can move as quickly as you, or as quietly. No one has better eyesight with which to watch out for enemies. Also, you're the smallest person here, which means that you're able to hide much better than anyone else."

"I'll do it, Master."

Overwhelmed with emotion, Orren embraced Haxel. Tears streamed down the boy's cheeks, and there was a lump in his throat. "Please be careful," he said. "I lost Richard. I can't lose you too."

"We'll let you out of the city as soon as night falls, brave Haxel," Shann-Rell said.

"And here," Grnoud added. He handed Orya, the gwell of fire, to the zhiv. "You'll also need this." The council translator then pulled a small sack out of his pocket. "Here's one of the brilliant Forest of Doom sacks you made for the gwellen," he said. "When Narx confiscated these sacks from you, he gave them to me to be their keeper. Take this one, Haxel, and I'll give the others to your friends."

Haxel held on tightly to the rope, while the yelia lowered him down from the city wall. It was a descent of about one hundred feet, so he did not look down until he felt solid, black earth beneath his soles.

He was somewhere on the city's western end. Letting him out here had been Shann-Rell's idea, because patrols of Berthus's men had been sighted, snooping around the main gate. The pitch-blackness of the Ghoul Vale was made worse by impenetrable clouds, which cut off all view of the moon and stars. Haxel was afraid, not of the ghouls, for he knew they no longer posed a problem, but of the possibility that Berthus's humans and wolfards were lurking about. He listened carefully for the sounds of footsteps, and when he heard none, he took out the gwell-sack, which he opened, and lightly touched Orya with his fingers. He willed the red stone to light up. The illumination shone through the sack, providing a dim, red light to guide Haxel through the darkness.

He had come well equipped. An ax was firmly fastened to the belt of his grass skirt, and a water skin was attached to his torso. His shlenki sack hung from his shoulders, and the folds of his shaspa were full of dried fruit and mushrooms, bread, and cheese. Shann-Rell had insisted on Haxel taking the food, for he would need it to replenish his energy, especially if he had to go far.

He sprinted across the black earth. He raced around dark lumps, and darted through gullies. He leapt over any pools of water he came across; for they reminded him of the time when he and Orren blundered into one, and a submerged ghoul grabbed him.

He was able to move much faster than either a human or a yelius could, so within minutes he reached the slope of Airen's Arc. He ascended, treading carefully so as to avoid dislodging rocks. Presently, he emerged from the cloudbank and saw the night sky, which was full of stars and a bright, full moon.

When he reached the top of the vale, he poked his head out over the rim, only to see masses of tents and campfires. Berthus's men were carousing. Haxel found a place where there was less light, and dashed behind a tent. He moved quietly through the camp, using the tents as cover. One time, he tripped over something that stirred, but it turned out to be a barely conscious drunkard. Using his very effective stealth tactics, the zhiv descended the arc, until he was beyond the edge of the Greymantles.

He pulled Orya out of its sack and concentrated on it. He cast his mental sight southward, to see if he could locate Quartz. Something else, however, entered his consciousness, and it was then that he realized that he was still too close to Berthus's camp.

In his mind's eye, he saw the Wicked One sleeping soundly in his tent. He shuddered at the memory of Berthus catching him, and was determined not to let it happen again.

The visual of Berthus faded, and another one took its place. He saw Shelton's face in a lantern light. The vile little thug was Berthus's right hand man. Shelton did not detect Haxel, however, for he was preoccupied with beating a female slave. A large-bodied, small-headed oaf was with Shelton, the one Master Orren referred to as Lumus. He was apparently Shelton's nephew, and right now he had a stupid grin on his face, for he clearly enjoyed watching his uncle torment the poor woman.

The vision of Shelton faded, and Haxel saw a bonfire, before which stood Dargun Rodrick. The young Drammite leader brandished a slaughtering knife in front of three slaves bound to stakes. He then saw the large shape of Jurgan, the bandit chief, who was drunk. Neither the dargun nor the big thug saw Haxel.

Suddenly, he felt a surge of malice, and saw a rider on horseback. He recognized Ramburgus, the magic sniffer. Ramburgus looked directly at Haxel, who felt the man's bloodlust feed his hex-seed. The zhiv's head began to buzz, an indication that his life was in danger.

Haxel shoved the gwell back into its pouch, and thus cut off his pursuer. He then set off as fast as he could go, through brush and woodlands. He could hear the sounds of hoof beats—Ramburgus was closer than he'd thought! He ran.

A massive black shape appeared before him. It was an elevated plateau similar to the one upon which the human city of Sherbass was situated. Haxel made his way toward it, and scrambled up a cliff. When he reached the top, he looked back the way he had come. He could see no sign of Ramburgus, and neither could he hear the man's horse. There was no buzzing sound in his head, and his hex-seed settled down.

Now was as good a time as ever to try contact Quartz. He drew Orya out of its sack, and concentrated on sending the Web southward.

"Master Haxel?" a welcome, familiar voice spoke in his mind.

"Big Friend, is that you?"

"Indeed it is, Master Haxel." Haxel received a visual of where Quartz currently was. A raging fire illuminated the rock giant's stony face. Behind him, a city was burning. Men and horses screamed, and weapons clashed together.

"Where are you, Big Friend? What's going on?"

"Relax, Master Haxel," the sholl said. "Baron Toynberg has everything under control. We are at Kasta, and the baron's knights have driven the Order of Dramm out of the city. You ought to see how these men fight, Master Haxel. Many Drammites have been killed, but not one single knight. The townsfolk and local villagers are coming to our assistance."

"But…the city's burning!" Haxel said.

"Only the Drammite section of it is," Quartz said. "The Drammites took the finest quarters for themselves. Now the luxury there is proving to be their doom."

"Big Friend, things are very bad up here," Haxel talked quickly. "Our friends are in danger. So are the yelia." He told Quartz everything that had transpired since the time they had parted company. So intent was he at letting the sholl know everything, that he did not notice the hoof beats coming up behind him, or the return of the buzzing sound.

"That's why the baron's got to hurry," Haxel said when he had finished the tale. "The Wicked One's about to use his magic on the yelian city!"

"It will take a few days for the baron to reach you," Quartz said, "but I will come immediately, together with Iskander. I just need a minute to inform the baron."

"And Perceval?"

"He is needed in Rivulein," Quartz said. "He is a great inspiration to the resistance fighters."

Haxel let out a sigh of relief. "That's good to know, Big Friend," he said, "I've missed you so much. I can't tell you—"

"Master Haxel!" Quartz screamed. "Behind you! Duck!"

Haxel ducked in time to avoid being decapitated. Ramburgus turned his horse around, and the beast bore down on the zhiv. Haxel rolled away moments before the hard hoofs could crush his skull. The horse passed him by.

Before the magic sniffer could turn his horse around again, Haxel leapt onto the beast's back. Ramburgus did not have time to react before Haxel swiped his claws across the man's neck. The magic sniffer let out a scream of pain, and fell from his horse. It only took Haxel a second to draw his ax, another second to leap from the horse's back, and a third to sink the weapon's blade into his pursuer's neck.

In his mind's eye, he saw Berthus sit bolt upright and scream, "Iranda! Something's happened to Ramburgus!"

Haxel heard another scream nearby. The buzz in his head went insane. He looked up in time to see the magic sniffer's horse rear up on its hind legs, and sprout claws.

Another equatrox!

He touched Orya to the earth and set fire to the fallen leaves and pine needles that covered the ground. When the fire reached the equatrox, it immediately consumed the monster.

Haxel scrambled over to Ramburgus's dead body, took the man's shiny blade, and put it into his shlenki sack. He then collapsed on the ground, exhausted, and gave tearful thanks to Tchafla for his narrow escape.

# CATASTROPHE

"He's dead!" Berthus cried out. "Ramburgus is dead!"

The Lord of the Corcadine felt like everything was collapsing around him. He should never have hit the magic sniffer and sent him away. Felix Ramburgus had contributed more to the success of Berthus's quest than any other person, and now he was dead. Berthus's Web was down to four individuals, himself included.

He searched frantically in the darkness for his lantern. When he found it, he quickly ignited it and stumbled, half blind, out of his tent. He needed someone to talk to, someone who could console him. He needed Iranda.

As fate would have it, however, the first person he encountered was Dargun Rodrick. Out of breath, sweating profusely, and not bothering to consider the fact that he looked weak in front of the Drammite leader, Berthus fell to the ground and wept.

"My Lord!" the dargun said, placing a hand on his shoulder.

"He's dead, Eric!" Berthus said. "Ramburgus is dead!"

"I know. I felt his death through the Web. I'm sorry, m'lord. Truly, I am."

"But...but you hated him," Berthus shot the dargun an accusing look.

Dargun Rodrick sighed, "We had our differences, to be sure, but Felix Ramburgus was a man of knowledge. His loss is keenly felt."

"I don't need false sympathy," Berthus growled. "Where's Iranda? I need to speak to Iranda. She'll make sense of all this. What's happening to my Web, Eric? First I lost Hemric, and now Ramburgus. Get Iranda now!"

"My Lord," the dargun took Berthus's hands in his own. "Please listen to what I'm about to say. The reason you keep having so much bad luck is because the swine boy planted someone in your army, someone who gained your trust, but who was doing your brother's work the whole time. I've finally found out who it is."

"Who, Eric?" Berthus grabbed the dargun by the collar. "Tell me now."

"It was the witch," the Drammite leader said, "It was Iranda."

"What?" Berthus was more perplexed than angry at the dargun's outrageous suggestion. "How can that be?"

"Come back into the tent, my Lord," Dargun Rodrick said, "I'll explain it all to you." He led Berthus back into the tent, took the lantern from him and put it on the floor. They both sat down on the cot, side by side.

"Think about this, my Lord," the dargun said. "Iranda appeared out of nowhere. She promised to bring you luck, but instead she led you to the edge of the Forest of Doom, where you lost the swine boy.

"She disappeared, and you had to travel around the forest without her. She should have convinced the Framguth lords to join forces with the Order of Dramm, but instead, she allowed them to revolt against you. This forced you to kill them, and thus you lost many of your most important allies. She was not present when you put down the revolt, and neither was she there to help you deal with the raids upon your camp, by the Prett faction within the Order of Dramm.

"You finally made it to the Greymantles, and there you caught the swine boy's goblin, yet Iranda convinced you not to kill it, but to use it to lead you to the swine boy. You caught the swine boy, but she talked you out of killing *him*, reasoning that you needed him to lead you to the gwellen. This gave him a chance to escape, and enabled his goblin to continue bringing us bad luck, while Marett Baines survived to continue plotting against us. Eventually, you lost the swine boy in the Ghoul Vale.

"We then searched for Nebi, and Iranda went with us. We caught the swine boy and his friends, and obtained the gwell too, but we lost the boy, his friends, and the stone once more."

The dargun let out a sigh and then continued.

"*You* found Kalsh without Iranda's help. *You* located Ru'i without her help. It was you and I who overcame the old dodder, and got Ru'i away from him—you and I, my Lord—not you, Iranda, and I. When the swine boy revealed the whereabouts of Hesh, Orya, and the lost elvish city, he did it because *you* wrung it out of him. Iranda had no part in that.

"She's brought you nothing but bad luck, and what you've accomplished, she had no part in."

"There's one problem with what you're saying, Eric," Berthus said. "Iranda's the one who convinced you and your order, that I was your liberator."

Dargun Rodrick shook his head in dismay and said, "That's what she wants you to believe—what the swine boy wants you to believe—but it's not true."

"What do you mean?"

"Darguns Telleri and Dromburdt were the ones who decided that the swine boy was the liberator and you, the anti-liberator," the dargun said. "I knew better, but no one listened to me, until the swine boy betrayed us all. I took over the order, and made sure everyone knew the truth. I just needed someone in your camp, someone close to you, whom I could use to bring you the message. Iranda fit the bill. I convinced *her*, my lord, not the other way around. She's been feeding you lies, and using her beauty to soften you up. You need to hand the woman over to me, for a witch must be burned."

"You're a filthy liar," a sharp female voice rang out in the darkness.

Iranda entered the chamber. The lantern light illuminated her flawless features and made her brown curls look like burnished copper. Her eyes flashed dangerously. She was beautiful, but

Berthus knew many stories of beautiful women beguiling unsuspecting men.

"This filthy Drammite is trying to turn you against me, Berthus," Iranda said. "It's because he wants to control you. He wants to make you a slave to his cult, and in the end, when he no longer has any need for you, he will sacrifice you to his god."

Iranda's words resulted in a yelling match between her and the Drammite. The commotion attracted a crowd of men, including Jurgan, Shelton, and Lumus. Within minutes, the tent was full of people, who started arguing among themselves. Berthus's head pounded from the noise and pandemonium, so he reached into his pouch, drew Kalsh out, and touched it to the earth. He sent a shockwave through the ground.

Everyone went silent.

"I have reason to believe the dargun," Berthus said. "He's a Web member, but I need to hear from the other Web members. Shelton, what say you?"

"Believe neither, m'lord," the little man said. "Your true hope lies in those who have been with you all the way from the Corcadine—people like myself and Lumus."

Both Iranda and the dargun started to protest, but Berthus held up a hand for silence. He cast threatening looks at both of them.

"Jurgan," Berthus said. "What do you think?"

"The Drammite is a liar, m'lord," the huge bandit said. "He's using his Duraline skills to persuade you, but you're the man of power, not him. Don't surrender your authority to a religious fanatic. Iranda is much more trustworthy than he is."

"Is that so?" the dargun retorted. "M'lord, let's see if what I'm saying is true. This woman appeared out of nowhere. Where does she come from? What's she doing here? What does she get out of her relationship with you?"

"Iranda," Berthus said. "Have you got answers for the dargun's questions?"

"I-I can't answer these questions," the woman said.

Berthus stood up and grabbed her. He shook her violently. "Answer the dargun!" he yelled.

"M'lord!" Jurgan roared. "You're making a big mistake!"

"Shut your mouth!" Berthus shouted. He continued shaking Iranda. "Who are

you? Did the swine boy send you?"

"If you believe that, you're a fool," Iranda said.

Berthus threw her to the ground and spat on her. "You can have her, Eric," he said. "Burn the witch. Sacrifice her to the Blood Master."

The dargun grinned. He reached for Iranda, but the woman spun away and kicked him in the shin. Other men attempted to seize for her, but she dodged them. One man caught her in a headlock, but Jurgan knocked him out. Iranda fled the tent and disappeared into the night.

Berthus pushed his way through the crowd, and looked everywhere for her, but she was gone. He wondered if he had made yet another mistake. He knew he would never see Iranda again.

He ran back into the tent. All his men went silent. Shelton whispered something in Lumus's ear. Dargun Rodrick was still sitting on the cot, his arms folded, and a smug look on his face. The Drammite's attitude angered Berthus, for he had used Berthus's fears to manipulate him into alienating Iranda.

"Shelton!" Berthus yelled. "Get the Gothma fighters and all my men from the Corcadine. Also, get the Framguth knights. We're gonna go into the Ghoul Vale and destroy that city once and for all. We'll come back here with Hesh, Orya, and Nebi." Then he turned to the dargun and said, "You, Eric! You and your Drammites won't be coming with us. You think you control me, but you don't. The swine boy may have gotten rid of the ghouls I sent after him, and he thinks he's won, but he hasn't. Neither have you, though, and you'll know it when we return victorious."

"We'll be here for you then, my lord," the dargun said in a submissive manner.

"That you will," Berthus said. "Shelton, let's march!"

Berthus returned to his tent to gird himself for war. Shelton started moving through the camp to mobilize his lord's army. Nobody noticed Jurgan sneak away, into the darkness.

Morning had come to the Ghoul Vale.

Orren was talking to various yelia, when one of them, a 50-year-old Kell named Lafshing, scurried out of the council chamber, desperate and panting for breath. Lafshing had been on sentry duty in nearby Prarx's Tower, the tallest building in Wardolam. Orren had been informed that Prarx's Tower commanded a full view of the Ghoul Vale's southern half. The building's summit was lost in the cloudbank, but apparently it contained an ancient crystal that enabled a lookout to see through the brown fog.

"O Shann-Rell," Lafshing blurted out. "Thousands of humans approach Wardolam. Lord Berthus is coming!"

Cries of dismay went through the yelian crowd. Almost all the Sun-Children were still assembled in the forum, for they were traumatized by their ordeal with the ghouls, and found safety and comfort in numbers. Orren and his friends were with them, and everyone had blankets and bundles of food.

"Take me to the tower," Orren commanded. "I have to see what's going on."

"I'll come as well," Shann-Rell said.

Lafshing led Orren and Shann-Rell into the council chamber. Marett, Anselm, and Jasper followed suit, as did Grnoud and fourteen other yelia. The red mastiff trotted alongside Shann-Rell's feet, and the falcon rode on her shoulder.

Yelian workers had cleared a pathway through the council chamber and the adjoining passageway. Skulls and bones were piled up on either side. Even so, the group had to walk in single file. Lafshing went first, followed by Shann-Rell, and then the red dog. Grnoud came next, followed by Orren, Marett, Jasper, Anselm, and finally, their yelian escort. The interior of the building and the hallway behind it were full of thick, choking dust, which caused everyone to cough and sputter.

They reached the spiral, stone staircase that ascended Prarx's Tower. The group climbed five stories, until they arrived in the observation chamber. A large window faced southward, and in front of it, set in a sconce, was the crystal. It was rectangular in shape, four feet long, four feet wide, and several inches thick. Orren gazed through it, and discovered that he could see everything up to the slopes of Airen's Arc. His heart sank when he saw that the vale was full of Berthus's army.

There were mounted Framguth knights in armor, ragtag Gothma fighters on foot, and ruffians of all kinds. Interspersed among the fighters were wolfards—their hideous, hairy forms towering over most of the humans. There were also numerous war mastiffs and greyhounds. Among the many warhorses were several that had predatory bearings, which indicated that they were equatrii. Hundreds of sordigryps flew above the army, disappearing into the cloudbank and then reappearing again.

The army was divided into two huge battalions, with an empty space between them. Berthus and Shelton stood side-by-side in that space, before the gates of the city. Berthus drew the brown gwell from his pouch.

"He's about to use Kalsh to knock down the gates," Orren said. "Someone warn the yelia to get into the tunnels. It won't take Berthus's army long to find the forum."

"I'll go," Grnoud said. He promptly left the chamber.

Orren racked his mind for a plan. He had to find a way to save the city, but he could come up with nothing. His frustration caused the hex-seed in his brain to expand until it filled his head. The seed took hold of his consciousness, and created a connection with the mind of Berthus, a connection that had nothing to do with any gwell.

For a second, Orren felt the familiar dread that he associated with his half brother, but he soon remembered the confrontation by the Fallagourn Falls, and the fear dissipated. Berthus was a mere man, not a god. He could be wounded and even killed. Hatred replaced fear, and Berthus returned the feeling.

"I'll kill you, your friends, and the elves," Berthus snarled. "The time has come. It's over, swine boy."

Suddenly, Orren spied a man atop the city gates. He took a closer look, and saw that it was Narx! The former ruler of Wardolam was covered in dust. His mane of white hair was now a matted gray, and he bore something in his hand—something green.

Orren then realized something terrible. Amid the chaos and trauma of the ghoul invasion, everyone had neglected to confiscate Nebi and Hesh from Narx!

Suddenly, both Orren's mind *and* Berthus's, made contact with Narx. The former council head's filthy face was contorted in demented rage. His golden eyes flashed in anger. Berthus reacted with rage as well, and started concentrating on Kalsh, while Narx concentrated on Nebi. Absolutely horrified, Orren knew what these two destructively ruthless individuals were about to do.

"Berthus! Narx! Don't do it!" The boy yelled at his brother and the former yelian ruler, both aloud and telepathically. "Put the gwellen away! Both of you!"

A mental blow from Berthus and a searing pain from Narx, caused Orren to fall to the ground, and he lost both connections. He picked himself up and tried contacting them again, but it was too late. Berthus sent a shockwave into the earth, which threw up a cloud of dust that blew toward the city. Narx intercepted the dust and activated thousands of living particles in it. The yelian villain collapsed onto the stonemasonry, and Orren saw him retch. However, he had succeeded in what he was trying to do. The magic of Nebi was activated, while Berthus still concentrated on Kalsh. The combination of both stones' powers shook the earth and agitated the brown clouds above the Ghoul Vale. What never should happen had happened!

Orren collapsed on the ground, clutching at his head and weeping. With all the effort he could muster, he said, "Two gwellen...used at once! Must...get into...tunnels."

His vision went black, and then Orren found himself floating outside his body, above the vale. What he saw below was horrifying.

The dust thrown up by the gwellen swirled in the air, at first slowly, but then faster and faster, until it turned into a cyclone. It pulled the brown clouds of the Ghoul Vale into itself, which caused it to expand, sucking in men and beasts. Sordigryps were yanked out of the sky, to explode in bursts of feathers. The dead bodies of men, horses, dogs, and wolfards were flung in all directions, as were rocks and sand. The cyclone consumed Berthus's army.

When the storm reached Wardolam's gates, it pulverized them to dust, and raged through the city. Everywhere, buildings fell, and tunnels were exposed. It only took a few minutes for the maelstrom to reach Wardolam's agricultural sector, where it tore trees and crops up by the roots. The livestock animals of the yelia screamed as they died. Within seconds, the city was strewn with dead sheep, goats, pigeons, chickens, hogs, and fish.

When the storm reached the forum, it grabbed all the yelia who had not been fast enough to reach the tunnels, and flung them to their deaths. Even many who were *in* the tunnels did not escape, for the cyclone exposed their hiding places and plucked them out of the ground. Hundreds upon hundreds of Sun-Children met their deaths in the twister's yawning maw. Surely this was the end—the end of the yelia!

Orren screamed in pain, anguish, and grief before losing all consciousness.

Berthus was carried out of the Ghoul Vale by five sordigryps. He had summoned the birds, using Ru'i, as soon as he saw the twister grow. Vomiting blood and gasping for air from having used the beast stone, he now lay on the lip of Airen's Arc, staring down into the vale, which had disappeared in a cloud of dust that filled the crater and the sky above it.

He cursed his brother, but then remembered that it was not the swine boy who made this catastrophe happen. It was that hideous elf, whose name Berthus had heard in his head as soon as their minds first met. *Narx.*

Narx, the elvish wizard, was responsible for what had happened. Narx hated the swine boy every bit as much as he hated Berthus. This Berthus knew, because he and Narx had inadvertently traded thoughts.

However, it wasn't only Narx's fault. Berthus had himself, in one single moment, destroyed everything—his army, his fortune, most of his allies. He wept when he recalled Shelton being sucked into the cyclone. There had been a look of abject horror on the little man's face as he saw his death approach. Berthus felt his right-hand man's death like a knife in his gut, especially when he considered the fact that he had never really valued Shelton as a friend.

He needed Iranda!

But no, he had chased her off! Giving into despair, Berthus wept hysterically, beating the ground with his fists.

Orren woke up to find himself lying on the stone floor, in the darkness.

"Hello?" he called out. "Anyone there?"

"We're all here, young man," Anselm's voice responded. The old man lit his lantern. "You've been out for two days."

By the lantern light, Orren saw Anselm, Jasper, Marett, Shann-Rell, Lafshing, and the other fourteen yelia who had accompanied them into Prarx's Tower. Everyone had a grave look on his or her face, and each person was covered in a layer of dust.

"Where are we?" Orren asked.

"Beneath the tower," Shann-Rell said. "As soon as the cyclone hit, we fled down the steps, into the deepest tunnels. We carried you with us, but now the tower has fallen, and the tunnels beneath it have caved in. I'm afraid, Orren Randolphus, that we're trapped."

# IMMINENT EXTINCTION

Night fell. Berthus lay on the edge of Airen's Arc, feeling ill from having used Ru'i without Dargun Rodrick's assistance. He had been forced to do so, in order to summon the sordigryps that had carried him out of the doomed vale; otherwise he would have died in the cyclone. The Corcadinian toughs, the magic sniffers, the Framguth lords and their knights, and the Gothma horde, were all dead, along with at least three members of Berthus's Web. Iranda—beloved Iranda—had been driven off.

And, after all of this, he still had only *two gwellen*.

He had no way of knowing what had become of the lost city. Even if it turned out that the cyclone had wiped the place out; that did not mean that the swine boy and his friends were dead. Somehow the little rat always managed to survive. Narx too, might still be alive. If the swine boy and the hideous elf had survived the cyclone, then Berthus would have to face both archenemies on his own.

He gave in to grief over his sorry state. His emotions brought back memories of Richard. What would the old steward think of Berthus now? Could he, a peaceful man, possibly comprehend the need to burn villages, enslave enemies, and to relentlessly pursue a fourteen-year-old boy across the wilderness? Could it ever have been possible for Richard to understand that he had spent those years protecting the monster that the swine boy was?

Dear, dear Richard. The grief Berthus felt when he recalled his mentor's death was still fresh. Richard was the one who had ensured that Berthus's childhood was not spent alone. Now, however, the Lord of the Corcadine was *truly* on his own.

Or was he? Berthus looked up. He thought he could make out the shapes of people in the dusty fog, and they were approaching him. As they came closer, he saw that they wore long robes and hoods. Then he remembered that he had excluded the Drammites from his foray into the Ghoul Vale. Could they have survived the catastrophe?

The Drammites drew closer, and it was then that Berthus realized how many of them there were. They came at him from all sides, but why? Then suddenly, Berthus remembered that the magic of a gwell could only move in one direction at any given time.

A lasso fell over his neck. He reached for Kalsh, but several dargas grabbed him before he could take the gwell out. They twisted his arms behind his back. Berthus protested loudly, yelling that he was their liberator and lord, but they paid him no heed. They forced him to walk down the slope of Airen's Arc. They entered a campsite, and led him toward one particular tent—his tent.

They pulled him inside, where he saw, by the light of several lanterns, Dargun Eric Rodrick. The young Drammite leader sat on Berthus's cot, his golden hair shimmering in the firelight. He smiled and said, "So, if it isn't my chosen brother in the Web, Berthus Randolphus."

"Eric, what's the meaning of this?" Berthus demanded. "Your men dragged me here as though I were a slave. What do you think you're doing?"

The dargun stood up and backhanded Berthus across the face once, twice, three times, and then four. Berthus tasted blood and felt his cheeks swell. He stared at the Drammite leader in shock.

"You've walked all over the Order of Dramm for too long, Berthus," Dargun Rodrick said, "and we allowed you to, because you had other factions in your army, which were hostile to us. We therefore had to tread carefully, but no longer. The other factions are dead, thanks to your own foolishness. So are all your Web members, except for Jurgan and myself, and Jurgan's disappeared; I've tried contacting him through the Web but to no avail. He clearly doesn't want to be contacted. Iranda too, is gone."

"You convinced me to send Iranda away!" Berthus yelled, "you traitor—" The dargun hit him again. Berthus saw stars.

"All you have left is the Order of Dramm," Dargun Rodrick said, "and now you'll do exactly what we tell you to."

"Eric," Berthus blubbered. "Why are you treating me like this? I'm your liberator."

"Let's examine the prophecy of the liberator again, shall we?" the dargun said.

> O dargas,
> Be vigilant
> For one of gold hair and fiery mood
> Who comes
> Bearing a stone of the sun's vanished brood
> And witness to him
> Shall be penitent nobility
> Casting off privilege to walk by his side.
> And the taméd beast
> Shall walk with him as well
> To attest to the mission of he who's my pride.

"A few sordigryp stragglers still fly around our camp," the dargun then said, "and we have equatrii as well—that's plenty of beast witnesses, so now we need a noble witness, which is where *you* come in."

"What are you talking about?"

"Well let's see," the dargun said. "You're lord of the Corcadine, and therefore noble, and you will be penitent after I'm through with you. Your anti-liberator brother—the swine boy, as you call him—is, thanks to you having chosen me, akin to my brother. I feel a kinship toward both of you, for I too am of gold hair and fiery mood."

Berthus gaped, horrified, at the dargun. "You, the liberator? You're crazy!"

Dargun Rodrick reached into Berthus's pouch and removed both Ru'i and Kalsh from it. "And now I bear the stones of the sun's brood, which is truly vanished now," he said, brandishing the two gwellen in front of Berthus's face. "Ru'i is my stone, but I figured out, through my own inference, exactly what Iranda's idea was. Now I'll turn that plan around onto you. You'll shoulder Kalsh's burden whenever I want to use it. So bound are you to that stone, that you can't help but assist me.

"Dargun van der Schelt is on his way here with over a thousand men, including Dramm-friendly magic sniffers. Should be here in four days, and then we'll search the ruined city for Hesh and Nebi. Oh, and while you were sleeping a few nights back, I was busy performing sacrifices, when I caught a visual in my mind's eye of the goblin conversing with the sholl, outside the Ghoul Vale. The goblin had Orya, and I have reason to believe that the rock giant has Magna, for I felt the presence of both stones."

"You can't take them!" Berthus yelled. "The gwellen are mine—all six!"

"You bore me, Berthus," the dargun said. "Men, take him away."

Four Drammite warriors ushered a horrified Berthus out of the tent that had once been his. They dragged him toward the 'Barrow', an ugly hunk of metal on cartwheels. It was originally the property of a now-dead Framguth lord and had been used to discipline recalcitrant slaves, who had been chained to it and forced to push it.

Now it would be used to discipline Berthus. The Lord of the Corcadine wept as the Drammites bound him to the misshapen vehicle, and left him out in the cold.

Haxel rode upon Quartz's right shoulder, as the rock giant silently descended the black, shale slopes of Galli's Arc. The first thing they both noticed was that the immense dust cloud, which had been visible many miles away, had settled. Also, it seemed that the vale's brown cloudbank was gone. This did not help visibility, however, for a cold, early spring fog had settled in, and it, together with the darkness of the night, meant that Haxel had to use Orya to guide their way.

Iskander had come north with them, also riding on Quartz's shoulders. When they approached Airen's Arc, however, Haxel did some spying, and determined that the giant ramp was covered in tents. Upon closer inspection, however, all he could see were dargas and Drammite warriors. When he reported this to Iskander, the young man asked to be dropped off, for he was about to investigate and, if necessary, infiltrate the Drammites as Perceval had done. He advised Quartz to give Airen's Arc a wide berth, and instead, to descend into the vale from the other side.

Sometime after Iskander disappeared into the camp, another dark-mantled figure picked up Quartz's trail, and followed him into the vale. Neither Quartz nor Haxel spotted or heard their silent pursuer.

Galli's Arc was identical to Airen's Arc in everything except length. When they reached the bottom, the familiar black landscape, dotted with mounds, came into view, but now there was also an overpowering stench in the air. There were thousands of rotting corpses of humans, horses, dogs, wolfards, and sordigryps.

"Big Friend," Haxel said, trying not to gag, "is this the Wicked One's army?"

"I think it is, Master Haxel," the sholl said, "but what happened?"

"More important, what about our friends and the yelia?"

"Our friends are alive, Master Haxel."

"How do you know that? We can't find them using the Web, because our hex-seeds are now too strong."

"I am bonded to Master Orren, Madam Marett, and Master Anselm," Quartz said. "I can find them wherever they are, and I am detecting their presence right now, which would not be the case if they were dead."

"Oh, yes," Haxel said, "I forgot about that."

"I can not, however, speak with the same confidence about the Sun-Children," the sholl said in a sad voice. "I did not have sufficient opportunity to bond with them, so I can not tell you whether any of them yet live."

Haxel let out a deep sigh. "We'll soon see."

They reached the walls of Wardolam, but something was amiss. The walls looked as though they had been ripped down. Quartz gingerly stepped over the destroyed fortifications, and entered the city. They both let out cries of despair when they saw the devastation.

Whatever catastrophe had wiped out the Wicked One's army had also destroyed the city. Not a single building was left undamaged. Dead livestock, uprooted trees, and devastated gardens lay about, causing Wardolam to stink.

When Quartz reached the place where the city forum had been, he and Haxel broke down in tears, for in that open space, were the broken corpses of over six hundred yelia. Haxel and Quartz bawled. Great sobs convulsed the sholl's giant body, while Haxel let out screams of grief and anguish. His hex-seed felt like a tumor.

After a few minutes, Quartz gently touched Haxel's shoulder. "Come," he said in a broken voice. "We must help our friends." He placed Haxel back on his shoulder and continued moving through what had once been Wardolam. More yelian corpses lay about, particularly in places where the catastrophe had ripped open the earth and exposed tunnels.

Haxel caught a glimpse of something dark moving in the ruins, but dismissed it as a trick of his imagination. The fog was now so thick, the night so black, and his eyes so full of tears, that he could not see properly.

They reached the ruins of a tall building. Quartz said, "Here is the place. Master Haxel, would you be so kind as to shine the light from Orya onto the ground, so I can see what I am doing?"

Haxel obliged, and the sholl worked furiously, throwing aside huge quantities of stonemasonry and rubble, until he exposed a tunnel.

"Who's there?" a voice called out.

"Good Sir Anselm!" Haxel's relief caused his hex-seed to shrink once again, and he knew from Quartz's emotions, that the sholl was experiencing the same thing.

"Haxel, is that you?" the old man asked.

"I am here as well, Master Anselm," Quartz said.

The old man poked his face out of the tunnel opening. Jasper was by his side. Both of them were covered in dust, but otherwise they appeared to be in good health.

"Orren and Marett are here too," Anselm said, "and Shann-Rell and fourteen others, and that dog and bird. Shann-Rell's now the council head, you know. Hey folks!" he called out. "Quartz and Haxel are here. We're saved."

Anselm and Jasper crawled through the tunnel opening, followed by Orren, Shann-Rell, the mastiff, and the other yelian individuals, who were evenly divided between Magg and Kell. Marett, ever the caretaker, came last. The peregrine falcon flew out of the darkness, and landed on Quartz's shoulder. Everyone looked about at the ruins of the once mighty city, with sorrowful bewilderment.

"We didn't see any other living yelia," Haxel said, his eyes downcast. "I'm afraid..."

"That my people are dead," Shann-Rell said. "I know, but some of them may have survived. We must find them. They all had food with them, so if they took refuge in the tunnels, they stand a chance."

"That's right," Anselm said, "don't lose hope."

Shann-Rell looked back at him with tenderness in her eyes. The old man nodded at her and smiled in encouragement.

"Thank you, Anselm," the council head spoke in a soft voice. "I need all the positive reinforcement I can get right now."

"Shann-Rell," Marett said, "My family lore says that certain yelian leaders could locate their people through a kind of meditation."

"I know how to do it," the yelian leader said, "but nobody has used it for hundreds of years."

"No one has had the gwellen for hundreds of years either," Marett said, "but now Quartz bears Magna, and Haxel has Orya. Surely the presence of the stones will help?"

"Indeed they will," Shann-Rell said.

"We also have the hex-seeds," Anselm said in a gloomy voice, "and those interfere with everything, including weakening our ability to use the gwellen."

"Even so, we must try," Orren said. "All five of us must put our heads together, and get the Web going as best we can." Then, turning to Shann-Rell, he said, "and we need help."

Shann-Rell gave instructions to her fellow yelia. Then to the gwell-bearers she said, "Hold your gwellen in your hands. Concentrate on the stones, and then, with your minds, scan the city with us. If you detect warmth, then you'll have found living yelia."

Haxel drew out Orya, and Quartz, Magna. The gwell bearers fixed their minds on the stones, and activated the Web. The yelia joined the telepathic effort.

The silvery Web light was most fragile, weakened as it was by the hex-seeds, but it held nonetheless. The yelian minds present helped to buttress the gwell-bearers as well. However, it was not enough.

*We need more strength,* Shann-Rell said. *You gwell-bearers must try harder.*

*We can't,* Anselm shot back. *The hex-seeds are too strong.*

*We need assistance,* Marett said, *but where can we get it from?*

*I know where,* Orren said. Haxel heard the boy speaking to someone or something.

Suddenly, a humming sound passed from Orren's mind to Haxel's. It weakened the hex-seeds until they were barely perceptible. Haxel knew from the feelings of pleasure and relief emanating from everyone, that all the gwell-bearers and their yelian supporters felt it.

The mysterious voice that Orren always talked about was here…for everyone!

"This way," Shann-Rell said, pointing in one direction, "Walk with me, while keeping your eyes open, but maintain your focus!"

Together, they approached a mound of rubble.

Haxel held up Orya. By its light, Quartz moved the debris away, until he revealed a single yelius—a tall, thin man covered in dust and soot. The yelius opened his eyes. They were bright gold, and full of defiance.

"That's Narx!" Shann-Rell exclaimed. "Seize him! Quick!"

Six yelia sprang forth and grabbed the former council head, who let out a string of curses and insults.

"Get the stones away from him," Shann-Rell said.

A middle-aged Kell male searched through Narx's pockets. He drew out Hesh and Nebi.

"Give Hesh to Orren," Shann-Rell instructed. "Who will take Nebi? Marett?"

The girl shook her head. "I'm sorry," she said. "When we found Nebi, I was in no emotional state to take responsibility for it. Since I rejected Nebi once, I don't think I can accept it now."

"Anselm, what about you?"

The old man refused. "The first gwell I ever found was Ru'i," he said. "I even used its magic once. In this Web, I'm Ru'i's bearer."

"Then I'll keep this gwell until we sort all of this out," Shann-Rell said. "and I will fix my mind upon it. Let's continue our search. Narx, I suggest you help us."

Narx, however, spat at her, so they carried on without him.

Shann-Rell led them toward the city forum, where they felt a great number of warm sensations. She instructed Quartz to dig, and within minutes, he revealed a tunnel in which there were fifty yelian survivors. Half were Magg, and the rest were Kell and Rau. The rescued yelia joined in the meditation and accompanying search.

Over the next three nights, the search continued, both for dead and for living yelia. Sadly, the dead were easy to find, for they lay about wherever the cyclone had ripped into the buildings and tunnels, and they far outnumbered the living. Burial rites were held, and the deceased Sun-Children were interred beneath the rubble of the city they had once called home.

By pre-dawn of the fourth day, 1,781 bodies were recovered, and disposed of in the traditional yelian manner. 462 yelian survivors had been rescued from the ruins. The tribal breakdown came to 147 Magg, 102 Kell, 90 Rau, 67 Haas, and 56 Nebb. Twenty-two yelia were still missing, which was upsetting in and of itself, but to make matters worse, no Orr had been found, engendering fears of that tribe being extinct.

Besides for Shann-Rell, the only tribal chief who had survived the disaster was Thraix, the bald, skinny Nebb chief. The bodies of Diduann, Warah-Hoolah, Sha-Rax, and Ordam were given the greatest honors possible; they were interred in the ruined council building. While clearing out their tombs, the yelia discovered the corpse of Grnoud. The council translator's clothes were ripped, and it appeared as though something had been written on the torn pieces.

Upon closer inspection, it was determined that Grnoud had not died immediately after being crushed by falling stonemasonry. He must have scratched his body before he expired, drawing blood, which he had used to write a message on his clothes, in the yelian symbol script. Shann-Rell read it, and translated it into the human tongue.

*Beloved Sun-Children*, it said, *I am dying, but should you find my body, please never give into evil as I did. Rebuild the yelian nation by bearing children, even if doing so requires Diffusion. I return to our Sun Father. Farewell.*

Everybody broke down and wept. After several hours of intense mourning for so many losses, Anselm asked Shann-Rell, "What does *Diffusion* mean?"

Shann-Rell did not answer, but instead, looked into the old man's eyes and said, "It's time to search for the last twenty-one Sun-Children. Please, everyone, let's meditate, and support the Bearers' Web once more."

Everyone but Narx joined in the search. The three yelia who had voted with Narx against his removal from office, were dead, so the former council head now saw everyone as his enemy. However, the combined efforts of the gwell-bearers and the yelian crowd, with the assistance of the mysterious humming voice, located the last yelia, who were trapped beneath the ruined Sundog Temple, in tunnels so far down that it took everyone's utmost mental effort to maintain contact.

Quartz began digging with his left hand, while holding Magna with the right. Suddenly, the sholl cried out in pain and dropped the yellow gwell. Haxel saw a spear lodged in one of the cracks that marred the giant's hand. Before anyone could do anything, a dark-clad figure darted out from behind a wall, grabbed Magna, and disappeared. Haxel chased after the thief, using Orya for light. He had nearly caught up with the fugitive, when the latter turned around and used Magna's power.

The zhiv slammed into what could only be described as a solid wall of compressed air. He was winded, and the fugitive escaped, but not before Haxel caught a glimpse of his face. There could be no mistaking the savage, bearded countenance of Jurgan the bandit.

There was nothing to do but warn everybody else. Haxel ran back toward the place where he had left Quartz and the yelia. The spear was gone. Shann-Rell was rubbing the sholl's hand, and whispering words of comfort to him, and Orren, Marett, Anselm, and Jasper were also by his side. At the same time, the yelia were rescuing their last trapped brethren. Sixteen of them were Orr, thus ensuring the little tribe's survival. Four were Nebb, and the last one was the small Kell male named Zarell.

Now that all the surviving yelia were rescued, an emotionally-charged hubbub broke out in their ranks. Orren, Haxel, Marett, and Anselm looked at one another in confusion, while Quartz nursed his wound. Before they had a chance to ask what was going on, Shann-Rell spoke in both the yelian and human tongues. She was addressing Narx.

"Narx," she said, "under your headship, we suffered tyranny, but we accepted it, because we were sure you had the best interests of the Sun-Children in mind. Your actions, however, have proven otherwise, and as Grnoud, when he was dying, wrote in his own blood, we must never give in to evil."

"It is evil, Narx, to use a gwell simultaneously with another gwell. In so doing, you are responsible for the deaths of more than 1,700 yelia. Our race is now the closest to extinction that it's ever been. When we attempted to find our lost brethren, you refused to help. You could have made some small atonement for what you did, but you wouldn't."

"Every single yelius is precious, particularly now that so few of us are left, from a race that once numbered in the millions. Even so, you, Narx, are a threat to our survival, but I will not countenance your execution, for you *did* once hold an office sacred to our Sun Father."

"Acting in my capacity as emergency leader of our people, I therefore expel you, Narx, from the community of Wardolam and from the race of the Sun-Children."

Narx shot looks of pure hatred at his people, which turned to humiliation and angst. He then let out a primal scream and disappeared into the dark fog. Everyone watched him go, their hearts heavy.

The silence was interrupted by horns blowing from outside the city.

Haxel ran toward the source of the sound. He soon reached Wardolam's ruined walls. Light permeated the fog, revealing the approach of dawn. The zhiv saw the shapes of hundreds of armed humans marching toward Wardolam. Some of them carried staffs, upon which were dargooks—the horned eyeball symbols of the Order of Dramm!

# FINDING COMMON GROUND

As soon as Marett heard that the Drammites were marching toward Wardolam, she was spurred into action. She grabbed both coils of rope, and threw their lengths down the hole where the Orr tribesmen had been hiding. She handed the end of one rope to Orren and the other, to Anselm. Several yelia came to their assistance.

"Shann-Rell, get everyone into the tunnels," Marett instructed.

The yelian leader did not panic, but orchestrated an orderly descent for all her brethren, as well as the mastiff, the falcon, and Jasper. Shann-Rell herself remained above ground, together with the gwell-bearers. They hid beneath the sleeping Quartz's skooch, which the sholl had rendered to make himself invisible among the ruins.

More horns blew, and the voices of numerous Drammites could be heard. They began chanting their deity's name. The 'Dramm, Dramm' refrain reverberated through the devastated city.

"Keep your gwellen in their sacks," Marett whispered to the others. "Only use them as a last resort. I'm leaving."

"Where are you going?" Anselm demanded.

"To find Dargun Rodrick," Marett said. "If I can kill him, I'll be cutting off the head of the Drammite beast."

Before anyone had a chance to protest, Marett ran off into the ruins. It did not take long for her to encounter two dargas, whom she ran through with her sword. She removed the robe and hood from one of them, donned them on atop her own clothes, and placed the veil over her face.

Wardolam was crawling with dargas and Drammite warriors. Marett caught snippets of their conversation, and thus she learned that the cult intended to sacrifice not only her friends, but also any yelia they found. She grit her teeth in anger, but quickly put it aside. She would need all her resolve in case the dargun caught sight of her.

She finally saw what she was looking for—a figure in red robes with a red face veil. Two black-clad dargas accompanied their leader, as he disappeared behind a partially collapsed wall. Marett set off in hot pursuit, and when she reached her quarry, she quickly dispatched the dargas. Dargun Rodrick swiveled around and drew his sword, but not quickly enough. Marett drove her blade into him, and he fell to the ground dead.

Desiring to see the face of her vanquished foe, she bent down and removed his veil, only to discover that she had *not* killed Dargun Rodrick. Instead, she found a middle-aged man with dark hair that was graying at the temples. Gritting her teeth in frustration, she stood up ready to resume her hunt, when something knocked her to the ground.

She rolled over in time to avoid being impaled by the *real* Dargun Rodrick's sword. He had a cruel grin on his face, and in his eyes, she saw a lust for blood. "So you came looking for me, did you, Marett Baines? Instead you killed Dargun van der Schelt, but you won't make the same mistake twice."

His sword came down toward her, but she parried it, momentarily throwing him off balance. It was enough to enable her to jump to her feet. He slashed at her again, but she parried successfully once more. They pushed against each other with their swords, both of them trying to maintain their balance as they attempted to outdo each other with brute force. Marett felt her strength giving out. Certainly she was very strong for a woman, but Dargun Rodrick was stronger still.

She felt something kick her in the back of her calf. Her leg buckled and she fell forward. Out of the corner of her eye, she saw that a large darga had approached her from behind, and had tripped her. He and Dargun Rodrick both stabbed downward toward the girl, but Dargun Rodrick let out a yell of pain.

A third darga appeared, and he leapt into action, quickly stabbing the darga that had attacked Marett. The man collapsed. Dargun Rodrick bled from his right arm, but he drew back and readied himself once more. Marett's unexpected ally removed his veil. It was Iskander!

"Back off, Eric," Iskander said in a menacing voice. "I won't hesitate to kill you."

"You always were a weak one, Cousin Iskander," the dargun said in a jeering tone, "and you will not best me with a sword, for I was taught by the best sword masters of our family. Now prepare to die—you and this girl!"

Berthus's hands were bound behind his back, and he was being roughly manhandled by two brutish dargas. Their names were Guida Fellini and Henry Voss, and they had been assigned by Dargun Rodrick to 'make the noble witness penitent'. Fellini and Voss were well known among the Drammites for their sadistic savagery. Berthus already had a black eye and numerous cuts and bruises all over his body, from the blows that they liberally dealt out. He quickly learned not to anger them, and he became sheepish and subservient.

Fellini and Voss had marched Berthus into the Ghoul Vale, kicking and punching him when he went too slowly. Dargun Rodrick instructed them to remain with Berthus, on the outskirts of the ruined city. The two men were in a foul mood, for they had hoped to take part in the hunting of elves.

It became increasingly clear to Berthus, however, that Fellini and Voss were idiots. A plan hatched in his mind. Dargun Rodrick would *not* get away with stealing the gwellen from Berthus and humiliating him!

"My esteemed teachers," he said in a meek voice. "Please may I eat? I'm starving."

Darga Voss kicked Berthus in the gut, and he fell down gasping for air.

"I'm not gonna sit here feeding you like a baby," the man growled.

"Please," Berthus begged. "I must eat if I'm to serve our liberator. You can untie my hands. I won't do anything, for I've seen the error of my ways."

"OK," Darga Voss growled.

"But if you try anything, you'll regret it," Darga Fellini added. He drew a knife, and cut Berthus on the back of his right hand. Berthus screamed and wept, but that was more a part of his act than from real pain.

Darga Fellini cut Berthus's bonds. "Henry, give him some of your food."

Darga Voss was reaching into his sack, when Berthus grabbed two handfuls of the thick dust that covered the ground of the Ghoul Vale. In two very quick motions, he threw it in his captors' faces, blinding them. He then fled into the ruined city, determined to find the usurping Drammite leader.

Marett and Iskander fought side-by-side, but it soon became clear to Marett that Iskander, while courageous, was not a skilled sword fighter despite being Duraline. This came as no surprise to her, for he had left his family at a tender young age, and perhaps had not had a chance to learn the skill to an advanced level. He was actually a hindrance, for he was getting in her way. It was all she could do to keep Dargun Rodrick from cutting him up.

Dargun Rodrick had a grin on his face, and he laughed, for clearly time was on his side. How long would it be before he wore both Marett and Iskander down? How long before the other Drammites found them, and came to their leader's assistance? Worst of all, Dargun Rodrick had a pouch at his waist, and it appeared to contain two objects the size and shape of gwellen.

Someone seemed to materialize in the fog, right behind the dargun. As Dargun Rodrick raised his sword against Marett, the newcomer pulled out a knife and drew it across the Drammite leader's throat. Dargun Rodrick's eyes rolled back in his head, and his blood flowed, but before he could fall to the ground, the newcomer caught him, and cut the pouch from his belt.

"The usurper is dead!" It was the triumphant voice of Lord Berthus Randolphus. Berthus pulled the gwellen out of the dargun's pouch. "Kalsh and Ru'i are mine once more!" he shouted.

Marett and Iskander stared in shock as Berthus bent down, touched Kalsh to the ground, and smiled at them.

"So you're the swine boy's girlfriend," he gloated. "Well, prepare to be buried alive—you and this friend of yours, and all the filthy Drammites!"

Suddenly, a tall, soot-covered figure bounded over a ruined wall, and assaulted Berthus. Marett and Iskander gasped as Berthus was sliced open with a sacrificial knife. The tyrant fell to the ground, screaming, as blood poured out of him. The assailant looked at Marett and Iskander, and then back at the wounded, bleeding Berthus. The attacker's face was blackened, but there could be no mistaking his cruel, golden eyes with their elliptical cat-pupils.

"Such will be the end of all naugai who dare handle the Sun-Stones," Narx said, as he kicked the groaning Berthus in the ribs. "And now, Berthus Randolphus, it's time for you to die, and for the gwellen to return to their rightful owner."

"No Narx!" Marett said, brandishing her sword in a threatening manner. "You've been expelled from your people. The gwellen are no more yours to take than they are his."

Narx glared at Marett. Marett stared right back up at him, determined not to let him have his way. The former yelian leader then spat on Berthus's contorted face, before swiveling around and disappearing into the ruins.

"Here's the Miss!" Haxel's voice rang out, as he, Orren, Anselm, and Shann-Rell appeared from behind a ruined wall. "And Iskander's with her!"

"Berthus too!" Orren cried out.

"Marett, what's going on?" Anselm asked.

"Berthus just killed Dargun Rodrick," Marett said, "and Narx nearly killed Berthus, and now Narx is nowhere to be seen. But why are you here? I told you to stay under Quartz's skooch!"

"We felt your desperation through the Web," Haxel said. "You think we're just going to let you face danger on your own?"

"But the Drammites will kill you!" Marett hissed.

"The Drammites are finished," Anselm said. "Baron Toynberg and his knights have just arrived in great numbers. They're cutting down the Drammites like straw."

As if to prove Anselm's point, Marett heard the sounds of fighting, screaming, and hoof beats.

"Orren, your brother's badly hurt," Iskander said. "He's losing blood."

"But I'm still strong enough to kill all of you," Berthus said, "The Drammites, the yelia, the baron's men, and especially you, swine boy." Berthus narrowed his eyes. His brow creased, and his face grit in pain, as he began focusing on the brown gwell.

"I'll let you live!" Orren said quickly, but emphatically. He stared down at his half brother with contempt. Berthus's fancy clothes were cut, torn, and blood-soaked. His face was pale. He clutched at his stomach with his left hand and, with his right, he held onto Kalsh, the gwell of earth. Berthus looked up at Orren with a look of both hatred and bewilderment.

"Let *me* live?" Berthus chuckled. "How can you do that, swine boy? Every second you remain alive is thanks to me, and don't you or any of your friends dare take a step closer."

"You're dying," Orren said. "You've lost most of your blood, and you don't have long to go. Narx really did you in."

"Are you jealous?" Berthus asked. "I'm sure you wish you'd done this."

"What are you talking about?" Orren asked.

"Oh, don't play stupid with me," Berthus said. "I know who and what you are. Your whole life exists for one reason only, and that is to kill me—to wipe me off the face of the earth."

"Are you crazy?" Orren was outraged. "Do you really believe what you're saying?"

"Father wanted me dead," Berthus said, "and he would have killed me had it not been for Richard. That's why Father had you. He wanted you to be around after he died, so that you could finish what he started. That's the reason you're alive."

Orren's entire body shook with anger. He clenched his fists. "That's a lie!" he hollered. "You're nothing but a liar. You were the one who tried to kill me. I never did anything to you!"

At this point, a large group of Alivadus knights arrived on the scene. Iskander held up a hand, and they, recognizing the young man, stopped to watch whatever was about to take place.

"You stole Father's love!" Berthus yelled at Orren. "You took away my inheritance, and then you stole my gwell."

"I never took anything from you," Orren growled. "Father did what he did, but I had nothing to do with it! I don't even remember Father; I didn't even know what he looked like until your memories of him entered my mind when we met inside that black cloud. Yes, I took Hesh, but it was never *your* gwell. You shouldn't have a gwell, because look what you've done with them!"

"What if I told you that Father was getting better," Berthus asked, "and that he died because I poisoned his drink. Yes, swine boy, you know I'm telling the truth. I can see it in your eyes, and you want to know something else? I'm happy I did it."

Orren gave into his rage. He drew his short sword and prepared to run it through his half brother, when suddenly, he heard the voice in his mind yell, *Stop!*

Orren froze in place.

*This is no time to give into your anger, Orren. Berthus is a hairsbreadth away from using Kalsh to wipe out everyone and believe me, he can do it despite the fact that he's dying, and he will do it. You already offered him life. Therein lies the only chance you have of getting the gwellen away from him. For everyone's sakes, you must put aside your memories and find common ground with him.*

Orren placed his sword back in its sheath. Common ground? What common ground could he possibly have with Berthus? The only thing they had in common was that Richard had loved them both.

That was it!

"Richard loved you," Orren quickly blurted out.

He saw a flicker of softness on his brother's face. "W-What did you say?" Berthus asked.

"I said that Richard loved you," Orren said. "I know he did, because I saw some of your memories when our minds met inside that cloud. Included in those were some memories of Richard, and that's how I *know* he loved you."

"He was the only one who loved me," Berthus said, tears streaming down his filthy face. "He protected me from Father, and taught me how to run the manor. Richard was the only good thing that ever happened to me. He was my whole world."

"Richard was my whole world too," Orren said through his own tears. "He protected me from you. He taught me how to survive in the wilderness, and he taught me how to love."

"There are many reasons why I should kill you, Berthus," Orren continued. "All the awful things you did to me over the years. The folks you enslaved, the villages you destroyed, the yelia you killed—the list goes on and on, but I can't kill you. It's not because you don't deserve to die. You do. But Richard loved you, and Richard loved me, and I loved Richard. I can't kill you, because I can't kill someone Richard loved."

Berthus looked at him with confusion.

"We'll heal you, Berthus, because Shann-Rell here," Orren pointed at the yelian leader, "has Nebi. We'll use it on you, and I'll make sure you get out of the Ghoul Vale alive and whole. This I swear on Richard's memory. All I ask from you in return, is Kalsh and Ru'i."

"I'm supposed to trust *you?*" Berthus asked.

"Yes," Orren said, "because Richard trusted me. I swear that no one on my side will harm you if I can do anything about it. Not me, not my friends, nor the baron or his knights, nor even the yelia, though you'll have to make sure you don't run into Narx again. He's been kicked out of the yelian race by his own folks, so I can't control *him*. I beg you to choose life, not for your sake, but for Richard's."

Berthus tried to sigh, but he was unable to do even that. He let go of the brown gwell. It rolled along the ground.

"Marett, pick it up," Orren said. "It's yours."

Marett did as Orren asked.

"And Ru'i too," Orren instructed Berthus.

Berthus released the purple gwell. "Anselm take it," Orren said. The old man picked Ru'i up.

"Shann-Rell, please pass Nebi to me," Orren said, "and I'll need you to help me—you, Haxel, Marett, and Anselm."

The yelian woman handed the green stone to Orren. The boy put the gwell on Berthus's skin. Haxel, Marett, Anselm, and Shann-Rell all placed their hands on top of his. None of the Web members was Nebi's bearer, and Shann-Rell was not from Nebi's tribe. Even so, working together to heal Berthus was worth it, if only to live up to the promise they made.

"Let's do this," Orren said. He concentrated on the stone, as did the others.

Orren felt the growth element flow from the stone, into Berthus. The body tissues healed themselves. New blood pumped through Berthus's veins and arteries, and his skin knit together. When the healing process was finished, there weren't even any scars where Narx had wounded him.

Orren tasted bile in his throat and his skin trembled. He and his friends all coughed violently. At that point, Shann-Rell asked Thraix, the Nebb chief, to join in the effort, for Nebi *was* the stone of his tribe. Thraix complied, even though he had doubts, due to his being unfamiliar with magic, or with the lore of the gwellen. These doubts could be felt by the gwell-bearers and by Shann-Rell, but even so, the Nebb chief's presence had a solidifying effect. Therefore, when the magic was finished, no one felt ill, and Berthus was completely healed.

Berthus got to his feet. He was too confused to express any emotions. He could not even look into his half brother's face.

"Swine boy, I—"

"That's Orren," his brother said. "Say it."

"Orren," the word was almost too painful for Berthus to utter. "I…I never knew…you."

"You know why you never knew me?" Orren said, "because this is the first time you and I ever had a confer–conserv–what's that long word, Marett?"

"Conversation," the girl said.

"Yes," Orren said. "That. We've never talked to each other, Berthus. Think about what might have been if we had."

"How can you guarantee that no one will kill me?" Berthus asked.

"I can guarantee it," a voice from among the assembled knights spoke. A man of medium height stepped forward. He was stocky, with brown hair and a goatee, and he wore chain mail.

"Who might you be?" Berthus asked.

"I'm Baron Alfred Toynberg of Alivadus," the man said, "and I guarantee that you'll leave this vale alive."

"Let your knights also look out for him," Orren said. "Otherwise Narx might try to kill him again."

"Done," the baron said. He gave orders to some of his knights, who left to carry the message to others.

"What now?" Berthus asked, his face full of confusion.

"Our lives have to go on," Orren said. "Go now, Berthus. Leave the vale, and go somewhere far away. We'll never see each other again."

Berthus turned around, and without another word, walked away through the ruins. When he reached the eastern edge of the city, he made his way through the vale, past the watchful eyes of Baron Toynberg's men, and the dead bodies of Drammites. He climbed Airen's Arc. As he did, the fog lifted, and the sun shone clearly.

When he reached the top, he turned around, and for one brief moment, looked back down into the vale. The ruined city was clearly visible now, for the cloudbank was gone, destroyed like so many other things, by the cyclone that Berthus and Narx had created together. Berthus then turned around and headed for the Hidden Pass. He knew not where he was going to go. Nor did it matter, for his mind was completely occupied by one gut-wrenching, heart-sickening, mind-haunting question.

What might have been?

# SPECIES TO SPECIES ENCOUNTERS

Orren continued staring into the ruins long after Berthus disappeared. A confusing mixture of emotions was affecting him. He felt relief at the fact that he had conquered his greatest fear, and at the same time, had prevented yet another disaster from taking place. The knowledge that Berthus would never again have any control over his life was empowering. At the same time, however, he felt sorrow, because Berthus, evil though he was, represented a living link to Richard.

Haxel placed a clawed hand on his shoulder, and Orren slowly turned around to face the zhiv. He tried to say something, but could not think of the words. Haxel nodded in understanding, while Marett, Iskander, Anselm, Shann-Rell, and the Alivadene knights looked on in silence.

Marett held Kalsh in the palm of her right hand. She looked uncomfortable with it, as if she had no idea what to do with a gwell.

"Do you know why I gave you Kalsh?" Orren asked the girl. "You used earth to get us out of the Forest of Doom. You threw clumps of earth at the giant snake, to save us. This is the gwell of earth, Marett, and I think you should bear it."

Marett closed her eyes and nodded. She placed Kalsh inside a gwell-sack, and gave Orren a warm hug.

Baron Toynberg stepped forward. "It is an honor and a privilege to have been so favored by the divine astra that they've allowed me to make the acquaintance of brave, noble heroes such as yourselves."

Marett and Iskander bowed their heads. Orren followed their cue and did the same thing, and the others copied his example.

"Iskander here has told me about all of you," the baron said. "Minstrels will sing your praises for centuries to come, for you've saved LeFain from unspeakable tyranny. Now, Orren Randolphus…"

Orren looked up at the baron.

"Everything Iskander, Perceval, and the rock giant said about you is true. I witnessed most of the exchange between you and your half-brother, and I'm impressed with the way you disarmed him. He actually forsook his opportunity for revenge. Despite his weakened condition, he could have killed all of us with that gwell, but you prevented it, and saved our lives."

Orren did not know how to respond to such praise.

The baron then turned to Haxel. "Druba Haxel…I can't remember the rest of your name…you have brought good fortune to the knights of Alivadus today. Never again may anyone in my barony teach that goblins bring bad luck."

"I'm most grateful, Honored Baron," Haxel said.

"Marett Baines," Baron Toynberg said. "You are wise, beautiful, and true. You're a credit to the Baines family name, as is your brother."

"You're too kind, my Lord," Marett said with tears in her eyes.

"Anselm," the baron addressed the old man. "Thank you for all the services rendered when you guided the gwell bearers over the mountains. You also deserve great honors."

Anselm bowed.

"All of you gwell bearers, including Quartz, would be welcome additions to the population of Alivadus," the baron said. "I offer you all, including Iskander and Perceval, new lives in my barony. Will you accept my offer?"

"Richard always wanted me to come to your city," Orren said. "Of course I'll come."

"I will too," Marett said.

"And I," Anselm chimed in.

"I can't," Haxel said. "I mean no offense, Honored Baron, but I can't live in human society. I need to be with my own kind."

"I certainly understand that," Baron Toynberg said, "and that brings me to what I wanted to discuss with the yelian leader." Turning to Shann-Rell, he said, "Greetings, my lady, forgive me for any breach of protocol, but I didn't know how to address the leaders of elves."

"I wish to express, on behalf of all my race, our gratitude for your invaluable assistance," Shann-Rell said. "You may just have saved our species."

"What are the plans for your people now, noble lady?"

Shann-Rell sighed. "There are only 483 yelia left in the world, most them in hiding at this present moment. We'll have to rebuild our lives and our community."

"You're not safe here," the baron said. "The cloudbank that once covered the Ghoul Vale is gone, as are the ghouls. With your small numbers, you don't have much hope of defending yourselves against enemies."

"I know," Shann-Rell said, her eyes cast downward, "but what other choice have we?"

"You can travel south with us," the baron said. "It just so happens that I can provide a perfect home for the yelia."

"Really? Where?"

"At the southernmost extent of my barony lies the Moreido Escarpment," the baron said. "Basically it's a series of steep limestone cliffs, atop of which grows a thick forest of rowan, elm, pear, hazelnut, and oak trees. Springs of clear water are there too. The Moreido's been uninhabited since a plague wiped out its human population centuries ago, and humans are superstitious about it. They won't resettle it."

"You'll have freedom there, and plenty of room, for the escarpment is over sixty miles long. To its south lie duchies and principalities that view my barony with envious eyes. If you'll consent to settle the Moreido, you can keep watch on these potential enemies for me. In return, the Moreido will belong to the yelia forever."

"My lord," Shann-Rell said, "The offer is enticing, especially because of the oak trees. In ancient times, acorns were a staple of our diet. I must speak to the Wardolam council before making such a decision. Doing that will require elections of new tribal chiefs, because with only one exception, all of the ones we had before, were killed in the storm."

"Then you can do that as soon as your people emerge from hiding," Baron Toynberg said.

"Just don't take too long to do it," Anselm said to Shann-Rell. "Remember that Orren, Haxel, Marett, Quartz, and myself are still under the Ghouls' Curse, and we only have forty-three days in which to find that big ape Jurgan, and get Magna away from him."

"It will not take long, Anselm," Shann-Rell patted him on the arm in an affectionate manner.

Baron Toynberg gave orders to a dozen knights, who escorted Shann-Rell into the ruins, to retrieve her people.

"What's the Ghoul's Curse?" the baron asked the gwell bearers. "What do you have only forty-three days to do?"

Orren and his friends told the baron everything that had happened, starting with their foray to the Fallagourn Falls, and ending with the cyclone. They explained the Ghouls' Curse, and how it affected them, as well as the foul hex-seeds that sat in their minds.

"So if you don't hand all six gwellen to Shann-Rell by the time the Moment of Reckoning arrives, you'll forever have to guard an empty city?" the baron asked.

"That's correct, my lord," Marett said, "and as it currently stands, I bear Kalsh, Orren bears Hesh, Anselm is Ru'i's bearer, Haxel is Orya's, and Shann-Rell carries Nebi, though she isn't that stone's designated bearer. Only Magna, of which Quartz *is* the designated bearer, is still at large, stolen by Jurgan. There's no telling where Jurgan could be right now."

"I wish I could be of more assistance," the baron said. "After everything you gwell bearers have done for the people of LeFain, it pains me that I'm unable to search for Magna myself."

"I'm afraid the only thing to do is pray to the astra," Marett said with a sigh.

"Well said," Baron Toynberg agreed with a smile. "Sadly, four of my brave knights fell today, as did eight of Berthus's former slaves. We'll bury them atop the arc. The funeral of a righteous person is a fortuitous time for prayer, because the recently deceased spirit can intervene with the astra, on our behalf."

An hour later, Shann-Rell and the knights returned with all the yelia, who were bewildered and nervous, as well as somewhat disappointed by the fact that the sky was cloudy, preventing them from seeing the Sun Father. The knights did not intend to be rude, but they could not help staring at the 'elves', who were supposed to be extinct. The yelia, however, did not notice, for they were too busy debating in their fluty tongue. Anselm explained to everyone that the Sun-Children were determining who should become the next tribal leaders and council members. It took only a few minutes for them to choose twenty individuals to represent them on the council.

Elections for tribal chiefs were held next. The Nebb was the only tribe not to have them, because their chief, Thraix, had survived the cyclone. Shann-Rell offered him Nebi, using as an argument the fact that he had already supported the gwell-bearers in their use of the green stone, to heal Berthus. Thraix, however, refused on the grounds that in his younger days, he been a shadow guard. He felt that given his problematic past, he was unworthy to bear a gwell, even if it *was* the gwell of his tribe. The other Nebb members were not versed enough in the lore of the gwellen to take on the responsibility either, for gwell lore had not been taught since the days of Shibbia. Ignorance, Shann-Rell explained, was how the past three council heads kept the yelian masses under control. Shann-Rell agreed to continue keeping the green gwell in trust, until such time as the Nebb received necessary instruction.

The sixteen Orr voted unanimously for the eldest member of their group, a blue-eyed male named Ful-Rax. The Rau chose a small, black-haired female named Relshing, and the Haas selected Grnalt, an older male who stood nearly seven feet tall.

The Kell vote presented a strange twist. Fifty-one members of the tribe supported Lafshing, and the other fifty-one supported Lafshing's sister, Laf-Nrell. Both were heroes, for Lafshing assisted the gwell-bearers, and Laf-Nrell had found a deep tunnel, thus saving the lives of sixty yelia.

"Siblings are nowadays almost unknown among the Sun Children," Shann-Rell remarked with a tear in her eye.

"Will the yelia honor Grnoud's last wishes?" Marett asked. "It would seem to me that the only way to do so would be to have children, and not just one child per family."

"I certainly hope that they will," Shann-Rell said, "and that our new home beneath the constant gaze of our Sun Father, would induce them to multiply."

In the end, the vote was resolved when Laf-Nrell stepped down in her brother's favor.

Shann-Rell then approached her own tribe and spoke to them. Anselm translated what she said so the humans and zhiv could understand. Shann-Rell, it seemed, did not approve of the offices of Magg chief and council head being combined in the same person. She advised her tribe to choose someone else as tribal chief, and they did. They selected a golden-haired, porcelain-skinned male named Eskwell, a distant cousin of the deceased Grnoud.

By the time the voting reached its conclusion, night had fallen. Quartz emerged from the ruins. The ruler of Alivadus then announced that with everyone present, it was time to leave the Ghoul Vale.

The knights numbered 630 in total, two hundred of them cavalry. The baron asked each mounted knight to transport an older yelius on his horse's back. Ten elderly yelia rode on Quartz's shoulders, and the sholl also carried the four dead knights. The younger Sun-Children walked alongside the infantry. Orren, Haxel, Marett, Anselm, Shann-Rell, Iskander, and the baron went with them, while Jasper and the red mastiff accompanied the yelian leader, and the falcon flew overhead.

They ascended the steep slopes of Airen's Arc, and when they all reached the top, they immediately dug graves for the four Alivadene knights and the eight rebel slaves who fell fighting the Drammites. The service was very moving. It was conducted in Classical Gothma and Alamene. After it was done, Haxel intoned zhiv prayers to Tchafla on behalf of the fallen. Marett recited a poem written by an ancestor. Quartz made an invocation to the Moon Mother, and the yelia held an elaborate ceremony of their own. It was a unique and meaningful cross-species experience.

After this was over, Orren called the other gwell-bearers over to initiate a search for Jurgan. Shann-Rell could not join them, despite the fact that she bore Nebi, because she was not a Web member. Therefore, Orren, Haxel, Marett, and Anselm concentrated on their respective stones, and activated the Web. Quartz, though not in possession of a gwell, joined them by tapping into the silvery light. Together the five gwell-bearers projected their minds outward.

Almost immediately, the hex-seeds flared up. They infected the Web, causing the silvery light to take on a mottled appearance. Nonetheless, Orren and his friends persevered. At last, they made contact with Jurgan, who could do nothing to conceal Magna, as he did not possess a Forest of Doom gwell-sack. Everyone felt the bandit's fear, and they heard him spur his horse to a gallop. After a few minutes they lost the connection.

"He's riding away from Sherbass," Anselm said, "and he's heading southward."

"We must set off at once to find him!" Haxel cried out.

"My masters, the night will be over soon," Quartz said in a despairing voice. "I will need to sleep beneath my skooch."

"Let's talk to the baron," Marett said. "Perhaps he can spare a few knights to go with us, and you, Quartz, can catch up later."

They approached Baron Toynberg and explained the situation to him, but the baron refused.

"I sent a detachment of knights north," the baron said, "and they've succeeded, with the help of the locals, in driving the Drammites out of the northern part of Rivulein. However, the order is still strong in the center and south. Only Kasta has been liberated. I will need all my knights with me, especially if I have any hope of driving the Drammites out of Sherbass. Once Sherbass is liberated, the Drammites will have lost their main stronghold. However, I can't allow you five to leave us before then. The countryside around Sherbass is on fire with civil war. It's just too dangerous."

"Quartz will take us," Haxel said. "He can protect us."

"No offense, but Quartz is not in any shape to even protect himself," the baron said. "Look what Jurgan was able to do to him! With these cracks all over his hide, it would only take one flaming arrow…No, I can't allow it."

"We have the gwellen," Haxel said.

"And I'll go with them," Shann-Rell said, "for I have Nebi."

"Don't be a pair of fools," Anselm snapped at the zhiv and the yelius. "The way these hex-seeds are, it's very hard to use the gwellen, and it will only get worse."

"So what are we supposed to do?" Haxel cried out.

"Here's what we do," Orren said. "We'll travel with the baron to Sherbass. We still have enough ability to use the gwellen so that we can help him take the city by magic. Then when Sherbass is free, we'll travel with the baron by day and with Quartz by night. Quartz can sleep in the day, and it isn't a problem for him to catch up with us by night."

"That is true, Master Orren," the sholl said.

"Moving in this way, we'll go much faster than Jurgan," Orren said, "because horses tire out, so we're sure to overtake him. It will take our best efforts, but we'll still track him wherever he goes. I say Shann-Rell and the tribal leaders should come with to help support us. Quartz *can* carry that many people."

"Can Jasper come with us, as well?" Quartz requested.

"Just what I was about to ask," Anselm said.

"I would like to have Jasper with me at all times, if that is acceptable to you, Master Anselm," the sholl said. "I would even like to keep her under my skooch at night. She seems hungry all the time, and I can assist her in finding enough food to keep her full."

"Fine," the old man said with a smile.

The little donkey nuzzled her master in gratitude. Jasper's lost eye had completely regenerated. She appeared to be broadening at the shoulders, and her head was wider than it had been before. Strangest of all, her tail appeared to have fused itself to her body. The Salve of Healing appeared to have produced some unusual side effects.

Shann-Rell left their company. She returned a few minutes later with an announcement. "The Wardolam council has voted to accept Baron Toynberg's offer," she said. "We will live upon the Moreido Escarpment and there, we'll bear children."

"Shann-Rell," Anselm said. "I don't mean to put a damper on all this, but there are very few yelia left, and most of you are old. How do you expect to be a viable species if you are already plagued by birth defects?"

Shann-Rell smiled and tapped Anselm's hand. "Do you remember the message Grnoud left?" she asked.

"Yes," Anselm said. "He mentioned something called Diffusion."

"Diffusion is one advantage of being a yelius," Shann-Rell said. "We can interbreed with members of similar sapient species, humans included. In ancient times, this was not unusual; some of the Regii had yelian siblings. If a yelius has children with a human, then some of the children will be human and some will be yelia, but they can't be both. You're either a yelius or you're not."

"You mean you'd marry a human?" Anselm asked.

"If necessary, yes," Shann-Rell said, "doing that would make our blood stronger, and the birth defects would disappear. Also, we yelia remain fertile well into old age."

Anselm's mouth dropped open. For the first time ever, Orren saw the old man go silent.

# THE LIBERATION OF SHERBASS

Marett was awakened by the sound of soft chanting. She stood up and went outside. There, she found the Sun Children—all 483 of them—gathered in the pre-dawn chill, facing eastward. The sky contained few clouds, and the stars were fading, as dawn approached. The soothing, ethereal refrain of the yelian voices seemed to flow into the ground and animate the snow-capped peaks of the Greymantles.

Anselm emerged from the tent, followed by Orren and Haxel. Jasper joined them, though it was impossible to say where she had come from.

"The yelia are greeting the Sun Father," Anselm said, "They're giving thanks to the Sun Father's spirit for enabling them to see this moment."

"It's amazing," Marett said. "The yelia have been deprived of something that has been an everyday occurrence in our lives. I'll never look at a sunrise the same way again."

"That's right, my girl," Anselm said. "Not a single yelius, save for the council heads that preceded Narx, has seen the sun in over four centuries."

The Alivadene knights awakened as well. They emerged from their tents, saw the yelia at prayer, and stood in respectful silence.

As the sky grew lighter, the chanting increased in intensity. Marett looked at the awestruck faces of the Sun-Children. Back in the Ghoul Vale, the yelia had been dour and humorless, but now, as the sky turned pink, their skin seemed to glow, their hair became glossier, and there was a pervasive sense of rejuvenation in their voices. Tears streamed down Marett's cheeks, for she had never seen anything so beautiful and profound. The expressions on her friends' faces, and those of the knights, indicated that they all felt the same way.

When the sun appeared above the mountain peaks, the chanting stopped, and there was pure silence. Every yelius stood still, basking in the rays of their Sun Father. After an hour of contemplation, Shann-Rell spoke a few words in the fluty tongue, and the ceremony ended. The yelia greeted each other and their human allies, and then awaited instructions from their leaders.

Shann-Rell and the tribal chiefs walked over to the gwell-bearers. They smiled at the humans and the zhiv, and Shann-Rell said, "Thank you, Orren Randolphus, Druba Haxel Spakiwakwak, Marett Reina Baines, and Anselm. Please also convey our gratitude to Quartz Moonchild when he awakens. Were it not for the five of you, this moment would never have come."

"But we also led Berthus to your city," Anselm said in a gloomy voice, "which is why you lost most of your people."

"Our numbers were far greater a few days ago, that's true," Shann-Rell said, "but what kind of existence did we have, suffering under tyranny, deprived of contact with our Sun Father, and heading inexorably toward extinction? The loss of so many loved ones is not your fault, but that of a wicked human bully and a ruthless yelian tyrant. Perhaps we're fewer now, but we have hope and, thanks to Baron Toynberg, a new home."

Baron Toynberg and Iskander approached on horseback.

"Gwell-bearers," the baron said. "A message has come from Perceval, carried by a raven." The baron took out a piece of parchment and read:

"Greetings from Sherbass. Drammites have city closed off. Intend to starve population into submission. People sacrificed everyday, and Drammites partake of offerings. Help needed urgently, but beware of Drammites at closed city gate."

"Does this mean the Drammites have become cannibals?" Marett shrieked.

"It would seem so," Iskander said, "that way *they* don't starve."

"This shouldn't surprise anyone," Orren said. "I can't tell you how many hymns the darguns forced into my head, which talked about the sweet blood and flesh of victims. When you have that drummed into your mind for hours and hours every day, you start looking at human flesh differently."

"Orren!" Marett cried out in shock.

"You don't know what they put me through, Marett," Orren said, "and I hope you never find out."

"How disgusting," Anselm spat. "Typically human. They always—"

Marett shot him a sharp look. Anselm said, "Sorry. Old habits, you know."

"We're setting off at once," the baron said. "Sixty oxcarts are waiting in the valley to transport the infantry, the yelia, and yourselves. We'll leave Quartz here to sleep, because he won't have trouble catching up with us when he awakens. He'll follow by using the bond he has to you gwell-bearers."

An hour later, Marett, Orren, Haxel, Anselm, Shann-Rell, and the yelian tribal chiefs were riding together in one oxcart. Baron Toynberg and Iskander rode alongside on horseback. Shann-Rell's red mastiff trotted alongside, while her peregrine falcon flew overhead. The combined company left Airen's Arc and the Ghoul Vale, and traveled through a landscape of mixed woods and farmland. By evening, they reached the Gress Plateau.

There was very little snow left on the ground, though patches of it were more common on the plateau. The air was cold and crisp, but it carried the scent of spring and new beginnings. Carpets of white wood anemone and lesser celandine in brilliant yellow covered the ground beneath the trees. Here and there, purple crocuses could be seen. Rain came frequently, and this, Marett knew, contributed to the abundance of wildflowers.

The first springtime birds had also arrived. White storks were common in agricultural land and meadows, where they fed alongside partridges and quail. In the wooded areas, the travelers heard cuckoos and woodpeckers, and everywhere, there were swallows, starlings, and swifts. The beauty of winter's end eased the hex-seed in Marett's mind.

The local people welcomed the baron and his knights as liberators. They greeted the Alivadenes with food, flowers, and supplies. Skirmishes with small bands of Drammites were frequent, but they always ended quickly, with the deaths of the cultists.

It took an entire day to cross the plateau, but by evening, they pitched camp at its southern edge, in clear view of the Braddon River. They ate supper and spent several hours conversing with the baron.

Marett found the baron to be a well-mannered, intelligent man, who never raised his voice or allowed his emotions to run away with him. He was devoutly religious, praying to the astra twice a day. His knights had the utmost respect for him, and would surely follow him to the ends of the earth. He, in turn, was actively concerned with the welfare of each one of them.

The baron was fond of Orren, and the boy came to look upon him as a father figure. Marett had often worried about the fact that, ever since Richard's death, Orren had no older, male role model in his life. Anselm, with his impatience and volatility was unsuited for such a job, and Quartz, though undoubtedly very old, was from a species that was nothing like humans at all.

In the morning, they woke to another beautiful sunrise, and more yelian chanting. Marett and her friends left the tent, and saw that Quartz was in camp, wrapped up snugly inside his skooch. Jasper's front hoofs poked out from the garment's edge.

The company descended the southern slopes of the Gress. They crossed the Braddon River at a shallow ford, located beside an old fortress town called Bomberg. There, their numbers were swelled by large numbers of Rivulene resistance fighters. They took a sharp turn eastward, and spent the rest of the day traveling toward Sherbass. They were delayed in Vitter, a town similar to Skaps, where they had to assist the locals in driving out a particularly nasty group of Drammites.

The next morning, they awakened, and once again found that Quartz and Jasper had caught up. By midday, they overlooked the Din Ravine and the old Gothma bridge.

Sherbass appeared even more forbidding that it had the last time Marett and Orren were there. The city gates were closed, and yellow flags with dargooks, flapped in the cold wind. The breeze carried the foul smell of smoke and burning flesh.

A raven flew onto Iskander's outstretched arm, with a piece of parchment tied to its leg. The young man read it aloud.

"Drammites in every tower. Things deteriorating, and people considering surrender. Need help quick."

"How will we get into the city?" the baron asked. "My men will be slaughtered ascending toward the gate."

"We can go through the catacombs," Iskander suggested.

"Not a good idea," Marett said. "For much of the way, people have to walk in single file alongside the main sluice. There are also areas where one has to crawl. Try doing that in armor! Besides, Iskander, the snow and ice are melting, which means that the catacombs will be full of water."

"So *then* what?" Iskander asked.

"Why not use one of the gwellen to knock the walls down?" an officer suggested.

"Because we can't see behind the walls," Marett said. "We have no idea where the Drammites are, and where the townsfolk are. We could end up killing many townsfolk."

"Especially since the city is full of refugees," Iskander said.

"Hang on," Orren said, "let me think."

Everyone went silent while the boy lost himself in thought. After about twenty minutes, he said, "Here's the first part of my plan. Only Marett, Anselm, and I will enter the catacombs. If they're full of water, I'll use Hesh."

"I'll to come too," Haxel said.

"I have to forbid that, Haxel," the baron was emphatic. "The city is full of uneducated, superstitious humans, and it's not safe for a zhiv. I also must forbid the yelia from participating, because with their small numbers, every one of them is needed to perpetuate their species. When Quartz arrives, he too, must stay out, because his size may cause panic, and he can't maneuver in narrow city alleyways."

"I want to do *something*," Haxel said, with his arms crossed, and a pout on his lips.

"You *will* do something," Orren put a hand on the zhiv's shoulder. "Shann-Rell, are yelia good at making clothes?"

"A number of the Rau and Nebb are skilled that way," the yelian leader said.

"Get them together," Orren said, "and Haxel, we'll need you too. Take some of the tents, and cut pieces off of them so they look like Drammite robes and hoods. If you strip off outer layers of the canvas, you should be able to make veils thin enough to see through. You'll be making dargas' robes. You'll have to work quickly, 'cause there isn't much time."

"Honored baron," the boy continued. "I think you should pick some of your men—maybe fifteen. They'll be disguised as dargas. Get another fifty men and shave their heads. Have you got any ink?"

"Yes," the baron said. "That's how I've been communicating with Perceval."

"Have you got any men who are good at painting?"

"The Kell are," Shann-Rell cut in.

"Good," Orren said. "Get the best Kell painters to put dargooks on the foreheads of the men the baron chooses. Baron, tell the men you choose, to turn their tunics inside out. Make them yellow with something—the local folks drink a light-colored beer; Kenner loved it…that could work. Haxel, you'll use Orya to light fires that will dry the tunics quickly. Don't worry if they get scorched a bit; that will just make it look like the warriors have been in battle."

"I understand, Master," Haxel said.

"When the tunics are dry, the Kell must paint dargooks over the hearts. That way you'll have fake Drammite warriors to go with the fake dargas. Then we need to take pieces from some of the hide covers of the ox carts. From them, Haxel and the yelia will make another robe, hood, and veil for Iskander. We'll need to dye these clothes red with something."

"Holly bushes," Anselm said. "Plenty of them grow along the edge of the Din, and they should still have red winter berries."

"Good," Orren said, "The yelia will gather some, and then they'll dye Iskander's robes red. Then, Iskander, put oil on your face and maybe some beer in your hair, so you look like your cousin."

"I have to pretend that I'm Eric?" Iskander raised an eyebrow.

"Yes," Orren said. "His hair was golden, while yours is white blond, so you need to make yours look darker. His skin was a tiny bit darker than yours, and his voice a little deeper. If you do all those things, the Drammites will think you're him. They can't know that he's dead. We killed all the Drammites we found in the Ghoul Vale, so how could they have gotten messages to the Drammites here in Sherbass?"

"This boy is brilliant," the baron said in an awestruck voice. Marett felt a surge of pride.

"You and the other fake Drammites will walk up to the gate," Orren said. "You'll tell the Drammites in the city to let you in, because you want to make peace with the Prett dargas, and you've also brought your very best fighters to help them destroy the rebels. Make sure you use lots of Dramm talk—you know, about blood and sacrifice and all that."

"Of course I know," Iskander smiled. "Remember, I was raised Drammite."

"When you get into the city," Orren said, "you'll kill the Drammites guarding the towers and gates, and then the honored baron will invade with his men. Baron, make sure you look out for city folks, who will be pointing you to places where there are Drammites."

"How will the city folks know to do that?" the baron asked.

"Because that's why Marett, Anselm, and I are going into the catacombs. Perceval can't arrange this on his own. He'll need our help. One last thing, Iskander. Write Perceval a message. Tell him to send someone to meet us by the millstone, where we first entered the catacombs. Then send the raven back with it."

A few minutes later, Orren grasped the rope and moved hand over hand into the

Din. Several Alivadene knights held onto the other end. As the boy descended, he noted how different the slope was, now that the snow on it had melted. There would be no avalanches today.

After a few minutes, he reached the bottom, and Marett and Anselm followed. The Din River was no longer iced over.

"Let's step on rocks to cross over," Orren said. "I don't want to use Hesh unless we really have to. Jurgan could be in the city, and he'd detect me using the gwell. I don't think he's there, but you never know."

They crossed the river and entered the catacombs, which, interestingly, did not smell as bad as they had before. The spring rains, it seemed, had washed them out. There was a great deal of water, as Marett said there might be, but in the larger tunnel it was confined to the sluice. They had to slosh through some of it when they reached the narrower side tunnel, and at one point, they had to crawl through it on their hands and knees. Soon they reached the hidden entryway, which was partially concealed by the millstone. They then pulled themselves upward, and into the city.

A green-eyed, rag-clad girl of nine, with soiled blond curls, met them beside the millstone. Meisie was the sister of Rolf, the leader of a band of urchins who had rendered invaluable assistance to Orren and Marett the last time they had been in Skaps.

"Meisie!" Marett said, "How good to see you again."

"Come with me," Meisie said, "My brother and yours are waiting."

She led them through the burned part of the city. People were everywhere, many of them sick. Their faces were pinched with cold and starvation. Their clothes were tattered. The stench of burning flesh from nearby sacrifices made Orren gag.

It was a challenge to keep up with Meisie, but they managed to do it. They followed the girl into the back of a partially ruined frame house. Meisie lifted up an otherwise unnoticeable set of floorboards, and revealed a ladder, which led down into some sort of basement. Orren saw a light shining in it. He climbed down the ladder, followed by Marett and Anselm. Perceval's seven ravens fluttered down into the ground with them, and then Meisie also entered, closing the trapdoor over her head.

They entered a chamber that had literally been dug out of the earth, and there, Perceval and Rolf sat on the floor with only a small lantern. The chamber roof was six feet high, which meant that Perceval, being above six feet, was unable to stand in it.

Perceval shifted himself over to his sister and embraced her. He then hugged Orren, and gave Anselm an awkward nod. The old man grunted. Orren and Marett then embraced Rolf, and introduced him to Anselm.

Orren explained his plan to Perceval and Rolf, both of whom were suitably impressed.

"Rolf, you must spread the word," Orren said in Vulgalquor. Perceval translated what he said into Allamene. "Tell your gang to get folks into the buildings and to wait beside the windows, on roofs, and in alleyways. You'll be showing the baron's men where to find the Drammites."

"But there are Drammites all over the city," Perceval said, "and some of them have disappeared into thin air. Cinda Lowny is one of those."

"Then we'll have to have folks all over the city," Orren said.

"Sounds like a plan," Perceval said, "Rolf, Meisie, get to it right away." The two street urchins scrambled up the ladder.

"Perceval," Marett said in what Orren thought was a somewhat accusatory tone. "You don't look like you're starving."

"The Drammites still think I'm one of them," Perceval said. "I move among them, so I must act like one of them."

"Are you saying you've partaken of their sacrifices?" Marett asked in a near shriek.

"I'm not the first Duraline who's been forced to develop a strong stomach," Perceval said. "I had to do it, sis, and being nourished is, I suppose, an unintended side benefit."

"I don't want to talk about this," Marett said. She was green in the face.

Orren and his friends had to be patient and keep a low profile, because it took Baron Toynberg and his knights three days to cleanse the city of the Drammite scourge. In the end, however, it was done. The baron and Iskander held public speeches in the city square, in front of the domed central church. Orren, Marett, Anselm, and Perceval stood by his side. The baron explained to the people, the need to rebuild their lives and to be faithful to the astra.

Suddenly, a woman cried out, "My children!"

Orren and Marett both gasped, as they saw Kenner and Fama make their way through the crowd. Much of Kenner's brown hair had gone gray. He now had an unkempt beard, and his hunch was more pronounced. Fama's face seemed to have acquired more wrinkles, and her greasy, blond hair was untidy. They were, however, overjoyed to find the adopted children they thought they had lost. They wept as they embraced Orren and Marett, and Orren and Marett embraced them warmly in return.

"Now we can be a family again," Fama said.

"No," Marett shook her head sadly. "I'm so sorry, Fama. I honestly wish we *could*, but you need to know the truth."

She led Fama, Kenner, and Orren away from the crowd and sat them down beside a wall. She told them an abridged version of their story. She did not tell them about Haxel, Jasper, and Quartz, and she said as little as possible about the yelia. Orren listened in silence.

"And now you know who we really are," Marett said. "You also know why we need to go with the baron, to Alivadus."

"One thing I don't get," Kenner said. "You say Boren…I mean Orren…made all those plans. How could he tell you his plans if he can't talk?"

"I talk," Orren said.

Kenner and Fama opened their mouths in surprise.

"I talk," Orren said, "but my Allamene not good."

"It was the only way we could avoid people getting suspicious," Marett said, "because if people *were* suspicious, they'd alert the Drammites. We're so sorry, Kenner, Fama. You should know that we really do love you."

Fama sighed and looked at her 'children' with tears in her eyes. "All that matters is that you're safe."

"What actually happened in Skaps?" Marett asked.

"We were distraught after you left," Kenner said, "but we were comforted in the arrival of Blood Master Dramm. Maybe he'd fight Mortistia and get you back. Darga Drugger entered our village, and consecrated the dirigon. That's when we realized something was wrong, for they demanded a sacrifice from among our own people. We were shocked at the demand, and no one stepped up, so they took Garberin."

"Nò!" Marett cried out. Garberin, the young man she had knocked out using the substance called *mursh*, had been stupid, but he was also faithful and kind.

"He screamed as he died, and they cut him up into pieces," Fama said. "From that time on, everything became worse. The Drammites took our property, and quartered warriors in our houses. We had to serve them, to give them most of what we produced. Anyone who protested was sacrificed. Chief Marvin got us to fight back. We killed all the Drammites we could find, but more came, and destroyed Skaps. Chief Marvin's dead, and his family too, and many others."

"We who survived fled into the woods. The rebels found us and took us to Sherbass. They asked us to join the rebellion there."

Orren and Marett went silent. The thought of all the kind folks of Skaps dying, inflamed the hex-seed in Orren's head. Marett's face registered her own pain.

"The Drammites are being hunted down all over Rivulein," Marett said, "but I don't think the nobles will ever come back either. You must gather all the folks from Skaps, and go back to rebuild it. The soil, air, water, and pasture there is too good to let go to waste."

"You're right," Kenner said, "but for Skaps to live on, there must be children. We can't help, because we have no children of our own."

Orren suddenly had an idea. "Kenner, Fama, wait here. Come Marett."

He and Marett made their way back into the city square, and found Perceval.

"Where's Rolf?" Orren asked.

"He doesn't like long speeches," Perceval said. "He's in that alleyway over there."

They found Rolf throwing stones against a wall. "Rolf," Marett said. "Get Meisie and all of your gang."

The boy ran off. He reappeared moments later, with his blond-curled sister and over a dozen other street urchins.

"Follow us," Marett said. She and Orren led the children to where Kenner and Fama sat. The peasant couple looked up at them with hopeful eyes.

"Kenner, Fama, you want children," Marett said. "Rolf, Meisie, how would you like to have parents again?"

"More than anything," Rolf said with tears in his eyes.

"Kenner and Fama," Marett said. "Rolf and Meisie are the best children you could possibly have, and you'll be giving them a better home, out in the country, where it's healthier. Find the other folks of Skaps. Knowing them as I do, they'll adopt all of these other children, and probably many more besides."

"They sure will," Kenner said. "Many villagers would be happy to adopt them, and together, we'll rebuild our beloved town."

Fama threw her arms around Meisie and hugged her tightly. Kenner did the same with Rolf.

"You're good folks," Rolf said. "I can see that in your eyes."

Kenner, Fama, Rolf, and Meisie all turned to Orren and Marett with tears of gratitude. "Thank you," they said. They embraced Orren, Marett, and one another. The other street urchins looked on, in hopeful anticipation of the new families that they too, would soon receive.

By this time, the speeches and ceremonies were finished. Orren and Marett rejoined Iskander, Perceval, and the baron. They entered a building that, as it so happened, was adjacent to the alleyway where Rolf had been throwing the stones. The baron bid them goodnight, and then Perceval and Iskander led Orren and Marett to the room where they would be staying. Anselm was already there, wrapped up in blankets, and fast asleep.

"You should tell her now, 'Skander," Perceval said.

"Marett," Iskander's eyes darted about nervously, "I have feelings for you."

"Yes," Marett nodded.

"And you have feelings for me too."

"Yes," Marett looked at the ground and nodded again.

"But I have to stay here in Sherbass," Iskander said. "The church needs

reorganizing, and so does the government, but when I'm done, I'll come down to Alivadus and join the baron's knights. Then we can be together."

"I understand," Marett said. She kissed him on the cheek and he kissed her back. She then wrapped herself in the blankets that had been left for her, but Orren saw tears in her eyes. Orren felt jealous of Iskander, but at the same time, was sad for Marett, that she would be separated from this young man she loved. The conflict of emotions made his head spin.

Why could nothing end smoothly? Orren remembered Rheudia, the red-headed girl he had fallen in love with in Thelican, and whom he had been forced to leave behind there. The pain he had felt at having to leave her came back to him. His hex-seed throbbed. He needed to clear his head, so he left the room and walked out the back door of the building, into the alleyway.

Strong hands grabbed him and forced something over his nose and mouth. He struggled, but his captors had a firm grip on him. He smelled *mursh*.

# THE ABDUCTION

Haxel felt a soft tap on his shoulder. He opened his eyes and sat bolt upright. The tent flap was open, and Quartz was peering in. The rock giant had a perplexed expression on his huge, stony face.

"Master Haxel?"

"What's wrong, Big Friend?"

"Something is very amiss, Master Haxel," Quartz said. "Master Orren is moving

away from the city, without Madam Marett or Master Anselm. Why would he go off on his own like that?"

"Is the baron with him?" Haxel asked. "What about Perceval or Iskander?"

"I am sorry, Master Haxel," Quartz said, "Much though I love the baron, Perceval, and Iskander, they are not gwell-bearers, and therefore I have no bond toward them. I cannot track them the way I can track Master Orren, so I am unable to determine whether they are with him or not. Master Anselm and Madam Marett are still inside the city."

"What about using the Web?" Haxel asked.

"My hex-seed is too strong to send the Web out as far away as where Master Orren now is," Quartz said.

"Mine's gotten worse too," Haxel said. "I think it would make more sense to follow after him. We mustn't get too close. That way, if he's carrying out some secret plan, we won't spoil it."

Quartz took Haxel out of the tent and placed the zhiv on his shoulder. Haxel then heard a whinny coming from the ground. He looked down and saw Jasper nuzzling Quartz's feet.

"I understand, Jasper," Haxel said. "I too, miss our masters."

"Master Haxel," Quartz said, "I do not believe that is what concerns her. I think she wants to come with us."

Haxel shrugged. "I see no harm in taking her."

Quartz picked up the little donkey and, holding her in the palm of his right hand, strode out of the campsite. He was careful to avoid disturbing the yelia and the knights who had been left behind to protect them. When they passed the tent where Shann-Rell was sleeping, they saw the red mastiff in the entryway. The dog lifted its head and watched them go.

When they reached the edge of the Din Ravine, Quartz said, "I am going to climb down the cliff. I sense that Master Orren travels southward along the river, and besides, if I travel through the ravine, I can avoid dense tree cover."

"Do what you think is best," Haxel said.

Quartz descended the slope, which was only three times his height. When he reached the bottom of the Din, he sloshed through the river water. The sholl had no trouble seeing his way in the darkness, and he followed the twisting, turning course of the gorge without difficulty.

After a few minutes of walking, Quartz and his two passengers reached a section where the ravine widened. The Sherbass Plateau still loomed large and dark on the east, but on the western side, the slopes were no longer steep. Instead, there were rolling, grass-covered hills, and small peasant villages surrounded by fallow fields. All the humans, however, were now asleep.

Suddenly, he stopped. "He passed this way, Master Haxel. He left the river here, and is now heading westward."

"Just a moment," Haxel said, "Let me down."

The sholl put him on the ground. Haxel examined the muddy bank, and found hoof prints. "Horses," he said, "and not just any horses. Miss Marett once told me about horses like these. They're small—just a little higher than my head, but they're very fast. The Master must be in a hurry."

"Then what do we do?"

"We keep going," Haxel said. "Even *these* horses can't go on forever. Sooner or later, the Master will have to stop. The horses will need to rest and graze."

They traveled overland for hours. Quartz avoided the wooded areas, because he

did not want the trees to slow him down. Instead, he kept to agricultural land and grassy meadows. Haxel knew that his giant friend was becoming increasingly worried, because the sun would soon rise, and he would have to bed down for the day.

"He has stopped," Quartz said at last. "I think I can catch up to him."

They ascended a tall hill. From the top, Haxel could see an open field, where five horses grazed, their human riders still on their backs. The moon provided enough illumination for the zhiv to see what was going on, so he took a closer look.

"Do you see Master Orren?" Quartz asked.

"Oh, I see him alright," Haxel said, "but he's asleep, and there's a man riding with him, holding him up in a sitting position. He has the Master all bundled up."

"Can you see who the other humans are?"

"They have no armor, so it can't be the baron or his men," Haxel said. "Iskander's not there either. The man who's holding the Master is big. Could be Perceval. We need to get closer."

Quartz descended the hill under the cover of darkness. Soon he was close enough so that he and Haxel could hear the riders' conversation. The humans appeared to be arguing with one another, but one thing was for certain. Perceval was not among them.

"Big Friend," Haxel hissed. "I think these humans have abducted the Master. They've knocked him out and are taking him away!"

Quartz charged.

The riders screamed in fear when they saw the rock giant coming at them. One of them, the big one who held Orren, whipped something out of his pocket. Too late, Haxel recognized Jurgan the bandit.

Jurgan sent forth a blast of air that carried Quartz backward and smashed his body against the side of the hill. The sholl dropped Jasper and Haxel, and let out a moan of agony.

The riders galloped away.

"Big Friend!" Haxel was frantic. "Are you hurt?"

"Master Haxel!" Quartz gasped. "They are getting away. You can catch up if you run. Now please *go!*" He said 'go' with such force, that it was like a command. Haxel set off at a sprint. He ran faster than he ever had in his life. After two minutes, he saw the horses, and this spurred him to go even faster.

Before long, he caught up with Jurgan's horse. He leapt onto its back, intending to kill the bandit as he had killed Ramburgus. Jurgan looked over his shoulder and let out a startled yell. Before Haxel could do anything, one of the other men pulled out a crossbow, aimed it at the zhiv, and shot.

Haxel heard a whoosh and a thud, and looked down with shock at the bolt protruding from his chest. It had missed his heart, but his blood was gushing out. He went dizzy, saw stars, and fell to the ground.

The woman rider wheeled her horse around, "It's a goblin," she said, "let's skin him!"

"We can't kill him!" one of the men said. "Our orders are that no gwell bearer may be killed. Jurgan didn't kill the giant, and the goblin will recover from this, but we can't take him with us, because we need the boy on his own. And now we've got to get out of Rivulein quick!"

The horsemen disappeared into the distance, while Haxel lay on the ground, trying to stem the flow of blood with his shaspa. His hex-seed grew until it occupied his entire head.

Jasper ran up to him, whimpering.

"Jasper," Haxel gasped. "You've got to go get the baron, Miss Marett, and your master. You're...our...only hope."

After saying these words, he blacked out.

Meanwhile, in the city, Marett woke up. She discovered that Anselm and Orren were gone, so she had a breakfast of bread and cheese by herself. She then went to look for her friends.

She found Anselm in the building's main entrance. He was laughing and joking with Baron Toynberg. It warmed her heart to know that after all the disappointment that the old man had suffered, he could still find enjoyment in life.

"Good morning, Honored Baron," she said. "Good morning, Anselm."

"Good morning," the old man and the baron both said.

"Where did Orren go?"

"Afraid I haven't seen him yet," the baron said.

"Haven't seen him since last night," Anselm added. "He's probably with that ridiculous brother of yours and the blond whippersnapper you've got eyes for."

Marett ignored the snide remarks. "Where are Perceval and Iskander?" she asked.

"I saw them a few minutes ago in the city square," the baron said. "Perceval was teaching Iskander the fine points of communicating with ravens."

"Thank you," Marett said.

She walked out of the main entrance, and into the city square. The sky was blue, with only a few clouds. The cold air carried the scent of spring, though this was filtered through the unwholesome urban odors of tanneries, raw sewage, and the still-pervasive smell of burned flesh, left over from Drammite sacrifices.

There were many townsfolk in the large, open space. The doors of the central church were open, and Marett could hear hymns being sung within. Flocks of pigeons were suddenly scattered by seven ravens. Marett heard a whistle, and saw the birds fly across the square to the opposite end, where Perceval waited.

She strode over to her brother and found Iskander with him. The two men were laughing. Iskander smiled at Marett, sending her heart aflutter, and she smiled back at him.

"Good morning, sis," Perceval said.

"Good morning," Marett said. "Is Orren with you?"

"Haven't seen him since last night," Perceval said.

"I haven't either," Iskander said.

"*No one* has seen him since last night," Marett shouted.

"What do you mean?" Perceval's face fell.

"Perhaps he's in the church praying," Iskander said.

"Orren pray?" Marett raised an eyebrow. "I don't think so."

"Nonetheless, it wouldn't hurt to look."

They entered the church together. About two hundred people were there, including fifteen Alivadene knights. Two young fraters led the congregation in singing hymns of praise to the astra. Perceval whispered something to the nearest knight, who walked over to his closest fellow, and whispered to him as well. Soon, all of the knights were searching through the crowd. After a few minutes, they all returned to Marett, shaking their heads.

"Orren wouldn't just go off without telling us," Marett said. "I fear something's happened to him. We must tell the baron!"

They all ran across the city square, and entered the building where they and the baron were staying. They burst into the baron's room. The ruler of Alivadus was still talking to Anselm.

"Nobody can find Orren!" Marett shouted.

"What?" the baron's eyes went wide.

"He's not in the church or the city square," Perceval said.

"Let's use the Web," Anselm said. "We must leave the city and go back to the camp. There we can meet up with Quartz and Haxel to activate it. Between the four of us, we may be able to muster enough power to overcome our hex-seeds."

"That depends on how far away Orren is," Marett said. "The Web has little effect right now, even with all four of us *and* Orren working together, thanks to these horrible parasites in our minds. How effective do you think it will be with only four of us?"

Suddenly, four knights entered the chamber, together with Shann-Rell and her dog, and a bedraggled, exhausted Jasper. The little donkey's tongue was lolling to one side, and her chest heaved.

"Shann-Rell," Anselm said. "Why are you in the city?"

"Jasper came to me this morning," the yelian leader said. "She looks exhausted. Look at her eyes. She's desperate to tell me something, but I have no idea what she wants, though I think it may have something to do with Quartz and Haxel disappearing from the camp."

"What do you mean Quartz and Haxel disappeared?" Marett shouted.

"Exactly that," Shann-Rell said. "No one can find them!"

"Orren, Quartz, and Haxel gone!" the baron said, "That doesn't sound right!"

"No it doesn't," Anselm said, "but instead of standing about yammering, we ought to be searching. That's why my Jasper was so desparate to get here."

"She's just an animal," one of the knights said.

"She's not just an animal," Iskander replied. "There's something special about
her, and Perceval and I were blind not to have seen it earlier. She surely knows something about our friends' disappearance."

Jasper, however, collapsed on the floor.

The baron turned to one of his officers. "Sergeant Riveldi, get water for this animal," he said. Sergeant Riveldi saluted and left the building.

The red mastiff walked over to Jasper and whimpered. Jasper grabbed the dog's floppy ear in her mouth and made soft whinnying sounds. When she was finished, the dog barked at the assembled crowd and ran out of the room. He ran back in, and then ran out again. This he did several times.

"Jasper told my dog something," Shann-Rell said. "The donkey's come a long way and is too exhausted to lead us, but my dog can do it instead."

Sergeant Riveldi returned to the room with a bucket of water. "Sergeant," Baron Toynberg said. "This donkey is very important, and I need you to care for her."

"Yes sir," the sergeant said.

"Captain Domberg!" the baron shouted out.

A tall, blond knight appeared at the door, "Yes sir?"

"Get twelve cavalrymen," the baron said. "This dog is intent on taking us somewhere, so we'll be riding after it. Get horses for Marett, Perceval, and Iskander. Anselm will ride with me on my horse. Give Marett a double saddle so Shann-Rell can ride with her. If anyone can understand the dog, it will be her."

Only minutes later, the assembled group rode through the city. They followed the red mastiff through the city streets. As they went, they yelled at the city folk to get out of the way, something the people of Sherbass, like the folk of all cities at that time, were good at doing.

They galloped out of the gates, down the hill, and across the old bridge. When the red dog reached the other side, he let out a yelp. Shann-Rell's falcon swooped out of the trees with a loud screech.

"My bird's helping too," the yelian leader said.

"My ravens will follow," Perceval let out a shrill whistle. The seven large, black birds flew into view. They landed on Perceval's shoulders. He closed his eyes and made clucking sounds at them. The ravens flew after the falcon, and the dog raced off into the woods, following the birds.

"Let's go!" Baron Toynberg spurred his horse after the mastiff.

The dog ran through thickets and woodlands, and the horses thundered after him. The company rode through carpets of lesser celandine and wood anemone, and past peasant villages. They splashed through the streams that fed into the Din River, and ascended and descended one grassy hill after another. Every now and then, Shann-Rell's falcon would circle back toward the riders with a screech, and Perceval's ravens would fly, cawing, after her. The mastiff never let any of the birds out of his sight.

After several hours, they reached the top of a hill, where the red dog yelped, and the falcon and the ravens circled about. Marett was the first rider to reach the summit. She looked down and let out an anguished cry.

Quartz lay on the hillside in a petrified state. His left arm was twisted behind his back at an unnatural angle, and the cracks in his body had worsened. It almost looked as though pieces of him were falling off.

They rode down the hill until they reached him.

"What happened?" Anselm cried out in anguish.

"He's dead," Shann-Rell wept. "If only we'd healed him of all his cracks before! But we were caught up in helping my people and the humans of Sherbass. We didn't even think of Quartz and his needs."

The baron and his knights bowed their heads in respect.

"Quartz never complained about anything," Anselm said. "He always put the needs of others before himself, to his own detriment, and now he's dead."

"Relax, everyone," Marett said. "Quartz is not dead. He may be seriously injured, but when sholls die, they crumble to dust, and all you find are their clothes."

"You listened well to Grandfather's teachings," Perceval said with pride.

"Why didn't he cover himself with that garment of his?" the baron asked.

"My guess is that he was too badly injured to wrap himself up in his skooch," Marett said. "He couldn't do it, and when the sun came up, he was petrified."

"Who could have done this?" Anselm shrieked.

"The only thing that could inflict such damage on a sholl is a gwell," Marett said, "so Jurgan did this, but before we deal with him, we must heal Quartz, and for that we have to wait for nightfall. I just don't know what he was thinking, chasing Jurgan with no one but Jasper for company."

There was a loud screech. Shann-Rell's falcon swooped downward, barely missing the baron's head. The ravens followed close behind. They dive-bombed the riders again and again, and the mastiff howled.

"What's the problem with these birds?" the baron asked.

"They want us to follow them again," Shann-Rell said.

"Let's go," the baron commanded.

They galloped across the meadows for several miles, following the dog and the birds. Suddenly, Marett yelled, "Sweet astra!"

She leapt off her horse and knelt beside Haxel. The zhiv lay in a pool of his own blood. A crossbow bolt protruded from his chest. He was still alive, but unconscious.

Everyone let out cries of dismay as they pulled their horses up to where Haxel lay.

"Anselm! Shann-Rell!" Marett said. "I need help."

The old man and the yelius dismounted. Shann-Rell pulled Nebi out of her
pocket.

"Oh, if only we'd brought Thraix along," she cried out. "I'm a Magg, and thus, not suited for this stone."

"Never mind that," Marett pulled the crossbow bolt out of Haxel's chest. It had missed the zhiv's heart by three inches. "We'll do what we can." She took the stone from Shann-Rell and touched it to Haxel's skin. Anselm placed his hand over hers, and Shann-Rell placed her hand over his. All three of them concentrated.

Marett became very sick, which caused her hex-seed to expand. She felt the presence of Anselm's hex-seed. For a moment, it seemed like the two gray entities would join together, which would be horrible. Nonetheless, they both concentrated, as did Shann-Rell, and the hex-seeds shrank once again.

Haxel's tissues knitted together and became whole, and then his leathery skin closed up. The zhiv coughed and opened his eyes. "Honored baron," Marett said, trying to keep herself from vomiting. "Bring food and water."

The baron held his water skin to Haxel's lips. The zhiv drank.

"Jurgan has Master Orren," Haxel said in a weak voice. "They must have knocked him out. He was bundled up, and Jurgan was riding with him. There were four other humans too, all on horses."

"Did you recognize any of them?" Iskander asked.

"There was a female named Cinda," Haxel said. "Isn't that the woman Perceval hates so much?" The zhiv then fell back into unconsciousness again.

"Darga Cinda Lowny," Perceval said. "My friends, this is not good. Jurgan has obviously made an unholy alliance with the Drammites."

"The only reason Jurgan took Orren was so he could get his filthy paws on Hesh," Anselm said.

"But Jurgan's *himself* a chosen person now," Marett objected. "He could have killed Orren and taken Hesh from his body. No, Anselm. Jurgan and the Drammites want him for some other purpose."

"Just a moment," Captain Domberg held up a hand. "Take a look at these hoof prints in the dust. They're small horses—most likely purebred Midani, prized for their speed. And see this crossbow bolt? It's of the variety used by skilled cavalry archers, whose aim is deadly accurate. If they'd wanted to kill Haxel, they would have had no trouble shooting him right through the heart."

"And Jurgan could have easily killed Quartz with his gwell," Perceval added. "But he merely left him incapacitated."

"So they *didn't* want to kill Haxel or Quartz," Baron Toynberg said. "They merely wanted to get Orren away from his friends, which means that they won't sacrifice Orren; they need him alive."

"They wanted to prevent Haxel and Quartz from influencing him, surely," Iskander said. "My friends, I think there can be no doubt that Orren was taken by the Prett Drammites."

"To revive his fulfillment of the liberator prophecy!" Marett said, "They're going to try mind twisting Orren again, far away from the support of his fellow Web members!"

"They'll have plans for all five of you," the baron said, "but for now, Orren is the one they want, probably because he's the leader of your quest."

"We have no choice but to follow them!" Anselm cried out. "We've got to find Orren and save him!"

"True," Marett said, "but since the Web is now too weak for us to find him with, the only person who can do it is Quartz, because of his bonding ability. Let's get back to Quartz, and when night falls, we'll heal him."

The baron gave the order, and everyone mounted his or her horse. Captain Domberg carried Haxel over his shoulder, and together they galloped back toward the petrified form of Quartz. The captain placed Haxel on the ground, and Marett, Anselm, and Shann-Rell all dismounted.

"Perceval, Iskander, seeing as you two are always sending messages to each other by raven, are either one of you carrying ink?" the baron asked.

"Yes," they both said, each one pulling little inkwells out of their pouches. "We now go everywhere with ink."

"Terrific," the baron said. "Captain Domberg, come here and bare your arm."

The captain did as he was bid. Baron Toynberg picked a strand of grass, and dipped it into Iskander's inkwell. He then signed his name on the captain's bare arm, after which he took a brass signet ring out of his pocket, and handed it to the knight.

"Captain Domberg, you've served me well for years," the baron said. "So as of today you're no longer a captain, but a colonel."

"Thank you, my lord," Colonel Domberg said with an enthusiastic salute.

"Keep your arm bare until the ink dries," the baron said. "The signet ring is an official sign of my favor, and the signature on your arm will be recognized by other officers, as my own. You're now in charge of my army, Colonel. I'm riding with seven of my men, to accompany Haxel, Marett, Quartz, Anselm, Shann-Rell, and Perceval, wherever they may go. We've got to ride as fast as we can if we're to have any hope of saving Orren from what could be a fate worse than death.

"Seven men will go back to Sherbass with you. You need to mobilize my army, both inside the city and outside. Bring my men after me, and the yelia as well, and don't forget Jasper. Perceval's ravens will keep you informed as to our whereabouts. Also, escort Iskander back to Sherbass. He's greatly needed there."

"Goodbye Marett," Iskander embraced Marett and gave her a tender kiss on the cheek.

Marett hugged him warmly. Tears streamed down her cheeks, and her throat felt like it had a lump in it. She turned her back, so she would not see Iskander ride away with the colonel and his men.

# A DUBIOUS PROPOSAL

Orren knew he was a prisoner, and that his captors were taking him somewhere. He was aware that he was riding a horse, his limp body supported by someone much larger than he.

Most of the time he slept, awakening only at mealtimes. The fare given to him consisted of bland gruel mixed with beans and bacon, with water to wash it down. He ate what was given to him, despite being aware that it was drugged; his only alternative was to starve. His vision was blurred, and he could not sit straight.

He welcomed sleep, because that was when the mysterious voice hummed in his head. When he was awake, he was plagued by worries about the friends he might never see again. Such gloomy thoughts caused his hex-seed to expand.

This state of affairs went on for…He had no idea how long.

One day, he woke up to discover that he was lying on something solid. The air was warm, and a pleasant breeze blew, carrying with it the scent of blossoms and the sea. He heard waves crashing against rocks, and the squawking of gulls.

The large person who had been riding with him, propped him up into a sitting position. Orren opened his eyes, and saw that he was sitting upon stonemasonry. In front of and behind him, were crenellated walls about six feet high. He figured that he was on a parapet of some sort.

"Ah," an elderly man's voice spoke, "our honored guest is awake."

Orren turned sharply to his right and saw a red-robed dargun whom he had never met. The Drammite leader was slightly older than Anselm, with a head that was bald, save for a few wisps of gray hair. He had a round face, and sharp, blue eyes. He sat on the parapet floor facing Orren and his captor, and smiled.

"Greetings, Orren Randolphus," the dargun said. "It's an honor to meet you at last."

"Do you always talk to folks before you sacrifice them?" Orren spat.

The dargun howled with laughter. He then shook his head and wiped his eyes. "Dear, dear me," he said. "You don't know who I am, do you?"

"No, I don't."

"I'm Dargun Philip Prett, the leader of the truest followers of our Blood Master Dramm—the ones who never lost faith in you, our Blood Master's liberator."

"Not this again!" Orren shouted. "I'm *not* your liberator!"

"Yes, you are," the dargun smiled. "Dargun Telleri knew it instantly, and he also recognized your witnesses, but he and Dargun Dromburdt made the fatal error of asking you to kill your witnesses. That's when they lost not only your loyalty, but also our Blood Master's favor. Thus it was that the order fell into the hands of that foul usurper, Eric Rodrick, who backed your brother."

"Now we have a chance to set things right. Drammites are being hunted down from the Greymantles to the borders of Salin. We need a sanctuary for our order, and thanks to this man," he pointed at Orren's captor, "we have one."

Orren looked over his shoulder. His heart froze, for he saw that his captor, the man who had held him during the long horse ride, was none other than Jurgan, the big, black-bearded bandit chief.

"Hail, Orren Randolphus, liberator," Jurgan said with what Orren knew was false piety.

Orren felt for the pouch at his waist, but it was empty.

Jurgan chuckled. He pulled Hesh out of his own pocket, and showed it off with an ugly grin. Orren tried to grab it, but Jurgan seized his hand in a vice-like grip that made the boy cry out in pain.

"Release him!" Dargun Prett commanded the big bandit. "Is that any way to treat our liberator?"

Jurgan let Orren go. The boy clutched at his aching wrist.

"What did you bring me here for?" he asked.

"Simple," Dargun Prett said. "You're going to fulfill the prophecy of our Blood Master. It won't be long before your friends—the goblin, the Duraline, the old man, and the giant—will come to rescue you. We'll allow them to join you, for they're your witnesses, as well as the members of your Bearers' Web. The goblin and the giant are the beast witnesses, and the girl is a noble witness. The old man I'm not sure about."

"He's noble too," Orren lied, mainly to protect Anselm's life in the event that the old man fell into Dargun Prett's hands. "He's the prince of a bunch of Jangurth tribes."

"So there you have it," the dargun said, "and Jurgan here is a witness too."

"He's *really* a beast witness," Orren said.

Dargun Prett laughed again. "As it happens," he said, "Jurgan comes from Salinese nobility. Throwing in his lot with the Order of Dramm makes him a perfect example of 'penitent nobility'. And speaking of penance, there are others here who you might recognize."

He clapped his hands three times.

It was then that Orren saw the stairwell, which was situated almost directly behind where Jurgan sat. Three individuals ascended the steps. Orren's mouth dropped open when he recognized Cinda Lowny, Stefan Drugger, and Ferrus Staffords.

"What are they doing here?" Orren demanded.

"Cinda is doing penance," the dargun said. "For she attempted to kill you and the Duraline. Now she'll serve you for the rest of your life." The ginger-haired female darga stared at the ground as the dargun spoke.

"Stefan Drugger too, must do penance," the dargun said, "for he was responsible for destroying Skaps, where you and your Duraline friend stayed." Drugger, a small, balding man who sweated profusely, also stared at the ground.

"And Staffords, who Berthus left in charge of the Corcadine while he was gone, must do penance for how he treated you during your childhood."

Ferrus Staffords had changed since Orren had last seen him. Orren had always known him as a huge, obese man with an unshaven face and patched, filthy clothes. He was the peddler for Randolphus Manor's pork products, and was constantly abused by Berthus. Unable to vent his frustration on his lord, he instead took it out on anyone whose status was lower than his own, be it Orren, a swinery worker, or any other powerless individual.

Since then, Staffords had lost a great deal of weight, and was thus no longer large. He had far more gray hair than he used to, and more wrinkles. His clothes were now fancy, though wine-stained. He looked battered, but he was defiant. Unlike Lowny and Drugger, he glared at Orren maliciously.

Jurgan stood up and punched the peddler so hard, he fell to the ground.

"Show respect toward the liberator!" the bandit snarled.

Staffords glared again, whereupon Jurgan lifted him up, and hit him again and again, before dropping him to the ground, where he kicked him in his side. Staffords gasped for air and clutched at his stomach.

"You can't treat me this way!" the peddler cried out, once he caught his breath. "Iranda said you have to respect me and be kind to me!"

"Iranda?" Orren demanded. "You mean Berthus's woman?"

"Yes," the dargun said. "She's here too. Men, take this filthy piece of rubbish away!" Three Drammite warriors roughly dragged Staffords back down the steps. The peddler cursed his tormentors in the foulest of language.

"I know what you're thinking," the dargun said. "Staffords' penance will fail. But we have plans for him. You see, Orren, ever since Staffords has been in our presence, we've been abusing him. You must admit that he deserves it."

Orren conceded that Dargun Prett had a point.

"Only one person treats him nicely, and that's Iranda. Eventually, Staffords will desire revenge upon all of us, and Iranda will offer it to him in exchange for something."

"What?"

"That he become her proxy," the dargun said. "You see, Lady Iranda is a rare type of witch. Her kind cannot handle a gwell, so in order for her to do so, she needs to possess someone else who can. As it turns out, when Berthus appointed Staffords to rule the Corcadine, he was a little bit drunk, and rather emotional about leaving the place where he grew up with Richard as his guardian. His parting words to Staffords were, 'be sure you take care of Richard's homeland, for Richard was a true father to me, and you…you're like my brother.' In that moment of weakness, Berthus conferred 'chosenness' upon Staffords. I know all of this, because Iranda told it to me, and Berthus told it to her."

"But all Berthus ever did was beat Staffords," Orren said.

"Yes, he did," the dargun nodded. "However, Staffords was essentially taking Richard's place as steward of the manor, and *that* fact pulled Berthus's heartstrings. The point is, Staffords can handle a gwell now, and Iranda will use his desire for revenge, to trick him into letting her possess him. When she does, he'll lose his free will, and she'll be able to handle a gwell through him. You need a sixth member for your Web, Orren. Iranda would do that well."

"I'm not letting that evil witch into my Web!" Orren was horrified.

"Have you ever considered the possibility that Iranda was on your side the whole time?" the dargun asked. "She was the one who persuaded the Rodrick faction of the Order of Dramm, to join Berthus's side. In so doing, she created the conditions by which Berthus had to destroy his main allies, the Framguth lords. Iranda was the one who tricked Berthus into not killing Haxel, and then she tricked him again, into not killing the three of you when you fell into his power. In the end, Berthus realized all of this, and kicked her out. You owe Iranda a great deal, and you should make her the sixth member of your Web. She'll have Staffords completely under her control.

"Under this new arrangement, everyone wins," the dargun continued. "We Drammites, who are being hunted down across LeFain, get a sanctuary. Jurgan and these others gain the penance their souls so desperately need. You and your friends get to live in finery and luxury for the rest of your lives, and in each other's company, while the Order of Dramm serves your every need. Jurgan will even hand Magna back to the sholl. Your Web will become complete with the addition of Iranda to it. Your lives will be peaceful and happy here in this wonderful place."

"But where are we?" Orren asked. "What place is this?"

"Stand up," Dargun Prett said, "and take a look."

Orren picked himself up and, leaning against the parapet wall, looked out.

He saw waves battering against the foundations of the battlement. The ocean spread out before him, boundless, before disappearing on the horizon. He looked toward the land and saw a little beach, and the forests of early spring. There were large oaks, elms, and beech trees, their boughs bright green, with tiny leaves and millions upon millions of catkins. Orren could also see pear and crab-apple trees, all of them covered in snowy blossoms.

Great mountains rose behind the forests, and these, too, were covered in the greens, whites, and pinks of early spring. Small, wispy clouds had anchored themselves to the sharp summits; they were the only clouds present in the otherwise clear, blue sky. Far off in the distance, Orren could barely make out a line of dark blue that could only be another part of the sea.

He knew exactly where he was.

"The Corcadine!" he exclaimed, with surprise, outrage, and nostalgia, all rolled into a confused emotional muddle. "You've brought me back to the Corcadine, and we're standing on Berthus's wall!"

"That's right, Orren," Dargun Prett said. "Welcome home."

"We rode for ten days to get here," Jurgan said. "All that time, you were unconscious, except of course, when we fed you."

"It takes much more than ten days to get from Sherbass to the Corcadine," Orren said.

"Not if you have Magna," Jurgan beamed with pride. He took the yellow gwell out of his pocket and caressed it. "Using this stone, I learned to create winds that pushed our horses, making them move much faster than they normally could. It wasn't an easy thing to do, and it tired me out, but it did the trick."

"And now, Orren Randolphus," the dargun said, "the time has come to return to the home and inheritance that was always rightfully yours. Let us leave this wall and return to Randolphus Manor, the home of our liberator."

Many thoughts raced through Orren's mind as Dargun Prett and Jurgan ushered him off the wall and onto the ground, whereupon they boarded an ox cart. As Orren sat down, thoughts, emotions, and contradictions swirled around in his head.

True, the future that Dargun Prett offered sounded attractive, but Orren still hated the Order of Dramm and everything it stood for. He would never forget the fact that the cult had ordered him to sacrifice his friends. He recalled Haxel and Marett describing how Ferthan the miller had been slaughtered. Then there was all the suffering that the cult had inflicted upon the people of Skaps.

There was not much he could do now, because he was completely under the Drammites' power...again. He had to play along as though he were accepting Dargun Prett's offer. However, to return to the Drammites was to betray Kenner and Fama, Rolf and Meisie, Iskander, Perceval, and so many others he had come to love. It meant turning his back on Baron Toynberg and his brave knights, as well as Shann-Rell and the yelia.

And, what of Jurgan? Orren did not believe for one minute that the big bandit chief had become a Drammite. Jurgan probably had a nefarious scheme of his own. For all Orren knew, he had filled the Corcadine with thugs and pirates, and was merely awaiting the right moment to strike both Orren *and* the Drammites.

And, what of Iranda? Could she really have been on Orren's side all along? Whenever he had encountered her, he found her to be utterly evil. Who was this Iranda anyway, and what did it mean that she was a 'rare type of witch'?

Besides for all of this, there was the matter of the Ghouls' Curse, which he had not mentioned to Dargun Prett. Twenty-five days were left until it took effect, and there was nothing Orren could do to stave it off.

All of these thoughts and emotions bombarded his mind, and caused the hex-seed to expand until it almost filled his brain. He clutched at his throbbing head. Surely all was lost!

*All is not lost.* The voice in his mind spoke. *Things are rough right now, Orren, and they'll continue to be so for the next few weeks, but they're not lost.*

*I can't think of anything,* Orren said. *Can you?*

*You have an important ally here in the Corcadine,* the voice said. *Or did you forget the one who inspired you to undertake this quest in the first place?*

*Carlenda!* Orren remembered the healing woman of Stoneybeach.

*You need her,* the voice said. *The Drammites are going to try mind twist you, depriving you of sleep and necessary aspects of your diet, but Carlenda knows how to make drinks that can alleviate the effects of bad nutrition, and others that will give you deep sleep so you obtain more rest than you would if you just sleep normally.*

*But how am I to send her a message?* Orren asked. *The Drammites are gonna keep me closely watched, and they'll get suspicious if I send for her.*

*There are other ways,* the voice said. *Look for help in the least likely place.*

*What does that mean?* Orren asked. *Why do you say so many unclear things? Who are you anyway, and why do you only speak to me and to Iskander?*

*Orren Randolphus,* the voice said. *I speak to all of your friends, though not directly, as I speak to you. Baron Toynberg receives my messages through contemplating the sacred teachings of his faith. Shann-Rell and the yelia follow me too, as do Haxel and Quartz, because the Sun Father, Moon Mother, and Tchafla all follow me. They're disciples of mine, so to speak.*

*Really?* Orren asked.

*Really,* the voice said. *Shann-Rell once spoke of the Sun Father's spirit. Quartz mentioned the Moon Mother's spirit, and Haxel has talked about Tchafla's spirit.*

*Yes,* Orren said. *I remember all of them saying those things.*

*I'm that spirit, Orren,* the voice said, *the spirit that guides the astra, gods of the light. Marett, Perceval, and Anselm follow me too, for I am the Wisdom Core of the Duralines and the Guiding Light of the Jangurth. Iskander may be a Duraline as well, but his upbringing was contaminated by Drammite dogmas, thus necessitating my direct intervention in his life, something you too needed after Richard's death.*

*Oh,* was all Orren could think of to say.

*You have to figure out everything on your own now,* the voice continued. *That's something you've proven more than capable of doing. You can prevail over your enemies despite the odds and the Ghouls' Curse. If this quest fails, or if you and your friends become ghouls, it will be because you or your friends have given into your weaknesses. Despite what Narx said, you won't be ghouls forever, but it will last a long time, and you'll turn more people into ghouls during that time. Believe me, you don't want to become ghouls; it's about as bad a fate as can possibly befall a person. That's why you, Orren, must make sure that neither yourself, nor Haxel, Marett, Quartz, nor Anselm, gives in to the temptations that will inevitably, up until the Moment of Reckoning, present themselves.*

*This is the last time I will speak directly to you, Orren, because you are now equipped to find your own way. However, that does not mean I won't be with you. I'll be there to provide you with strength and courage; you need only ask.*

*Sleep now, Orren Randolphus, and know that no matter how insane and warped things get, I love you and am always with you.*

# HELP FROM AN
# UNLIKELY SOURCE

Orren was given a luxurious room on the third floor of Randolphus Manor. He slept on a fine, goose-down bed, and had a spectacular view of the eastern ocean, the sea cliffs, and the Tidesdale harbor. The Drammites catered for his every need.

His days, however, were very long, and they were spent being indoctrinated by Dargun Prett and Darga Drugger. This lasted for hour after hour. It kept his hex-seed strong, to the extent that he often lost his ability to see color. Despite the beauty of his surroundings and the comfort of his lodgings, his world became gray and bleak. It was all he could do to keep himself from falling into a depression. Moreover, he did not get the sleep he needed, and what the Drammites fed him, while tasty, was not nutritious enough for his needs. They were clearly trying to mind-twist him again, exactly as the voice had predicted would happen.

A few times, the barrage proved too much, and Orren allowed his temper to get the better of him. When that happened, Dargun Prett had Jurgan whip him savagely, so that he bled, and he was then thrown into the swinery for a few hours. One night they forced him to sleep there, in the mud and muck. The next morning, the dargun brought him out, cleaned him up, and allowed him to return to his luxurious chamber.

"I hated doing that to you," the Drammite leader said, "but you need to learn proper respect for our Blood Master and his servants."

It was while he was in the swinery that he learned that all the swinery workers who had worked for Berthus before had been sacrificed to Dramm, along with their families. Human sacrifices were taking place daily in nearby Tidesdale, and sometimes, when the wind blew southward, Orren smelled the stench. The new swinery workers were polite but hollow-eyed, for they had no hope. Orren asked them if they could contact Carlenda for him, but they replied that they could not, for they and their families dwelt in stockaded camps, and Jurgan's thugs monitored their movements.

Orren's own movements were also constantly watched, and he was heavily guarded. He had little privacy, because someone was with him all the time, even when he slept. Sometimes it was Darga Lowny and other times, Darga Drugger or Darga Schuenn, who was Dargun Prett's right-hand man. Orren therefore had no opportunity or means to send a message to Carlenda.

Sneaking Carlenda into Randolphus Manor, he felt, would not be difficult, especially if it were done at night. All it would take would be for Carlenda to be disguised as a Drammite. Even if the guards at the manor gate demanded to see her face, the scheme would work, for there were several older female dargas who looked quite a bit like Carlenda. The problem was actually getting the message to the healing woman, that he needed her help.

Late on the tenth night of his captivity, Orren was awakened by scuffling sounds. He saw a shadow moving about in the darkness. He was about to ask who was there, when he felt a weight on his back, and a knife at his throat.

"Shut your mouth," Orren's heart sank when he recognized Staffords' voice.

Staffords roughly pulled Orren's hands behind his back, and bound them with cords, which bit into his flesh. The peddler then lifted him to his feet, and kept the knife at his throat.

"Get moving," he said, "and if you utter one sound, it'll be your last."

Obediently, Orren walked in silence. Staffords marched him out of the room, past the prostrate forms of two toughs, who had clearly been knocked unconscious. They entered a doorway that Orren had not seen before, and descended a hidden staircase, which led outside. The wind blew through Randolphus Manor, carrying the scent of crab apple and cherry blossoms, and a hint of incinerated human flesh. The stars and a sickle-shaped moon shone brightly in the sky above. A barn owl screeched as it flew over their heads.

Staffords brought Orren to another staircase that cut along the side of the manor house, where the building's edge touched the southern cliff. They ascended until they reached a pathway, which was narrow, because tall bushes hemmed it in. They had to walk in single file. Not for one second did Staffords pull the knife away from Orren's throat. Presently, they reached a rocky ledge, which hung out over the darkened sea, hundreds of feet below.

"Like this place, swine boy?" Staffords' sarcastic tone was full of rage. "I've come to know every square inch of this manor, including its secret passageways. I promise you, no one will hear you, if you scream for help."

The peddler turned around and punched the side of the cliff. He then started to rant.

"It all revolves around *you*, doesn't it? *You're* the liberator. The Drammites have all their hopes pinned on *you*. Well, not anymore, 'cause I'm about to spoil their plans. I've had enough of being beaten and abused, first by Berthus, and then by Jurgan and the Drammites. I'm a noble, I am…from an old Albinese family, but since the mainland Framguth invaded Albina and took our lands from us, we had to wander about as traveling peddlers. Then things got too dangerous on the mainland, which is why I came to this nasty little peninsula, only to end up being punched and kicked around.

"Before Berthus left the Corcadine, he said in his drunken state, that I was his brother. Why? Because I was now in charge of this place, which was Richard's home. I became ruler here, but I was a kind ruler, and the people came to love me. Richard's name had been mentioned, so I took care of what was his. Still, Berthus could never be a brother of mine. I would willingly throw him off a cliff if I ever got a chance to. And that's exactly what I'm about to do to you."

"Richard wouldn't want you to do this," Orren said, thinking fast.

Staffords spun Orren around and pressed his face close. Orren nearly gagged from the reek of beer on the peddler's breath.

"You're not worthy to speak Richard's name, swine boy," Staffords snarled, though Orren could see, by the moonlight, a soft expression in the peddler's eyes, at the mention of Richard's name. Something clicked in Orren's mind, and he remembered what the mysterious voice had said. *Look for help in the least likely place.*

"Staffords, I'm in your power now," Orren said. "If you want to kill me, I can't stop you. But it won't help you. You'll go back to the manor, and the Drammites and Jurgan will still treat you badly. You'll be under their power, just as I'm under yours. And you'll have killed the one person who could have stopped them."

Staffords started to tremble. His grip on Orren slackened. "What do you mean you can stop them?" he asked.

Orren patiently told Staffords about the Bearers' Web, though he did not inform Staffords of what Dargun Prett had told him—that Berthus had inadvertently conferred chosen status upon the peddler. He informed Staffords about the Ghouls' Curse and the Moment of Reckoning. Finally, he revealed what Iranda's plans were. The peddler went pale and shook all over.

"You're not lying," Staffords said. "Somehow I know you're not. I've always wondered why Iranda was the only one to treat me well, but at the same time, she worked closely with those who tormented me. It makes sense now."

"You're not a thoughtless killer," Orren said in a soft voice. "If you were, then you would have thrown me off the cliff without telling me all about yourself first. You have simply put your anger on the wrong person, because you're confused."

Staffords fell to his knees. "But I know no other way to be," he said in a shaking voice. "And I don't know what to do to stop all of this."

"I only have fourteen days left until the Moment of Reckoning," Orren said. "If me and my Web members can't get the six stones back into the council head's hands by that time, then we'll become ghouls. If that happens, Jurgan and the Drammites will become unstoppable."

A desperate, pleading expression appeared on Staffords' face, and Orren saw an individual who was consumed not by hatred, but by fear.

"What can I do?" The peddler's voice was meek.

"Well for one thing, you can stop bullying folks," Orren said. "I saw the way Berthus treated you. He bullied you, and then what did you do? You found anyone with less power than you, and bullied them. You took out your anger on folks who did nothing to you, and who couldn't fight back. That's what you're doing to me now.

"I always thought you were just a brute, Staffords, but you loved Richard, as I did. Richard brought out the best in all of us, even Berthus. When Berthus put you in charge of the Corcadine, you could have treated the folks here really badly, but you didn't, and for one reason only; because Richard's name came up.

"When folks who bully you have power, you become a bully. Once they're gone, you're not a bully anymore, because that's not who you really are. Now the bullies are back. Staffords, it's time to turn around and stop the bullies who are beating on *you* in the first place."

"But how?" Staffords pleaded.

"I'm so tired," Orren said. "The Drammites don't give me enough sleep or the foods that I need. Dargun Prett is trying to break me down and twist my mind so he can do what he wants with me. I can't escape, because they watch out for me everywhere. I don't know how much longer I'll be able to fight this, especially since the hex-seed in my mind is making me weaker and weaker each day. I need someone who can give me a special drink or something like that, which can help my body deal with what's being done to me. The only person who can do that is Carlenda."

"Richard's sister?" Staffords said with reverence. "The great healing woman from Stoneybeach? You know her?"

"She helped me escape Berthus," Orren said. "And she can help me get deeper, more restful sleep out of the few hours the Drammites allow me. She can heal the cuts and bruises from my punishment. I need her, Staffords. Do you think you can get her for me?"

"Yes," Staffords said, "and I could give her some dargas' robes and a veil, and get her in here. If the guards at the gate demand to see her face, they'll think she's Darga Tullini, or Darga Batricia, or maybe even Darga da Metrina."

Orren smiled.

Staffords had, by himself, come up with Orren's own plan!

"Just give me two or three days to find Carlenda and bring her here," the peddler said. He cut through the cords that bound Orren's hands.

"Everything you said about me was right, swine b—I mean Orren. You don't deserve what I did to you over the years, and for that I'm...I'm sorry. I would bring you with me if I could... you know, help you escape, but with their eyes on you all the time, I dare not even *try* get you past the gate. The Drammites don't pay much attention to me, 'cause they see me as a stupid drunkard. They think I'll just blindly walk into Iranda's trap, and become her puppet, but I'll show them! Anyway, before I go, I'll do something that will take the Drammites' minds off of you for a while, and maybe you'll get some rest."

Not long after Staffords returned Orren to his room, Orren smelled something burning. Within minutes, he heard crackling flames, and people running around screaming and barking out orders. A few dargas came to check on him. Once satisfied that their young liberator was fine, they left to join in the effort to put out the fire.

For the next four days, nobody paid Orren much attention, besides for checking up on him, and bringing him food and drink. They didn't always keep a close watch on him, so he was able to raid the kitchen to get better food.

By listening to their conversation, Orren discovered that all the manor's outbuildings had been consumed in the conflagration, and that the swinery had been severely damaged. It took a great deal of effort to stamp out the flames, and now the Drammites were trying to rebuild everything that had been destroyed.

Clearly, Staffords, who Berthus had always referred to as that 'fat, useless lout,' was not so useless after all! Underneath his brutal, bullying exterior, there was a core of goodness. It only needed someone to tap into it.

Four nights later, under the cover of thick fog, Orren watched as Staffords entered the room accompanied by a person with the black robes and veil of a darga. The newcomer removed her veil, and the boy was overjoyed to see Carlenda's wrinkled, warm face.

"Good evening, Orren," Carlenda said.

"Madam Carlenda," Orren replied, "Thank you for coming."

"Delighted to. I've heard of the great things you've done. You heeded my words and saved us all from your half brother."

"But now Jurgan's got two gwellen," Orren said, "and the Drammites are helping him."

"Then it's up to you to find a way to defeat them," Carlenda said. "After all, you devised a plan to get me here."

"I've got Staffords to thank for that," Orren said.

The peddler then did something Orren had never seen him do. He smiled.

"He's not so bad," Carlenda patted Staffords on the shoulder. "When he became governor, we thought he'd simply carry out Berthus's wishes, but he left folks alone, reduced taxes, and even assisted us residents of Stoneybeach in rebuilding our town."

Orren smiled. Carlenda's arrival could not have come at a better time, for the repairs to the swinery and outbuildings, were nearing completion. It would not be long before Orren's 'reeducation' resumed. The boy's hex-seed had also grown back, particularly with the knowledge that a mere ten days remained until the Moment of Reckoning.

Carlenda drew a large sack from within her shapeless dargas' robes. "In here I've got herbs, poultices, and elixirs," she said. "Whatever else I need is easily obtainable in Tidesdale." She pulled a water skin out of her sack, and gave it to Orren. It was full of goat's milk that had been enriched and flavored with various herbs. The boy drank deeply. He felt the liquid course through his body, giving him strength.

"Now lie down," the old woman said, "and relax."

Orren did as she asked. With Staffords' help, Carlenda scrubbed his body with a thick cloth. She then applied poultices to cuts he had received from the whippings Dargun Prett had administered. When the old woman was finished, she lovingly brushed a calloused hand through his hair. Orren looked up at her adoringly. She was so much like Richard! Tears streamed down his cheeks.

"It's OK," Carlenda said. "You've been through a lot."

At that point, Orren told her all about his adventures, from the time he fled the Corcadine, to his abduction. He talked about Haxel, Marett, Quartz, and Anselm, as well as the other good people he and his friends had encountered. He then explained to her the phenomenon of the Bearers' Web, and described the Ghouls' Curse as well. Finally, he spoke about the mysterious voice.

When he was finished, Carlenda ruffled his hair and said, "What a terrific boy you are, so brave, loyal, and intelligent, not to mention handsome. No wonder my brother loved you so much. Now goodnight and get some sleep. I must leave this place, but I'll be back soon."

Orren's "reeducation" continued the very next morning. He was dragged out of bed, and Dargun Prett and Darga Drugger preached to him. They bombarded him with questions about the Blood Master and his worship. Orren decided that the best thing to do was to make it seem as though the mind-twisting was succeeding. By the end of the day he was worn out, but the herbs and potions given to him by Carlenda enabled him to bear it. Late at night, Staffords snuck Carlenda into the manor once again. The old woman put more poultices on Orren's skin, and administered more of her potent drink.

This state of affairs continued unchanged for six days. On the sixth night, Jurgan, Dargun Prett, Dargas Drugger and Lowny, and Iranda, all came to Orren's room. The boy looked at them with a blank expression.

"Good news, liberator," Dargun Prett said. "Your friends are on their way."

"They are?" Orren felt a surge of hope.

"Yes," the dargun said. "They're traveling with the baron of Alivadus and his knights, and are no more than two days away from reaching Berthus's Wall. We'll be there, awaiting them with a grand reception. Jurgan has placed a barrier of air in front of the wall, so no one can enter or leave the Corcadine, but he'll remove it in order that your four friends may enter."

Orren nodded.

His next project, he decided, was to convince the dargun to allow Shann-Rell to also enter. Then all the gwellen would be in one place, and the handing-over ritual could commence. Dargun Prett, however, did not seem like one easily influenced, which was a serious problem, because only four days remained until the Moment of Reckoning.

# INTO THE HANDS
# OF VILLAINS

Orren's friends were determined to get him back, to the extent that the Ghoul's Curse and the ever-present hex-seeds were no longer of paramount importance. Using the Web to connect with the boy was not possible, but as far as Quartz was concerned, this made no difference. The sholl's bond, a phenomenon unique to his race, enabled him to lead the other gwell-bearers, and the baron and several knights, right across the wilderness of LeFain. Perceval came with, as did Shann-Rell, and both of them brought their respective pets along. Quartz's leadership of the group, however, meant that all traveling had to be done by night.

The sholl led everyone out of Rivulein. They passed Quar-Qeissang, the extinct volcano that marked one end of the Forest of Doom, and entered the southern extremity of Sardalian. It was there that Sergeant Riveldi caught up with them. Jasper was with him, trotting alongside his horse. The little donkey had captured the officer's heart, and somehow he had learned to understand her. That was why he assisted her as best he could to move ahead of the rest of the army, and thus rejoin her friends.

Jasper had changed considerably. She was broad and heavyset now, and her tail had fused to her body. Her head was thick and bulbous, her hoofs splayed outward, and her fur had matted to form what could only be described as shingles. Not even Marett or Perceval could explain these bizarre changes.

Springtime was in full force. The larger trees were full of buds and catkins, while certain smaller species, such as wild pear and cherry, and rowans on the hillsides, had burst into a riot of blossoms. Woodlands, fields, and agricultural land were full of wildflowers, and the countryside echoed with birdsong. By night, the travelers saw herds of red and fallow deer, as well as wild boar and hedgehogs, and they heard owls hooting and nightjars calling.

Baron Toynberg's presence was a calming and stabilizing factor. Something about the man gave the four friends hope, as if he were able to make things right. The gwell-bearers found time to converse with him, and thus, they learned a great deal about Alivadus, including the affairs of state, and the threats that the barony faced. Perceval too, lightened the atmosphere with his sense of humor and his stories.

An unusual dynamic developed between Anselm and Shann-Rell. The old man and the yelian leader spent many hours together, conversing in the strange fluty tongue of the Sun-Children. At campsites, they often sat side by side, with Anselm's arm draped around Shann-Rell's shoulders. They also, however, bickered a great deal, and sometimes had screaming matches that disturbed everyone. After these fights, they avoided each other, refusing to speak or even make eye contact for a day or more. In the end, however, they always made up, enjoying one another's company until the next blow-up.

Spring rains hit the Sardalian, thus forcing the travelers to take refuge in copses. The Gotai River was bloated with runoff, and the squalls that swept across the countryside undermined embankments, turned meadows into bogs, and made traveling impossible. The weather dampened the gwell-bearers' moods, because for them, time was running out. However, it did provide enough of a pause in the traveling to enable the rest of the baron's army, along with the yelia, to catch up. This was fortunate, because bands of Drammites still plagued the countryside, rendering it unsafe for small groups. Many skirmishes broke out with the cultists, which always resulted in victory for the Alivadene knights.

Quartz led the army across the Gotai and into Innland. This was a friendly region, ruled by Framguth lords who had been converted to the Astralite faith. The baron and his army received support and much-needed provisions there. After a week of traveling through Innland, however, they reached the eastern Selera River. On the other side was Marchland, a chaotic region teeming with various noble households that were constantly at war with each other. The gwell-bearers learned that the Marchlanders were so belligerent that they could not even agree as to which river was the Selera. Both the river that bordered their land on the west *and* the one on the east shared the same name. In fact, one of the bloodiest wars in LeFain's history had been fought over that very issue.

"Totally irrational," Marett said, "and very human."

"You've got that right," Anselm said in such an emphatic tone that it caused peals of laughter on the part of anyone who knew the old man's story.

"That's why we must head south," the baron said. "We'll travel close to the border of my barony so we can stay out of all of this nonsense. I hope Quartz agrees to this."

"I do, Honored Baron," the sholl said. "It does not matter where we travel, as long as we continue westward, for that is where Master Orren has been taken."

They crossed a fortified bridge, which was garrisoned by Alivadene knights, and entered the Land Betwixt the Rivers. The next night, they were ambushed by forces loyal to Lord Ambrose Strank.

Strank had become one of the strongest Framguth lords in the region, ever since many of the others had been killed by Berthus. He had steadily taken over demesne after demesne until his realm straddled both sides of the western Selera. He did not care for the idea of Baron Toynberg crossing his lands with so many knights. The trouble, Colonel Domberg explained to the gwell-bearers, was that fighting Strank off would waste a great deal of precious time.

As soon as the colonel said these words, Quartz picked himself up, willed his skooch to go black, and disappeared into the darkness. A few hours later, messengers came to Baron Toynberg to inform him that Strank's forces had broken up. It seemed that a gigantic shadow had ploughed into the enemy camp, tossing men and horses about like straw, and causing terrible damage. Those who escaped fled in panic, certain that something demonic had fallen upon them.

A few minutes after this good news was received, Quartz reappeared in the baron's camp, very pleased with himself. He then led the army through the Land Betwixt the Rivers, in a southwesterly direction.

One night, after a full month of traveling, they reached Reenmark, a miniature state in the southern extremity of the Land Betwixt the Rivers. Lord Stephen Kleinholt of Reenmark was a vassal of Baron Toynberg, and he, accompanied by six of his cavalry knights, rode out to greet his lord's army. Kleinholt quickly dismounted from his horse, and prostrated himself on the ground.

"Rise, Stephen," Baron Toynberg said. "You look agitated. What's wrong?"

"Oh, my lord Baron," Lord Kleinholt said, "Thank Soter you've returned. The bandit warlord Jurgan, and the Order of Dramm, have taken over the Corcadine Peninsula. They've made it a haven for pirates and brigands. The waters around the Corcadine are as full of pirate ships as the air is with birds. Across the isthmus that connects the peninsula to the mainland, there's a magical barrier that I can only describe as solid air. Every day, the pirates carry out raids on the mainland, and I have reason to believe that some of the people they kidnap are sacrificed by the Drammites."

"So they've taken Orren back to the Corcadine!" Marett exclaimed.

"That air barrier—Jurgan made it for sure, using Magna," Anselm said. "How can we get across it? And the Moment of Reckoning is only three days away!"

Nobody answered, but all the gwell-bearers felt their hex-seeds throb. Worse, however, they started to feel each other's gray nodules of despair.

"This is as I feared," Marett clutched at her head.

"What?" Anselm asked.

"There are vague references to this in my family lore," Marett said. "People joined together in a magically sealed, mutual pact eventually gain the ability to sense one another's pain."

"This is a terrible thing that Narx has done to you," Shann-Rell said. "Your hex-seeds are starting to merge into one. It will become a big hex-circle that will encompass all your minds together. That's how you'll know the Ghouls' Curse is beginning to take effect."

Haxel let out an anguished cry. Quartz began to shiver, which was felt by all the others.

"Well thanks for all the good news," Anselm snapped at the yelian leader. "The next time I want a dose of positive thinking, I'll know just who to ask." Shann-Rell placed a reassuring hand on the old man's shoulder, but he rudely brushed it off.

"Stop it!" Perceval shouted. "You're not helping yourselves in this manner. I'm sure all of us would take some of your burden upon ourselves if we could. I know I would, but it simply isn't possible. It is therefore up to *you four* to maintain your focus."

"Listen to Perceval's wise words," Baron Toynberg said. "You must do what he says, if not for your sakes, then for Orren's. Don't you think that's what *Orren* would do if he were here with you right now?"

"Perceval and the baron are correct," Marett said. "Up until now, we've relied on Orren to provide the leadership. We became dependent upon him, and assumed that he would always be there to make plans for us. Well now he isn't, so it's our turn to do it instead. We owe him at least that much."

"Aye, that we do," Anselm said. "The four of us need to keep it together, even if our hex-seeds combine."

"We must try to think like the Master," Haxel added.

"There's much that we can learn from that remarkable young man," Anselm said, "and while we're at it, why don't we kick a few boulders and punch some trees?"

Everybody laughed. The humor lessened the hex-seeds somewhat.

A full night of travel brought the baron's army to the isthmus that connected the Corcadine to the mainland. Most of the flat, narrow piece of land was covered in dense, sweet-smelling woodlands. Box and tamarisk, strawberry trees, elders and spindle grew in profusion. Under the cover of this growth, the baron pitched camp, and Quartz bedded down, because the pillar of dawn was visible over the eastern sea.

When the sun came up, Haxel, Marett, Anselm, Baron Toynberg, Perceval, and Shann-Rell climbed a hillock that, while low, afforded a good view of the isthmus. The sea was perfectly visible on both sides, and about two miles to the south, was Berthus's Wall, looming dark and forbidding, and straddling the entire breadth of the isthmus, from one shore to the other. It was not the wall of stone that worried everyone, however, but the wall they could *not* see—the magical air barrier that Jurgan had created.

"M'lord!" Colonel Domberg ascended the hillock with a mousy little Gothma man in a straw hat. "This is Bolo. He's come from Jurgan and Dargun Prett, bearing a message."

"Let's hear it," the baron said.

Bolo bowed respectfully. "I bear greetings, Noble Baron of Alivadus, from the new Lord of the Corcadine, Jurgan de Burnoisse, and Dargun Philip Prett, the leader of the Order of Dramm. Lord Jurgan and Dargun Prett also respectfully greet the esteemed gwell bearers, the witnesses to the liberator's prophecy."

"Oh, not this liberator stuff again," Haxel groaned.

"What did you expect?" Marett asked. "Dargun Prett is the one who continued believing in Orren, and he clearly wants to use him to reestablish the prophecy."

"Never mind all that," Anselm snapped. "I want to know what they've done with him."

"Lord Jurgan and Dargun Prett wish to assure you that Orren Randolphus is alive and well, and in good health," Bolo said. "He's at Randolphus Manor, being educated in the ways of our Blood Master."

"Mind-twisted is more like it," Marett said.

"We want to see him!" Anselm demanded.

"And that's precisely what Lord Jurgan and Dargun Prett want as well," Bolo
said. "They wish to invite you to enter the Corcadine, and come join the liberator at his home. Lord Jurgan will withdraw the air barrier for a brief moment, to allow the four gwell-bearers safe passage into the peninsula's gateway."

"I must come too," Shann-Rell said.

"Orren Randolphus desired that you should come, elf-leader," Bolo said with a bow, "but Dargun Prett said it wasn't possible at this time."

The four gwell-bearers all cried out in anguish.

"What should we do?" Haxel asked the others.

"We take up the offer, that's what we do," Anselm said.

"That's right," Marett concurred. "The Moment of Reckoning approaches, and it's imperative that we, and the stones, be together, whether we're in friendly hands or in the hands of villains."

"Anxious as I am to go," Anselm said, "we must wait until evening for Quartz to wake up."

"So be it," Bolo said. "Upon the moment the rock giant rises, I will escort you into the Corcadine. Now I must ride back to my lord, and relay the excellent news that you agree to grace us with your presence."

As soon as the sun set over the western sea, Quartz threw the hood off his head and unclasped his hands. As if on cue, Bolo reappeared on a white horse. The baron and his men stood at attention, and saluted the gwell-bearers. He bid them farewell. The gwell-bearers said goodbye to him, Perceval, Shann-Rell, and the others, including Jasper. The donkey whimpered as they walked away, and Anselm took one long last look at Shann-Rell.

Quartz then placed Haxel, Marett, and Anselm on his shoulders, while Bolo mounted his white horse. The sholl followed the Corcadinian messenger toward Berthus's Wall. All of the gwell bearers felt a whoosh of air as the invisible barrier opened to allow them through. Bolo then led them toward the only gate that had been built into the wall. It swung open. Quartz had to duck to get through.

A large group of bandits and Drammites waited for them on the other side, carrying enough torches to turn night to day. Their leader was a middle-aged darga with light brown hair. "Greetings, gwell bearers," he said. "I'm Darga Kurt Schuenn, assistant to Dargun Prett. It's my privilege to escort you to Randolphus Manor. We'll spend the night traveling southward, and tomorrow, we'll sleep in Stoneybeach."

"I've seen maps of the Corcadine, so I know where everything is," Marett said. "Surely it doesn't take long to reach Randolphus Manor. Orren told us that it overlooks Tidesdale."

"He told you correctly," Darga Schuenn said, "but the Lady Iranda has established a schedule for you, and it's imperative that we stick to it."

"Berthus's Iranda?" Marett asked in shock.

"What's *she* doing here?" Haxel demanded.

"Berthus drove her off," Darga Schuenn said. "She joined forces with Jurgan and Dargun Prett, and has been most instrumental in creating this sanctuary for our order, right in the liberator's home territory. Jurgan has given her many duties, and among them is arranging your schedule."

"You can't stop us, if we decide to go ahead," Marett said.

"Actually, Madam Marett, I can not go ahead," Quartz said so that only the other gwell-bearers could understand. "Master Jurgan—"

"Oh, it's *Master* Jurgan now, is it?" Anselm asked in a testy voice.

"Yes, Master Anselm," Quartz said. "Every gwell-bearer is my master, and I must serve him or her. Anyway, as I was saying, Master Jurgan has a gwell, and I cannot do anything to counteract his wishes. Lady Iranda's wishes are Master Jurgan's wishes, so I dare not disobey her while she is under his orders. If I do, then I disobey *him* and may bring down his wrath upon me."

"Do you see what Iranda's doing?" Marett asked. "She's orchestrating all of this so we're forced to face the Moment of Reckoning."

"Just who is she anyway?" Anselm asked, "and how would she know about the Moment of Reckoning?"

"I don't know," Haxel said, "but I don't like it."

By pre-dawn, they reached Stoneybeach, a rather unattractive town surrounded by a wooden palisade, exactly as Orren had described it. Quartz bedded down on the town's outskirts, while Darga Schuenn pitched a camp, and gave Haxel, Marett, and Anselm a luxurious tent and a meal that, while delicious, went unappreciated.

They spent the next night traveling at a maddeningly slow pace, reaching Tidesdale by dawn. Quartz slept on a hill overlooking the city, while the others ate and rested for the day. Everyone was able to feel everyone else's hex-seeds, and now Orren's was also discernible. It seemed that channels had opened up between the five hex-seeds, and negative thoughts and feelings flowed freely from mind to mind. The dreaded hex-circle that Shann-Rell had mentioned was coming together.

Quartz slept fitfully beneath his skooch, while Haxel, Marett, and Anselm spent the day in brooding silence. The knowledge that this was the last day before the night of reckoning, pressed down on their minds as though it were the weight of the world. As the hours went by, the gray dreariness increased, and it even affected their senses. By the late afternoon, the gwell-bearers were no longer able to see in color, and their senses of smell seemed to have disappeared. The whole world now existed in varying shades of white, black, and gray. It was depressing.

As soon as the sun set, Quartz woke up, and told the others that the dreary, dull grayness hit him all at once. His reaction was to sink into misery, and he brought everyone else down as well.

"Don't give in to it," Anselm told the rock giant.

"I suppose the best thing to do is to keep going," Quartz said with a sigh. He placed Haxel, Marett, and Anselm on his shoulders again.

"Let's be off," Marett said to Darga Schuenn.

To everyone's surprise, the Drammite did not argue. He led the sholl up a winding dirt road, which cut through a forest of holly, tamarisk, and spindle. After half an hour, they reached Randolphus Manor, which was exactly as Orren had described it—a collection of buildings set on a wide ledge that overlooked the sea.

Darga Schuenn led them into the manor gate, which was wide open. Inside was a large, open space, which sat between the great manor house, the soaring cliffs, and an enormous structure that could only be the swinery. The place was ablaze with torchlight, and hundreds upon hundreds of Drammites and assorted thugs were present.

At the front of the crowd stood Jurgan, huge and brutal-looking as ever, though his clothes were now elegant, and his long, black beard had been carefully combed and powdered. To his right was Iranda, her beauty dazzling even to people in a state of sensory deprivation. Her long curls cascaded over her shoulders. She wore a white gown with trimmings of gold or silver—the gwell-bearers could not tell which. The garment shimmered in the torchlight. Attending Iranda was a sad-faced, unkempt-looking man in clothes that might once have been resplendent, but had since been stained.

On Jurgan's left, there was a dargun—an older man with a bald head. He could only be Dargun Prett. He was attended by two dargas, one male, and one female. Haxel recognized Darga Drugger, and Marett whispered that the woman was Darga Lowny.

"Greetings, noble gwell-bearers and witnesses," Dargun Prett said. "It's an uncommon pleasure to have you with us, to usher in our Blood Master's reign."

"Where's Orren?" Marett demanded.

"Oh, he's right here." The reception committee parted to allow the boy through.

Even in the dismal grayness, Orren cut a fine figure. His tunic and hose fit him perfectly, and he also wore a cape and a pair of shining, knee-high boots. His hair had been slicked back, and he looked healthy and well fed. His eyes, however, had a haunted look of despair, and the hex-seed that emanated from them, pierced the others' minds.

Haxel, Marett, and Anselm climbed off Quartz's shoulders and approached their beloved friend.

"How sweet is the reunion of friends," Dargun Prett said with a smile. "Now here's what's going to happen."

"No," Jurgan interrupted the Drammite. "I'll tell you what's going to happen."

"Excuse me?" Dargun Prett asked in shocked disbelief.

Jurgan raised his right arm. Two crossbow bolts whistled through the air and struck Dargas Lowny and Drugger. They both fell over dead, their eyes wide in shock.

"Jurgan!" the dargun shrieked. "What's the meaning of this?"

"You Drammites have been in control for too long," Jurgan said. "I've had enough of your pious mouthings and extravagant rituals. I'm sick of smelling burned human flesh. I've cooperated with you until now, because I needed to abduct Orren from Sherbass. Cinda Lowny there," he kicked the woman's dead body disrespectfully, "knew her way around Sherbass, and Stefan Drugger was able to use the order's connections to afford us safe passage through Rivulein. I needed you Drammites to support me in my takeover of the Corcadine, but now that the peninsula is full of *my* kind of folks, I need you no more."

"This is treachery!" Dargun Prett hollered.

"Then it should be familiar to you," Jurgan said. The big bandit then ran Dargun Prett through with his sword.

The Drammites were not about to go down without a fight, however, and thus, pandemonium erupted. Many of Jurgan's men fell to the dargas and cult warriors, but the Order of Dramm's representatives at Randolphus Manor were hopelessly outnumbered. Little by little, the thugs cut them down.

Quartz wrapped his fingers and skooch around Orren, Haxel, Marett, and Anselm in a protective embrace, while for more than an hour and a half, the battle raged. When it was over, the manor grounds were littered with bodies. Jurgan stood tall, proud, and victorious, but Iranda and the sad-faced man had both disappeared without a trace.

The big ruffian walked confidently up to Quartz, and looked at the giant's folded hands, behind which the other gwell-bearers huddled. They were now under the bandit lord's power. That realization caused their hex-seeds to begin merging.

"Grab the boy!" Jurgan commanded. The bandit used Magna to create a wave of air that knocked Quartz to the ground.

Then a mass of thugs scrambled over the sholl's hands and seized Orren. They dragged the struggling boy back to Jurgan's side, and surrounded Quartz, Haxel, Marett, and Anselm, with weapons drawn.

Jurgan grabbed Orren's shoulders and forced him to kneel.

"OK, swine boy, the good times are over," he said. "I'm going to create a Bearers' Web of my own, and you'll be part of it, but you won't carry Hesh. Instead, you're going to help me use its magic whenever I want to, and its burden will be yours." He explained to Orren how the dependency aspect of Berthus's Web had worked.

"What makes you think I'll agree to this?" Orren yelled.

"Because your friends here are going to be taken away from you," Jurgan said. "They'll be hostages. You will do what I say and be part of my Web, because if you don't, harm will come to the goblin, the giant, the girl, and the old man. They won't be in my Web. Instead, I'll find other members. One will be Iranda, using Staffords as proxy, just like the Drammites originally planned. The others will be...I don't know...maybe pirate chiefs who come here. The Corcadine will, under my rule, become a paradise for pirates, bandits, and slave-traders of all kinds, and you, my young friend, will help make that possible."

At those words, shockwaves passed from Orren to his friends and back. The hex-circle engulfed all their minds.

# THE MOMENT OF RECKONING

Orren watched helplessly as Jurgan's men plucked Haxel, Marett, and Anselm out from behind Quartz's hands. There was nothing the sholl could do to prevent this from happening, because Jurgan held Magna in his right hand. Quartz was powerless against the will of a gwell-bearer, as was always the case with his kind.

Jurgan then activated the gwell's magic, and created a shield of air in front of the rock giant. He walked around Quartz in a circle, and administered the same magic on each side, until the sholl was completely imprisoned in a force field of air.

"You can see him here whenever you want to," the bandit chief said. "I'm not telling you where I'm taking the others; all you need to know is that they're hostages."

The Moment of Reckoning was a mere three hours away. Jurgan did not know it, but when midnight arrived, Orren and his friends would all become ghouls. They would escape the bandit chief's clutches—even Quartz would manage it somehow—only to return, as undead prisoners, to the barren, lifeless Ghoul Vale. There they would forever guard the ruins of an empty city. The gwellen, with the possible exception of Nebi, would all fall into Jurgan's hands, because Orren and his friends would lose the ability to pick the stones up, and would thus be unable to take them with to the dreaded vale.

The hex-circle encompassed the minds of all five gwell-bearers, and it swirled around like a gray, dreary whirlpool. In its torrent were the negative thoughts and feelings of each person— Orren's sense of helplessness, Haxel's self-pity, Quartz's self-blame, Marett's regrets, and Anselm's anger toward the world. As the minutes passed, and time ran out, this whirlpool would undoubtedly get darker and heavier, and it would drag all of them down.

Orren fell to the ground. Through his peripheral vision, he saw Jurgan's men march Haxel, Marett, and Anselm toward the thug leader. Jurgan put Magna inside a pouch that was attached to his tunic belt—the same pouch in which he also carried Hesh. He then grabbed Haxel, rifled through the zhiv's shaspa, and drew forth Orya. The thugs then pulled Haxel away, and marched him toward the manor gate, while Jurgan pocketed the gwell of fire.

Marett was brought to him next, and Jurgan searched her as well, paying no heed to her dignity. When he found Kalsh, he took it out, and told his men to remove the girl. The earth stone joined the other three gwellen in the pouch, which was now filled to capacity.

When Anselm was brought to stand facing Jurgan, he spat in the bandit chief's face. Jurgan clobbered him, and the old man cried out and went limp in his captors' grip. Orren had to admire Anselm's nerve, despite the fact that it did him no good. Jurgan triumphantly pulled Ru'i out of the old man's pouch. The thug then placed the gwell of animal spirit inside a pocket of his cloak.

"Only one gwell left," Jurgan said, "and you, swine boy, will tell me where it is. Where's Nebi?"

Orren stared up at Jurgan with a blank expression on his face. His head throbbed from his friends' thoughts, and his vision was growing darker and drearier. He could not smell anything, and his hands and feet were numb. He therefore did not care what the bandit did to him.

"Didn't you hear me?" Jurgan roared. "Where's Nebi?"

Orren did not answer, but watched with indifference as the man's right foot attempted a savage kick to his ribs. The blow, however, did not come. Instead, Jurgan howled in pain and clutched at his leg.

Ferrus Staffords appeared, and he positioned himself between Orren and his tormentor. The ragged peddler brandished a club and growled, "Leave Orren alone or I'll clout you again!"

"You filthy lout!" Jurgan cursed. "I'll kill you right where you stand. I'll—"

Before any of Jurgan's men could come to their leader's assistance, however, Staffords swung the club and hit the big thug in the stomach. Jurgan fell to the ground, and Staffords, dodging several arrows, scrambled underneath the larger man. Using the coughing Jurgan as a shield, he drew a knife, and pressed it up against the bandit chief's jugular.

"Not one step closer!" the peddler roared at the assorted bandits, toughs, and pirates. "And if I hear one bow twang, Jurgan gets it!"

The thugs did nothing. They were confused and helpless without their leader telling them what to do.

"Orren," the peddler pleaded. "I don't know how long I can hold him, but you've got to escape."

"I...can't," Orren clutched at his head.

"Whatever's happening to you, Orren, you've got to stop it," the peddler said. "I broke free of Iranda. I told her I wasn't interested in having anything to do with her, and that I wouldn't put myself under her power. You must do the same. Don't give into your weakness."

*Don't give into your weakness.* That was what the mysterious voice had also said.

Mustering up his strength, Orren picked himself up. So strong was the whirlpool in his mind that it weighed his body down. He needed to break off contact with his friends, for their negative emotions were preventing him from taking advantage of what little hope there was left.

*Get out of my mind!* He yelled at them. *All of you!*

The hex-circle lessened until it became five hex-seeds once again. These hex-seeds still engulfed the minds of their respective hosts, but the connection between them had been minimized. Orren knew that as the Moment of Reckoning drew nearer, the hex-circle would reestablish itself, and then cutting it off like this would no longer be possible. He therefore had to act quickly.

*Help me find hope,* he called out to the mysterious voice, wherever it was.

A peculiar warm sensation emanated from the ground. It was the same sensation he had felt when Shann-Rell directed him and his friends to search for yelia trapped beneath Wardolam's ruins. With every passing second, the sensation became stronger. It could only mean one thing.

There were yelia in the ground! Dozens of yelia…no, scores of yelia, perhaps even hundreds of them. The yelia were heading in Orren's direction, and they were coming from beneath the earth. How this was possible, he had no idea, but it was happening!

However, if the yelia emerged above ground, they would find themselves surrounded by pirates, toughs, and bandits. The villains would entrap the Sun-Children if Jurgan was able to bark out commands, but without his leadership, they would be discombobulated. It was therefore necessary to get rid of Jurgan now. The lives of numerous yelia depended upon it.

"Kill him, Staffords!" Orren ordered. "Kill him now!"

The peddler drew the knife across Jurgan's throat.

At that same moment, the ground in front of Orren seemed to open up, and a great mass of armored knights poured out. Accompanying them was a creature, the likes of which Orren had never seen.

The knights fell upon Jurgan's confused and disorganized men. The thugs fought back, but more and more armored men emerged from the ground. The bizarre creature ran around the hole, and seemed to be digging, so as to make it wider. It used some sort of shovel-shaped apparatus that it held in its mouth.

It was then that Orren realized that the creature was Jasper. How odd she now looked! Her body was completely covered in armor-like scales, and her head was square-shaped. Each of her hoofs had split into five parts, which looked like stiff fingers, and her tail was gone. The digging apparatus in her mouth was the Shovel of Tunneling, the last of the talismans given to the gwell-bearers by the yelia. Orren had forgotten that Jasper had taken it.

When the hole was big enough to satisfy the donkey—if you could still call her a donkey— she pulled back to allow more knights to come through. Immediately, the Tunnel of Shoveling crumbled to dust, which was dispersed by the sea winds.

A large knight barked out orders. Orren recognized the voice of Perceval. Other knights spoke in the fluty tongue of the yelia, and it was then that Orren realized that among these knights were numerous yelia. *They* were the ones he had detected. Baron Toynberg must have given them arms and armor, thus enabling them to join the battle. Why would he do that, when he refused, on the grounds that they were an endangered species, to allow them to participate in Sherbass's liberation?

Shann-Rell's red mastiff was with them, as was the peregrine falcon, swooping through the night sky.

Orren called out to Perceval. When he had the man's attention, Orren shouted, "They've taken Marett, Haxel, and Anselm out of the manor!" Perceval issued more commands, and a group of knights and yelia accompanied him out of the manor gates, while the rest of the company continued fighting. Before long, there were no more thugs left on the manor grounds. Many knights and yelia entered the manor house itself, in order to hunt the thugs inside. The dog and the falcon went with them.

One knight approached Orren.

"Are you hurt?" It was Baron Toynberg.

"No, m'lord," Orren said. The baron gave him a hand and helped him to his feet. Staffords pulled himself out from beneath Jurgan's body, and stood by Orren's side. Jasper joined them, and Orren pet the donkey-creature. He then approached Quartz, who was still imprisoned inside the air barrier.

"I'll get you out of there," the boy said. He rifled through Jurgan's corpse, and took out Magna, Hesh, Kalsh, Ru'i, and Orya. He prepared to use Magna to remove the force field that imprisoned the sholl.

*No Master Orren,* Quartz spoke in his head. *Magna isn't your gwell. The Moment of Reckoning comes, and we cannot afford to have you go ill. I saw Shann-Rell come out of the tunnel, though I have lost sight of her. Let her remove this barrier.*

For over two hours, the fighting inside the manor house and outside the manor grounds, raged. A great mass of thugs suddenly burst out of the building, chased by knights and yelia. Some of them made their way toward Orren and Staffords, their knives drawn, and bloodlust in their eyes. The red mastiff bounded out of the manor house and fell upon them. The dog caused pandemonium, as Jurgan's surviving followers tried to avoid its slavering jaws. The falcon swooped down to assist. It tore at the enemies' faces with its beak and talons, and defended the dog against those who tried to attack it. The two animals were of tremendous assistance to the baron's men. Before long, Jurgan's combined force of toughs, pirates, bandits, brigands, slavers, and troublemakers were so many corpses littering Randolphus Manor's grounds and buildings.

Orren heard a cry of dismay from Quartz, and saw that an arrow had skewered the falcon. The bird had fallen to the ground. The red dog was severely wounded in many places, and it collapsed on its right side, bleeding and panting for breath.

"Help these animals!" the baron called out. "Take them to Madame Carlenda!" A yelius gently picked up the falcon, and pulled the arrow out of its body. Several men lifted the big dog. Both animals were removed from the manor.

Perceval and his men entered the gate a few minutes later, accompanied by Marett, Haxel, and Anselm. Carlenda was also with them.

"It's over for Jurgan's men," Perceval said. "Colonel Domberg is cleaning the last few pockets of thugs, out of Tidesdale. The townsfolk have come to their assistance. Soon all of the northern and central Corcadine will be free of their scourge. You're probably wondering what the yelia are doing here; well, they insisted on joining the fight. You gwell-bearers did so much for them, they said, that they only felt it right to do their utmost to rescue you. So the baron outfitted them with arms and armor."

"And how did you find Carlenda?" Orren asked.

"She's been encamped in the forest since I brought her here to care for you," Staffords said. "I've been supporting her, and as for how your friends found her, I think it more likely that she found them."

"Indeed she did," Perceval said. "As soon as we rescued Marett, Haxel, and Anselm from Jurgan's thugs, she approached us and identified herself, and we remembered her from everything you told us, Orren."

"How did you all get past Jurgan's air barrier?" Marett asked.

"Jasper did it for us," the baron said. "Ever since you five left, she was highly agitated. She kept on trying to tell us something, but we could not understand her. My officers and I convened a war council in an attempt to figure out how to get into the Corcadine. In it, Sergeant Riveldi insisted that we listen to the donkey. We did not pay heed to him at first, but he kept haranguing us. Finally, we asked Jasper what was wrong. She turned around and kept trying to bite the sacks that she carried. We took them off her back, and she nosed around in them until she found the shovel.

"We asked Shann-Rell what the meaning of this was. That's when she explained about the talismans. We let Jasper activate the shovel, which created a long tunnel that went underneath the air barrier and Berthus's Wall, and enabled us to come here. Jasper guided us the whole way. How she knew where to go, I have no idea."

"And where's Shann-Rell?" Anselm asked.

"She came with us," the baron said. "She was by my side the whole way."

"So where is she now?" the old man demanded.

"We need her," Haxel said, "and she's got Nebi, the green gwell."

"We also need her to free Quartz," Orren added.

No one, however, seemed to know where the yelian council head was.

"Here she is," a female voice rang out.

Iranda appeared on the edge of the manor outbuildings, the trimmings on the beautiful woman's white gown sparkling in the torchlight. She had Shann-Rell in a headlock, with a knife pressed up against her throat. The yelian council head's arms were tied behind her back, and there was a look of both fear and determination in her eyes.

"Get all the other yelia out of here," Iranda demanded, "and the baron and his knights—they must leave too. Leave only the gwell-bearers. Obey me or this yelius dies!"

"You heard her," the baron commanded. "Everyone, let's go."

The mass of knights and yelia exited the gate, and Jasper, at Anselm's instruction, went with them. Staffords refused to leave Orren's side.

"You too, Staff," Iranda said. "Since you rejected me, I have no more use for you."

Staffords looked to Orren for guidance. "Do as she says," Orren said in a soft voice. Reluctantly, the peddler left. Orren, Haxel, Marett, and Anselm stood next to one another, facing Iranda and Shann-Rell. The five gwellen were at the gwell bearers' feet. Quartz, still trapped within the air barriers, stood behind the evil woman and her desperate prisoner.

The hex-circle flared up again, and encompassed all their minds exactly as it had before. Only forty minutes were left until the Moment of Reckoning.

"What do you want with her, Iranda?" Orren demanded.

Iranda smiled and flashed her cruel, dark eyes.

"Brilliant, isn't it?" she asked in a mocking voice. "During the mayhem, I snuck up on Shann-Rell and grabbed her, but I didn't take her just for the sake of having a prisoner. I have a proposal for you gwell-bearers, which you'd be foolish to refuse."

"Say it," Anselm snapped.

"I want to be the sixth person in your Bearers' Web," Iranda said, "but I can't handle a gwell myself. I need a proxy, that is, a living body with a soul still attached, to bear it for me. I also desire a Bearers' Web so that I can access the magic of any gwell I choose.

"My original plan was to join *Berthus's* Web, and for one of its members to be my proxy—I was considering that dullard Lord Hemric. When *that* option disappeared, I encouraged Jurgan to create a Web of his own just in case things didn't go well with Berthus. Dargun Rodrick overheard me taking to Jurgan, and outed me to Berthus, which is why Berthus kicked me out. Jurgan stuck with me, however, and I instructed him and the Drammites to abuse Staffords, so that he, intent on revenge, would make a deal with me. I intended on making Staffords my proxy."

"I know," Orren said. "Dargun Prett explained it to me, but Staffords rejected you. He refuses to be your puppet, so you can't do what you want with him. In fact, you can't do anything with him."

"Exactly," Iranda said, "I can't use him if he's unwilling, so I needed to find someone else who *is* willing, and now I have just such a person."

"You're lying!" Anselm cried out in anguish. "Shann, tell her she's lying!"

"Why would Shann-Rell agree to something like that?" Marett asked, "and what kind of witch are you, that you think you can possess someone's body?"

"In order to avoid the Ghouls' Curse, you gwell-bearers each have to place your respective gwell in the council head's hands,"

Iranda said. "But I have her hands tied, so she can't accept them. Her only alternative is therefore to give herself over to me."

"You're a liar!" Haxel cried out. "Shann-Rell's too smart to agree to something like that!"

"Ah, but she did," Iranda said. "Didn't you, my lovely?"

"Yes," the yelian leader responded in a sad voice.

"Shann," Anselm cried out. "Why?"

"It's the only way to save you gwell-bearers from becoming ghouls," Shann-Rell said, "but I require that you too, agree to it."

"My masters," Quartz said. "Shann-Rell is offering herself up to this witch in order to save us. She is sacrificing herself for our sakes. How can we allow this?"

"You can allow it because Shann-Rell's living body will be payment from you," Iranda said. "I can remove the Ghouls' Curse. I can absorb the hex-circle that afflicts you. Then you'll be free. All I need is for one of you—just one—to agree to these terms, and to let me have Shann-Rell as my proxy."

"Why just one of us?" Anselm asked.

"Because the hex-circle has bonded all five of you together," Iranda said. "You five are now one organism. Your fate is shared. If one of you becomes a ghoul, all of you do. Similarly, if only one of you accepts my offer, all of you will, even if the others refuse. That's the nature of a hex-circle."

"Surely that would also mean that if one of us *refuses*, all of us do?" Haxel asked.

"Good try, Haxel," Iranda said, "But Shann-Rell has placed herself under my power. All I need is her consent, which I have, and yours, which will happen if only *one* of you agrees to it. The combination of Shann-Rell's assent and your own, gives her over into my hands."

"I'm afraid what she says is true," Marett said. "I remember something like this from my family lore."

"I would, of course, prefer that all five of you accept," Iranda said. "But only one is necessary. Acceptance of my offer achieves three things. First, you'll make Shann-Rell a part of your Web, and by extension, myself. Second, you'll hand the hex-circle over to me and be free of the Ghouls' Curse. Third, I'll have access to the power of all six stones. Think about it, gwell-bearers, but don't take too long. Only half an hour is left until the Moment of Reckoning."

"What makes you think we believe you?" Anselm asked.

"And why can she not handle a Sun-Stone herself?" Quartz chimed in.

In answer to that question, Iranda's body began to glow, and her eyes shone.

"What kind of witch is she?" Orren asked.

"She's no witch!" Marett cried out. "What a fool I've been for not having seen it before! I know exactly who she is. The name 'Iranda' is 'Adnari' backwards. My friends, this is Adnari the Temptress—one of the last odia remaining on earth."

"Correct, Marett," Adnari the Temptress said. "I am a goddess!"

"An evil goddess," Anselm growled.

"Nevertheless, a goddess," Adnari flashed a dazzling smile.

"And odia cannot handle the gwellen," Marett said. "An odius like Adnari here can't even *touch* a gwell, lest the stones harm her."

"For centuries I've searched for a way around the limitations that the astra imposed upon me," Adnari said. "Particularly concerning the Sun-Stones. Now I've found a way, thanks to Shann-Rell here!"

"None of us will have any part in this," Orren said. "So be gone and go drown yourself."

"Orren Randolphus," the evil goddess turned her beautiful eyes toward the boy. Orren could not help but be entranced by her. "Think about your friends. They embarked on this quest because of you. They made your struggle their own. If they're doomed to an existence that forever hovers between life and death—never being able to eat or drink or to enjoy anything that the senses delight in, never appreciating beauty, or experiencing love, or having hope, then it will all be your fault. Do you really want to have that over your head forever? Reach out to me and embrace me instead, and you and your friends will be free."

Orren collapsed on the ground at the weight of her words. Guilt pressed him down, and all the other gwell-bearers felt it too.

"Druba Haxel Spakiwakwak," Adnari looked into the zhiv's eyes, through which all the others could see as well. "Would you really sacrifice your life for a yelius? Do you not know of the hatred that prevails between your race and theirs? Observe if you will."

Suddenly the hex-circle filled with images. There were zhivi toiling as slaves under harsh yelian taskmasters. A pitched battle took place between zhivi and yelia, with the death cries of many zhivi echoing through the minds of the gwell-bearers.

"These are ancient enemies, Haxel," Adnari said. "So why are you making common cause with them? Reach out to me instead."

"Marett Reina Baines," The goddess's eyes bored into the girl's soul. "The yelia have been playing you Duralines for far too long, and what did you gain from it? You weren't even designated chosen ones. No wonder you've declined in numbers and influence through the centuries. As if that wasn't bad enough, it was the yelian leader Varshing who created the dark Duraline pact."

The terrible sting of shame that Marett felt when she first learned about the dark Duralines was palpable to all the gwell-bearers.

"Do you think Varshing acted alone? No, Marett. He had the full support of the Wardolam city council. That's how it always has been with these yelia. They care only for themselves, and consider all others to be tools. Don't sacrifice yourself and your friends for a yelius, especially one who, in essence, is a disciple of Varshing and Narx."

"None of what she says is true!" Anselm shouted. "Shann-Rell didn't do any of those things."

"But let me tell you what she *did* do, Anselm," Adnari said. "She stood by idly while you were used. The yelia called you a slave and treated you as a slave. You carried out difficult errands for them, often undergoing deprivation and hardship. All of it was worth it, you thought, for the promise of becoming a yelius. Then you found out that such a thing wasn't possible. Did Shann-Rell ever warn you that this would happen? Did she make you aware of what was going on? Or was she complacent while Narx made you do his dirty work for nothing? Don't waste your life on her, Anselm. Reach out to me instead."

Anselm's wrath, shame, and anguish passed to everyone else.

"And Quartz," the goddess said, "Talk about being used as a tool. That's all your entire species was ever used for. You sholls served the yelia faithfully and whole-heartedly, but what did they ever do for you?"

"A sholl's duty is to serve and obey," Quartz said in a voice that indicated faltering resolve.

"The Moon Mother created you sholls to serve the yelia—that's true, but the yelia were instructed to cherish you and to care for you, but they never did. They fed you enormous amounts of food and drink, figuring that you were just big, stupid animals, whose only concern was to fill their stomachs. They did nothing to ensure your survival as a species, which is why no sholls were ever brought down into Wardolam. No wonder you're the last one left."

Quartz began to weep, and the suffering that came from the loss of his species cut him to the core. Adnari smiled, for the giant was falling for her arguments.

"The yelia are not the legendary, heroic beings you all thought they were," Adnari said. "They're conniving, manipulative, and small-minded. No wonder they put you under the Ghouls' Curse. Don't sacrifice yourselves for them. Embrace me, and be free."

Orren remembered what the voice had told him about not giving into temptations and who could tempt better than Adnari the Temptress?

"No," the boy said.

"No what?" Adnari asked.

"I won't do it," Orren said. "I was told not to."

"And who, pray tell, told you?" Adnari asked in a mocking voice.

"Someone who's greater and stronger than you could ever hope to be," Orren said. "Someone whose voice has always spoken in my mind."

"Does that 'someone' know that only twenty minutes are left until the Moment of Reckoning?" Adnari asked. "And then you will fail, Orren Randolphus. And you'll have failed all your friends."

"I'll fail only if I give into you," Orren said. "And the same goes for all of us. If any one of us allows you to tempt us, then we'll have failed. But I won't do it, you goddess of manure and vomit. So my answer is no."

"It doesn't matter," Adnari said with a laugh. "You're just one person among five. If any one of you reaches out to me, then that person will pull the rest of you in."

"I won't do it either," Marett jumped in. "Being a dark Duraline or a light Duraline is a choice, and if I were to choose to go with you, I'd be merely strengthening the dark Duralines. So, Adnari the Temptress, my answer to you is also no."

"What about you, Haxel?" Adnari asked.

"The wars between us zhivi and the yelia," Haxel said, "are because of bad ideas. The time has come to put these aside. I've come to love these humans here like they were brothers and sister. I can do the same with the yelia no matter what happened long ago. So my answer to you is also no."

"What about you, Anselm?" Adnari asked. "You love Shann-Rell, do you not? Even though she betrayed you for many years. If you reach out to me, she lives. If not, she dies."

"I love her," the old man said in a weak voice, "but I love her as she is, not as something you'd make her into. I have grown, and she has grown. She lived in fear, which is why she never told me the truth. I gave into spite for many years, but no more. We've both learned life's lessons, and are greater than what we were before. Therefore, I spit on you, foul odius, and I say no to your rotten proposal."

"Quartz," Adnari hissed, "You're the last hope that the gwell-bearers have. Will you fail them? Think about your duties."

Everyone felt the sholl debating within himself.

"Hurry up, Quartz," Adnari said. "A mere fifteen minutes remain until the Moment of Reckoning."

Orren suddenly knew what he had to do.

"Quartz's duties are to fellow sholls, yelia, and gwell-bearers," the boy said. "He has no duty to odia. Isn't that right, Quartz?

"That is correct, Master Orren," the giant said, "nonetheless, what the goddess says makes sense. I would like to try reaching out to her, but I cannot, for I am trapped within this prison of air." Then turning to Adnari, he said, "Great Goddess of Power, I must be released from this prison. Only Shann-Rell can do it, for she is a Magg, and can activate Magna's power. Release one of her hands and let her take the stone, so she can remove this air barrier. Then I will be able to reach out to you."

"Very well," Adnari said. She pulled Shann-Rell over to where five of the six gwellen lay. "Pick Magna up," she said to the yelian leader, "but don't dare try anything."

With Adnari's knife still at her throat, Shann-Rell bent down and picked up Magna from the ground. Adnari then walked her over to the air barrier. The yelian leader activated the gwell's magic, and Quartz's prison of air was soon no more.

"Thank you very much, Great Goddess," Quartz said. "I am most relieved, and now I can reach out to you."

"Quartz, no!" Orren, Haxel, Marett, and Anselm all chimed in. They tried to flood his consciousness with their thoughts, but to no avail.

To everyone's abject horror, the giant reached with his enormous right hand toward the goddess. Then suddenly, he stretched out his index finger and grabbed Adnari's knife with it. The blade sunk into his rocky fingertip, but there was no crack there, so it did not affect the sholl. With one deft and incredibly dexterous swipe, Quartz flung it out of the goddess's grip. With his left hand, he grabbed Shann-Rell, and pulled her out of Adnari's grasp.

"Quartz, what's the meaning of this?" Adnari shouted.

"I cannot lie," Quartz said, "and I do not know exactly what it means to lie, but I think I understand how it *might* work. I love my masters, and I must obey them, for the Code of Duties that we sholls live by, says I must serve my masters, even if it means 'lying' for their sake—yes, even to a goddess—a goddess who I am not duty bound to obey. Therefore, Adnari the Temptress, I say no to you!"

With that, he grabbed the goddess in his right hand and flung her as far as he could, out of sight. Adnari sailed over the manor house, and fell screaming into the sea far below.

Quartz placed Shann-Rell on the ground. The yelian elder was trembling, but she nonetheless managed to place Magna back where it had sat before, next to Hesh, Kalsh, Ru'i, and Orya.

"Shann-Rell!" Orren cried out. "Get Nebi out of your pocket too, and toss it to me! Quick, there's only three minutes to go!"

Shann-Rell did as the boy asked. Orren placed Nebi on the ground next to the other five gwellen.

"Gwell-bearers, quick!" Shann-Rell said. "Each of you must hand his or her chosen gwell to me."

Quartz deftly picked up Magna. He placed the yellow gwell in the council head's outstretched hands. Shann-Rell put Magna inside her robe, where she had several folds that served as pockets.

Anselm and Haxel came next. They each picked up their respective stones. Haxel placed Orya in Shann-Rell's right hand, and Anselm placed Ru'i in her left. Shann-Rell pocketed these gwellen as well.

Marett then picked up Kalsh, and Orren, Hesh. Marett placed Kalsh in Shann-Rell's left hand, and Orren placed Hesh in her right. These stones too, disappeared inside Shann-Rell's robes.

"What do we do now?" Anselm cried out. "Nebi has no bearer!"

"And less than one minute is left!" Haxel wailed.

"Quartz!" Orren cried out. "Pick up Nebi and give it to Anselm!"

The rock giant lifted the last remaining stone. He held it between his thumb and index finger, and placed it in Anselm's outstretched palm.

"Now give it to Haxel!" Orren shouted. The zhiv received the gwell from the old man.

"Give it to Marett!"

Haxel placed the gwell in Marett's hand.

"Now give it to me!" Orren said.

Only ten seconds were left until the Moment of Reckoning. Marett gave Nebi to Orren. Orren then placed the gwell in Shann-Rell's hand.

The hex-circle and the Ghouls' Curse both shattered like so much glass, and disintegrated into the cosmos. A pleasant breeze blew, bringing with it the smell of the springtime forest and the salt spray of the sea. The heady mixture of sensations and intense relief, were almost too much for the gwell-bearers to take in at once. They all fell to the ground.

The gates of Randolphus Manor opened. Baron Toynberg, Perceval, and the yelian elders all entered, along with Jasper, Staffords, and Carlenda. With them came several score knights and yelia. Orren noticed that many were wounded, but that they had been patched up.

"Greetings, gwell-bearers," the baron said. "We all felt the curse lift. You've saved LeFain. We owe all of you a tremendous debt of gratitude, and also to this fine lady here." He patted Carlenda on the shoulder. "After we left the manor she began tirelessly treating my men *and* the yelia, and she's been teaching us what to do to treat ourselves. She even gave instructions on how to care for the red dog and the bird."

"All of the Drammites and Jurgan's thugs have been killed or driven out of Tidesdale," Perceval added. "The oppressors have been forced into the southern Corcadine."

Then Thraix, the chief of the Nebb, appeared, along with the other tribal chiefs. Thraix called to Shann-Rell in the fluty yelian tongue. Shann-Rell walked over to the chiefs. A discussion ensued in the yelian language, and everyone waited in silence to see what the outcome would be.

"Honored Baron," Shann-Rell said, "The gwellen were created to provide us yelia with magic by which we could protect ourselves, but you have saved our race and provided us with a home. We therefore wish to extend the Sun-Stones' protection to all of Alivadus."

"What about finding a sanctuary for the stones?" Anselm asked.

"There will always be a sanctuary for the gwellen among the Sun-Children,"

Shann-Rell said, "but the best sanctuary for them is among members of a Bearers' Web, made up of trustworthy individuals. Such individuals will not abuse the stones' powers, and will use the gwellen only when absolutely necessary. A Web of that nature will enable the gwellen to more effectively serve Alivadus than would be possible if the stones were with us, in isolation, on the escarpment. It is therefore our unanimous wish that this noble Bearers' Web we have before us, carries on. We would like to give Hesh to Orren Randolphus, Orya to Druba Haxel Spakiwakwak, Kalsh to Marett Reina Baines, Magna to Quartz Moonchild, and Ru'i to our dear benefactor Anselm, a slave never more.

"But you need a sixth member of your Web," the yelian leader added, "and I can think of no better candidate than this wise and faithful healing woman, Carlenda. Nebi is a healing stone, a stone of growth and rejuvenation. There will always be room for healing arts of all kinds, but their knowledge can be enhanced if Nebi is in the right hands. Madame Carlenda, sister of Richard of blessed memory, we, the Sun-Children wish to confer upon you, chosen status, and designate you as bearer of Nebi, gwell of plant spirit. Will you agree to it?"

"I would be honored to," the old woman said, "and it would be a rare privilege to join Orren's Web. I promise to use Nebi for the good of all."

"Madame Carlenda," Shann-Rell said to her, "we, the Sun-Children, choose you to be a gwell-bearer." She placed the green stone in the healing woman's hand. Carlenda smiled and looked at the gwell with awe and wonder in her eyes.

"My friends," Orren said, "let's activate the Web."

He sent forth the silvery light, and in his mind's eye, saw the cords envelop himself, Haxel, Marett, Quartz, and Anselm. Then all five friends sent the light forth and drew Carlenda into their embrace. Feelings of love and devotion passed between the six gwell-bearers, as the Bearers' Web became complete.

A horrible, cruel laughter shattered their reverie. Orren and his friends looked up in time to see Adnari the Temptress appear atop the roof of Randolphus Manor. The evil goddess leapt to the ground.

"Did you think it was so easy to get rid of me?" she asked. "I may have failed in accessing the powers of the gwellen, but I can make sure that if I can't control the Sun-Stones, then no one else will be able to either!"

"You have no power in our lives," Haxel said.

"And never will," Anselm said. "Even though in your pathetic, deluded state, you're convinced that you will. What a poor excuse for a goddess!"

"Anselm's right," Marett added. "You odia can only control those who accept your control."

"Ah," Adnari cackled, "but many have done so."

She raised her arms above her head, and when she did, the dead bodies of Jurgan and all of his thugs, rose to their feet. More of the dead crawled over the walls of Randolphus Manor and the outbuildings. The gwell-bearers, the yelian elders, and the baron and all his men who were present, were soon completely surrounded. Hundreds of dead eyes stared blankly at them, and hundreds of dead arms bore weapons.

"All these people placed themselves in my power while they were still alive," Adnari said with a laugh, "and they can fight my fight after their death. And now it's time for all of *you* to die!"

# REALIZATIONS AND REVELATIONS

Orren activated the Web and through it, issued a desperate call to Haxel, Marett, Quartz, Anselm, and Carlenda. *Surround our friends! Protect everyone!*

Baron Toynberg and all the knights and yelia present, as well as Jasper and Staffords, were hemmed in on all sides, while the masses of dead thugs closed in on them. The corpses moved slowly, for their mistress clearly wanted to savor her victims' terror. The dead eyes stared blankly; dead hands clutched weapons. It was like the Ghoul Vale all over again. Meanwhile, the evil Adnari cackled with glee.

"Ready your weapons!" the baron commanded. His men and the yelia had their swords drawn and their battle-axes at the ready, but it was a pathetic gesture. Their foes could not be killed, for they were already dead.

Orren positioned himself in front of the baron. Marett stood in front of Perceval, Anselm shielded Shann-Rell, and Haxel, the whimpering Jasper. All of the gwell-bearers had their weapons drawn in one hand, and their gwellen in the other. Quartz stood like a massive barrier on the western side of the group, cutting off the largest number of dead thugs from their intended victims. The Web shimmered and glowed in the gwell-bearers' minds, and thoughts were freely communicated. All six of them knew that the others would willingly serve as the first line of defense against the gruesome enemies. This was even true of Carlenda, despite the fact that her fear was compounded by confusion.

*What am I to do?* The healing woman asked through the Web. *I've never used a gwell. Besides, Nebi is a stone of healing. How can I fight with it?*

*Nebi is the gwell of plant spirit, Auntie,* Marett said. *It governs the capacity for growth. Anywhere plants, even tiny ones, are present, Nebi's magic will work.*

*Concentrate on Nebi,* Orren said. *Touch it to its element and think about what you want it to do.*

*Just remember that its magic can only move in one direction at a time,* Anselm added.

*And never use it when someone else is using a gwell,* Quartz said. *The Web is here so everyone in it knows what everyone else is doing. That way we make sure that two gwellen being used at once, does not happen, with disaster resulting.*

*I will remember all this,* Carlenda said. *Right now I'm going to use Nebi. Quartz, cover me.*

The sholl shielded Carlenda with the hem of his skooch, while the old woman crouched down and touched Nebi to the soil. She concentrated.

The grounds of Randolphus Manor were covered in mud, which contained untold amounts of pollen, seeds, and spores that had drifted in, on the winds from the surrounding woodlands. Nebi activated all of these, and within seconds, they grew into a seething mass of vines and jungle. The vegetation grabbed the dead bodies that approached from Carlenda's side, and held them tight. The corpses struggled, hacking away at the growth. Sooner or later, they would free themselves, but Carlenda had temporarily immobilized them.

*Good going!* Anselm cheered. *Let me have a go!*

The old man stood on the opposite side of the group from Carlenda. All the Web members felt him activate Ru'i and project his mind out to sea. Suddenly the sky above the manor house was filled with gulls. The seabirds descended upon the animated corpses that approached Anselm's side, and began gorging themselves on their dead flesh. The corpses tried to claw the birds off, but there were too many. Whatever gulls *were* thrown off simply wheeled around in the air and returned, intent on the feast.

Adnari laughed. "Very amusing!" the odius said, "but you'll have to do much better than that!"

*If that's how she wants it,* Marett's thoughts expressed themselves.. Then aloud, she said, "Perceval, cover me." She then bent down and touched Kalsh to the earth. A tremendous fissure opened up in the ground, and all the dead thugs on Marett's side plunged into it. She then closed the earth over them. Adnari scowled.

"Temporary setback," the goddess said, "but there are many other corpses, and besides, the ones you buried will claw their way out."

Quartz then used Magna to create a wind barrier that shielded the entire company on his side. He sent forth a great tempest that blew bodies away, over the manor walls. When he was finished, Haxel ignited the ground on his side, and a great conflagration arose, consuming the dead in their path.

"Burning them won't stop them," Adnari jeered, "They will be reborn from their ashes, and now I've had about enough games. The end has come."

*Keep going!* Orren said to the others. *You all know what to do, so keep the corpses busy. I'm about to use Hesh, so make sure you all stop when I start.*

*But Master,* Haxel said. *There's no water here.*

Orren did not answer. Instead, he broke away from the crowd and charged Adnari. He raced between Haxel's flames and Quartz's air barrier, until he reached the goddess. He grabbed Adnari's cloak and hung on tight.

"No water," Adnari said with a smirk. "There's nothing you can do to me."

"You're an odius," Orren retorted, "and no odius can even *touch* a gwell."

Adnari screamed and tried to brush Orren off, but he touched Hesh to her clothes. It did not matter that there was no water in them. The mere contact of a gwell was detrimental enough to her kind. Orren felt Adnari's body melt beneath the garments. The goddess, now desperate, fought back with her mental power.

*Help me!* Orren called out to the Web. His friends sent forth their power. The silvery light flowed from Haxel, Marett, Quartz, Anselm, and Carlenda, into Orren, and from him into the gwell. Orren leapt onto Adnari's shoulders, and shoved Hesh into her scalp. Her brown hair sizzled and melted, and the odius screamed in agony.

Orren felt the goddess's body expand. Her divine blood boiled within her. Her limbs moved away from one another, for she was literally coming apart. Waves of power assaulted Orren, and it was all he could do to keep himself on Adnari's shoulders.

*Get off her now!* Anselm shouted. *Or you'll die!*

*She's about to explode,* Marett said.

*And she'll take you with her,* Carlenda added.

His friends' warnings came too late, however. Orren felt shockwaves pass through his body. Charges went through the air. Adnari was about to be blown apart, and Orren would explode with her. He prepared himself for the end.

Suddenly, a pair of brilliant white arms wrapped themselves around him and pulled him off Adnari's melting shoulders. An enormous man—over eight feet tall—embraced Orren. The boy saw more beings of light on either side of his rescuer. They stood between the disintegrating, combusting Adnari, and her intended victims.

Adnari the Temptress exploded. The shockwave passed through both earth and air. Orren heard rocks falling and parts of buildings collapsing. However, his ethereal benefactor enveloped him in light, and did not allow Adnari's explosion to hurt him.

The other light beings shielded all of Orren's friends, so that they too, were not harmed.

Then it was over. Orren looked up to see the light beings shoot into the night sky like rockets. His own rescuer let him go. Orren's head reeled and his world spun around. He tried to focus on the man of light, but the effort was too much.

The last thing he saw before he blacked out was Richard smiling down at him.

Orren woke up to discover that it was night time, and that he was on a soft mattress. He rolled over, opened his eyes, and saw that there was a distant torch. Its light filtered into the place where he lay.

"Hello?" he called out. "Anyone there?"

"Master Orren, you're awake." It was the voice of Ferrus Staffords. The peddler entered the chamber. He had a smile on his face, and carried the torch, which he set in a sconce on the wall. Staffords wore a clean set of clothes, though his unshaven face still made him look unkempt.

"Where am I?" Orren asked.

"Look around you, Master Orren," Staffords said.

Orren took a deep breath of fresh, sea air. He sat up and saw a clean set of clothes on the pedestal next to the bed. His short sword and hunting bow had been propped up against the wall, next to Hesh, the gwell of water. He was in a small room with a wooden floor and a wardrobe, as well as the bed, which turned out to be a four-poster.

He recognized this place. It was Richard's old room!

There were several poultices on his skin, all of them now cold, and he had been bathed. Staffords ushered him out of the room, and toward a small chamber where Orren could see to his toileting needs. After that, the boy returned to Richard's room.

There, Staffords waited with honey cake and a jug of goats' milk. Orren ate and drank heartily, and thanked the peddler, who momentarily left the room while the boy dressed himself in the clothes provided. These consisted of a fitted green tunic, brown hose, and a pair of dark green shoes. He girded his short sword to his tunic belt, and placed his bow around his shoulders. Then he put Hesh inside the pouch attached to the belt.

He opened the wardrobe and found the mirror, wherein he had first seen his own reflection. By the torchlight, he saw that his red-blond hair had been cut short, and he had grown considerably since he had been in this room the last time. In his new clothes, he cut a fine figure.

"It was my suggestion that you be brought here," Staffords said. "I thought that being in Richard's room might help you, Master Orren."

"*Master* Orren?" He looked at Staffords with confusion. "Only Haxel and Quartz call me that, and they do it even though I've asked them not to. Why are you now calling me that?"

"Haxel does it because he sees you as his master even though he's actually your friend," Staffords said. "Quartz, I think, does it out of habit. I do it because you truly are my master."

"Since when?"

"Please allow me to explain," Staffords said. He let out a sigh and said, "That night when I took you to the edge of the cliff, intending to kill you, you said things to me which forced me to take a good, hard look at myself. It was like you were a mirror, and when I looked in it, I hated what I saw."

"I've been angry my whole life, Master Orren—angry about what was done to my family and to myself. I took my anger out on others who were weaker than me, but your words taught me something. Bullying others does me no good, and it certainly won't restore my family's holdings in Albina. All it has done is make me unhappier, and a worse person."

"At that moment, I resolved to turn my life around, which is why I helped Carlenda reach you. However, I still felt terrible remorse at the way I abused you during your childhood. My guilt was eating me up, so, soon after you left, I went to the baron and told him everything. Whatever punishment he would decree for me, I would happily accept, even if it meant being put to death."

"And what did the baron do?" Orren asked.

"Baron Toynberg is the kindest and most just of men," Staffords said. "He said this to me, in his exact words. 'Ferrus Staffords, you've done very noble and heroic things for Orren, but that can't erase what you did before. You must pay for your wrongs.

"'I oppose slavery,' the baron said, 'and there are no slaves in my realm, but I'm going to make an exception in your case. You will be Orren's slave, serving him for at least two years, and doing whatever it is he wants you to do, no matter how menial. If after two years, he chooses to free you, you may go free. If you serve him faithfully, you'll be rewarded, and a fief of your own would certainly not be out of the question.'"

"I don't need the fief or the reward, Master Orren," Staffords continued. "I need to become a better person and to atone for my evil. The only way to do that is to be your slave. I should have learned from Richard's example. I should have befriended you and done what I could to make your life easier, but I didn't. Instead, I acted like Berthus did, and hurt you whenever I could. For that, I'm so very, very sorry. Please allow slavery for me. I don't want freedom. I don't deserve it."

"I understand how you feel," Orren said. "OK. You can be my...uh...um..."

"Slave," Staffords finished the sentence.

"Whatever," Orren said.

"Master Orren," Staffords said. "Everyone's worried about you, for you've been asleep for three days. I've been here the whole time, waiting outside your room, hoping you would awaken."

"Staffords, where are my friends? Is everyone all right? What actually happened that night?"

"Iranda—that is Adnari the Temptress—exploded," Staffords said. "The gwell destroyed her. She could have killed many with her explosion, and indeed, parts of the manor house and swinery sustained considerable damage. But some strange people appeared—they were very tall, and looked like they were made of light. They protected everyone, including you."

"I saw them," Orren said. "The one who grabbed me had Richard's face."

"It *was* Richard, master," Staffords said with awestruck reverence. "In his new heavenly form. We saw him as well. And the others? They were astra. The gods of the light came down from the heavens to protect us.

"The corpses, being deprived of the goddess who raised them, crumbled into dust. Nothing remains of them; not even bones. Lady Marett says that the powers of the gods simply vaporized them. As for Adnari, all that remained of *her* was the dress she wore, with the shiny trimmings. Sir Haxel took it as his final shlenk."

"Did he?" Orren smiled. "That's very good!"

"After we put you to bed here," Staffords continued, "the baron continued his campaign into the southern Corcadine. All of Jurgan's surviving thugs are down there, along with the remaining Drammites, led by Darga Schuenn. They actually have joined forces, because both parties know the end is coming for them. Yesterday, they were driven out of Sandspitton, through a brilliant attack that the baron arranged from the sea. The folks of Lintas rose up and killed the ones who were in their town. At this time, reinforcements are on their way, to ensure that the thugs and Drammites don't take Lintas back. The filth is being forced up into the corkwoods above the sea cliffs. However, Master Orren, there's more news that you should hear. I think you ought to call your friends through the Web."

Orren did as Staffords suggested.

*So! The princeling awakens from his beauty sleep at last!* Anselm's answer teased Orren through the Web.

*Nice of him to grace us with his presence,* Marett added. *To what do we owe the honor?*

*We owe it to honey cake and goats' milk,* Carlenda said. *Gets them up every time.*

*Where are you all?* Orren asked.

*In the drawing room,* Marett said.

*We've been waiting for you, Master,* Haxel said.

Orren raced down the stairs. He entered the drawing room—the same place where he once hid behind the couches and stole Hesh from Berthus. This was the room where the quest began, for the act of stealing the gwell had set into motion the entire, mind-boggling chain of events.

There were more couches in the room than there had been before. Torches set in sconces lit up the chamber. The tall windows were open, and pleasant sea drafts blew in. Upon the couches sat Haxel, Marett, Anselm, Carlenda, Baron Toynberg, Perceval, Sergeant Riveldi and several other officers, Shann-Rell, and all six yelian tribal chiefs. Shann-Rell's falcon was perched upon her shoulder; the bird's wing was in a cast. The red mastiff lay on the floor; there were bandages all over his body.

"Come sit down," Baron Toynberg made room for Orren between himself and an officer. Orren sat.

"It's so great to have you all here," the boy said, tears of joy streaming down his cheeks. "I only wish Quartz could fit inside this place too."

"Did I hear somebody call my name?" the sholl's voice rang out. Orren looked over his shoulder. By the light of the torches he could barely make out the rock giant's face, as it stared into a window. There was something different about him though. Orren stood up and went to investigate.

He took a torch off the wall so he could see Quartz better. His heart leapt with joy.

All of the fissures and cracks in the sholl's hide were gone. Instead, his rocky exterior was whole and smooth, and even his skooch, and the mail tunic beneath it, appeared to have a luster that they had not had before. His appearance was spectacular!

"Do you like my new look, Master Orren?" Quartz asked. "Madame Carlenda healed me, using Nebi. She also gave me many wonderful things to drink, and fed me all kinds of fruits and roots…and seaweed. I have never tasted seaweed before, but I really like it."

"I like your look very much," Orren said, "and I'm so happy to see you this way. I only wish I could have seen Carlenda heal you, but I was sleeping."

"Master," Haxel said. "We thought you'd never wake up, but now we've got lots of news for you. Good Sir Anselm, you have your say."

"First, thanks for deigning to grace us with your presence," Anselm said with a comic roll of his eyes. "Shann-Rell and I have an announcement to make, and everyone's heard it except you."

"What?"

"We're going to be wed," Shann-Rell stated.

Orren's mouth dropped open.

"Don't do that," Anselm ragged him, "you'll catch flies. Shann-Rell and I are getting married. She doesn't seem to mind an old man of sixty-seven like me."

Shann-Rell smiled. "I think a young lady of ninety-three like me, could manage you."

"That's amazing!" Orren cried out. He gave Quartz's nose an affectionate pat, and then returned to sit back down next to the baron.

"We were waiting for you to wake up before we went through with it," Anselm said, "but there's more news. Why don't you start telling him, Carlenda?"

The old healing woman had a smile on her brown, wrinkled face.

"After Richard and the astra saved us all from being blown up," she said, "Richard gazed at all of us, and Anselm said, 'I know this man from somewhere.' Then he and I started to talk. Anselm asked me where I learned so many of my healing skills, and I told him that Richard—my brother—and I, were raised by an old forest witch who lived on her own in a cave, and taught us many skills. Her name was Sereida."

"Where have I heard that name before?" Orren asked.

"That was the witch woman who took in my siblings and myself," Anselm said. "Then I ran away from her and them."

"What are you saying?"

"What we're saying, Orren, is this," Carlenda said. "You always thought that Richard and I were Gothma. That's what we wanted everyone to think, for they would not have been pleased, had they known we were Jangurth. The name 'Richard', you see, was given to my brother by your father, but it's a Framguth name, for your father was Framguth. My brother's Gothma name was Ricardi, and even *that* was an adaptation of his Jangurth name, Rigedd. Likewise, Carlenda is the Gothma version of my Jangurth name—Klida."

Orren's heart leapt. "Anselm!" he cried out. "You're Richard and Carlenda's long lost brother!" He leapt up and enthusiastically embraced the old man. "All this time, I've been traveling with Richard's brother!"

"And you're squashing him to death," Anselm said. "So can you please back off just a little?"

"Sorry," Orren let him go. "I'm just so…so…"

"You thought Richard left you," Carlenda said, "but he never did. He was watching over you the whole time, and he descended from the heavens, together with the astra, to protect you. Not only that, but both of Richard's siblings are members of your Bearers' Web, and they helped you blow up Adnari the Temptress."

"I killed a god?" Orren asked.

"No," Marett said. "You can't just kill a god unless you're another god, and even *then* it isn't so easy. No Orren. You destroyed Adnari's physical form and have made her weak. It will probably be centuries before she rises again. Until then she'll be a miserable wraith, searching for power-hungry, ruthless people to latch on to. Such people, including your brother, are what give her strength. It's no wonder she found Berthus."

"Never mind her," Orren said. "Anselm, you need to know something. Richard was the one who made me what I am today. If it weren't for him, I would have jumped off these cliffs to my death. Richard died thinking he had failed Berthus, but it was Richard who gave Berthus the little good he actually had. I was able to get through to Berthus, and make him give up Kalsh and Ru'i, *because* of Richard. As for your sister here, she treated my wounds after I was whipped badly, and she was the one who got me to go on this quest. Also, she healed me from the whippings Dargun Prett gave me, and made drinks so I would sleep better, and not get mind twisted.

"I know that Carlenda and Richard treated you badly when you were young, but they're not like that anymore. You've got to forgive your sister, Anselm, and Richard too."

Carlenda's lower lip quivered as she turned to face Anselm. "Ansai," she said, "I'm so, so sorry. The way Rigedd and I treated you—we thought you were endangering our relationship with Sereida, but that's no excuse. I want you to know that we searched for you for months afterward, but you were gone. The guilt we felt about what we did to you, has haunted us ever since. Richard died with it. But it was that guilt, Ansai, which prompted us to live our lives helping others. That's why I became a healer, and Richard mentored a man who wanted to make the world a better place.

"That man, however, had a blind spot with respect to his older boy, so Richard became the father Berthus never had. When Berthus started victimizing Orren, Richard protected and looked after Orren the way he'd done with Berthus."

"Orren," Anselm said in an uncharacteristically tender voice. "You and I have had our differences, but you really are a remarkable young person, and my brother Richard is to thank for that. Carlenda saved you. How could I ever remain angry with two people who do things like that? When we were young we were foolish. Now we're old and, I hope, wise. Of course I forgive my siblings. How could I do otherwise?"

His voice broke at these last words and he turned to Carlenda. The two siblings stood up and hugged each other. There wasn't a dry eye in the room.

"And now I've got a *new* sister," Carlenda said, as she reached a hand toward Shann-Rell. The yelian leader stood up and took her hand. Carlenda pulled her into the embrace.

"I have news as well," Quartz's voice from outside, filled the room. "I have not yet announced it, because I have been waiting for Master Orren to awaken first." Everyone turned to look at the giant's face, which was pensive as he peered through the window. "Give me one moment," the sholl said. He disappeared, only to reappear moments later, with Jasper in hand. He reached through the window and placed the donkey-creature inside.

Jasper's appearance was even weirder than it had been before. Her hoofs were now huge, and they appeared to be turning into hoof-hand hybrids. Her front legs had grown long. Her head was no longer recognizable as that of a donkey, for it was shorter and more rounded.

Shann-Rell's red mastiff trotted over to Jasper's side, and the falcon fluttered onto her back.

"Jasper now sleeps beneath my skooch every day, while the sun is up," Quartz said. "She can no longer go out during the daytime, so I am giving her shelter from the sun…at least until she grows a skooch of her own."

Cries of amazement went through the crowd.

"You mean—" Orren began.

"Exactly," Quartz said. "Jasper is a sholl-spirit."

"No wonder Jasper knew where to lead everyone to when she used the Shovel of Tunneling!" Marett cried out. "Being a sholl, she is bonded to gwell-bearers just like Quartz is! It was easy for her to find us."

Now it was Anselm's mouth that dropped open.

"Anselm," Orren said with a mischievous smile. "Flies!"

"How…" was all Anselm could get out.

"Jasper has told me everything about herself," Quartz said. "You see, my masters and friends, she once served a Haas community, which was wiped out in the wars of Aigorn. She was so depressed about this that she mourned for an entire night, and never saw the sun rising. She turned to stone, and let me tell you, she crumbled much quicker than I did.

"Her sholl-spirit was forced to wander until it found an appropriate body, that of a dying donkey. Thus it was that she took her donkey-form, but she had no one to serve until she stumbled across Tiuvang, the Wardolam council head who was Shibbia's predecessor. Tiuvang was running an errand, as was the way of the council heads prior to Narx. Jasper followed him back to the lost city, and has served the Sun-Children ever since, though they had no idea who or what she was.

"Master Anselm, your love for and devotion to Jasper is very great, and you must have a deep connection to her sholl-spirit, as evidenced by your naming her 'Jasper', for that is in fact, her real sholl name."

"It is?" the old man's jaw dropped open.

"Yes, Master Anselm," Quartz said. "Remember, we sholls are always named after the rocks and minerals of the earth." Quartz then turned to Orren, Haxel, and Marett. "My other masters," he said, "do you remember me saying that I detected a sholl-spirit as soon as we left the Forest of Doom?"

"Yes."

"Jasper was that sholl-spirit," Quartz said. "Realizing it, however, was not so easy. You see, a sholl can detect another sholl-spirit from far away, but that does not necessarily mean he will recognize the sholl-spirit close up. It is a complex thing, and it has to do with many factors—the emotional state of the sholl-spirit in question, the mood he or she happens to be in, how well he or she has eaten, the weather patterns, the position of the moon in the sky, and so on and so forth. Conditions have to be just right, and they *were* that night, but it did not last, and thus I lost my ability to detect her. I certainly never discovered what form she had taken. I did not even know that she was a female sholl-spirit; she might as well have been male, for all I knew."

"When did you discover who she was?" Haxel asked.

"I long suspected it," Quartz said, "but we sholls are so used to being disappointed, that we tend not to get our hopes up until we see hard, solid evidence. It was only when she emerged from the ground, carrying the Shovel of Tunnels, and looking so bizarre, that I no longer had any doubts."

"Quartz, that's wonderful," Marett said, "but how did this happen? You told us that you've never heard of a sholl regaining his or her sholl-form."

You are correct, Madam Marett, when you say that I never heard of it happening," Quartz explained. "But the possibility of it happening has always existed, for our Moon Mother decreed it so, and spoke of it to us sholls when she gave us our Code of Duties. It requires an act of tremendous self-sacrifice on the part of the sholl-spirit, one that will please the Moon Mother. Jasper performed exactly such an act when she ran through the tunnels of the Kegelmont, distracting the sordigryps, who otherwise would have killed you, my masters, along with our friends, Perceval and Iskander."

"So now you can rebuild your species," Baron Toynberg said.

"There is something else, Honored Baron," the rock giant continued. "We sholls are divided into two clans—Clan Sediment and Clan Volcanic. Membership in either clan begins when a sholl has his or her Coming of Age Ceremony. That is when the Moon Mother bestows clan membership upon us.

"I am a member of Clan Sediment. Any sholl who is also a member of Clan Sediment is my brother or sister, and is thus off limits for marriage and the begetting of offspring. It is necessary, therefore, for a Sediment to marry a Volcanic, and vice versa. As it so happens, Jasper is, like me, a Sediment."

Everyone let out disappointed groans.

"Do not be downhearted my friends and masters," Quartz said. "For the Moon Mother has directed two Volcanics right into our midst. In fact they are both there with you in the room."

The red mastiff walked over to the window, together with Jasper, who had the peregrine falcon on her back. Quartz reached into the room with his index finger, and petted the dog and the bird.

"Meet Diamond," he said, indicating toward the dog. "And this is Onyx," he pointed at the falcon.

"You mean, my dog and my bird are *also* sholl-spirits?" Shann-Rell asked.

"Yes. Honored Council Head," Quartz said, "and they are both Volcanics. I do not know how they came to be in Wardolam, for they have not yet transformed to the extent that they can tell their stories to me."

"No wonder they've been eating fruits and vegetables ever since they recovered," Shann-Rell said, "and *a lot* of them too. Why, my falcon here—Onyx, I guess her name is—got into a huge sack of flour in the manor kitchen and ate all of its contents in one go! So white was she that she became a small gyrfalcon!"

Everyone laughed.

"Will they get back their sholl-forms?" Haxel asked.

"That is already beginning to happen, Master Haxel," Quartz said. "Diamond and Onyx fought very bravely to protect the Sun-Children, the Honored Baron and his men, and the Web members."

"Aye, that they did," Perceval said. "These brave animals put themselves in harm's way and saved many of us from being wounded or killed. The dog was cut and wounded in many places, and the falcon was shot by an arrow. Thanks to Madame Carlenda's healing skills, they are recovering."

"And thanks also to Madame Carlenda, they will live and regain their sholl-forms," Quartz said. "Like Jasper, Diamond and Onyx sacrificed themselves in a way that pleased the Moon Mother. It will not be long before you see them regaining their true sholl-forms, as is happening with Jasper right before our eyes. When they are fully restored, I will marry Onyx and Jasper will marry Diamond. We will thus be able to rescue our species from extinction, much as the yelia have."

"And you'll do it right atop Moreido Escarpment," Shann-Rell said. "You sholls will live with us forever and we will cherish you this time, and never take you for granted again."

Baron Toynberg stood up and turned to face the giant. "Quartz, are these your plans?" he asked. "Will you and your fellow sholls make a home together with the yelia?"

"Yes. Why do you ask this, my lord baron?"

"Because the Moreido Escarpment is a big place," the baron said. "The yelia, few as they are in number, will take many generations to repopulate it. I hereby deed it to you and your species as well. How you sholls and the yelia divide it up, is for your parties to decide."

"That wasn't really necessary," Shann-Rell said. "We are the children of the Sun Father. The sholls are the children of the Moon Mother. Our two species are used to coexisting in the same place. This time, however, we will live not as servant and master, but as equals. Wherever the yelia go, the sholls will go as well, and whatever fate and fortune brings us, will benefit them too."

"Nonetheless, esteemed council head, the baron's gesture means a great deal to Diamond, Onyx, Jasper, and myself," Quartz said. "By giving us this place as our home, he has granted us leave, within his realm, to rebuild our species. Sholl-spirits from miles around can hopefully come to the escarpment to find their people, and we can look for ways to restore their sholl-forms to them."

"My Jasper, a rock giant!" Anselm shook his head in disbelief and smiled.

"Master Anselm," Quartz said. "When Jasper regains her sholl-form in full, she will also regain the ability to speak like a sholl, and you will be able to have conversations with her. The same will be true for Diamond and Onyx, but later. After all, *they* are still able to walk about in daylight."

The old man rushed forward and embraced the now-oddly-shaped donkey.

"My big rocky friend, Quartz," Anselm said, "I share in your joy as you share in mine."

"That's right," Perceval said. "Quartz and Jasper coming together is a family reunion every bit as much as Anselm and Carlenda coming together is, or for that matter, myself and Marett. There is much we have to be grateful to the astra for, my friends, and among them are the reunions of our respective family members."

Everyone cheered except Orren. He knew that Perceval had not intended it this way, but his words cut like a knife.

True, Orren had many dear and beloved friends now, but none of them shared his blood or his family history. Therefore, for Orren Randolphus there could be no family reunion.

# Springtime of the Spirit

The wedding of Anselm and Shann-Rell took place the day after Quartz's and Anselm's revelations. It was conducted in the Tidesdale church, where the late Frater Berlissi had once preached. There were two ceremonies, one was Astralite, done in accordance with the teachings of the church, and the other was a traditional yelian wedding with invocations to the Sun Father. The former was carried out by Baron Toynberg, who as it turned out, was an ordained frater. The latter was conducted by a Haas named Abalatrax, who, being 407 years of age, was the eldest surviving yelius.

A great feast and celebration was put together by the folk of the Corcadine.

Soon after the wedding, Colonel Domberg brought the news that his men were having great difficulty dislodging the thugs and Drammites from the thick corkwoods of the southern Corcadine. Eleven knights fell in battle, and the thugs were using their positions above Sandspitton and Lintas, to shoot flaming arrows into both towns. These landed upon houses with thatched roofs, which caught fire. As a result, several score locals were killed.

Anselm let out a string of curses, and he asked the baron for permission to enter the fray. Quartz agreed to transport him into the corkwoods, and Jasper also went. Orren, Haxel, Marett, and Carlenda stayed behind in Tidesdale, but it was not long before news came back of their friends' exploits. Apparently, Anselm used Ru'i to summon every single field mouse, bush rat, and vole in the vicinity, until they swarmed in their hundreds of thousands.

As the thugs and Drammites attempted to fend off the tidal wave of rodents, the baron's men galloped into the cork forests, and cut the enemies down. Those who survived were driven out onto the Fingerpoint. This was a barren, rocky miniature peninsula on the Corcadine's southwestern extremity, surrounded on all sides by the tallest sea cliffs on the entire continent of LeFain.

The assorted thugs fought to their deaths, which came quickly. The Drammites, however, had other plans. Following Darga Schuenn's lead, they carried out a final act of blood sacrifice to their deity. They leapt off the cliffs, and fell from dizzying heights into the rough seas more than two thousand feet below. Thus it was that the Drammite occupation of the Corcadine came to an end.

While all of this was going on, Orren spent the time relaxing. He particularly enjoyed Carlenda's company, for the old woman had much to teach him about healing arts and the properties of various plants. She also told him his father's life story, and how Lorien had fled from his own family of northern Framguth nobles. It seemed that Richard and Carlenda assisted him in doing so, and in the process, became acquainted with members of House Randolphus.

Though Orren was fascinated, the information Carlenda imparted was also very disturbing. The Randolphuses, it seemed, were odia-worshippers and drunkards, whose bad habits actually caused them to lose most of their family fortune, and sink into poverty. They ended up eking out their survival through banditry, slave trading, and other foul pursuits. The way Carlenda described them, Berthus sounded angelic by comparison. All of this drove home to Orren the fact that he had no family worthy of being reunited with.

As soon as Anselm, Quartz, and Jasper returned from the south, the people of Tidesdale gave them a heroes' welcome. The newly reconstituted Corcadinian Council then beseeched Baron

Toynberg to make their peninsula a province of his barony. The baron accepted, whereupon Carlenda approached him.

"My lord," she said. "I am an old woman, and am no longer given to excessive travel. Might I remain here in the Corcadine? This place is my home, and these are my people. I will make the peninsula a center for medicine and healing."

"Madame Carlenda," the baron said, "I think you would also make a most effective governor for this province. The people here love and respect you. Of course, this depends upon whether you and the Corcadinian Council will agree to it."

The council held a vote, and it was unanimous in favor of Carlenda acting as governor of the peninsula. The baron and the council held a joint investiture ceremony. The discussion then turned to where the seat of government should be. After much deliberation, one of the council members proposed transforming Randolphus Manor for that purpose. Carlenda's residence would be there as well, together with a healing center.

"I can't agree to any of this," Carlenda said, "Randolphus Manor belongs to Orren. It was willed to him by his father."

"I don't want it," Orren said.

"Why?"

"My childhood there was awful," Orren said. "The place is full of bad memories, and besides, I won't be living there. True, Richard was there too, but the best times I had with him, were spent up in the high country, not on the manor. His last wish was for me to go to Alivadus to enter the honored baron's service, so that's what I'll do. Richard was the one who ran the manor, so I only think it's right that it should belong to his sister."

"Orren," Carlenda began. "Do you really want to—"

"Yes," Orren said, tears streaming down his cheeks. "It's a beautiful place, Carlenda. You'd love it, and you could do so much good with it. Just promise me you'll keep the swinery workers' jobs."

"I most definitely will," Carlenda said. "I don't know the first thing about raising hogs, but I've got a very dear friend in Stoneybeach named Rinald, to whom I'll send a message immediately. He's good at raising everything, and works well with people. I'm sure he'll be happy to run the swinery for me, and he'll make sure the workers are taken care of. But Orren, you should know that there will always be a home in the manor for you. If you ever want to come live with me here, you're more than welcome. I'll set up a nice room for you."

"I'll take a room too," Anselm piped up, "and I'll take it now."

"Just how do you propose to be in the Moreido *and* the Corcadine at once?" Carlenda asked. "Shann-Rell can't spend inordinate amounts of time here, you know. She'll have her hands full, establishing new settlements for the yelia and the sholls."

"She'll have her hands full with me too," Anselm said. "Mother used to say I was a little terror. Well, dear sister, I still am. I would like to stay here with you for maybe two months or so. We have so much catching up to do after all these years. Then when you get sick of me, as inevitably you will, I'll leave, and return to the Moreido to live with my wife. I promise you that after a few months, Shann too, will be happy to see the back of me, whereupon I'll come back here to spend more time with you."

"You always were impossible, Ans," Carlenda shook her head and rolled her eyes. "That clearly hasn't changed. You'd like to be away from your wife for months on end? What kind of basis is that for a marriage?"

"A very good one, I'll say," Anselm cracked a mischievous smile. "Just ask any of your fellow gwell-bearers what it's like having me for company day in, day out. Ask Shann how much we argue and bicker. I promise you, dear sis, it's better this way. Besides, the Jangurth spirit never left me. I'm a nomad and a wanderer by nature—can't stay in one place too long. Jasper will tell you all about it when she regains her ability to speak."

"And you have no problem with this?" Carlenda asked Shann-Rell.

"Carly, I love your brother very deeply and dearly," Shann-Rell said, "but at times, I'm sure I'll love him more when he's far away. After a while, I'll miss him and pine for him, and then he'll come back to me."

"Then that settles it," Carlenda shrugged. "Anselm will stay with me for a little while until I practically kick him out. Meanwhile you go build your life in the Moreido, but Shann, you have to promise me that you will *also* visit when you get a chance. I'd come to you, but at my age, I'm not about to go traveling long distances. Oh, and bring Jasper also...and Quartz...and whomever else you wish."

"I do so promise," Shann-Rell said. Then the old woman and the yelian council head embraced warmly.

Baron Toynberg desired to give Anselm a reward for all he had done, but the only thing the old man wanted was a place for his people—the Jangurth. The baron then announced that he would set aside some empty lands to the east of his capital city. These, he proclaimed, would be henceforth called Jangurthsheim, and they would serve as a place where the wandering nomads, regardless of what clan they were from, could feel safe and at home, and could work the land if they chose. He then invested Anselm with the official title of Lord of Jangurthsheim.

A moving memorial service was held for the fallen knights, after which Baron Toynberg announced that he and his army would return to Alivadus on the morrow. Their intention, however, was to escort the yelia and sholls to the Moreido Escarpment. Thus, preparations were made for departure. Ox wagons were loaded up, and horses were shoed. While this was taking place, Orren led the other gwell-bearers up into the mountains above the manor. He showed them the cave where he and Richard stayed during their forays into the high country. Then Quartz climbed to the top of Cloudwisp Peak, the highest mountain in the Corcadine, with Orren, Haxel, Marett, Anselm, Carlenda, and Jasper in his pockets and on his shoulders. From that vantage point, much of the Corcadine was visible, including all of Tidesdale.

The next day, they departed. Everyone said tearful goodbyes to Carlenda and Anselm. Many local folks stood with the two siblings to give their new lord a grand farewell. These included all the members of the Corcadinian Council, and Carlenda's friend Rinald, who, in response to Carlenda's message, had ridden to the manor on a fast horse.

Orren was all choked up and unable to speak. He rode in an ox cart together with Marett and Haxel, as well as Shann-Rell, the dog-sholl named Diamond, and the falcon-sholl Onyx. Both sholl-animals were well provided with fruits, grains, and vegetables. Quartz and Jasper did not come with, for it was daytime, and they had to stay behind, to sleep beneath Quartz's skooch. Orren sat in the rear, looking backward at Richard's two siblings, until the convoy rounded a bend in the road, and Carlenda and Anselm were out of sight. Their absence created an aching void in his heart. True, his friends were all accessible through the Bearers' Web, but it was not the same as actually having them physically present.

The Corcadine Peninsula was now alive with springtime blooms. The tamarisks sported bunches of tiny pink flowers, and the green woodlands boasted white blossoms of crab apple and wild pear. In the undergrowth, brooms, hairy brooms, and bladder sennas blazed in full golden-yellow glory, while carpets of periwinkles added splashes of blue to the ground cover. The hollies too, were in flower, with bits of white decorating their shiny, green leaves. Purple-and-white lady orchids jutted up from the forest floor.

There were birds everywhere, including thrushes, robins, nightingales, tits, finches, blackbirds, and various warblers. Buzzards and kites hunted in the skies above the Corcadine, and woodpigeons filled the forests with their soft cooing. Wild boar and hedgehogs scuffled about in the undergrowth.

The baron and his men left the Corcadine by way of Berthus's Wall. After four days of riding eastward along the coast of the mainland, they reached a number of peasant villages, in the midst of which sat an old castle built of light-colored stone. It overlooked the sea. Flowering vines grew all over its walls, and it had a generally pleasant and inviting appearance. The land in the area seemed to be agriculturally rich, with numerous orchards and vineyards.

"Welcome to Orchardine-by-Sea," the baron said. "This is one place of which my family is proud."

"It looks to be of excellent quality," Marett said, "and would be a most pleasant place to live one's life."

"I'm happy to hear you say that," the baron said, "for it has been my intention to give it to you and Perceval as a fief."

"My lord, you're too kind," Perceval said.

"The local people have to agree to it, of course," the baron said, "but I think they will. You see, my young friends, Orchardine was originally deeded, by my father, to my first cousin, Lutbrand. Lutbrand was, however, a scoundrel of the worst kind. He exploited the local folk most cruelly, and became an odia-worshipper. One of the first things I did after my father's death was depose him. Lutbrand has absolutely no conscience or morals whatsoever. I therefore forced him to live in the Monastery of Driehook Isle, under the stern control of the Monks of Manschaad, astrum of the dead.

"The people of Orchardine have suffered greatly from bandits and pirates. I have come to their aid as much as possible, but what they really need is a powerful lord who is always here. I promised this to them, but also told them that such a lord would be of only the highest moral caliber. That's why I would like to propose that Orchardine become the home of Duraline House Baines."

"I will agree to it if the people do," Perceval said.

"So will I," Marett added. "I could do a great deal with this fine land, and could put our family lore's knowledge of the soil, to work."

Baron Toynberg convened a meeting of the elders, leaders, and fraters of the surrounding settlements, and explained what his plan was. The locals warmly greeted Marett and Perceval, and hailed them as the new lord and lady protector of the region. They held a feast in honor of the two Duraline siblings, and though the fare was basic—pork, turnips, bread, cheese, and pigeon pies—it was touching to see the enthusiasm with which people greeted their new leaders. Then an investiture ceremony took place, which was attended by thousands of people from all over the region.

Three-dozen young knights elected to stay with Marett and Perceval, and to form the nucleus of their future garrison. Immediately, work began on restoring the castle to its former glory. Peasants, knights, yelia, and fraters all pitched in to help, as did Quartz and Jasper during the night. It did not take long to make the castle habitable.

After a three-day sojourn in Orchardine, Baron Toynberg decided that the time had come to continue traveling southward, toward the Moreido Escarpment.

"The backs of the pirates have been broken," he told Marett and Perceval before his departure, "but that doesn't mean they'll disappear forever. I think that I've given you and your brother enough of a window, during which you can build a navy, before the pirates make a comeback."

"We'll start working on it right away, my lord," Perceval said. He and Marett saluted the baron, and hugged each other. It warmed Orren's heart to see the love and affection between them, but it made him feel empty, for he knew he was about to leave them behind.

"Take good care of yourself, Orren," Perceval said, as he hugged the boy.

"And visit as soon as you can," Marett said. They fell into each other's arms and wept.

Many tears were shed when the time came for the baron and his entourage to leave Orchardine. After emotional farewells, everyone rode away, and Marett and Perceval stood, arms around each other's shoulders, until their friends were out of sight. Before long, the hills blocked off all view of the ancient seaside castle. Orren, Haxel, Staffords, the baron, and the yelian leaders kept conversing for hours about the girl whose wisdom contributed so much to the success of Orren's quest, and her remarkable brother, who infiltrated a dangerous cult.

Due to the fact that springtime storms hit the coastal lowlands with great ferocity, the baron was forced to travel eastward, inland. His entourage passed through a beautiful landscape of rolling green hills and forests interspersed with meadows and farmland. There were charming villages with stone cottages, hedgerows, and barns. Sheep, goats, and cows grazed in fields of tall grass, vetch, clover, and dandelion. Pea vines and ivy grew on old walls. Wild irises and pansies, dog-violets, blue veronicas, and white borage graced the meadows. Roses had been cultivated by the locals, alongside their homes' walls. Rooks, jackdaws, and white storks abounded in cultivated fields, where they fed side by side with the livestock.

Everywhere, there were butterflies, from checkered skippers and yellow swallowtails to orange-banded admirals, painted ladies, and little blues. The delicate, gossamer insects seemed particularly attracted to the sleeping form of Quartz, when he wrapped himself and Jasper in his skooch. Also common were beehives, and the air was filled with the buzzing of bees, wasps, and hornets. The forests were mostly oak, elm, and beech. In the undergrowth, snowdrops, wood spurges, and bluebells were in full flower, and large herds of deer grazed.

On the sixth day out from Orchardine, the baron's entourage ascended a line of hills, and found themselves overlooking the floodplain of a small river called the Iberi. The Moreido Escarpment was visible on the far side of the river, behind a forest. The cliffs rose some five hundred feet above the trees, and atop them, many more trees could be seen.

"There it is," the baron said to Shann-Rell. "Your new home. We'll ride there now, and then we'll set up camp for the night. Then, when Quartz and Jasper catch up with us, you can begin ascending the cliffs."

"Sounds good," the yelian leader said.

The horses and their riders rode off the hill, followed by the ox carts. They crossed a wide meadow, and forded the Iberi, which was shallow. They were about to enter the woods, when the trees came to life with hundreds upon hundreds of armed zhivi.

The knights drew their swords and readied their crossbows. The zhivi, however, were every bit as well armed as the humans were. They carried shields of elaborately interwoven, woody vines. Their ranks bristled with spears, axes, long bows, and quivers full of arrows.

"Don't do anything!" the baron called out. "We don't know what they want yet."

The knights and the zhiv army left a gap between them, about two hundred feet wide. Neither force advanced toward the other, or made any threatening moves. After a few minutes of stalemate, a trio of zhivi walked out from among their force, and strode into the unoccupied space. All three were female, and not one of them carried a weapon.

The first female was of a fairly advanced age. Her voluminous hair was gray, and she walked with the aid of a stick. Her knee-length, grass skirt was decorated with feathers, as was her shaspa, which she wore over both shoulders. The second zhiv female was much younger, with umber brown hair and a similar, knee-length skirt. Her shaspa was unadorned, and she wore it wrapped around her torso, though it left her right shoulder bare. She actually looked very much like Haxel.

The third individual was enormous for a zhiv. She stood over four-and-a-half feet tall, and was attired in a similar manner to the older female. Her hair was jet-black, and her skin dark. Her features were so fine they looked as though they had been chiseled by a sculptor. She could only be described as beautiful.

"Tiowa! Muppah! Grispel!" Haxel cried out in jubilation. He charged out from amid the baron's ranks, and ran toward his loved ones. He threw his arms around Muppah, nearly bowling his sister over. He then embraced his aunt. Finally, he flung himself into Grispel's arms. The big, dark female lifted Haxel into the air, hugged him tight, and planted a kiss on his long nose. There was much excited chattering in the zhiv tongue amongst the four of them.

"Master Orren! Come here!" Haxel called out.

Orren walked toward Haxel and his relatives. Haxel introduced everyone to one another. Orren awkwardly touched palms with Tiowa, Muppah, and Grispel; he was happy to meet them, but was nervous, for he did not want to inadvertently offend them, particularly with so many of their armed brethren present.

"Haxel has spoken often of the three of you," Orren said. "You should know, he loves you very much and…" He gulped, for he painfully recalled Rheudia. "Grispel, he…he wants to spend his life with you."

"And I want to spend my life with him," Grispel said with a warm smile, "but the next time Haxel goes on any adventures, I'm coming with."

"We've heard all about the great things our Haxel has done," Tiowa said.

"He's brought great honor and prestige to the Druba glunk," Muppah added.

"You want to see the shlenki I got?" Haxel asked.

"Not yet," Tiowa said. "We want to be with you and your friends first."

"That's right," Muppah said. "Shlenki can wait. You, my Haxel, are more important than any shlenk."

"I was about to say the same thing," Grispel chimed in.

Haxel placed his hand in Grispel's, and gazed up at her. The look between them was one of pure love.

"Tonight, you'll meet the big friend, Quartz," Haxel said with childlike enthusiasm, "and Jasper too. I only wish Miss Marett, Good Sir Anselm, and Carlenda, the wise lady, could be here."

"We'll meet them one day," Muppah said. "We already know about Marett and Anselm. The wise lady you mention, we don't know, but we'd like to meet her too."

"How do you know so much?" Orren asked.

Tiowa smiled and let out a shrill whistle.

The zhiv army parted to allow three more zhivi to pass through. One of them was a big female, only slightly smaller than Grispel. Her hair was red, a feature that, Orren noticed, was completely absent among Haxel's dark-haired colony members. The other two were smaller, armed males, whom Orren did not know, but it was obvious that they were the red-haired female's guards.

"Rudub!" Haxel said. "How did you get down here?"

"Mother Tiblitz and Father Veshkel sent us," Rudub said. "They felt it important to inform the Southland zhivi of Haxel's heroism, and the loyalty of his brave companions, who are friends of the zhivi."

"This is the first time we in the Southland Colony ever saw a zhiv with red hair," Tiowa said with a smile on her wrinkled face. "When we saw Rudub, we knew she had to have come from far away. It gave credibility to whatever she said."

"I'll tell you the rest of our long story later," Haxel said to his family members. "Come. You must meet Baron Toynberg and the leaders of his knights, and Shann-Rell and the yelia too."

After introductions were made, Baron Toynberg made an announcement.

"I have endeavored to reward the gwell-bearers and their companions for everything they have done; for their bravery, loyalty, and faithfulness," he said. "To Quartz and the sholls, I have deeded the Moreido Escarpment, for them to share with the yelia. To Madame Carlenda I gave governorship of the Corcadine. To Anselm, I awarded Jangurthsheim, and to Perceval and Marett, I gave Orchardine-by-Sea. My brave knights will each receive plots of land and promotions, upon our return to Alivadus.

"It is therefore my desire to reward Druba Haxel Spakiwakwak as well," the baron said. "Sir Haxel, you may choose of any land in my realm that you desire."

"That's very kind of you, Honored Baron," the zhiv said, "but I desire no land. I only want to be with my own kind. Our Southland Mountain home borders your lands, so I will do whatever I can to protect your realm. Don't forget, I've got Orya. So if anyone tries to invade your lands from the east, I'll burn them to a crisp."

The baron laughed. "Nonetheless," he said, "I will reward you with a title. It is necessary for good relations to prevail between our species. I therefore give you, Druba Haxel Spakiwakwak, the title of Official Laison to the Zhivi. And, as a token of my gratitude, I offer you one last shlenk."

An officer then handed the baron something that shimmered in the torchlight. The baron placed it in Haxel's hands. It was a spider made entirely of gold, with eight pearls for eyes.

"I had a smith in Tidesdale make it for you," the baron explained.

Haxel's eyes teared up. "This is too kind of you. Tchafla bless you and your realm."

All the zhivi cheered, and the knights and yelia followed suit.

There was much laughing, joking, and conversing by the light of hundreds of torches, as humans, yelia, and zhivi freely intermingled at the base of the Moreido Escarpment. Orren and Staffords sat conversing with Haxel, Tiowa, Muppah, and Grispel.

The baron and his officers were discussing urgent matters of state with Shann-Rell and her fellow tribal chiefs, and a number of zhiv leaders. It was a beautiful thing to see the three species, which had for so long been mortal enemies, creating alliances and friendships.

Suddenly, many of the zhivi started to scream in terror. A massive, black shape emerged from the forest. Haxel ran toward his people, reassuring them that everything was fine, and that the sholls had arrived.

Quartz looked incredible by the firelight. His rocky countenance was smooth and polished. Jasper, for her part, was really starting to look like a sholl. She walked upright now, and had grown larger. She stood some eight feet tall, and though she appeared tiny next to Quartz, she towered over everyone else. Her donkey face was flattening, and her shingles had grown into a proper chain mail tunic and leggings, similar to what Quartz wore. She still had her donkey's mane, but it had grown wooly and long, and was showing the first signs of becoming a skooch. Interestingly, the packs and rope coils were still tied to her shoulders, and she still carried them with pride.

Diamond trotted over to Jasper's side, and Onyx flew onto Quartz's shoulder. It was then that Orren noticed that the dog and the bird were both becoming heavier set, and that their faces were flattening out.

"The time has come, my masters," Quartz said. "My people and the yelia must claim our new homes."

Orren's heart sank.

The boy and the zhiv then walked over to Quartz and hugged his hands. Jasper positioned herself behind them, and they turned around and touched her hoof-hands.

"Always believe in yourself, big friend," Haxel said through his tears. "And you too, Jasper."

"You taught us to do that, my masters," Quartz said. "I will never forget those lessons."

"Goodbye, Quartz and Jasper," Orren's voice broke.

"Goodbye, my friends," Quartz said.

Quartz then placed fifteen of the elder yelia on his shoulders. Onyx flew to the top of his head. Jasper allowed three yelia to climb onto her shoulders, along with Diamond. The two sholls walked over to the cliffs and ascended them, their hands adhering to the rock like magnets on iron.

When they reached the top, they threw down the ropes that Jasper carried. Some of the younger yelia used these to ascend, and they climbed hand over hand with surprising agility. Quartz and Jasper descended once again, and took more of the older yelia to their new home. Meanwhile, the humans and zhivi looked on in awed silence.

Shann-Rell and the tribal chiefs were the last to go. They bid Orren, Haxel, the baron, and the assembled knights and zhivi, goodbye. Then they too, ascended the ropes until they reached the top. All the yelia and sholls disappeared into the Moreido's forests and rocky outcrops.

For four days, the baron and his knights traveled north, together with the zhiv army. Most of the zhivi parted company with them some twenty miles south of the city of Alivadus, and returned to their colony in the Southland Mountains. Haxel, however, insisted on carrying on. Grispel went with him, but Muppah said she needed to get Tiowa home, so she bid Orren, Staffords, and the baron goodbye. About twenty young zhiv warriors—ten male and ten female—came with Haxel and Grispel, as did Rudub and the two Greymantle males. All the zhivi traveled on ox cart, as they were nervous around the horses.

One fine morning, the entourage ascended a hill, which was covered in flowering tamarisks. It commanded a view of a wide, open plain, full of orchards, farmland, and villages. Orren saw, some eight miles away, a large, walled city of light-colored stone, with tall towers, and what appeared to be pennants flapping in the breeze.

"There it is," the baron said. "The city of Alivadus." He turned to Haxel and said, "I'm going to have to forbid you from coming any farther. You see, the peasant folk are superstitious. They're not inclined to the same sort of rationality as my knights are. I fear that your life and those of your fellow zhivi may be in danger."

"But my lord," Haxel said. "I promised to see my master to the big human city."

The baron pointed to a four-foot tall, white stone sticking out of the ground, which was situated between three tamarisks. "Do you see that?" he asked.

"Yes," Haxel said.

"That's the boundary stone marking Alivadus's old border," the baron said. "In my grandfather's time, that was the full extent of this state. My father, however, greatly expanded the barony. The old state—my grandfather's realm—has been incorporated into the city of Alivadus, which means that all the villages you see from up here are part of the Alivadus municipality. What it also means, brave Haxel, is that you've fulfilled your duty. You've escorted Orren successfully to the 'big human city.'"

"Oh, Master Orren, I'll miss you," Haxel's eyes welled up with tears.

Orren took Haxel's leathery hands in his own. "Haxel," he said, "you've fulfilled the duty Tchafla gave you. That means I'm not your master any more. From now on, you should just call me Orren."

"OK…um…Orren," Haxel said.

Overwhelmed with emotion, they threw their arms around one another, and cried on each other's shoulders. They stood like that for some time, while Baron Toynberg, Staffords, and the knights looked on in silence.

"Enjoy serving the baron," Haxel said. "We'll see each other again. I hope soon."

"You better believe that," Orren said. He let Haxel go. He then bid Grispel and the others farewell, while Haxel did the same for the baron and his men. The zhivi then walked away. Before they disappeared into the bushes, they waved goodbye one last time. Then they vanished into the foliage until it seemed that they were no more than a dream that had passed.

The void in Orren's heart gnawed at his stomach. Tears streamed down his cheeks, as he watched Haxel, his closest friend in the world, vanish into the greenery.

# Sanctuary at Last

The walls of Alivadus were some fifty feet high, and were constructed of a light-colored stone. The battlements included towers that were almost triple the height of the walls, from the tops of which blue pennants fluttered in the breeze. These did not sport Baron Toynberg's family emblem, but instead, the Volcano Man symbol of the Astralite Church.

A wide road led into the city's main gates. The thoroughfare cut through green pastures, filled with clover and dandelion, which in turn, were surrounded by woodlands of oak, elm, pear, and beech. The sky above was pure blue, and there was a soft breeze, which made for very pleasant weather. Birds, bees, and butterflies were everywhere, and red squirrels chattered in the trees.

Orren was riding upon a bay mare, alongside Baron Toynberg, who rode a chestnut stallion. The boy had picked up the basics of horseback riding during the course of their travels around the Barony of Alivadus. The knights trotted behind their lord on their own mounts, together with ox carts, which rumbled through the idyllic spring landscape.

The countryside was beautiful, the peasant villages quaint, and Alivadus itself had a welcoming charm. Though it was similar in size to Sherbass, it was otherwise completely unlike that dark, forbidding northern city.

Orren, however, could not shake his melancholy. His friends were no longer with him, and he was now in the company of strangers. True, the baron was warm and friendly, but he was nonetheless an authority figure, a commander of men. Orren had come to Alivadus to enter the man's service, in fulfillment of Richard's last wish. That was the only reason he was here.

"Orren?" the baron asked. "I can see you're unhappy. Would you like to talk?"

"I don't want to trouble you, my lord," the boy said.

The baron stopped his horse and held up his hand for everyone to halt. He then called out to Staffords. The peddler, who was now Orren's slave, dismounted from one of the ox carts. He approached the baron and kneeled.

"Yes, my lord?"

Baron Toynberg dismounted. He walked over to Orren and motioned for the boy to dismount as well, which Orren did.

"Staffords," the baron said. "I want you to take my horse and Orren's, and lead them into the palace stables. Feed them and give them water. The knights will show you exactly where everything is."

"As you wish, my lord," Staffords said with a bowed head. He then took the horses by the reigns, and led them away.

"Everybody else," the baron said. "Ride into the city without us. Your families have missed you for long enough."

The men saluted and did as their lord had instructed them.

"Orren," Baron Toynberg said when everyone was gone, "Let's go sit in the shade of that oak tree over there."

Dragging his feet, Orren followed his lord. They both sat down in the grass beneath a beautiful, spreading oak. The boy fiddled with fallen leaves, and stared at the ground.

"Orren," the baron said in a soft voice. "I understand that you miss your friends. I miss them too. Please tell me if there's anything I can do to make you feel welcome in Alivadus."

Orren shook his head. He then reached into his pouch, and pulled out Hesh. He caressed the blue stone, and then spoke his mind.

"This stone is what started everything," he said. "I stole it from Berthus. Berthus chased after me to kill me and get the stone back, and then one thing led to another. When I stole Hesh, Berthus was a great lord with lots of riches, and I was a filthy boy without a home or a friend. Now I'm in the service of a great lord, and Berthus is the one without home or friend."

"He actually thought I was trying to kill him, my lord. He thought I lived to destroy him. Can you believe that? And he led an army full of the worst thugs and human-sacrificing Drammites through the mainland, causing death and suffering along the way, all because of what he thought I was."

"Then I healed him. I wanted to kill him, and maybe I should have, but I didn't, because I needed to get Kalsh and Ru'i away from him. But the other reason I didn't kill him was because I wanted to prove him wrong. When he was healed, he stood up and left the Ghoul Vale, but before he went, he took one last look at me. His eyes no longer had hate in them, but sadness. I knew he was sorry for everything he did, and that he wished he'd done things differently, but it was too late. He left, and somehow I knew that I'd never see him again. I still know it."

"I feared Berthus more than anything else in the world, but when I saw him lying there in his own blood, I understood how stupid my fear was. Berthus was just a man, after all. I defeated him, and when I did, I defeated the thing I feared most. It was *because* I defeated my fear that I was able to face and defeat much worse enemies than Berthus—a dargun who did his best to turn me into something I'm not; a big, bullying bandit chief who for a short time, became the leader of all thugs; and finally, an evil goddess!"

"But those enemies still frighten me less than Berthus did, because Berthus and I both come from the same place. We're alike in many ways—we look alike, we both have tempers, we're both leaders, and we both know how to solve problems and make plans, no matter what you throw in our way. After I healed Berthus, he went his way and I went my way, but we didn't just go different ways because we wanted to get away from each other.

He went his way, I'm sure, because he couldn't face everything he'd done to me, and I went my way, because I knew we could never be brothers."

"I know you two can never be brothers," the baron said, "but you have to know that none of what happened was your fault. Berthus convinced himself that you were his enemy. He never challenged his own stupid belief. It's like humans who think zhivi bring bad luck. They're superstitious about zhivi, and Berthus was superstitious about you. Nothing you could have done would have changed that. It was Berthus's responsibility to find out if what he believed was true or not, but he chose not to, and now he's suffering the consequences."

"But Berthus could have been my family," Orren said, "and if there's one thing I've learned from my friends, it's that family's something very special. Family is what you come from, and what you can always go back to. What makes folks your family is that you can always love them again, even after things don't go so well, and they will love you too."

"There are other Randolphuses around," Orren continued, "but Carlenda told me all about them. They sound as bad as Berthus, if not worse."

"She's right about that," the baron said. "I've encountered a few of them myself. Not the kind of people you want as family."

"Look at Anselm and Carlenda," Orren said. "No matter how badly Carlenda and Richard treated Anselm when they were young, they were still family. Carlenda and Richard spent their whole lives trying to make up for what they did to Anselm, and in the end they did. Carlenda and Anselm came back together and now they have each other."

"Then there's Marett. She had all the wrong ideas about Perceval, but when he explained to her what he was really trying to do, she took him back. When they came back together as a family, then it was like they both came home."

"What you say is correct," the baron said.

"Haxel was forced to leave his family," Orren said, "especially after he brought so much shame to his glunk. It wasn't that Tiowa or Muppah wanted him to go. The glunk elders gave them no choice. Haxel wandered around, but in the end he came back, and both of them—and Grispel also—were really happy to see him again. The shlenki didn't matter—you heard what Muppah said—what mattered was that the person in their family, who they loved, came home to them.

"Quartz didn't even know that Jasper was his family. I'm not sure that he even met her in the old days, before they both turned to stone. But when he found out she was from his clan, he knew that she was a sister to him. So Quartz and Jasper are family too, and they have each other."

"Is that what's troubling you?" the baron asked. "The fact that all your friends have family of their own, but you don't?"

"In a way, yes," Tears streamed down Orren's cheeks. "Because of their families, they all have places where they belong. Don't get me wrong; I'm really, really happy for them. I share in their joy, which all of them deserve, but would it be too much to wish that I could have some of that for myself?"

"No, it's not too much," the baron said, "and Orren, I'm glad you brought this up, because it's important. I have something to tell you, and I've been waiting for the right moment. Now is that moment, so listen to what I have to say."

The baron let out a sorrowful sigh, and said, "I understand what it's like to have no family."

"You do?" Orren looked at the man with curiosity.

"Yes," the baron said. "Most of House Toynberg was wiped out in a plague that swept through this region sixty years ago. The only survivors were my father, Gerald Toynberg, and his brother, Oscar. I was my father's only child. Uncle Oscar had two children, of whom only one is still alive, and that's Lutbrand. I told you all about Lutbrand, and I told you why I gave his old fief to Marett and Perceval."

"I remember," Orren said. "Is he really that bad?"

"He's the Berthus of my family," the baron said, "and he's truly evil. He never repented of anything he did, so he's no family to me, especially after the betrayal."

"What betrayal?"

"Lutbrand was offered a great deal of money by an enemy Framguth lord, in exchange for information about a secret passageway into Uncle Oscar's castle. The enemy lord's men raided the castle and killed everyone in it, including Uncle Oscar. The only person who was spared was Lutbrand's younger sister."

"They didn't kill her?" Orren asked.

"No," Baron Toynberg said. "Lutbrand's sister was a girl of fifteen. She was tall and very beautiful, with lustrous, golden hair and features that could only be described as perfect. The wicked lord took her to be a servant in his castle. You see, Orren, the Framguth lords like to impress one another with fancy and beautiful things—beautiful clothes and tapestries, chariots, jewelry, pedigreed horses and hounds, hunting falcons, and vicious-looking weaponry—all of these things are status symbols to them, and beautiful people are as well. They like having exquisite women and handsome men as servants, because they can show them off to their fellow lords as status symbols. And so it was that Lutbrand's poor sister became a showpiece and a slave. Eventually, the wicked lord's daughter chose my cousin to be her handmaid, and whenever she went looking for suitors, she brought the girl with her as part of her dowry."

"That's terrible," Orren said.

"The wicked heiress eventually married a powerful lord, and moved into his castle, taking Lutbrand's sister with," the baron said. "The marriage ended in disaster, but the husband fell in love with my cousin, the handmaid, and took her as his second wife. She found happiness, though it was brief, for she died soon afterward. However, she bore that lord a son."

Orren's mouth dropped open. His eyes went wide.

"Yes," the baron said. "The evil lord to whom Lutbrand betrayed his own family was Alaric Klehr. His daughter was Rowana, Berthus's mother. Rowana married your father, Lorien Randolphus, and my cousin…my beautiful cousin, was your mother, Marda."

Orren's eyes welled up with tears. "Then that means—"

"I'm your family," the baron said. "To be exact, I'm your second cousin, but Orren, I don't want to be just that."

"What do you mean?"

"My dear wife Loretta is a kind, loving, and devout woman," the baron said, "but the astra have never opened her womb. I therefore have no children and no heir. Orren Randolphus, you and I are family, but I want you to be more than just a cousin. I want to adopt you, and make you my son. Then one day, when I die or abdicate, you'll be the next baron of Alivadus. I can think of no one better than you, to become the lord over all these beautiful lands."

Orren was speechless. Unable to control his emotions, he threw his arms around Baron Toynberg. The baron hugged him as well, and stroked his hair. "I can't wait to introduce you to Loretta," he said with great enthusiasm. "She's going to *adore* you."

The baron let Orren go, and stood up. He offered the boy a hand, and lifted him to his feet. He then placed an arm around Orren's shoulders, and Orren put his arm around his new adoptive father.

Together they walked through the meadow, back onto the thoroughfare, and into the city gates.

*Get more of*

# CURSED QUEST

*and*

## THE SIX STONES TRILOGY

Full-size color maps, coats of arms for key characters, and more extras for the Six Stones Trilogy are available for free at http://www.nathowler.com. The website also features a blog, reader reviews, updates on the book series, and a biography of Nat Howler. Become part of the readers' network, enjoy special offers, and add your own comments and reviews!

http://www.nathowler.com
http://www.facebook.com/nathowler

# e|LIVE

## listen|imagine|view|experience

### AUDIO BOOK DOWNLOAD INCLUDED WITH THIS BOOK!

In your hands you hold a complete digital entertainment package. In addition to the paper version, you receive a free download of the audio version of this book. Simply use the code listed below when visiting our website. Once downloaded to your computer, you can listen to the book through your computer's speakers, burn it to an audio CD or save the file to your portable music device (such as Apple's popular iPod) and listen on the go!

How to get your free audio book digital download:

1. Visit www.tatepublishing.com and click on the e|LIVE logo on the home page.
2. Enter the following coupon code:
   5965-99aa-888b-e5fd-f507-ad00-c505-8a19
3. Download the audio book from your e|LIVE digital locker and begin enjoying your new digital entertainment package today!